Languidly, she lifted her lashes to behold his face, and behind his head the shadow of the mosque loomed. Gwen clutched his sleeves, not wanting him to draw away. An odd premonition struck her in the frightening magic of the night, and she whispered, "Who are you, Morgan Riff . . . who *are* you . . . ?"

He straightened and searched her expression as if pondering the cause of her question. Then, with gentle hands, horseman's hands that could wield a rifle like no other, he refastened the pearl buttons of her blouse. While she gazed at him with the question still in her eyes, he guided her toward the steps of the house. He looked directly into her face and touched her quivering lower lip, which his kisses had made red.

"Don't you know?" he asked. "Don't you know who I am?"

She shook her head even while foreboding visions told her that she lied.

Some emotion crossed his face, putting a slight but tormented frown between his brows. In an even voice he said, "Then I shall tell you."

She waited, held her breath, felt her chest squeeze.

"I am the Squire of Hiraeth."

"Look for the name Satinwood among the top-ranked authors of the genre along with Spencer, Garwood, Miller, soon, very soon!"–

—Heartland Critiques

DEBORAH SATINWOOD

ARABESQUE

ZEBRA BOOKS
KENSINGTON PUBLISHING CORP.

ZEBRA BOOKS are published by

Kensington Publishing Corp.
475 Park Avenue South
New York, NY 10016

First Printing: February, 1994

Printed in the United States of America

Here is the crux of our two lives:
Without the other, neither thrives.

from the *Honeysuckle Song*
by Marie de France, 1230

Author's Note

Writing *Arabesque* gave me particular enjoyment because of its exotic settings in Tangier and the Atlas Mountains of Morocco, locales which were interwoven with a touch of the mystique of Wales. I would love to hear your comments about the book. You may write to me in care of Zebra Books, 475 Park Avenue South, New York, New York, 10016. Please include a self-addressed, stamped envelope for a reply.

Prologue

Perhaps the sea would fill up, slither above its black jagged cliffs and send a flotilla of waves to wash away the land—even Ardderyd.

Such things happened. The cold Welsh waters made many things disappear. The oldest books said whole villages had vanished beneath the tides, and kingdoms had been swallowed up. Some even said the ancient city of fairies lay beneath the water-weeds just offshore, its towers aglitter with tarnished gold, its algaed bells tolling in the ears of fishermen lost.

Even now a tempest hurled sheets of water against Gwenllian's window, hammering it with such force she feared the glass would break. She scurried away from it, her cold-numbed hands faltering on the fastenings of her frock, missing two hooks in a row. She had not had time to light a lamp, and so dressed in darkness, fumbling about to find petticoats and stockings and warm black boots. Only minutes ago Papa had roused her from sleep, bade her get up and dress, and with a cryptic smile, announced that he was taking her on a journey.

Gwenllian quickened her pace, pulling on her boots without sitting down, hopping and stepping until her heel slipped inside the leather. Thunder rent the heavens, shook the centuries-old manse until the porcelain ponies on her mantelshelf danced.

"Holy Leaping Toads!" she swore, her six-year-old voice affecting a sea captain's drawl.

"Daughter!" Sir Gerald bellowed, stumping down the gloomy corridor. "Are ye not ready yet?"

"Yes, Papa!" she called, trying to walk while she tied her boot laces. "I'm coming!"

He hastened through the door, shielding a candle with his hand, its flame casting gyrating shadows across his mustachioed face. "Great Elysium, girl! Why didn't ye light a lamp? 'Tis as dark as the underside of hell in here. Do ye have yer cloak?"

Feeling her way to the wardrobe, she rifled through its contents, finding by touch the brown woolen garment and flinging it round her shoulders.

"Where are we going, Papa?" she asked with wide eyes while her window rattled in its frame.

Raising the candle, Sir Gerald moved forward to take her arm, his burly form throwing a bearlike silhouette on the wall above the door. "We're going to visit Hiraeth."

He could just as well have said, "We're going to visit Hades or the Cyclops' Cave or the dark side of the moon." Gwenllian stared at him with her mouth agape.

Taking hold of her arm, speaking above the fu-

8

rious din outside, he guided her by the light of the candle to the stair. "Can ye believe it, daughter? After all these years the young Squire of Hiraeth has appeared on his doorstep without so much as a by your leave. The gatekeeper there said he arrived in a hired coach, soaked to the bone, and with his clothes all bloodied up."

Gwenllian looked at her sire in both horror and astonishment, stumbling on the stair. Sir Gerald had to grasp her by the hood of her cloak to keep her from somersaulting down.

A squire of Hiraeth had come home at last?

She had always been fascinated by the estate and its disappearing squires in the way most children are fascinated by all things dark and mysterious. For at least three generations the imposing edifice on the cliffs had stood alone, slowly deteriorating beneath its terrible weight of neglect. Gwenllian had come to think of it as a living thing, a proud dying beast who no one but a caring master could save. Many times she had wished for a fairy's wand, so that with one magic word she might brandish it commandingly and rescue Hiraeth herself.

"Where did the new squire come from, Papa? Where has he been? Is he terribly injured?" she questioned in a breathless torrent of words.

"I don't know, Gwen. I don't know." With his daughter in tow Sir Gerald traversed the hall, nodded to the sleepy-eyed butler, who, after snapping open an umbrella, unlatched the oaken front door.

Immediately a caterwauling wind thrust itself inside, forcing them to turn their heads to avoid its stinging raindrops. Upon the flooded drive their old coach swayed in the buffeting gales, its lanterns feeble arcs in the downpour, its driver huddled in a glistening greatcoat with water trickling from his hat brim.

Sir Gerald ducked beneath the butler's upheld umbrella, scooped Gwenllian up in his arms, and together with the servant, dashed for the coach. Seconds later the vehicle lurched forward through the mud, its four wild-eyed horses bunching their haunches and proceeding straight into what could have passed for the maws of hell.

"How old is the new squire, Papa?" Gwenllian shouted before her father had even got the umbrella closed.

"Not much older than yerself, by my reckoning—that's why I allowed ye to come. But the gatekeeper said he was a belligerent little devil. Speaks some foreign kind of English, and not a word of Welsh. The servants up at Hiraeth don't know what to make of him. I said I'd get him settled in and fetch the trustees tomorrow. They've been trying to locate him nearly four years now, since word of his grandfather's death." His voice changed suddenly in the darkness, grew distant. "Years ago the old squire's daughter ran away with some barbarous foreigner and bore an heir. She never returned. The child is seeing his birthright for the first time tonight."

"Will he stay and be a proper squire, Papa?" Gwenllian asked. To her mind the most important thing in life was caring for the Welsh land, and those who lived upon it.

Her father snorted and shook his head. "Never a one of 'em has stayed put since my great grand-

10

father's day. Adventurers, rogues, wanderers, all! The careless scoundrels. They've let the finest estate in Wales go to rack and ruin these last threescore years and some."

It was no secret to Gwenllian that her sire disapproved of the absent neighboring heirs, and in the way children inherit their parents' beliefs she had grown to feel the same.

After a harrowing quarter hour's journey, during which the coach had to be twice heaved out of knee-deep mire, the travelers drew up before the proud facade of Hiraeth. Gwenllian buried her head against her father's wet wool coat and he galloped her to the door, rapping furiously with the iron knockers. When none of the skeleton staff answered, he put a shoulder to the portals and forced his way inside, propelled by the wolfish wind.

The two of them stood in the hall, a freezing, dank-smelling place whose towering walls were lit only by three fluttering sconces. Gwenllian shuddered with excitement, her eyes focusing on a smoke-dimmed painting high above her head. Upon its canvas a fierce warrior slashed his sword in some ancient battle, his blood spilling redly on churned Welsh earth.

A slight movement caught her attention then, and she swung her gaze to the curving stair. Upon the second step a figure sat alone. Small he looked against the vastness of his hall, and yet his presence was oddly prepossessing.

She peered closer.

In an attitude of defensiveness he clasped his arms about his legs, and with a wary, hostile stare

11

watched his guests in silence. She wondered if he had had his face buried against his knees before they entered, for he blinked painfully as if the light hurt his eyes. Not a move did he make to rise and show respect.

Sir Gerald noticed his presence and stepped forward. "Lad . . . ?"

At first, the Squire of Hiraeth made no reply, flexed not a muscle, nor batted an eye. Then, slowly, he raised up on the second step, his height just matching the man's.

The appearance of the boy struck Gwenllian forcefully, assailed her with vivid impressions never to be forgotten. Tall for a boy, the young squire wore a crimson sash cinched round his waist, and both water and mud spoiled his soft hide boots. His white ill-fitting garb was of a type she had never seen before, and splattered with scarlet drops.

Her stomach lurched, for she had an aversion to the sight of blood.

He was thirteen or fourteen, she figured, well-formed and handsome. And yet, there was about his face a wildness that she could only compare to the wildness in nature—like the storm outside, or the dangerous cliffs rising up from the sea. Her gaze moved upward. His hair was as black as any Welshman's, his eyes even bluer and more haughty than her own. And yet, she swore their lashes shimmered with the beads of recent tears.

She shivered, experiencing a strange fascination for this boy, a compelling impulse to stretch out her hand and touch him.

Her father stepped closer. "And what is yer name, boy?"

"Rhaman." Lifting his chin, he articulated the word arrogantly, as if defending the strange appellation.

Gwenllian wanted to ask him what sort of name it was; it hardly sounded like a proper title for a squire to her.

"We are yer neighbors," Sir Gerald explained. "Come to see ye settled. On the morrow I shall go to Dyfed and notify the trustees of yer estate that ye've arrived. I'm sure ye'll want to know the details of yer inheritance, an' all." Eyeing the boy's odd, sodden costume, he finished, "And I'm certain they'll be interested to know how ye came to be here."

Twisting his mouth into a humorless smile, the boy replied, "I shan't stay in this godforsaken country, you know. Live in this—" he swept out his hand— "crumbling mausoleum. I came only because my mother forced me to."

Gwenllian gasped at his rudeness, at his sacrilege to Wales and Hiraeth and all they represented.

Beside her Sir Gerald growled, his short-fused temper exploding. "It hardly surprises me. A poor lot ye last squires have been. Negligent, taking from the land, never giving back. The place falls into ruination and none of ye take heed, none care for the history in these stones, the blood yer own ancestors shed to keep it prosperous and whole." He snorted contemptuously. "Tainted blood, I say."

The boy glared at him, and Gwenllian thought

13

that if he had a sword at his side he would have drawn it.

"A more precious blood than theirs was shed to-night," Rhaman uttered through his teeth, his voice with its odd accent as hard as any man's. "My own mother's blood."

Sir Gerald's face paled. "Good God . . ." He took a step backward and muttered in a softer tone, "My apologies, lad. But here—we should go by the fire, speak awhile. Ye must tell me all about this tragedy."

"She was murdered on the road from Dyfed. That's all you need to know." Rhaman said the words curtly, then lowered his lashes and added, "It was me they meant to kill."

While Gwenllian reached to clutch her father's coattails, Sir Gerald stiffened. "Murdered . . . ?" he gasped. "Have the authorities been notified?"

The boy laughed, sending a harsh sound echoing round the hall like a saber clash. "Believe me when I say your authorities could do no good. Only *I* can avenge my mother's death." His eyes hardened while his fists clenched at his sides. "And I *will* avenge it, even if I must give my own life to see it done!"

Sir Gerald made a move to take his arm. "Now see here—calm yerself. There's no need to—"

Angrily the boy shook off his hands, then grasped the lion-headed newel post as if for support. Lines of fatigue hollowed his youthful face, and his thin squared shoulders seemed to slump with a burden of strain. "You may stay here for the night if you like," he murmured in a poor attempt at gracious-ness. "I bid you good eve."

14

Observing the set of his rigid young back with a baleful eye, Sir Gerald let him go.

At dawn, when the palest fingers of lavender brushed the clearing sky, Gwenllian rose from a high baroque bed on which a king of England had once reposed. Raising up her arms, she smiled through a yawn and a delicious thrill chased down her spine. At last, she had actually slept within the mysterious, magical walls of Hiraeth!

Pretending she was a princess of the realm, she pattered regally to the leaded window. Far below, the landscape stretched to the cliffs, its rippling mirror of floodwater reflecting the awakening radiance of heaven.

"Glorious . . ." she breathed, thinking God and his angels would materialize at any moment against such a majestic Welsh sky.

But instead of some deity, she beheld another, quite earthly figure strolling there. For a while the tall, solitary boy stood staring out to sea, watching the colors of sunrise turn from pastel to fire. Then he pivoted, and facing Hiraeth, tilted back his head. He seemed to scan its every stone and shingle, its every turret and gargoyle and spire as if to commit them to memory forever. Then his eyes lingered at Gwenllian's window, discovering her there.

She raised a hand, half suspended the fingers, but if he saw the tentative greeting he did not acknowledge it.

That was the last she saw of the boy who called himself Rhaman. Before the sun had risen fully off the ocean's curve, the Squire of Hiraeth had disappeared.

And Gwenllian never quite forgot him.

One

Papa had taken her on another journey. Only this time, she was not at all sure she would enjoy it. Never had she been out of Wales, never had she set her dainty foot upon a distant shore, heard spoken a strange tongue, or seen anyone who appeared overly different from herself. Between her loyalty and unworldliness, she felt certain no land was as beautiful as that of home, no language so enchanting as Welsh. And Papa contended that the earth held no faces as charming as those blue-eyed, pointy-chinned ones of her native realm.

But in spite of her sheltered upbringing, the prospect of seeing the country called Morocco excited Gwenllian Evans. As they sailed toward its sunglazed shores, she had to admit she had never beheld waters so bright, with depths the color of the aquamarine necklace concealed beneath her blouse on a twisted gold chain. She was suddenly glad that Papa's old friend, Colonel Carstairs, had invited her to enjoy a holiday in Tangier while her

17

father conducted business. As an added delight, Papa had allowed her to bring her future husband, Robyn Breese, and her dearest friend, Sophie.

Hugging her arms to herself, Gwen thought of the tours they would take together through the ancient streets, of the colorful people they would meet. The four of them would have a marvelous time shopping and dancing and dining in this exotic land. They would enjoy a holiday far more exciting than the jaunt to dull old London Sophie had wanted to take.

As the steamer *Sebou* chugged along, bucking on the wind-driven tide, a shower of sea foam eddied from its mother wave and splashed over the bow, stinging Gwenllian's cheeks. She shivered at its coldness, then started as a series of sharp, piercing whistles rent the pristine air smelling of salt and fish. The ship was heralding her approach into port!

Squinting her eyes against the shimmer of the glittering water, Gwenllian struggled to get a first glimpse of Tangier. She put a hand to her brow, blocked the sun's saffron glare, then gasped aloud.

Ahead rose a dazzling collection of minarets, their spiraling tops pointing graceful fingers of gold at vast blue heavens. Ringing the edifices, white walls and terraces vibrated with the sun's reflection, while atop the tallest mosques, tiles of green sparkled like square-cut emeralds set in polished bezels. Standing sentinel over all, luxuriant trees nodded in a lazy wind, nests for the soaring birds that wheeled and dipped like kites above the town's ancient ramparts.

The whole of this paradisal illusion seemed to

rise up out of the sea like a come-to-life fairy tale kingdom; indeed, Gwenllian mused, with goose-flesh prickling her arms, from her distant aspect the city could have been the lost realm of the *Tylwth Teg*, that fairy clan of Wales that she had so raptly read about in childhood.

"Your parasol, Gwen," a voice behind her said, dispelling her pleasant fancies. "This blasted sun will turn your face brown in the space of a day, if you're not careful of it."

Smiling, she took the ivory-handled sunshade and gave the lacy shield a reckless twirl. Her reply held a coquettishness unusual to her more serious nature. "Wouldn't you like me brown like a savage, Robyn?"

The slender, expensively attired young man leaned closer, speaking low in her ear. "I would like you any way at all, and well you know it."

"Fiddle-faddle!" Gwen scoffed, and raised her chin to show the curve of a delicate jaw. "You like your ladies pale and refined. I already know my days of traipsing about the estate in my old boots and rough woolens are numbered."

He chuckled and put an elegant hand atop her wrist. "Will it be so dreadful, my dear?"

She stared ahead, scanning the magical skyline of Tangier, and wondered. *Would* life be dreadful lived beside Robyn Breese? Would she awake on misty morns beneath the embroidered canopy of the squire's bed at Ardderyd and be discontented? Would she regret standing beside him at the christening of future blue-blooded heirs? He was the likely choice for her, after all, and Papa heartily approved of the union. Her cousin twice removed,

Robyn would inherit Ardderyd at her father's death since Sir Gerald had no male issue and declared no intention of marrying and begetting any. Of course, Robyn had not officially proposed to her yet, but that would come with their return to Wales next month, followed by all the pomp and ceremony the society-conscious young earl felt necessary to sanctify the occasion of his betrothal.

Gwen had known him since childhood and they got on together well enough, probably because he spoiled her just as outrageously as Papa did, giving in to her whims with little more prompting than a sulkily down-bent head and lowered lashes. He was nice looking, too, in an urbane, fastidious way, with the smooth hands of an aristocrat, and rarely a hair out of place.

Yet, where she was imaginative, he was prosaic. Robyn could never enjoy staring up at the stars and wondering aloud at their mystery, or abide reading a page of Plato, or find interest in poking about the waterweeds looking for relics of the lost Welsh clans.

"Robyn," Gwenllian said suddenly with a wistful tug on his arm. "The view of Tangier there . . . squint your eyes. Now, can't you just imagine it as the lost kingdom of the *Tylwth Teg*?"

He smiled at her fondly, his lower lip flattening. "You and your fancies, Gwen. I swear I've never known a girl who dreams and *thinks* so much. As for myself, I prefer more tangible pursuits." Putting his hands on her narrow waist and squeezing it, he added, "I shall show you what I mean before long."

Gwenllian leaned back against him, risking impropriety, for she wanted to feel some burgeoning

20

of ardency just as any young girl would yearn to do in the arms of her intended. Through instinct, she knew that a man with a stronger will would be a better match for her than the malleable Robyn, but such a prospect had never come her way. Besides, she did not want to lose Ardderyd, and if an amicable marriage would keep her in her ancestral home, she would go to the altar with no more than the usual maidenly qualms.

"What do ye think of it, daughter?" Sir Gerald strolled up behind her on the rocking deck, his steady gait revealing his past years in service to Her Majesty's Royal Navy. "Are ye excited to be landing on foreign soil for the first time in yer life?"

"You know I am," Gwen answered, tucking a strand of straggling black hair beneath the brim of her stylish hat. "And yet, already I miss the cool Welsh mists."

"Ye'll miss them even more before the month is out," he predicted with a slow nod of his wild-maned head. "I spent time on these shores during my days as a tar, and never felt air so parching or sun so hot." He inhaled deeply, squinted his nut-brown eyes to view the approaching chalky walls of Tangier. "But the place has a rare beauty of its own, ye'll see. Colonel Carstairs assures me that he and his missus are both quite taken with it."

"Is Sophie still below?" she asked her father with a concerned frown.

"I fear so. She does not have the—er—constitution," he phrased delicately, "for sailing choppy waters."

"Oh, look!" Gwen exclaimed in sudden excite-

21

ment, her eyes as bright as the sequined sea. "There's the pier!"

On the weathered planks ahead a group of coffee-skinned men climbed into waiting rowboats and pointed in the steamer's direction, nodding their turbaned heads and signaling with waving arms. After unshipping the oars, they speedily made their way toward the *Sebou* as the ship lurched and hove to. Moments later, the pier hands accessed the steamer like energetic monkeys and gesticulated wildly while speaking Arabic in vociferous voices.

After scooping up her little dog Buff to keep him out of harm's way, Gwen scurried to fetch Sophie and stood with the white-faced girl on the quarterdeck while the Arabs busily hauled up their trunks, and with no particular care, cast them into the bobbing rowboats. Robyn moved assertively close, scowling as the black-eyed workers openly ogled the fair Western ladies in their billowy pastel skirts.

Sophie put a handkerchief over her nose and whispered faintly to her friend, "Good heavens, I can smell those men from here."

"It's no wonder," Gwen replied, eyeing the gleaming mahogany faces and fanning herself with a flapping hand. "The sun's so dreadfully hot."

"I can't wait to get to the Carstairs' house and lie down again," Sophie fretted. "I swear I've never been so miserable."

Gwenllian scarcely heard her. She was staring hard at the Arabs, at the loose white garments falling from their shoulders in generous folds and at the sashes cinched loosely about their waists. The sight pricked a vivid memory.

"The Squire of Hiraeth . . ." she breathed, putting a hand to her throat in wonder.

Sir Gerald caught only her last word. "What did ye say, daughter?"

"Their clothes." She nodded to indicate the busy Arabs.

"The burnooses?"

"*He* wore the same kind of garment—the Squire of Hiraeth."

Sir Gerald glanced sharply at her and raised a brow. "Ye still remember him?"

Gwenllian observed the group of Arabs wielding her brass-bound trunks, her gaze filled with images of a tall enigmatic boy possessing expressive eyes of blue. Softly she replied, "I've never forgotten him."

Once they disembarked, the foursome proceeded to the Customs House, and, after laboriously communicating with the Arabic-speaking officials there, were finally cleared to go ashore. When Gwenllian at last stepped out upon the streets of Tangier and faced the swarming city baked by the sun, she felt as if she had crossed into another universe. Foreign sights, smells, and sounds assaulted her senses with such dizzying force that she stepped backward in reaction. Her dog squirmed in her arms and whimpered.

The streets teemed with life. Moors and Arabs bustled about in white burnooses, bargaining and arguing at colorful stalls burgeoning with exotic merchandise. In skull caps and sturdy sandals, knots of bearded Jews wended through the crowd, passing a straggling line of Negroes balancing baskets upon their jet-black heads. Amidst the jumble of pedestrians, teams of oxen lumbered, goaded by stick-toting masters who lashed the animals' flanks with braided whips. Sheep bleated in skittish flocks guarded by bare-legged shepherds, while groaning camels knelt with heavy loads strapped to their mountainous backs. Here and there shaggy donkeys stood tethered, viciously kicking out at the mangy stray dogs scampering close to their heels.

Gwen had not expected to see such sights, and stared with chagrined wonder at the wandering toothless beggars who whined for alms on every corner and accosted the passersby who came their way. In buzzing circles swarms of flies hovered over the muddy pavement strewn with animal dung, while the odor of exotic spices floated so repugnantly on the steaming air that Gwen clamped a hand to her nose to keep nausea at bay. How far she had come from the fresh counties of Wales where the scent of heather and fertile earth encouraged lungfuls of air!

"My God, this is a devil of a place," Robyn commented beside her, his eyes scanning the traffic and the squalor.

"We can take a proper tour later," Sir Gerald said, his enthusiasm for the jaunt obvious. "We should be on our way now. Just pray that my memory serves me right and I can lead us straightaway to Colonel Carstairs' house. He'll send servants later to transport our trunks." Bending down, he retrieved the slim portmanteau he had refused to leave behind with the other baggage and marched forward through the throng with Sophie on his arm.

"Can't we take a carriage, Papa?" Gwen asked. In distress she glanced at the mud already edging the hem of her new lilac skirts.

Her sire pushed aside the persistent beggar clawing at his sleeve. "Did I fail to mention to ye that there are no carriages here? I doubt that ye'll see even the crudest dray."

His three companions stared at him.

"Come now, Gwen," Robyn cajoled as if feeling it his masculine duty to be stoic. "You never minded walking."

"It's not the walking I mind." Wrinkling her nose, she lifted her skirts and stepped into the odiferous mire. "I should have worn the old boots I save for tramping over the bogs at Ardderyd."

Already, she had determined that Morocco was inferior to Wales, for where were the proper manners, the cleanliness and the order? She had never seen such a populated place. The narrow, mazelike streets she so gingerly traversed were literally packed with unwashed people and noisy animals. Countless cavelike shops with yawning doors and lounging vendors stretched everywhere in crooked rows, interrupted here and there by long white walls smudged with the oil of many hands. Moorish cafes abounded, sending out aromas that blended appallingly with the putrid smells of animal carcasses left to rot in foul heaps upon the streets.

Gwenllian kept her handkerchief to her nose and slapped away the grimy hands of supplicants daring to tug at her new silk blouse. "Great Elysium,

25

Robyn!" she hissed between her teeth. "Where has Papa brought us?" Glancing at her intended, she was annoyed to see him more stricken by the stench than she. His usually sanguine complexion had almost drained of color, and he dabbed a handkerchief at the perspiration dripping off his eyebrows.

Taking hold of the earl's elbow with sudden vexation, she noticed that her father strode ahead quite unaffected by the disgusting sights, with poor tripping Sophie clinging to his arm in a half-swoon.

"Look there at the mosque!" he exclaimed over a pointing finger. Thrusting a hand in his coat, he pulled out his pocket watch and checked the time. "The *muezzin* should be giving his call to prayer at any moment. Five times a day he does it on perfect schedule."

As if on cue, a shrill cry pierced the air. Chilled, the foursome stopped and squinted their eyes against the lemon glare, alert for a glimpse of the holy figure. On the balcony of the minaret he appeared and, after hoisting a white flag upon a pole, began to utter strange words in a loud and mournful voice. *"Allah Akhbar! Allah Akhbar!"*

All around, people stopped what they were doing and prostrated themselves in the act of worship, kneeling upon the dusty ground or upon prayer rugs hastily thrown down. Where once the streets had clamored, stillness reigned. But when Robyn would have moved forward to continue their progress in the lull, Sir Gerald stayed him with a rebuking hand. "Better not," he murmured.

Gwenllian stood awed, held captive by the whining chants. She felt suspended in time suddenly, as if a spell had whisked her across the boundaries of another dimension. She had never witnessed a religious ritual performed in the midst of bustling city streets or seen worshipers so faithful to a call. The sight of the countless forms with lowered heads and outstretched arms lying in the shadow of the green-tiled mosque sent a shiver down her spine.

Finally, the crowd began to stir and commence its industrious hum once more. Leading his party on, Sir Gerald zigzagged through lines of camels and pointed out various places of interest to his flagging companions.

"Yonder is the marketplace," he said. "Or, the souk as they call it here. I think ye'll find it quite entertaining, though we won't have time to browse the shops until tomorrow. Likely we'll be an attraction there. Don't be surprised to find yerself bothered by opportunistic Arabs offering a variety of services for a 'little token,' as they say."

Gwen scarcely heard him. Between sidestepping dead fowl and avoiding beggars, she had little attention to spare.

They approached a large square where every item and food imaginable was displayed by eager-eyed salespersons tempting passersby with a taste or a closer look. Spitted meats hung from makeshift rafters. Eggs, butter, figs, dates, sugar, tobacco, and spices sat in open crates or boxes; burnooses and multicolored kaftans billowed from wooden pegs beside glinting bridles and spurs. Red Moroccan slippers, braided thongs, and coarse carpets of Rabat wool all vied for the attention of shoppers, and everywhere guns were sold along with collections of swords, poniards, and knives.

Gwen held her squirming Corgi more securely, struggling to keep him from jumping out of her arms and into the shifting press of sweating bodies. Sophie released Sir Gerald's arm and, dropping back to join her friend, spoke in a thin distressed voice. "Those children—have you ever seen such a pitiful sight? Just *look* at them!" With horror mirrored in her unworldly eyes she indicated the huddle of scarecrow forms sitting on the pavement dabbling their feet in a puddle.

Gwenllian had already noticed the naked, dirty youngsters, and was loath to take a second glance. How shocked and disappointed she felt! Tangier was scarcely the delightful holiday spot she had envisioned while packing in Wales.

"It's an outrage, isn't it?" she said. "I had no idea this was such a horrid place, Sophie, or I would never have discouraged your plans to holiday in London. Conditions here are positively uncivilized."

"Uncivilized is too kind a word," Robyn cut in. "Try barbaric."

Gwenllian glanced at the red-faced young earl, sensing that he was intimidated by this world he did not know, a world far from the refinements of Oxford, the green order of his estates and the sumptuousness of his London gaming clubs. For the first time, and with an unexpected dismay, she thought him unmanly.

"Ah! Do ye see, daughter?" Sir Gerald shouted above the clamor. He waved off the persistent Moor offering to carry his portmanteau. "I told ye we would see a snake charmer, and by Jove, we didn't have to wait long for the treat!"

Peering through a herd of goats, Gwen saw a man with matted black hair chanting and beating a drum with his long-nailed hands. Beside him another performer played a bamboo flute in accompaniment, his eyes closed in ecstasy while his slender body slowly swayed. To the rhythm of their strange and lurid beat, a third man leapt about on long bare legs, his naked torso agleam with sweat and his eyes wild above pointed eyebrows. He held a large braided basket and, after dancing round the gathering crowd several times, flung open its decorated lid in a dramatic gesture. Thrusting an arm into its secret depths, he yanked out an enormous, writhing serpent.

Sophie hid her head rather than look at the hideous creature, and Robyn murmured a hissed "Egad!" while Gwenllian stood in morbid fascination.

The charmer held the undulating cobra high and displayed it with a flourish to the cringing crowd. Unwilling to miss the show, Gwen inched close to her father, mesmerized by both the gyrating charmer and the frightening serpent, which moved its head in tandem with its master's taunting wand. The eyes of the beast and the man seemed locked together in a daring game. And then, just as the snake twined about the muscled shoulders of its bearer, the charmer seized its flexing tail and took the end of it between his teeth.

The crowd applauded and tossed coins, encouraging greater feats of recklessness.

Clutching Buff tightly in her arms, Gwen leaned

forward and watched in sheer aversion as the charmer inserted a finger inside the open jaws of the baited reptile. Repeatedly the snake sank its fangs into its master's flesh, but the man only teased it more with the circling wand. Then with his black dancing eyes meeting those smaller slitted ones, the charmer thrust his face toward the danger of its gaping mouth.

Aghast at the dreadful drama, Gwen swayed. The charmer's cheek streamed with blood, and the horrible vision prompted a memory of a hunting trip with Papa long ago. She remembered a pack of hounds tearing the flesh of a fox. Papa had severed the brush with his knife and presented the bloody tail to her as the customary trophy. Ever since, the sight of blood had made her sick.

"Are ye alright, daughter?" Sir Gerald asked anxiously, his voice just penetrating her consciousness. He took her arm, put something to her lips, and bade her drink it.

Never one to indulge in feminine vapors, Gwen sipped the whiskey her father offered from a silver flask and tried to gather her wits. "I'm fine . . . really," she breathed, shaking her head when Robyn asked if he should pick her up and carry her to shade.

The pugnacious little Moor who had been following them held out a sliced lemon in his dirty palm, offering it to her with a wide yellowed smile.

"No, please . . ." Gwen said, repulsed, tugging at her sire's arm. "Let's just continue on. It's only the heat bothering me."

But as they pushed through the dispersing throng

a sound like thunder reverberated off the frescoed columns framing the market square. A horse approached, and its galloping hooves struck the hard baked earth in a rumbling beat. Still queasy, Gwen blinked her eyes and peered through the shifting crowd in curiosity.

The rider's garments shimmered with the waves of heat rising up from the ground, making him appear miragelike as he passed beneath the courtyard arches. The still air stirred beneath the horse's hooves, swirling the dust of the street into a cloud of ivory. People parted in respect or fear of the rider, and as they fell back, Gwenllian received a clearer view.

She held her breath, dazzled like the rest. The steed was the most magnificent animal she had ever seen, far finer than the best thoroughbreds for sale at the Dyfed fairs. Its intelligent eyes rolled with fire above reddened nostrils, its mane swished like silk over a high arched neck, and its rippling tail brushed the earth like a banner. Caparisoned with costly saddlery, the gray beast glistened with a layer of sand as if it had traveled hard and far. Even the silver-chased rifle case hanging from the saddle was filmed with dust. Foam flecked the horse's mouth and streamed over the wide reins which its master held in check.

Gwen raised her eyes and followed the line of the leather upward.

The master of the beast was not dressed richly. He wore only a simple chestnut-colored burnoose and breeches, yet his tall bearing and handling of the spirited animal suggested a natural authority.

Although a white *haik* was drawn across his face in the fashion of a Moroccan traveler, he sported fine English boots. And his spurs were of the type Papa wore rather than the more wicked ones displayed in the market stalls. By contrast, a sheathed saber hung from his hip, rocking slightly to and fro with the easy gait of the horse. Considering his inconsistencies of attire, Gwen studied the rider more closely, her gaze drawn to his half-concealed face, where only the eyes gave a hint of his looks.

And what startling eyes they were! Brilliantly incisive beneath a pair of straight black brows, their alertness was so entire they seemed to note every movement in the market, whether slight or obvious. For a brief second they scanned the faces of the crowd before meeting Gwen's gaze with a quick and assessing flicker. She felt disquieted by them, for they were light-colored, not black as she would have expected.

"You like him, missy? Some call him 'the English.'"

Gwen started at the sound of the informative voice. The persistent Moor pressed close to her side and smiled. Dismayed, she turned to find her father, but he was no longer standing at her elbow.

Wheeling about, she looked frantically for Robyn and Sophie in the crush of dark-skinned people. Where were they? She stood on tiptoe and again scanned the faces of the milling crowd, seeing no sign of her companions. Nor did she hear any fretful voices calling out her name.

In her distraction she forgot Buff and the opportunistic pet sprang from her arms in an energetic bound. To her horror, the dog darted beneath the hooves of the nervous gray horse, startling it. Quickly the rider hauled back on the reins to keep the stallion from trampling pedestrians, while, undeterred, the foolish cur dashed for a butcher's stall stocked with sheep carcasses hung on long wicked hooks. With no hesitation, Buff sank his pair of greedy jaws into the merchandise.

The infuriated vendor seized a stick and raised it as if to maim the thief, but Gwen screeched out a wrathful protest so loud it echoed off the whitewashed walls. Running across the square with furiously waving arms, she berated the man, creating such a spectacle that people began to stop and stare.

In astonishment, the vendor glared at the brash, shrill-voiced attacker in her Western gown, his seamed face turning darker. Incensed over her audacity to admonish him, he began to curse her in Arabic, raising the stick again to brutalize the dog. Alarmed, Gwen rushed forward to try and stay his arm, screaming out a most unladylike threat to flay him with her parasol. But before she could grasp the sleeve of his filthy burnoose or wield her lacy weapon, a pair of hands seized her about the waist and hauled her easily to one side.

Outraged, she objected to the affront, but the man called English ignored her, and in a calm voice began speaking to the vendor with his palms spread out in commiseration. Although he used a language she did not know, his tone was undeniably cajoling, so that all those watching the entertainment turned their eyes to Gwen and laughed. Beneath such derision she felt her already sunburnt cheeks turning a deeper shade of crimson.

After tossing a few coins to the now placated butcher, the self-possessed rider knelt down, and in English called to Buff, who was happily chewing his ill-gained booty. The dog pricked his ears and wiggled the tip of his tail before sheepishly trundling forward to be scooped up and retained in the crook of a strong arm.

Turning to Gwen, the rider pinned her with his extraordinary eyes. Then he strolled forward and, presenting her with the troublesome pet, spoke in a cool voice. "Hold tightly to that which you treasure here, miss. Else, you may find yourself without it."

Gwen seized the pup and hugged him protectively to her breast, speechless in the presence of the disconcerting foreigner.

Behind her the gray horse snorted, and his master gathered up its reins. Then he hesitated with one boot in the stirrup, and glancing at her over his shoulder, seemed to decide that his European acquaintance needed one more piece of advice. "And just so you'll know," he said with sternness, "in Morocco, a woman never berates a man."

When she stared at him, he winked and added, "Not in public anyway."

He made to vault into the saddle, but before his leg had quite cleared the cantle, a sound arrested him. Gwen glanced up, instantly thrown into a spine-chilling whirl of confusion. Three riders swooped into the square like vengeful demons, their fierce-eyed steeds trampling and felling any who could not flee their barreling pace quickly

34

enough. Ear-splitting screams rent the air while vegetable crates and makeshift booths crashed to the ground like tumbling matchsticks.

Even while she stood dazed amidst the sudden bedlam, the man called English thrust her forward into the butcher's stall. With rifle in hand, he joined her, pushing her more securely beneath the shield of hanging carcasses. To her dismay Buff escaped again, darting through her legs just as one of the pistol-brandishing horsemen flew forward on a viciously spurred steed.

Gwen screamed at the man beside her, thinking he was about to meet a most terrible end. But with practiced skill he raised his rifle, aimed and fired, all in the space of a second. His aim proved true. The savage attacker tumbled from his saddle.

As he fell his panicked horse bolted through the swinging carcasses in Gwen's direction, and before she could react, her quick-handed guardian dragged her closer to his side, where she huddled in sheer terror and prayed aloud for a merciful deliverance.

All about the ravaged marketplace women shrieked and men shouted as the two remaining riders circled the butcher's stall with their weapons poised and firing. Amidst the chaos and the choking dust, the English's rifle cracked again in answer. Lead flew, and the tall young man knelt down upon one knee to better sight his target. He hit his mark, and a dying cry met Gwen's ears while another riderless horse careened past with foam flying from its brutally sawed mouth.

Daring to raise her head a bit, she saw the third

demon rider thunder forth. In a dreadful clash, his horse collided with the English's gray steed, the point of their massive shoulders meeting in a bone-crushing thud. Amidst a tangle of legs, both animals crashed to the ground and rolled, unseating the surprised rider.

"Get down!" the English bellowed, shoving Gwen to the ground and shielding her with his body. "Or do you want to lose your head?"

His concern for her safety cost him a crucial second of time. With a bloodcurdling howl, the now unhorsed rider leapt over the upturned table and throttled the English with his bare hands. Swinging his rifle, Gwen's protector knocked the assailant to his knees, but the undaunted demon swiftly produced a slender saber.

Numb with fear, Gwen crawled further beneath the table, cowering there while the English unsheathed his own sword and prompted a dreadful contest of power and ferocity. The two determined men lunged and parried, not in the polished way she had seen at London exhibitions, but with savage strength and brutal purpose. She judged the English younger than his opponent, for his large but graceful body moved with more agility, and his sword arm swept in dextrous arcs that displayed an athletic vigor. After several deft feints and lunges he thrust the weapon home, cleanly piercing the chest of his enemy.

Gwenllian cried out in reaction to the death, her eyes fixed in horror upon the body lying at his feet. The gruesomeness and the freely flowing blood sickened her, and with a helpless moan she lowered her head toward the earth and heaved. On her knees and bent double, she was only dimly aware of the pair of boots planted just inches away. But after a moment a hand grasped her arm and drew her to her feet with a steady firmness.

"It's over now. You're safe."

She heard the calm voice of the English, but continued to shiver and pray that he would go away. He did not. He put a hand atop her lowered head and said, "Your courage has not deserted you now, has it? When you were battling the butcher, I could have sworn you were as fierce as I. Find your bravery again. You'll need it here."

She could not meet his eyes, for her own were fastened in revulsion to his scarlet-spattered burnoose. She shuddered, her nerves stretched to a snapping point over the violence she had witnessed. All at once her outrage at this man and his country burst from her lips in one branding word, which she spat at him with harsh contempt. *"Barbarian!"*

Every soul in the marketplace seemed to freeze. Even the animals stood still. Like an audience witnessing a play with the actors on center stage, the crowd watched awed, staring at the intrepid rider, the three bodies he had felled, and the bold-tongued European woman.

The English did not flinch at the slur but leaned to retrieve his rifle with his usual composure and cradled it in the crook of his arm. He inclined his head and answered her with perfect civility. "As you say, miss. As you say."

The marketplace was a near ruin, strewn with shattered pottery, blowing kaftans, and trampled melons. And in the midst of its wreckage, the splendid gray horse lay struggling to stand, its dust-covered legs flailing empty air and its spirited eyes glazed.

The man who had proudly ridden it into the square less than a half hour past slowly made his way to its side. For a moment he regarded his mount with expressionless eyes, though his wide shoulders slumped at the sight of the noble beast humbled with its shattered leg. And then he knelt down on one knee and, extending a hand, touched the flared muzzle with no less compassion than he might show a well-loved friend.

He stood. In the hollow of his arm he carried the rifle. Gwen saw him shift it, then hesitate with one hand upon the barrel. The horse snorted and, as if showing its master the full degree of its mettle, attempted to rise once more before falling back helplessly with heaving sides.

His decision made, the English raised the rifle and, looking down the barrel, positioned it in its deadly aim. As his finger moved to squeeze the trigger, Gwenllian turned away and sobbed. She was only vaguely aware that her father had rejoined her to murmur soothing words and countless apologies. But his hand on her arm was solid and familiar, and she clenched it frantically for support.

Then in a hoarse voice, she begged him to take her away from the carnage in the marketplace, and from the stranger she had called a barbarian.

Two

"I want to go home."

Sitting before a vanity vigorously brushing out her hair, Gwen regarded her father by way of the tilted mirror, her deep blue eyes blazing. Now that she was bathed and dressed in a fresh peach gown, her spirit had returned and she intended to use it full force in an effort to get her way.

Earlier she had closed the shutters of the guest room with a preemptory snap, blocking out the hateful view of blistering streets and crumbling arches. But the sly sun managed to find slivers of clearance through the slats anyway, defiantly striping the floor with hot saffron. As if to add to her misery, the *muezzin* had cried the call to prayer again, prompting her to clap her hands over her ears to smother his eerie whine. And those were not the only aspects of Morocco the shaken girl yearned to shut out, but unfortunately the bloody scene in the square was still too vivid to be eradicated simply at will.

"I had no idea Tangier was such an uncivilized

39

place, Papa," she continued peevishly, coiling her black hair and pinning it in a heavy chignon. "Else, I would never have come. It's filthy, backward, and populated by fiendish barbarians. I know you must stay to conduct business with Colonel Carstairs, but Robyn can accompany Sophie and me home just as soon as our passage is arranged."

Sir Gerald ran a hand over his thick whiskers and paced the length of the room, feeling ill-equipped as usual in the face of his daughter's petulance. "But, Gwenllian," he argued in his most patient tone, "we've been here only a matter of hours. The experience ye underwent in the souk was an unpleasant one, of course, but—"

"Experience?" Gwen echoed, giving her father a look of incredulity complete with gaping mouth and widened eyes. *"Unpleasant?* I was nearly killed, for heaven's sake! You saw all the dead bodies scattered about the square, and that—that savage who cut them down. It was something out of the darkest chapters of *Arabian Nights*. And amidst it all I lost Buff," she added fretfully, her lower lip aquiver. "It positively chills my blood to imagine *his* fate."

Sir Gerald had the grace to appear remorseful. "I know, my dear, and to help comfort ye, I'll get ye a new pup just as soon as we arrive home—one of Squire Melvyn's. In the meantime, we'll only be staying in Tangier a month, and 'tis most unlikely ye'd be involved in another such unfortunate encounter. Indeed, if yer uncomfortable going out, ye could find feminine occupation in the house here with Mrs. Carstairs and stay safely indoors all during yer visit."

"Stay confined? Papa, you know I'm not one for needlework and female chitchat. I should go mad cooped up with such sedentary tasks. Do you forget I'm accustomed to riding every day and walking, overseeing the entire domestic staff at Ardderyd?"

"But you are on holiday now—"

A light rap on the door and a discreet clearing of a throat interrupted the impasse. Relieved, Sir Gerald opened the portal to find Lord Breese lounging on the threshold.

"Ah, Robyn!" he exclaimed with more than usual enthusiasm. "Come in, come in! Perhaps ye can rationalize with Gwenllian where I have failed. She insists upon going home on the very next steamer, with yer escort."

"Perhaps this will help soothe you, Gwen." Immaculate in his fresh change of linen, the earl sauntered in and, setting down a roughly woven basket, flipped open the lid. Delving into its depths, he withdrew a squirming, bright-eyed Buff.

"Oh!" the young woman cried, snatching the errant dog and clutching him joyfully to her breast. "Where ever did you find him, darling Robyn?"

"Unfortunately, I can't claim credit for his discovery. The Carstairs' servant found the basket abandoned upon the doorstep a few moments ago. It's a mystery how it arrived."

Gwen frowned, pondering the puzzle before lifting her shoulders in dismissal. "Ah, well. It little matters, does it, just so my precious Buff is safe and sound."

"Well, daughter," Sir Gerald inquired with his

41

brows hopefully raised. "Are ye appeased? Will ye stay on?"

"What do you say, Gwen?" Robyn prompted, leaning with crossed arms on the edge of a writing desk. "I confess, Tangier is hardly what I expected it to be, but Carstairs assures me there are pleasant diversions in the more civilized avenues frequented by Europeans. Think of the shopping expeditions we had planned," he reminded her temptingly. "I haven't forgotten my promise to buy you a trinket or two."

Gwen was not eager to relinquish her position so easily. Besides, mention of the shopping spree only reminded her of the marketplace with its blood and death. As for the man called English, she could scarcely permit her thoughts to dwell upon him at all. At least the particulars of his fierce appearance were beginning to dim. During her encounter with him she had been too dazed to register many details, remembering above all that he possessed a savagery equal to his country and a dispassion surely found only in heathens. How had he remained so unruffled after strewing bodies about the souk? A civilized man would have at least displayed a modicum of remorse, or acted distressed in the aftermath of such carnage.

"What do you say, Gwen?" Robyn prodded again. "Shall we stay?"

"You behave as if you'd enjoy the prospect," she pouted, feeling betrayed.

He shrugged. "I'm game. And, frankly, Gwen, I'm surprised at you. I've never known you to be unadventurous. 'Tis usually you pulling me across

Ardderyd, begging me to go on treasure-hunting jaunts or archaeological explorations."

Gwenllian turned her back upon him, catching a glimpse of the earl's face in the mirror as he exchanged a conspiratorial nod with Sir Gerald. Realizing she had lost the battle but delaying the moment of surrender, she temporized, asking in a sulky tone, "How is Sophie, Robin?"

"Still resting with a cool cloth to her head. But I believe she intends to recover before dinner. Mrs. Carstairs just happens to be serving her favorite dessert."

Knowing herself outnumbered, Gwen turned her back and grumbled with ill grace, "Oh, very well, then. I won't have it said *I* spoiled the holiday."

Like a pair of soldiers who had just claimed some hard-fought victory, Sir Gerald and Robyn grinned at each other, unaware that the mirror reflected their smug faces across the room.

Maintaining her petulance for their benefit, Gwen closed the door with energy enough to rattle the lock. Then she sighed in resignation and let Buff jump to the floor, idly contemplating the basket in which he had so mysteriously arrived. While she was leaning to close the lid, a scrap of paper caught her eye. It was wedged between the slats reinforcing the oval bottom, and curious, she pulled it free.

Set down in boldly penned letters were a few scrawled lines.

Have you regained your courage? I hope it was easier to find than your pet. The scoundrel led me on quite a

43

merry chase before his penchant for mutton got the better of him. May I suggest a collar and leash?

Libby Carstairs proved to be a most gracious hostess in spite of her rather irritating fussiness. Kind but ineffectual, the plump Englishwoman had a way of making herself oblivious to the unpleasant, for when Sir Gerald related Gwen's ordeal, Libby clucked once or twice before neatly changing the subject to one of social news from home. Perhaps, Gwen thought, the woman had endured military life by adopting such an attitude, or maybe unpleasantries were so commonplace in the uncivilized places of foreign service that she had become inured to them.

At least her dining table was as nicely laid as any in an English brownstone, with nary a crack in the flowered dishes that had traveled all over the world. Gwen welcomed the familiar sight of Waterford crystal, lace napkins, and plainly cooked beef. Had the pungently spiced fare she had smelled earlier in the streets been set before her, she would have lost her appetite.

The shutters had been flung wide in the dining room, permitting a breeze to skip across the tiled floor, and providing a view of serpentine walls and looming mosques brushed with the gloom of twilight. Instead of appearing softer, less sharp with the limelight of a pitiless sun, the city only seemed more ominous, more secretively sly, able now to hide its threatening horrors from unsuspecting innocents. And somewhere, Gwen thought, a man called

44

English walked the streets without a horse, his burnoose spattered with blood . . .

Perhaps her face revealed distress, for when the party was all seated and served by Libby's maid, Colonel Carstairs cleared his throat and said, "Terribly sorry about your unfortunate experience in the souk today, Miss Evans. Truly dreadful for a gently-bred lady like yourself, but not likely to happen again. Why, Mrs. Carstairs ventures to the market with her maid almost daily, and has never suffered such an ordeal. Of course, there are dangerous characters roaming the streets, and one must take proper precautions."

Spreading butter on a crusty roll, he went on. "You will be quite safe in the neighborhoods suitable for tourists as long as you make no display of yourselves. You must understand that the natives are rather fanatical in their faith and tolerate Westerners only to a degree. It takes little to incite them."

"I've heard tales about Christians being murdered," Robyn commented, leisurely sipping his second glass of red wine. "Wasn't there a Major Liang brutally killed a few years ago?"

Sophie's face lost its precarious reserve of color again and Colonel Carstairs hastened to gloss over the account. "That was earlier in the century and done by a hostile tribe. Such things rarely happen in Tangier these days, especially if one is careful. Now, the outlying regions are a different matter—"

Pausing, he glanced through his spectacles at the ladies and seemed to amend the last half of his statement. "Well, Europeans must be discreet in all matters of religion."

Gwen thought of the *muezzin*'s call to prayer, of the rows of worshipful souls she had seen lying face-down in the dust, and could well believe the colonel's warning.

"I should never want to venture out into the countryside," Sophie declared with a delicate shiver of bare white shoulders. "I'm quite content staying within a mile of the British embassy, thank you."

"I should like a tour of the country," Robyn drawled, the fading light touching the sheen of macassar oil on his hair. "What a lark it would be traveling in one of those caravans and riding a camel over the dunes."

"It's a mistake to romanticize it," the colonel said to temper his guest's enthusiasm. "A brutal land lies beyond the ramparts of this city—harsh, alien to anything we Europeans know. I've made a few expeditions myself and, although they were exciting, I admit they quite tested my endurance."

Gwen noted that her father's eyes shone with an eager light, as if his sense of adventure were suddenly roused. "Papa," she whispered, leaning forward with concern, "you don't have some mad intention of going on a trek through the desert, do you?"

"Don't concern yerself, daughter. Just relax and make the most of yer holiday."

Gwen thought her holiday far beyond salvaging, but too well-bred to say so at the table, mustered a thin smile and politely took another bite of peas.

By the time the fruit and cheeses were served,

the city view beyond the open shutters had dimmed into a soft palette of amethyst and wisteria, with the sea a distant stretch of sapphire between tapering minarets. The candles had been lit, and playful breezes made the flames dance over the polished silver plate and faceted crystal. Mrs. Carstairs was chattering on about her brilliant nephew from Manchester who had just been promoted to captain in the Grenadier Guards, when a manservant discreetly passed a message to the colonel's hand.

"Ah, he is here!" Carstairs exclaimed upon perusing the note. "Invite him in. And bring us a bottle of brandy."

A moment later Gwen heard the quick rap of footsteps. Glancing up, she saw a gentleman enter the room, and the succulent slice of orange she had just lifted to her lips stayed suspended. Her eyes widened.

The meager light of the candles and the evening gloom cast only a faint illumination upon the man's features, but the glow was adequate enough to show the guest's considerable attributes. Judging by the quality of his black trousers and jacket, he was European. He possessed a face similar to those immortalized on the visages of Roman warriors clashing swords across Italian friezes, his dark skin and black hair completing the striking image. Gwen found his mouth especially charming, for it was finely shaped and bracketed with rugged lines.

The visitor's eye-catching looks, extraordinary in a more masculine than handsome way, caused even Robyn to straighten abruptly in his chair, as if his own male vanity were challenged by the mere presence of the other. Next to him, Sophie sat with her hand frozen upon her wineglass, obviously too enchanted to move.

Before a word could be spoken, the guest's eyes took in not only the face of every diner around the table, but the contents of their plates, so that Gwen fancied he could have detailed the type and amount of fruit each was eating. She thought his gaze dwelled upon her face a fraction longer than necessary, but perhaps that was because her own was equally interested and direct. Indeed, disconcerted over her own enthrallment, she lowered her head and toyed with the napkin in her lap. Then, unable to help herself, she raised her lashes for a second look.

The guest's eyes were still fixed upon hers and she took a wondering breath. She felt connected to him in a strange, almost frightening way. It was as if something for which she had been unconsciously but diligently seeking had appeared all of a sudden, in a most unexpected place and in an unpredictable way.

Pushing back his chair and standing, Colonel Carstairs began the greetings, introducing his guest as Mr. Morgan Riff. The wide-shouldered visitor shook hands with the gentlemen and bowed to each lady in turn, his deference a trace more pronounced toward Gwen, his fierce eyes lingering upon hers significantly longer, so that she had the odd notion that he, too, experienced an equal fascination.

"I'm a bit early," he said with an apologetic smile. "Forgive me for interrupting your meal."

"Oh, no, no!" Libby Carstairs protested, her

plump hands instantly aflutter, a sign perhaps that the matronly woman was no more immune to the charm of the guest than the younger females. "Actually, we were a little late sitting down, Mr. Riff. Sir Gerald and his family only arrived in Tangier today, and on the way to our house Miss Evans had an—an experience in the souk." Her tongue seemed to gather speed. "With so much talk about *that,* we have lingered long over dinner. But please do sit down and have dessert and coffee. Or would you rather have some brandy?"

As he seated himself across from her, Gwen watched Morgan Riff with interest, assessing his reaction to the gushing attentions of his hostess, thinking a smile of amusement would curl the edges of his mouth at any moment. But he maintained a serious demeanor, graciously accepting overgenerous helpings of chocolate torte, raspberry sorbet, and black coffee. He even managed with no change of expression to conceal the fact that the flustered maid unconsciously spilled hot coffee in his lap.

After he had taken a napkin and discreetly dabbed at the mess beneath the cover of the table, he caught Gwen watching him. Unabashed, he winked at her like a conspirator, and she bit her lip upon a smile.

"Well, Morgan," Colonel Carstairs said, leaning back in his chair, "how was your journey to Fez?"

The guest set down his cup, whose porcelain forget-me-nots seemed precariously delicate in his long-jointed hands. "No more eventful than usual. And no less warm."

The colonel chuckled in appreciation, but his wife frowned with sympathy.

"Oh," she said, "I can just imagine the pitiless temperatures there. Of course, I've never been upon the plains myself, but I've heard they're positively intense. And these poor delicate girls from Wales—" she flapped her braceleted wrist—"why, they were both wilting beneath our Tangier sun today. The sweet dears, so accustomed to the cool air of Britain. Why, it's a wonder neither is prostrate, especially our Miss Evans, after her *dreadful* ordeal on the way to our house."

Gwen hoped her hostess would not detail the whole gruesome tale again and make her the object of Morgan Riff's full and disconcerting attention. Already she was having difficulty keeping her eyes from his face, and each time she dared glance up, she found his gaze already pinned upon hers.

"I'm sorry to hear it, Miss Evans." His voice came warm and smooth. "What happened, exactly?"

Before Gwen could open her mouth to reply, Robyn coolly answered. "Miss Evans found herself in the middle of a fray between four men. They were members of opposing tribes—or so Colonel Carstairs believes. I witnessed most of the killing from a distance, regrettably having been separated from Miss Evans in the chaos. One of the men possessed a remarkable skill with a rifle and sword. I've never seen the likes of it before."

The earl lifted an indolent shoulder. "I shouldn't wonder, I suppose. The fellow was obviously no more civilized than the red Indians of the American West we read so much about."

As if uninterested in his lordship's comments, Morgan Riff turned to Gwenllian again. "What was your opinion of the fellow, Miss Evans?"

Agitated, she rotated the stem of her wineglass, her eyes fixed upon the warm red liquid swirling in its crystal. "He was—"

At her pause Morgan lifted a brow inquiringly, and Gwen was struck with the oddest notion that it was on the tip of his tongue to try and supply the term she sought. Out of politeness perhaps, he refrained and allowed her to finish.

"Barbaric," she said with the same contempt she had used in the marketplace.

"My apologies." At his tone Gwen frowned, and he added politely, "For your harsh introduction to Tangier, of course."

Colonel Carstairs turned the conversation back to lighter topics then, and when the last bottle of wine had been drunk, he explained that Sir Gerald and Mr. Riff had business to discuss with him in the library.

Libby took her cue and herded Robyn and the girls into her English parlor with its mauve-striped sofa and horsehair arm chairs, where she spent an hour extolling the virtues of her clever nephew. Drooping with fatigue, covering yawns behind a languid hand, Sophie withstood the dragging evening as best she could before begging leave to retire. Wanting to make certain the windows were latched against the night air, which she insisted could cause dreadful maladies, Mrs. Carstairs escorted Sophie to her room while Gwen stayed on with Robyn. The young man's company was dull, for he had just finished a bottle of excellent claret and sat dozing with his head lolled back.

Restless, Gwen left her chair and wandered about the room, idly picking up an item of bric-a-brac here and there, wondering why she was not as exhausted as Sophie. She suspected sleep would be elusive tonight, for surely the violence of the afternoon would come to haunt her as soon as her eyelids closed. And no doubt another image would keep her wide awake, as well . . . a more pleasantly disturbing one.

In the next room she could hear the low murmur of lively dialogue as the men conducted their business, and her ear strained to catch the calm, deeper tones of the youngest man's voice. She wondered what sort of business the three discussed, or what problems they argued, for from time to time heated outbursts punctuated the conversation. Morgan Riff seemed to be the peacemaker, his level voice often interrupting the escalating disputes.

Glancing at Robyn's insensible sprawled form in the corner chair, at his sagging jaw as it vibrated with a snore, Gwen felt unfaithful. Thoughts of Morgan Riff would not leave her.

The terrace doors stood open to the night, and wanting to escape her cousin's presence, or the guilt it brought her, Gwen strolled outside, drawn to the now cool air. The exotic flowers released fragrances strong enough to overcome the repugnant odors of the city, and she stood at the white jasmine-covered wall looking out, staring at the streets. She felt isolated suddenly, enveloped in darkness, faced by a vast unwelcoming land that she could not like.

Suddenly lonely, she realized how much she already missed Wales and Ardderyd, missed their cold rains and rolling mists. She wished she had never sailed to this strange and violent land where death had so quickly touched her, wished she were at home now, standing at her window saying a silent but loverly good night to the moors and cliffs that were her neighbors. If the moon were high she would be able to glimpse the towers of Hiraeth to the south, that forsaken fortress she had secretly loved, and coveted, all her life.

Footsteps sounded behind her, almost noiseless in their tread over the flagstones. She did not have to look up to know who had come, for her sense of him was unaccountably strong considering their brief acquaintance.

"You are homesick." His remark was not posed as a question, but uttered in a quiet, perceptive way.

"Hiraeth . . ." she answered with softness in her voice, still gazing out over the wall toward the sea that could take her home. "In Wales, it's our word for homesickness."

Morgan Riff made no comment, but put his hands next to hers atop the rough plaster wall. She saw the strong darkness of them, and for several moments contemplated their shape and size, thinking she would like to touch them, like them to touch her. And though such thoughts were wicked and disloyal to Robyn, she blamed them on Tangier, for surely its heathen air had already changed her, stripped away a layer of her propriety to make her as indecent as it.

Looking up at the constellations, which were

strewn like sequins across a field of black satin, the man beside her jerked his head and commented, "There's Pegasus up there . . . see? Trace the stars and you'll find him galloping across the heavens."

Gwen shifted her gaze, looking not at the sky but at Morgan Riff. His voice had been melancholy, full of a poignant sort of sadness, and as she searched the rugged profile of his face, she noticed that he studied the heavens with an air of brooding, as if seeing something more there besides the tiny blinking stars.

"The winged horse," she remarked.

"Who was never truly mastered."

"Bellerophon rode him."

"True," Morgan said, "but only briefly."

"That's because Bellerophon was foolish," Gwen scorned. "If he hadn't tried to ride to heaven, he would never have been thrown."

"You would condemn him for his high aspirations?"

"Certainly."

Morgan Riff seemed to reflect upon her answer, continuing his contemplation of the universe.

Gwen frowned, never having had such a conversation with a man before. It touched her in some way that Morgan Riff spoke musefully and with no superficiality, as if she were not a stranger but a friend of long standing.

"Do you live in Morocco, Mr. Riff?" she asked with sudden intentness, still using the hushed tones they had both adopted. She did not know what clue had made her think he resided in this country, for his dress, manners, and speech all suggested Europe.

He replied with no elaboration. "Yes."

Studying him askance, Gwen sensed he was deliberate with words, rarely impulsive. She also guessed he was straightforward and fair. She longed to speak with him about Tangier. Studying the night-shaded city walls and imagining the ugliness hiding behind their shielding shapes, she chose her words with care, loath to offend him but unable to mask the genuine mystification in her voice. "How do you countenance it all, Mr. Riff—the squalor and the backwardness, I mean? How do you stand the brutality here after the refinement of Europe? I find it appalling."

For the first time Morgan Riff moved his head to look down at her face, and although she could not discern the color of his eyes in the dimness, she could feel their incisive regard.

"I assure you, there are places in Europe less civilized than this, Miss Evans."

The words hung between them, not spoken as a challenge, but as a simple statement uttered by a man who knew. "It's all a matter of understanding really, isn't it?" he added. "Or a matter of wanting to understand."

Perhaps, Gwen thought, he meant to chastise her after all. But she did not feel chastised, merely more aware of her own prejudice.

"Look there, for example," he said, lifting a hand to indicate the time-worn ramparts, the spiraling minarets, and the watchful citadel outlined against a backdrop of sapphire blue. "Is there not beauty there? If you were to investigate by day you'd be astonished at the charm beneath your nose. There are secluded courtyards shaded by almond trees, countless fountains, large terraces where dark-eyed women tend their children—and the flowers here—their perfumes are just as sweet as any of those in England."

He leaned against the wall in a relaxed posture, folding his arms against his chest. "There's an ancient story I particularly like about Tangier, one that describes the four walls of the city in a very beautiful way. It says they were once decorated with precious stones—jasper, sapphire, chalcedony, and emerald—"

"Mr. Riff," Gwen admonished with a smile, detecting the change in his voice from solemnity to humor. "You're describing heaven according to Revelation."

He grinned readily, showing perfect teeth. "So I am, Miss Evans. So I am."

Although their conversation had evolved into lighter tones, Gwen sensed there was still an underlying seriousness, an obscure but no less significant meaning to everything Morgan Riff said. At the same time she knew her unworldliness and even her snobbery did not offend him, for he had moved closer, confidently so, as if knowing he would not be rebuffed. When he placed a hand atop hers on the wall, she closed her eyes, absorbing its warmth, its vitality, fearing to move lest he take it away.

At last he spoke, dispelling the quiet bond between them, and his breath lightly stirred her hair. "Unfortunately, I must say good night now."

She opened her mouth to speak, wanting him to stay and reveal more about his life, talk to her about the constellations, explain how he had come to live in this city. Most of all she yearned to know if she would see him again. But such a question would hardly be circumspect for a lady, especially a young lady promised to another man.

Slowly, she slid her hand from the harbor of his palm. "Good night then, Mr. Riff."

He nodded and stepped away, his tall form outlined against the light of the open door as he paused and said quietly, "I'll be seeing you again, Miss Evans. Soon."

And for the second time that evening, Gwenllian knew he had caught her thoughts, caught them just as easily as if they had been loose pages set afloat upon the hot Moroccan air.

Three

Colonel Carstairs was an avid proponent of the wisdom that, once thrown, the surest way to conquer the fear of falling off a horse was to speedily mount up again. With this attitude in mind, he proposed that Gwen go out into the streets the very next afternoon and see that Tangier, while admittedly uncultivated, was not always as savage as it had proved to be upon her arrival. Although Gwen relented under his gentle pressure, Sophie did not, declaring it her desire to simply sit upon the shaded terrace and sip lemonade with her hostess.

The colonel expressed regrets that he would be unable to accompany Gwen and Robyn about town, since he and Sir Gerald had a call to make at the embassy. But he had arranged for his guests to have a tour in his absence with the escort of none other than the charming Mr. Riff.

Gwen was standing in the foyer when the colonel made his announcement, and she was so astonished by the news that she had to turn her head to hide a smile of purest pleasure from Robyn. All through the sultry night she had thought of Morgan Riff, relived their time together in endless remembered vignettes, thinking about his voice, his hands, and the unfathomably strong attraction they shared. But most of all, she had pondered their unquestioning acceptance of that attraction.

Before she had time to gain breath at the thought of seeing him again so soon, a light rap sounded upon the door, and a white-coated servant opened the portal to admit the expected guest.

When he breached the threshold Morgan Riff looked directly at Gwen as if nothing else in the room were of importance to him. She met his eyes, finding them brilliantly blue with the pupils rimmed in black and the lashes thick. Unlike Robyn, who wore his London tailored jacket and embroidered waistcoat, Mr. Riff wore riding breeches, boots, and a white shirt of lightweight fabric more appropriate for walking in the dusty heat. He greeted Colonel Carstairs affably, but his greeting to Robyn was cool, and after his eyes had flicked over the earl's person, Gwen suspected that Lord Breese had been found lacking in more than one important quality.

Stepping in front of Robyn, Morgan took her hand and raised it to his lips with little regard for propriety, his eyes never leaving hers. "Did I arrive soon enough?" he murmured against her knuckles.

Flustered, she glanced askance at Robyn and spoke so that no one else could hear. "You seem to be a man of your word."

"I try to be."

Behind them the perturbed earl cleared his

59

throat while the colonel frowned at Morgan, giving him a look Gwen could not interpret just before he bade them all a hasty goodbye.

"Shall we go?"

At her escort's question Gwen smiled brightly, then frowned at Robyn's sour expression and gave him a discreet jab in the ribs with her elbow. The threesome set out in an awkward silence then, and the moment Gwen stepped from the Carstairs' English-flavored house with its lace tablecloths and quilted tea cozies, she felt her sense of safety waver. Like yesterday, the broken pavement blazed with a hot sun, and white-draped figures in flopping sandals scurried up and down the walk while riders on slow-footed donkeys vied for space in the chaotic traffic of the avenue. A few feet away a pair of dogs tugged at opposite ends of a camel carcass.

Hastily turning her eyes away from the disgusting sight, Gwen allowed Robyn to take her arm. With Morgan in the lead they passed a pair of richly robed Moors riding sleek mules, then a group of Negresses who bore upon their heads huge loaves of bread in wooden platters. The faint sound of distant hooves echoed off the undulating white walls, and instantly fearful, Gwen searched the street for signs of demon riders.

But she found nothing threatening and was glad when Morgan sensed her distress and took a place at her side opposite Robyn. She felt comforted by the pistol he wore at his hip, and by his solid presence. He moved with the same air of confidence as the high-ranking cavalry officers Papa often invited to Ardderyd, and displayed a natural attitude for leadership and command, although she suspected he was far too independent to ever be subordinate to any military system.

Beside her Robyn increased his grip upon her arm with a proprietary air and said, "I would appreciate it, Riff, if you could direct us to a reputable jeweler—there *are* reputable jewelers here in Morocco, aren't there? I'd like to purchase a trinket or two for Miss Evans, and although I don't mind paying a good price for it, I don't relish the thought of being cheated by some dark-skinned swindler."

"Buying jewelry here is a bit like gambling," Morgan Riff said without missing a step, his eyes fixed straight ahead. "As you are no doubt good at that, I'm sure you'll get a bargain."

Glancing askance at him from beneath the brim of her hat, Gwen guessed there had been tongue-in-cheek humor hidden in her escort's bland remark. But Robyn seemed not to notice; he was too preoccupied loosening his starched white collar and threading his way through the rubbish on the streets.

They turned left, then right, and zigzagged through several narrow streets in a meandering fashion, and as they walked Gwen sensed their route to the market was a circuitous one. After some thoughtful observation she surmised that Morgan sought to spare them as many unpleasant sights as possible. Unlike yesterday, they encountered no malformed children or sore-ridden lepers, and only an occasional beggar wandered close enough to risk their escort's frown. The avenues were tranquil beneath the scorching heat, and as they strolled deeper into the city, she caught many glimpses of tiled courtyards and flower-dotted terraces, from which chiming feminine laughter drifted in lazy waves.

Morgan was obviously giving her the opportunity to find beauty here, if she cared to look for it. And Gwen thought that if the horror in the marketplace had never occurred, she would have gazed upon the cherry laurels and ochre villas with an appreciative eye; as it was, their loveliness seemed tainted with the stain of lurking savagery.

"Why are there no carriages in Tangier, Riff?" Robyn inquired, mopping his brow with a silk handkerchief. "Devilishly stupid, if you ask me. People carry everything either on donkeys or atop their own heads as if it were the Middle Ages instead of the nineteenth century. Even a cart would do—for Miss Evans's comfort, of course."

"Maybe the folks here enjoy the exercise," came the dry reply. "You could stop one of them and ask."

While Gwen hid a smile at the sarcasm, Robyn scowled and failed to watch his step. He almost tripped over a huddled Arab napping on the street.

The disturbed sleeper jumped up and, realizing that an infidel had interrupted his peace, began waving his arms and shouting in guttural Arabic. Ignoring the ranting fellow, Morgan continued his imperturbed pace, halting only when Robyn seized his sleeve and demanded an interpretation. "What in heaven's name is that filthy vagrant saying to me?" he barked.

The taller man pinned him with cold eyes. "He's

saying you're a son of a dog and a dog of a Christian. And a few other compliments I'd be happy to pass on if a lady weren't present."

Robyn's face flushed deep red with indignation and he wheeled about to confront the furious Arab who was still shouting obscenities at him a few yards away. But before he could step forward, Morgan seized his arm to stay his unwise progress.

"Would you pick a fight with half of Tangier?" he hissed. "Touch that fellow and you'll have a dozen more upon your back before you can bat an eye. Consider your options before you decide to land the first punch." Releasing Robyn's arm, he turned about and added over his shoulder, "I'm not particularly in the mood to shoot anyone on your behalf."

The frustrated earl clenched his fists and shouted at Morgan's back. "Had we been in Britain I would have laid the black-skinned heathen flat!"

Morgan kept walking. "No doubt you would have."

Tugging at her cousin's elbow and hissing for him to be quiet, Gwen glanced with unease at the staring pedestrians. Robyn still hesitated, and loath to be more than a few steps away from Morgan's side, she yanked him forward and turned a deaf ear to his complaints about both the obnoxious Arab and their arrogant escort.

They crossed the street after Morgan, panting with the exertion of jogging in the ruthless heat. He led them past a collection of shops selling wares of tin and brass where the sound of hammers beating metal filled the stifling air. Against the wall of one shop Gwen noticed a group of men lounging beneath a strip of shade, and something about their confident stances caught her attention. Each wore a burnoose dotted with multihued tufts of wool that was cinched with a crimson sash. Shod in sandals of goatskin and equipped with powder flasks and poniards, the men leaned casually upon long-barreled muskets with ivory butts, their long arms exposed and well-muscled. Agleam with sweat, their ferocious faces were dark from the Moroccan sun, but, oddly, the fine-boned features suggested a Gallic ancestry.

It seemed to Gwen that everyone in the street gave them wide berth, and had she not been paying close attention she would have missed the abrupt straightening of their stances and the brief nods they exchanged with Morgan Riff. Frowning, she scrutinized their burnooses with a more discerning eye and realized that the garments were similar to the one worn in the market yesterday by the man called English.

"Those men—" she faltered in an anxious voice, speaking to Morgan. "Who are they?"

"Berbers. Mountaineers from the Amazirgh tribe."

"Really? But some of them are so fair skinned. I saw two with red hair and light-colored eyes."

"That's because they're of Aryan descent."

She looked back at them over her shoulder. "They're intimidating with those weapons and fierce looks. Do people fear them?"

Morgan's mouth curved. "Only those who have reason to."

She stared at him, unsatisfied with the answer, but in his typically taciturn way he made no further comment.

After leading them around a corner he directed them into a small square where the sound of splashing water provided a welcome melody. Peering ahead through the jumble of milling pedestrians, Gwen was delighted to see a fountain with its jet of clear water cascading into a huge public pool of green tiles. Groups of veiled women dipped earthenware vessels into the basin and, after hoisting them upon their narrow shoulders, glided away with their provocative, kohl-lined eyes cast down.

Europeans knelt at the pool, too, flushed and perspiring as they filled their metal pails and then took sips of the cool water from long crook-necked dippers.

The square was cleaner than any Gwen had previously seen, and she noticed a substantial number of Britons ambling about with open guidebooks, some led by French-speaking escorts who pointed out items of either historic or commercial interest. Situated among the native shops was a British post office, and beside it, a billiards room whose clash of balls and laughing male voices drifted out to blend with the cacophony of hawkers' cries. Much of the same merchandise Gwen had seen in yesterday's market was displayed in the stalls here, but it seemed of better quality, especially the trays of necklaces, earrings, and anklets that all vied for a stroller's eye in a circle around the fountain.

With his hand firm upon Gwen's arm, Robyn made for the nearest goldsmith, perusing delicate filigreed charms, dangling earrings and flat-linked chains. Speaking imperfect French, the vendor encouraged the purchase of a coral ring for the lady, which would, he assured, ward off the evil eye and keep her safe. Or would madam prefer to have a gold pendant set with the claw of a tiger or the tooth of a cheetah?

Her gaze ever drawn to him, Gwen watched Morgan. He idled against a nearby wall with his arms crossed in a negligent fashion. But his eyes perpetually tracked the movements of the crowd with an alertness she found unrelenting. She began to realize he was known in the square but, curiously, was never directly approached; people either nodded with deference at him, or nudged elbows in a silent communication of his presence to another. None came near. She wondered at their subtle show of respect, for according to Colonel Carstairs, Europeans were either stiffly tolerated or utterly despised.

Her attention was forced back to Robyn and his shopping, and she feigned interest in perusing the jewelry for a time, her eye alighting upon a small silver flask etched with an arabesque. She studied the design of twined leaves and flowers, running a finger over the engraving and wishing suddenly that Robyn would buy it for her. It was the only thing she had seen in Tangier that she would like to take back to Wales. Intrigued by the function of the container, she uncorked the lid and found it filled with a strange black substance she could not identify.

"Kohl," the vendor said helpfully, pointing to his

eyes and making a circular motion with a forefinger. "Kohl."

Robyn took it from her hand and recorked the lid with distaste. "You don't want that."

A bit regretfully she watched while he replaced it, wondering why the graceful vessel created for some dark-tapered hand with hennaed palms so intrigued her.

At Robyn's prompting, she finally settled upon a bracelet fashioned of beaten gold discs, and as he slipped it upon her wrist, his smooth hand squeezed hers in a meaningful way. She thought of the proposal of marriage that would be forthcoming; indeed, if his present ardent expression were any indication, he might even speak before the return to Wales.

As they turned to face the square once more, Gwen met Morgan Riff's keen eyes, and knew he had witnessed the intimate exchange. She held his gaze for a moment and felt a sudden remorse over her commitment to Robyn—that, and a fleeting unease sparked by a sharp but elusive memory.

"I'm parched!" Robyn declared, interrupting her disturbing train of thought. "Is there a place here to get refreshment, Riff?"

Uncrossing his arms, Morgan straightened from his leaning posture, and Gwen noticed the controlled energy in his movement which suggested that his body was unaccustomed to idleness. He did not waste breath to answer Lord Breese, but set off across the sprawling bazaar in his long-legged stride, so that the other two had to trot a few steps or be left behind.

Near the billiards room, the door to a Moorish cafe stood propped open by a broken stool, and ducking his head in order to clear the lintel, Morgan preceded them inside. Gloom pervaded the place, made all the more dense by the haze of pungent smoke, but Gwenllian could make out an earthen floor spread with rough-woven mats upon which diners sat smoking pipes. Unpolished lamps hung from the ceiling and food stained every surface, attracting a swarm of insects. In the center of the room a copper urn steamed upon a crude brick oven.

Their welcome by the waiter was civil enough, but Gwen suspected it was due only to Morgan's presence, which seemed to demand regard wherever he went. Wrinkling her nose at the stench of a dozen or so unwashed bodies, the smoke, and the sharp odor of unidentifiable fare, she hung back, taking great gulps of the warm but breathable air wending in from outside.

Morgan spoke a few low words to the waiter, apparently ordering a special drink for Robyn, for the earl was promptly handed a glass containing a dark amber liquid instead of the black coffee the other patrons consumed.

"Would you like something to eat?"

At Morgan's offer, Gwen shook her head vehemently, and her escort's handsome lips curved into a sympathetic smile. "I thought not. How about some water from the fountain?"

Her eyes slid uncertainly to Robyn. The young man had made himself comfortable upon a hide-covered divan in the corner of the cafe, away from

68

the native patrons who ignored his presence, but Gwen bit her lip in concern, for he seemed glaringly out of place and vulnerable.

Noting her worried frown through the pipe smoke, the earl raised his drink and called, "I won't be long. Let Riff give you a tour of the square if you like."

Morgan raised a brow and offered Gwenllian his arm. "How about that? Your beau has given me his permission."

Still unsure about abandoning Robyn but shamefully eager to be alone with her enthralling escort, Gwen accepted his arm, her hand sliding over it in an easy and natural way. When they returned to the sunshine outside, she had a strong suspicion that he had neatly turned the circumstances to suit himself.

At the fountain he flashed his brief but effective smile and, borrowing a dipper from a European woman, plunged it beneath the pool and offered it to Gwen. She sipped from it delicately, letting its welcome coolness relieve her dry throat and, with her lips upon the rim of the copper dipper, regarded Morgan from beneath the violet shade of her hat. Her attraction for him was a forceful thing, she realized, having been born the moment he had entered the dining room last evening, and burgeoning at an alarming pace that threatened to escalate beyond her control. Where would it end? She feared her own good judgment could not withstand it, and Morgan would have no scruples at all where Robyn Breese's claim to her was concerned. Already he had dismissed the other man as if he were no obstacle, making his own interest in her clear.

As he took the dipper from her hand, he let his fingers close over hers until he felt the answering quiver he seemed to want. Then he tilted the utensil and drank with the sun highlighting the blackness of his hair.

"What do you know about horses?" he asked her suddenly, returning the dipper to its owner.

Caught off guard and still dazzled by his allure, Gwen stammered, "Why, I—I've gone with my father to the Dyfed horse fair every year since I could walk . . ."

His voice held good-natured challenge. "Good. We'll see what a Welshwoman knows."

He offered his arm again, but Gwen hesitated and shifted her eyes to the little cafe with its ominous, cavelike door. Morgan watched her, still with his elbow extended. She wanted to protest, to argue that it was improper for her to leave Robyn and traipse off on the arm of a man she had known for less than twenty-four hours.

Torn, she glanced at the crude dusty streets full of kneeling camels and decaying fowl and half-naked children. She looked at the indifferent pedestrians and the scurrying women wrapped in their voluminous white shrouds and gauzy veils. Who would know or care what she did? What was English convention here? Besides, Robyn had told her to go with Morgan, hadn't he?

She raised her eyes to meet the blue ones staring back at her. And then, lifting a hand, she threaded it through Morgan's arm. The muscles beneath her

70

fingers tautened in response, and in that instance she knew that she had just committed an irrevocable act of will.

Silently they strolled along. He slowed his steps for hers, and the well-matched couple drew curious, clandestine stares not only from male eyes, but from eyes lined with heavy kohl.

Before long they passed beneath a looming horseshoe arch where a few men squatted on their heels and smoked. Just beyond them, Gwen saw dozens of makeshift pens strung with hemp ropes, and each enclosure contained scores of horses. She gasped at the sight of so many animals. Everywhere men bargained and haggled over the price of horseflesh, putting a surefooted pony through its paces or running knowledgeable hands over sleek hocks and withers.

Leading her to a pen in the very back, Morgan paused and indicated a small bay mare with four white stockings and a blaze. "What would you say about her?"

"Her ears are too large. And her chest is not deep enough for speed. She would give you a rough ride, I think, with those straight pasterns."

Morgan's mouth deepened at the corners before he pointed out a second horse. "And that one there?"

"Spavined, and too high at the withers."

On and on went his test of her judgment until they had toured almost every pen. Perspiration ran in rivulets between Gwen's breasts and dampened her blouse, and her hair straggled in loose curls about her face, adhering to her brow beneath the hat. She had examined the mouths of so many horses that her hands were sticky, but she hardly noticed the discomforts, for she knew her observations had been sound. And she knew she had impressed Morgan Riff.

Finally they approached the last pen, which contained a single horse. Gwen lowered her head so that her hat brim would better shade her vision from the glare, and smiled, knowing the best had been saved for last.

The animal moved about the small space as if unused to confinement, as if the muscles of his well-formed legs yearned to stretch and run. Like most of the others, he was an Arab, that ancient breed known for intelligence, speed, and endurance. His head displayed the distinctive dish-shape of his breed and his widely set eyes were full of fire. With an impatient step he glided from one end of the pen to the other, and the sun gilded his coat to a color that was no less bright than the polished copper vessels for sale in the marketplace.

"He's without flaw," Gwen said quietly, awed by the showy movements of the beast. "At least, one would have to be better schooled than I to find a blemish."

The animal wore a halter of braided cloth spangled with bright tassels which waltzed with the bobbing of his head, but Morgan made no move to grasp it. Instead, he fished a dried fig wrapped in waxed paper from his pocket and offered it to the beast from his palm. Gwen examined his extended hand with its long fingers and fine joints, and knew

72

it was a horseman's hand, as used to clasping reins as some hands were used to holding pencils.

Still maintaining a distance, the highly strung horse pricked its ears and flared its nostrils. Its muscles tensed with wariness. But Morgan waited and, speaking in a low coaxing voice, repeated words in a tongue Gwen did not know. At last the animal took a few cautious steps forward, then stretched out its glossy neck.

Morgan made no threatening move but allowed the treat to rest with seductive availability in his steady hand. With velvet lips the animal seized upon it and, while chewing, permitted the man to grasp the halter. At Morgan's offer, Gwen moved to run her fingers down the silky copper jaw, feeling privileged to touch such an animal.

"Horses are held in high regard in the East," Morgan told her. "Owning a fine steed is considered a mark of nobility, a reflection of the owner's position. Even horse dealers are esteemed and usually of gentle birth, not the often unscrupulous breed found in other countries."

"Will you ride him?" she asked, hoping he would.

For answer Morgan put two fingers to his mouth and whistled shrilly, catching the attention of an Arab standing under the shade of the arches. Without delay the fellow hurried forward toting a saddle of the Eastern type, with high cantle and pointed pommel. Ducking beneath the ropes of the pen, he settled it upon the back of the sidestepping chestnut. Once the girth was fastened and a silver-chased bridle buckled, Morgan led the horse out and, with a swift and easy vault, mounted up.

73

Bunching his muscles, the steed quivered with readiness to run, but Morgan checked him with a firm hand, forcing him to maintain a controlled walk until they had gone beyond the pens. And then he eased the beast into a canter, reining him in nimble figure eights with the unconsciously coordinated motions of hand and knee that only those born to the saddle can perform.

Gwen watched, spellbound over the athletic beauty of the pair. She followed every movement Morgan made, admiring his straight bearing and easy skill. Perspiration gleamed upon his face, giving its sculpture a polish, and his thin white shirt stuck to the valley between his wide shoulders to reveal the bronze of his flesh. If she had not already known it last night in that baffling moment when he had entered the Carstairses' dining room, Gwen knew now . . . knew that she was in love with Morgan Riff.

When he rode back to her and entrusted the now lathered horse to the waiting Arab, she asked with eagerness, "You're going to buy him, aren't you?"

Taking her arm, he steered her back through the arches and toward the bazaar. "I registered the bill of sale this morning—at dawn, before anyone else had a chance to get a glimpse of him."

Gwen's jaw dropped, and for a moment she felt offended, thinking he had been making sport of her these last few hours. Why had he asked her opinion of so many horses when he had already made his choice?

At the sight of her expression Morgan grinned, and the grin was so engaging Gwen could not help but allow a little laugh to escape her lips. "I should be angry with you, you know."

"Perhaps. But I'm glad you approved of my choice." His eyes were fastened to her face. "All in the space of a day I've discovered your opinion is important to me."

"Have you, Mr. Riff?"

A trace of affected moodiness still marked her tone, and he reached to touch her sulky mouth with a finger. "Yes."

In the bazaar he bought pomegranates and oranges for them and, finding a pool of deep blue shade, stood with her beneath it to enjoy the lusciousness of the tender fruit. Peeling an orange for her, he put it to her mouth. His fingers, damp with juice, brushed her lips. It was a liberty, but not one made in disrespect. Gwen knew he was not a man who had set out to take advantage of an unworldly girl, but simply a man who had made up his mind what he wanted and found no reason to hide it.

They washed their hands in the fountain and laughed together as two children splashed their feet in the midst of a water fight, then sipped glasses of tart lemonade purchased from a passing vendor.

There was no sign of Lord Breese in the square, and Gwen voiced her concern. "Could Robyn still be in the cafe?"

Morgan stood up from his seat at the fountain, and with a strong hand pulled Gwen to her feet as well. "I've no doubt that he's still in the cafe. But I'll put your mind to rest just the same. I don't like to see you fret."

They entered the shadowy den to find Robyn

sprawled on the same divan upon which they had last seen him. He was drunk and snoring.

"Before we left I told the proprietor to keep an eye on him and see that he came to no harm," Morgan said. "When he can hold his head up, he'll be plied with coffee and escorted home."

Gwen stared at Robyn's insensible form, rumpled hair, and wrinkled clothes with both pity and disgust.

"He has a weakness for drink, you know," Morgan said bluntly. "I'll wager that before he's forty he'll have to be carried to bed every night by a pair of footmen."

Gwen glanced at him sharply, ready to defend her cousin. But she held her tongue, realizing that Morgan spoke not out of malice but out of truth.

They stepped outside and began strolling through the labyrinth of stalls again. The sun had passed her zenith long ago and her heat had faded, prompting pedestrians to leave the shade and go about their shopping with more industry.

"I should take you home," Morgan said. "It will be dark soon and your father will worry. We've just the last section of stalls to see."

Although the mention of their inevitable separation wrenched her, Gwen did not protest, wanting to make the most of these last fleeting minutes with Morgan. She let him show her the tables of wares they had not seen before, and noted that the sale of weapons was brisk, even though most of the firearms were antiquated and not of the fine quality of the American-made revolver Morgan carried. But the variety of swords, sabers, and lances impressed her, for many of them were encrusted with precious jewels and trimmed in silver or gold. She looked away from the wicked curved scimitars whose edges were dark with dried blood.

Morgan was showing her a knife inlaid with ivory when an argument between two men interrupted them. Several stalls down, a man wearing a green turban shouted angrily at one of the shopkeepers, pointing with disdain at a rifle propped against the tent pole of the stall. The shopkeeper shook his head and whined as if to deny the charge made against him.

Morgan set the knife aside and continued their leisured pace, and although he appeared uninterested in the argument, Gwen suspected his ear was keenly attuned to it. All at once, she saw a man in the crowd point to him and then call out an alert to the perspiring, still protesting shopkeeper. People paused and stared, and Gwen nervously gripped Morgan's arm.

"Stay close to me," he murmured.

The panting shopkeeper came running up to them and, halting as if in deference or fear, addressed the tall young man in a hysterical rush of Arabic.

Morgan listened patiently, but with a firm shake of his head, denied the desperate plea.

Again the vendor implored him to relent, and clasping his hands before his breast sank to his knees and begged with a slavish persistence.

"What does he want?" Gwen asked in confusion.

Morgan's eyes shifted to the green-turbaned man waiting irritably at the stall. "That gentleman over

77

there purchased a gun from the shopkeeper, and says it's faulty. He's a city official, and threatens to haul my friend here to jail."

"Can you help him?"

"I think so. Follow me."

Saying nothing more, he started toward the stall. As he walked in his purposeful way, the curious gawkers parted to give him clear passage, bringing to Gwen's mind the analogy of Moses and the Red Sea. She trailed a little behind, standing to the side while Morgan bent to retrieve the rifle in question and examine it with a knowledgeable eye. His deft hands skimmed over its barrel and stock, then checked its ammunition.

Those witnessing the scene grew silent with anticipation, their eyes following every movement made by the man in European dress. Gwen could not fathom the respect he received wherever he went, and continued to ponder its cause while wondering what he could possibly do to solve the dispute.

She was not left to wonder long. Morgan raised the weapon to his shoulder in a smooth motion as if testing its weight. Then he lowered his head and, sighting some target, moved a finger to the trigger.

She shook her head in disbelief, for the object he had chosen seemed to be a goatskin drinking vessel hanging by a cord in a distant stall. It swayed unpredictably beneath a sluggish breeze, obscured in part by a billowy kaftan. The onlookers shifted their feet with excitement and placed wagers with a hurried clinking of coins.

The rifle cracked.

Waiting not a second, the Arab shopkeeper sprinted toward the drinking vessel with his striped burnoose flapping above his sandals. Hopping up, he yanked it from its hook and scrutinized it. Then, with a loud whoop, he raised the trophy high above his head and shook it in triumph before dashing back to show it to the scowling official.

Gwen sidled closer, standing on tiptoe to peer through the other spectators pressing for a look. She saw that a design of beadwork covered the face of the goatskin vessel, a pattern of red and blue with a sunburst in the middle. And there, just in the center of the sunburst, was a neat hole made by Morgan's bullet.

Exclamations and gasps of incredulity issued all around as the container was passed from hand to hand for closer inspection. Instead of displaying anger over being proved wrong, the official possessively snatched up the rifle and stalked off with it.

Gwen had watched her father at his target practice often enough to know that Morgan's accomplishment had been an extraordinary feat of marksmanship. She found herself awed by it, but, for some reason she could not quite grasp, disturbed as well. Who was Morgan Riff?

Ignoring the hoopla, he pushed through the crowd and took Gwen's arm.

"You're a marksman," she said inanely.

"In this country it's wise to acquire such a skill." He elaborated no further, and Gwen yearned to question him, ask why he was so well known and yet so carefully avoided. But an unwillingness to examine Morgan Riff's life too closely seemed to freeze her jaws, and instead of delving, she nestled her hand in the intimate place between his arm and his ribs and let him lead her onward.

The devilish sun was setting rapidly, descending in the cerulean sky like a great orange disc before hovering just above the ancient city ramparts. Gwen realized Morgan was taking a direct route to the Carstairs house instead of the more circuitous one earlier traversed, and the sights they passed were not gentle to her eyes. Even the wash of early evening could not mask the pitiful stare of the blind beggars, the canker-ridden faces of ragged children, or the group of lepers huddling near the worn steps of a mosque. The odors were equally distressing, and Gwen had to put a hand over her nose to stifle the nauseating stench of rotting refuse.

"I'm sorry we don't have time to take the more pleasant route," Morgan said with his shrewd ability to know her thoughts. "But I'd rather not shield you from the darker side of Tangier, Gwen. I want you to judge the city with a knowledge of both its beauty and its squalor."

She had judged already, yesterday. And she found her hatred of Morocco firm. Saying nothing, but knowing he read the workings of her mind, she pressed closer to him as if to apologize. He put a supporting hand to her back, and although the touch was steady and warm, it relayed his disappointment.

The sun vanished, and as a fading talisman of day, left behind a smear of apricot on the distant horizon. They crossed into more agreeable avenues where mimosas quivered in the breeze and shed delicate flowers of pink over the pitted pavement. Morgan slowed his steps and his hand curled about Gwen's waist. She leaned closer to his solid and comforting side, feeling the physical tension between them blossom painfully. She did not want to part from him and hear his resonant goodbye, even though she knew their time apart would be brief. The tension in his hands and the fierceness in his eyes whenever they gazed into her own told her that he would soon be back.

Before they arrived at the Carstairs' front steps he pulled her into the shadows of a lemon tree and, taking both her hands in his, searched her face for a moment with his eyes, telling her wordlessly that if she allowed it, she would become his and his alone, and nothing about her life would ever be the same again.

She should have hesitated, or even turned away. What of Robyn? What of prudence? What of the mystery in Morgan Riff's eyes? She should question that mystery, she told herself, question it now.

And yet when he bent his head to kiss her, she found that she no longer cared about wisdom or sanity. Tangier had robbed her of those saving graces.

Dragging her hat from her head, Morgan put his hands on either side of her face and kissed her with a consuming purpose, his roughness tempered by the tender words he spoke in his own language. He touched her with an intimacy that Robyn had never dared. It was unstoppable, this yearning that made them strain together and, she knew she had been waiting for it, knew that her path had been directed here across the seas so that she could find this man.

With thoroughness, his hands roved over her surrendering form, and she arched against him. She could feel his flesh through the fabric of his shirt and it was as hot as the air. She could taste both the salt of his body and the tang of orange on his lips, hear his hard breaths as he clasped her closer.

His mouth moved over her throat and found the hollow beneath her ear, then trailed to the open collar of her silken blouse and lingered there. Across his back, beneath her wondering fingers, his muscles flexed, rippled like those of the copper horse. His hands pressed against her hips and she closed her eyes. Then, his fingers released two pearl buttons of her blouse, and with reverence, he bent his head to the parted garment.

Languidly, she lifted her lashes to behold his face, and behind his head the shadow of the mosque loomed. Gwen clutched his sleeves, not wanting him to draw away. An odd premonition struck her in the frightening magic of the night, and she whispered, "Who are you, Morgan Riff . . . who *are* you . . . ?"

He straightened and searched her expression as if pondering the cause of her question. Then, with gentle hands, horseman's hands that could wield a rifle like no other, he refastened the pearl buttons of her blouse. While she gazed at him with the question still in her eyes, he guided her toward the steps of the house. He looked directly into her face and touched her quivering lower lip, which his kisses had made red.

"Don't you know?" he asked. "Don't you know who I am?"

She shook her head even while foreboding visions told her that she lied.

Some emotion crossed his face, putting a slight but tormented frown between his brows. In an even voice he said, "Then I shall tell you."

She waited, held her breath, felt her chest squeeze.

"I am the Squire of Hiraeth."

Four

He bade her goodbye shortly afterward, walking off in his effortless way until he vanished into the Tangier night. Experiencing both the exhilaration of a love newly born and the wonder of Morgan Riff's astonishing revelation, Gwen stared after him. Somehow the magic of her childhood dream had culminated here in Morocco after a long sail over the sea, and the miracle of it surely proved she was meant to be the squire's lady and return with him to Hiraeth.

As she savored the tang of orange still lingering upon her lips, she caught sight of the mosque crouched in the distance. It seemed to point to a heaven more remote than that one gazing down upon her native land, and she shivered, searching the shadows for another glimpse of the squire and wishing that the strength of her desire alone could call him back. When it did not, she turned away and entered the house.

Hearing male voices, she wandered into the parlor where her father and the colonel lounged with wineglasses in their hands.

"Ah, Gwenllian!" Sir Gerald said. "Ye have arrived in time for dinner. We were waiting for ye. Er—daughter . . . ?"

At the question in her father's tone Gwen put a hand to her hair, belatedly aware that she had left her discarded hat outside beneath the trees.

"Are ye alright?" he asked with concern.

"Oh, yes, Papa. I'm fine."

"Where's Robyn?"

"He'll be along in a while. Why didn't you tell me, Papa? Why didn't you tell me Morgan Riff was the Squire of Hiraeth?"

Her father's mustachioed lip twitched and he exchanged a sidelong glance with the colonel, who, after setting aside his glass of wine, quietly left them to a private conversation.

"He told ye who he was?" Sir Gerald asked in surprise, locking his hands behind his back and watching her beneath bristly black brows.

"Yes . . . just now. Outside, before he left."

Her sire regarded her closely for a moment, then shrugged his sloped shoulders in their tobacco-colored jacket. "Frankly, I didn't think the piece of news was significant enough to mention, Gwen. After all, the squires of Hiraeth have never been anything to us."

"Except our neighbors!" Failing to understand her father's apathy and more than a little suspicious of it, Gwen spread her hands in exasperation. "I can't believe you considered his presence so unremarkable that you let me sit through dinner last

85

night with no notion of his identity. Especially when you know I have always been—" She halted abruptly.

"Infatuated with the disappearing squires?" Sir Gerald finished for her, his voice going from testy to harsh. "Well, ye'd best stop romanticizing them, Gwenllian. I have always told ye plainly what they are and have ever been. Adventurers, rogues, blackguards all."

"Are you branding Mr. Riff a blackguard?" she asked, unable to mask her indignation. "Why, he is a friend of the Carstairs, a man the colonel seems to respect enough to invite to dinner and ask to be my escort."

"Ye know little about him," Sir Gerald argued, setting his jaw.

"I know enough to believe that you have no cause to be uncivil to him, Papa."

Sir Gerald's eyes narrowed as he examined her flushed cheeks. Turning his back, he regarded the shadowed city through the open window for a moment as if gathering his thoughts with care. When he spoke again he affected the cajoling tone he often used to placate her. "Yer emotions are obviously high tonight, my girl. Bringing ye here to Morocco has been a considerable strain upon yer nerves. Why don't ye go to yer room and rest before dinner is served, eh?"

Gwenllian raised her chin, irritated by his easy dismissal of her concerns. She squelched a sharp retort, reminding herself of her father's lifelong disapproval of the absent squires of Hiraeth. Voicing her new feelings for Morgan Riff would only spark his wrath and precipitate a stormy quarrel.

Bitter words would follow, for Gwen's emotions were indeed high tonight and her father's temper had always been fiery.

She hesitated in indecision. Should she end the conversation now, keep silent about the feelings of her heart? If so, her silence would be a form of deceit that would only grow more complicated until the secret was eventually forced out. And what then?

"Forgive me, Papa," she breathed, making her decision, beginning her tangled duplicity. "I did not mean to speak to you that way. I believe you're quite right. Tangier has put a strain upon my nerves. Perhaps a bath would be the thing now, and a little glass of wine at dinner."

Sir Gerald turned about at that, circling her shoulders with gentle arms and releasing a blustery sigh. "Jolly good idea. Off with ye now, ye minx."

Relieved to have avoided a scene yet saddened by the rift forming between them, Gwen trailed to her room. Staring at her straggling hair in the mirror, she backtracked in search of Sophie, intending to borrow a few hair pins for her toilette. Before she had gone many steps, she heard the low, private murmurs of her father and Colonel Carstairs as they conversed down the corridor. Hearing her name spoken, she paused to listen.

". . . will not invite him to dine again then," the colonel said. "And I'll keep his visits here brief and late if you deem it prudent, Gerald."

"Aye," Gwen's father agreed. "Best to keep her away from the fellow as much as possible."

"I'm told he turns all the female heads. It's natural your young Gwen would follow suit. Schoolgirl crush. Nothing to concern yourself about, I'm sure. Regardless of his insolence, Riff is surely honorable enough to keep his hands off."

"Perhaps ye're right. But I don't want to tempt fate, if ye know what I mean."

"I've never had a daughter, of course, but I can quite appreciate your concern."

Gwen's eyes darkened at the exchange. She felt angry over the conspiracy meant to keep her separated from Morgan. Although she hated to circumvent the well-meaning wishes of a sire she adored, her youthful heart, sore with love, acted as fuel for her rebellion. She would do whatever necessary to continue her relationship with Morgan Riff, regardless of the consequences.

The following morning, as dawn arrived and brought with it both the *muezzin*'s early call and a demonic heat, Gwen kicked off the damp sheets and tiredly got up from bed. She had rested little. But in spite of her exhaustion she looked forward to the day. Hoping her lover would call, she donned her prettiest gown of azure silk and asked Mrs. Carstairs's maid to style her hair. Just as the servant finished the task, Libby and Sophie entered bearing a tray of cocoa, cinnamon buns, and sliced fruit.

"Did you sleep well, dear?" her hostess asked.

"Fine, thank you."

After setting down the breakfast tray, Libby lingered, eager to gossip. "How was your afternoon with Mr. Riff yesterday? I've been dying to ask you in private. Isn't he enthralling? I declare, he had eyes only for you at dinner the other evening. He could scarcely tear that dazzling blue gaze away from your face, my dear. Sophie and I both noticed it."

"That we did," Sophie agreed, moving to straighten Gwen's lace collar at the nape. "And I think Robyn was more than a little incensed over it. I saw him glower every time he caught Mr. Riff watching you."

Uncomfortable with the subject she knew she must protect, and yet inordinately pleased that Morgan's attraction had been so apparent, Gwen went to the breakfast tray and busied herself with pouring out the rich dark chocolate.

"Well . . . ?" demanded Sophie in an excited voice. "What happened on your tour yesterday? Did Mr. Riff make advances in front of Robyn? He seems the type to make his interest known—very bold and sure of himself. I heard you arrived home with him alone, as a matter of fact, and left poor Robyn half-foxed in a cafe somewhere."

Gwen lifted the cup to her lips, sipped, then spoke in a voice she hoped was nonchalant. "Mr. Riff was the perfect gentleman."

"Tell that to Robyn," Sophie quipped.

"The earl may well be miffed," Libby cut in. "But you are not officiously betrothed to him yet, are you, Miss Evans?"

Gwen shook her head and smiled, realizing her hostess already hoped for a different match.

Sophie strolled to the terrace doors, and pushing them wide, leaned to gaze out at the distant sea before sighing wistfully. "How fortunate you are, Gwen. I think Mr. Riff is so—so—"

"Splendid?" Libby finished with feminine honesty. "I haven't met a woman yet whose heart doesn't palpitate at the sight of him. Myself included." She laughed in a girlish way until her gray curls bobbed. "If he's interested in you, dear Miss Evans, count yourself honored, for you are the only European lady he has ever noticed, as far as I know, and many beauties have thrown themselves at him during his infrequent visits to Tangier. It's assumed he prefers the native women."

Color rose high in Gwen's cheeks and she hastily bit into a tangerine slice only to have the juice run down beneath the curve of her lower lip. After mopping it up with a napkin, she affected a casual attitude. "What else do you know about him, Libby?"

"Very little, truth to tell," the woman admitted, smoothing out her plum-colored skirts before nestling down in a chair like a ruffled hen. "Very close-mouthed, he is. And rather elusive, too. He rarely attends social gatherings. My European friends know practically nothing at all about him, although they certainly wish to, for their daughters' sakes. Colonel Carstairs is no help either—exasperating man. When I question him about Mr. Riff he either claims to know nothing or says he will not stoop to gossip about a gentleman's personal life just to appease the curiosity of husband-hunting women. I do know Mr. Riff stays at the Hotel La Villa de France when he's in town."

Gwen took another sip of cocoa. "When we walked through the streets yesterday people seemed to know him."

"What, dear?"

"Yesterday. Almost everywhere we went the natives seemed to know him."

"Believe me, what the natives know and what the rest of us know in Tangier are two different things," Libby replied.

"Do you know anything of his mother or father?" Gwen asked. All night she had pondered the boy Rhaman, recalling his arrival in Wales so many years past. The picture of his fierce young stance and his vow to avenge his mother's death had never left her memory.

"No, dear, I'm afraid not. He's not a garrulous gentleman by any means. Prefers not to talk about himself."

Feeling guilty all at once that her mind had been so preoccupied with Morgan, Gwen asked, "Have you seen Robyn yet this morning?"

"No. But his valet requested a pot of coffee earlier and said the earl had quite a sore head on him. It seems Mr. Riff took him to one of the Moorish cafes yesterday. Alcohol is served there to Europeans—Muslims avoid drunkenness. But hashish is commonly smoked in those places. Poor Lord Breese. He was probably quite overcome."

"Probably," Gwen muttered, remembering Robyn sprawled in a stupor upon the divan.

Sophie still stood outside upon the terrace watching the traffic. "Pardon me for changing the subject, but why are there so few women on the streets? And why are they so careful to keep their faces covered with veils? Some even have their eyes concealed."

"It's a part of their culture," Libby explained.

91

"From the time they're born they're kept secluded and are seldom allowed to go out of their own apartments. It's said they feel embarrassed by the gaze of strangers. You'll find that the women coming in from the country to sell their goods are a bit less modest, but still hide at least the lower half of their faces."

"How dreadful to be confined all one's life."

"Oh, yes. Muslim men are quite jealous and consider their wives personal property—I believe it's called 'tillage' in the Koran. And they can own many wives, of course."

Sophie followed the progress of two scurrying women in their voluminous costumes. "It's a very strange country compared to Wales."

"Isn't it?" Gwen took another bite of her cinnamon bun. "I shouldn't want to stay here long. What of you, Mrs. Carstairs? Will the colonel get a transfer soon?"

"Within the year, I hope. He's been promised a term at the British embassy in the United States. I do hope he receives it." She stepped out upon the terrace with Sophie and shook her head at the sight below. "Look there. Someone's tossed out a pile of broken furniture upon the street, and a pallet as well. It's probably crawling with vermin."

Sophie drew squeamishly back from the wall, but the older woman only shrugged, her experience of foreign places leaving her resigned to unpleasantries. "Ah, yes, my dear," she said. "The fleas are as numerous here as sand."

An hour later Libby invited the girls to accompany her to the fruit and vegetable market with her male servant Selim acting as an escort. The older woman gave both girls a floppy straw hat to protect their pale complexions from the sun, and a basket for carrying produce. They went out into the street, and as soon as the traffic swallowed them up in its odiferous, stifling press, Gwen found herself searching for danger among the lines of camels and turbaned pedestrians. Without Morgan at her side she felt more fearful and kept a constant watch of the activity around her, looking for fierce-eyed horsemen and a barbarous native called the English.

The vegetable market was situated in a part of the city overlooking the sea, and while the other women perused a stall fragrant with ripening fruit, Gwen paused to breathe the fresh salt air, clearing her nostrils of those other horrid odors permeating the less breezy avenues.

As she stood looking out at the distant waves, a group of idling men lewdly ogled her flapping skirts and unveiled face, while ragged urchins shouted insults at her which she could not understand but which were surely curses. Determined to stand her ground and behave with no intimidation, she lifted her chin and ignored them all.

Sophie and Libby were still picking through boxes of limes and lemons, and Gwen wandered a short distance to collect pomegranates from an open crate. After a moment she caught sight of a silk kaftan rippling seductively upon its peg, and ambled close to admire it. The marketplace had grown quiet, for the ferocious sun had encouraged shoppers to seek shade and refreshment in the cafes.

Glad for the lull, Gwen held the kaftan to her shoulders for size, paying scant heed to the solitary horseman entering the square. But when he reined his steed so close that the odor of his unwashed body pricked her nostrils, she glanced his way in irritation.

At the sight of his grotesque visage the kaftan slithered from Gwen's fingers to the ground. Mesmerized, she met the black gaze of the stranger and saw that he had only one eye; the other lid was puckered and scarred, set in a face seamed by countless summers of brutal sun. Her glance flickered over his filthy turban and burnoose, over the crude necklace strung with animal claws clasped about his corded neck. In one hand he carried a modern rifle, and his lathered, rawboned horse shifted restively beneath the threat of evil spurs set with glittering rowels.

Gwen's flesh crawled, for the rider seemed to have singled her out from everyone else in the square. Clutching her basket, she took a trembling step to go behind him, but he only backed the horse with a cruel jerk of the reins and barred her route. Remembering the bloody horror she had witnessed two days ago and growing frantic, she changed direction and tried to run in front of the snorting steed, but the rider only maneuvered his mount so that its hooves nearly stamped on her toes.

At the man's obvious ominous intent she stood paralyzed. Pinned against a wall by the nervous horse, she was afraid to scream lest her action prompt some violent reaction from the fiend whose motives she could not fathom. Even as she stood quivering like a helpless rabbit awaiting his next move, she glimpsed two figures approaching with long-barreled rifles clutched in their hands.

Gwen pressed her spine against the wall and cowered. Did they mean to join her tormentor in his cruel and taunting game, or fight him in some gory clash similar to the one she had witnessed before?

Rooted in place, still hemmed by the restless, wild-eyed horse, she stared at the two men, struck by the features of their faces and the color of their rough burnooses. She was certain they were members of the armed band she had seen on her tour with Morgan yesterday, members of the Berber tribe he had described.

They halted a few paces from the rider, the soft scrape of their goatskin boats catching his attention. He twisted in his saddle and tensed at the sight of them, his hand clenching the rifle on impulse. They exchanged no words, and although the rider glared at them with malice, their ivory-butted weapons gave him pause.

At last, after a heart-stopping interval, the rider sawed the mouth of his horse and wheeled the abused animal about in a swirl of black tail and quivering haunches. Spurring it through the passageway, he left behind nothing more than dust.

In fear Gwen turned her eyes to the pair of Berbers still standing a few feet away. But they merely gave her brief and respectful nods, then strolled to a spot of shade beside a frescoed column where they lazily leaned upon their rifles as if nothing untoward had occurred.

Unstrung by the strange episode and failing to

understand its significance, Gwen hurried across the street to join Sophie and Mrs. Carstairs. As she ran, pomegranates spilled out of her basket and rolled over the dust in every direction. Grabbing the women by their arms, she spewed out the terrifying tale.

"Are you certain the man was bent upon mischief, dear?" Libby asked uncertainly, putting a freckled hand to her cheek and gazing about the peaceful square. "Perhaps your imagination has become a bit overactive since your arrival here."

Sophie inched closer, uneasy over her friend's vehement insistence that she had not exaggerated a trivial encounter.

"I tell you the rider singled me out!" Gwen persisted, her face pink from sun and distress. "Heaven only knows what he would have done had the Berbers not arrived."

Libby's face puckered in anxiety and after hurriedly popping one more orange in her basket, she nodded for Selim to pay the stall keeper. "Perhaps we bad better go home then. I really don't know what to think. Of course, European ladies are not much respected here, and because we go about unveiled the native men believe we are . . . well, promiscuous. The odious man was probably only leering at you. After all, you *are* very pretty, and naturally attract masculine attention." Her hands fluttered. "But let's do hurry home, for now that I think on it, there have been stories about young European women being captured and sold into harems. Oh, dear! Perhaps bringing you out was unwise."

At her words, Sophie let out a little squeal and Libby locked arms with her charges in a motherly fashion, herding them along the street while Selim trotted close behind. They had to backtrack once, for a large pile of refuse had been dumped in the middle of the narrow lane and caused a traffic snarl. The women hid their noses in their perfumed handkerchiefs and scurried in the opposite direction.

"Filth, harems, barbarous men," Gwen muttered through the lace of her hankie. "Dreadful, cursed country. Surely there's no more vile place upon the face of the earth."

That evening the Carstairs invited friends from the British embassy to dine with them, and although Gwen joined in the conversation with dutiful sociability, she could not keep her mind from the disturbing scene at the vegetable market. The colonel expressed concern over the incident, but did not think it serious enough to keep the women confined.

Nevertheless, to dispel haunting visions of the disfigured rider, Gwen concentrated on thoughts of Morgan, wondering when she would see him again. Although she yearned for his presence, she worried that he might arrive unexpectedly and be coldly received by her father.

Dessert had just been served, and her eyes met Robyn's across the crystal trifle bowl brimming with brandied cherries. All evening the young earl had watched her with speculation in his small green eyes. When he had seated her at the table earlier, he had made his desire for her obvious, caressing her waist with a discreet but intimate hand. She feared he would soon propose marriage, and she did not know what reply to give. How could she tell Robyn that she belonged to the Squire of Hiraeth?

In spite of her own strong feelings, doubts assailed her. Did Morgan feel that they belonged together? What if her time with him had been a kind of wistful dream, a child-built fantasy that the wild atmosphere of Tangier had recreated and strengthened? Had she read in his eyes some intent that was not really there? If he were truly smitten with her, surely he would have come knocking at the door by now.

After dinner she sat with the female guests in the parlor, watching the clock with a sinking heart, disappointed that her lover had not called. As time ticked by she began to give credence to Libby Carstairs' suggestion—perhaps she did suffer from an overstimulated imagination.

At ten o'clock the guests finally took leave, and although the other women retired, Gwen was too restless to sleep. She consented to play a game of chess with Robyn, but could not keep still in her seat or concentrate long upon the black and white pawns. The earl remarked upon her distraction, and receiving her murmured complaint about the heat, excused himself with a bottle of claret in hand.

A while later Sir Gerald peeked into the room to discover Gwen pacing to and fro across Libby's cabbage-rose carpet. He frowned at her. "Has everyone else gone to bed?"

"I believe they have, yes."

"Then why haven't ye, girl? Are ye not exhausted? It's quite late."

Gwen lowered her lashes and averted her face lest he somehow read her thoughts. "I'm not sleepy, really."

"Well, ye should be," he declared in his blustery tone, taking hold of her arm. "Here, let me escort ye to yer room. At least lie down and rest until sleep comes to ye. I hope ye're not sickening for something."

She wanted to tell him she was sickening for a certain tall young gentleman he did not approve of, but docilely permitted him to guide her down the corridor.

"Good night, girl." Turning back, he added gruffly, "I love ye."

She stood on tiptoes to kiss his bewhiskered cheek before shutting the door behind him. With a sigh she then ambled out upon the flagstone terrace and searched the dark avenues, seeing ghostly forms flitting past the yawning alleys. Chilled by the thoughts of the horrible secrets they hid, she hugged her arms and sank down into a garden chair.

She did not know how long she had been dozing when she heard male voices drifting from the open window at the opposite end of the house. She stilled, then jumped to her feet and leaned far out over the terrace wall to listen. Catching a familiar resonant tone, she closed her eyes and smiled.

A moment later she crept from her room and slipped down the corridor in the direction of the library. The portal to the small chamber stood ajar and permitted lamplight to splash the tiles at her feet. Avoiding the amber glow, she sidled near the threshold and peered inside.

With his back to her, Morgan sat at a circular table beside the two older men, one hand resting atop a large unfurled map and the other holding a pen. He raised a forefinger and slid it over the colored chart, following a dotted line drawn from one point to another.

Gwen's eyes traveled over the curve of his generous shoulders, then over the line of his leg where it stretched out from under the table. Light brushed his head at the crown, and when he turned to speak with her father, she could see his partial profile, the hard plane of his cheek, and the hollow beneath his ear where the point of the jaw cast a shadow.

Though the other two men faced her, their attention was so fixed upon the map that they failed to notice her presence. She remained still and barely breathed, loath to interrupt. But Morgan twisted his head, and his eyes swung with unerring aim to find her face in the shadows.

Gwen's breath caught upon her lips at his uncanny senses. How fierce was his look! Its heat made the flesh rise along her arms in natural response. Starved for the sight of him, she continued to stare at the blue gaze that seemed more startling than ever beneath the lowered black brows.

In one fluid move, he stood up. "Good evening, Miss Evans," he said as she stepped tentatively across the threshold. Though the greeting was simple, no more than a polite acknowledgement of her entry into the company of gentlemen, it came as quietly off his lips as an endearment.

Aware of her presence now, the two older men rose, clearing their throats as if caught off guard by her unexpected visit. "Gwenllian!" Sir Gerald interrupted. "I thought ye had retired."

Taking a step forward, Gwen tore her eyes away from Morgan and fabricated a hasty excuse. "I—I just came for something to read. I couldn't sleep."

Her father frowned and replied with uncharacteristic brusqueness. "Well, perhaps ye are not trying hard enough."

A hint of a smile inclined the corners of Morgan's mouth. "I often have that trouble myself, Miss Evans. Do you mind if I select a book for you?"

"N-no." She glanced nervously toward her father. "Of course not."

Colonel Carstairs smoothed over the awkwardness with a genial smile. "By all means, recommend a good book to the lady, Riff. I have quite a decent selection here."

"Then pardon me, gentlemen." He stepped between them to the well-stocked shelves that marched from floor to ceiling, scanning several rows of leather-bound volumes as if hunting for one particular title.

Behind him Gwen wrung her hands and smiled vaguely at the colonel while her father rocked on his heels and eyed the unfolded map waiting upon the table.

The Theory of the Divine Right of Kings," Morgan

pronounced at last, holding up a weighty tome. " 'A complete history of the last eight centuries of English rule in Britain and abroad.' If I remember correctly, it's guaranteed to put you to sleep in—" he lifted a brow and arranged his face into a thoughtful expression— "no more than thirty minutes."

He walked forward, and with the book extended, waited for Gwen to reach out and take it. His nearness made her heart beat faster and her hands quiver. He placed the volume in her palm, not letting go of it until she had a good grip of the heavy red binding. Their fingers touched.

"Thank you, Mr. Riff," she replied in a whisper, hugging it to her breast. "I shall begin to read it . . . immediately."

"Immediately," he repeated with a polite smile.

Sir Gerald took her arm and steered her toward the doorway. "I'll see you in the morning then, daughter. Now don't ruin yer eyes by staying up and reading late."

"No, Papa. I promise that I'll put the book down in half an hour—maybe sooner."

Her father nodded and, eager to return to his map, failed to see the anticipation lighting his daughter's face and the last fleeting glance that passed between her and the Squire of Hiraeth.

Five

A quarter hour . . . twenty minutes . . . a half hour. Time ticked by with a maddening disregard for impatience. And then, among the honeysuckle that twined like long green ribbons upon the latticework below, Gwen spied him. From her place upon the terrace she followed his easy progress with her eyes, watching while he paused and raised his head to find her. All at once, in a fleeting second, she pictured him in a different setting from this sultry one, imagined him standing upon the wild black cliffs beside Hiraeth as master of every stone and shingle of the mystical fortress she loved so well.

Lifting her skirts, she descended the iron stair, running across the courtyard in a step light and eager, her face soft with expectation. As she approached, Morgan held out his arms, and into their circle she flew. He did not say any words. He simply stood with her, and they came to better know the feel of the other's shape, while the rise and fall of their yearning breaths blended with the hot night sounds. And then he kissed her, his manner tender yet more thorough and prolonged than it had been beneath the lemon trees.

At last he took his mouth away, and with a gentle hand cradled her head against the ridge of his shoulder. "Your father will make an obstacle of himself in this," he whispered. "You know that, don't you?"

She pressed her cheek against his shirt and wished he would not speak of it. "Yes."

"I can't ask you to defy him for me, Gwen."

"I've made my decision. If I must deceive my father, I will."

At her stubborn declaration he lifted her chin, and his tone was sober. "I won't sneak about like a thief again. That's not my way."

She hung her head and reached to toy with a strand of honeysuckle from the tangle that concealed them from the house, twirling it about her finger. "I don't like to be furtive either, but Papa has an unreasonable prejudice against the squires of Hiraeth. He always has. He resents their neglect of the estate."

Morgan slowly pulled the vine from her finger, and as it unwound, its velvet leaves descended to his feet. "Perhaps he objects to me for some other reason."

"What other reason could he have?" she asked with genuine mystification.

"Why don't you ask him?"

"Perhaps I will. We'll have a lengthy discussion, and then he will be made to come round."

Morgan laughed, and the sound was deep and

pleasant in the darkness. "Does you father bend to your will so easily, Gwen?"

She cast her lashes down in a demure sweep, but lifted one shoulder in an eloquent shrug that suggested no lack of feminine guile. "He can be persuaded to see my point of view in the more important issues, that's all."

Morgan ran his hands up and down her arms. "I fear you'll have a more difficult time with me. I'm not easy to sway."

She lifted her lashes, and the silver light of the garden made her glance so provocative that Morgan reached out to touch her face, as if to be certain that its loveliness was real. "However . . ." he said with his lips descending again, "at the moment, I believe you could persuade me to do anything."

They spent long moments kissing, and finally the restraint between them weakened to such a degree that Morgan had to cool his ardor rather than cross a boundary of intimacy he was not yet ready to breach. Wondering at his sudden rigid control, Gwen allowed herself to be guided to a sheltered bench and seated. Morgan stood a little apart with one boot resting atop the bench and an arm draped across his thigh. The breeze blew, ruffling the lilac bush behind him and interrupting the rhythmic tinkle of the fountain pulsing in the nearby courtyard.

"Do you remember seeing me at Hiraeth long ago?" Gwen asked softly, gazing up at his shadowed face. "When you were a boy?"

He nodded and a smile touched the corners of his lips. "I remember well. You stared at me with

105

those wide blue eyes of yours as if I'd materialized from another universe."

She turned her head to look at the mosque framed by the feathered tops of countless palms. "Hadn't you?"

"Perhaps."

"You called yourself Rhaman then."

"It's the name my father gave to me, a name common to his people. My mother always called me Morgan. I guess it was her way of remembering her homeland. I honor her by using it whenever I'm in the company of Europeans."

"I've always wondered about your mother . . ." Gwen hesitated, wanting to be delicate with her questioning.

He looked toward the sky and its constellations as if she had turned his thoughts to a distant place and time. "An enemy of my father murdered her."

"How horrible." She wanted to touch his hand, but he had straightened and clasped them together behind his back. "You told Papa and me that you would avenge her death. Have you . . . ?"

His eyes shifted to the sky again, and they were as remote as the twinkling stars. "No."

Gwen sensed that she should question him no more, sensed that he intended to keep a part of his nature guarded, and rather than feeling frustrated over a thwarted curiosity, she was strangely content to live with the unanswered riddles. She wondered if she was unprepared for the truth.

A moment later, when he bade her good night with a light kiss to her brow, she watched him vanish into the obscurity of the courtyard, realizing that she was just a little frightened of Morgan Riff's mystery.

For three days she did not see him, and the interlude was fraught with restlessness and slumberless nights. It was as if she were plagued by an ailment with no cure save that of Morgan's presence. And yet his mystery continued to make her uneasy. The Welsh half of his nature she understood, for it was like her own. But the Moroccan half had its roots here in this place of scorching heat and stinging sands, and it caused her apprehension. She yearned to find a way to diminish it, make it subordinate to the other. Perhaps there was a way.

She knew she possessed a strange and sensual power in Morgan's arms, for she had seen it soften the hardness of his eyes, felt it make his hands quiver with need. Although she had no experience of the dark and rapturous passions that stirred them both, she would test her power, and if it proved strong enough, she would make the Squire of Hiraeth return to the place where he belonged.

Thinking such thoughts, she lingered long over breakfast in her room one morning, absently feeding bits of toast to Buff.

Robyn knocked politely at the door. "May I come in?"

She set the wicker tray aside and welcomed him. "Would you like chocolate? There's an extra cup here."

"No thank you. But will you come to the parlor with me? I wish to speak with you."

She rose and smoothed down her skirts, observing him askance with an uneasy curiosity. "Of course."

Robyn followed her down the corridor. The parlor was empty, and he closed the door so that the maid who was polishing silver in the dining room could not hear their conversation.

"What is it, Robyn?"

He came forward and took her hand, turning it over, playing with the fingers. "I had planned to speak with you later upon our return to Wales but I see no reason to delay."

Gwen's heart sank. She knew what was to come, but did not know how to respond to it.

"Will you be my wife?" he asked bluntly, caressing the back of her hand. "I've already spoken with your father. Last night we conversed at length, and he heartily approves of the match. But you already knew that, of course."

"Of course."

"Well, what do you say? Can we announce our betrothal this morning?"

"Did my father put you up to this?" Gwen asked with sudden suspicion. "Did he prompt you to speak now instead of waiting until we returned to Wales?"

At the resentment in her tone the earl stiffened and released her hand. Hurt shone in his eyes. "Does it matter?"

She bit her lip, distressed. She had grown up with him, after all, and he was her distant kinsman. Her

108

fondness for him had not wavered. But in this strange savage land, she had discovered that she did not love him—at least, not in the wild and painful way she had come to love Morgan Riff.

She walked out onto the terrace and he followed in her wake, staring at her troubled profile when she stopped to gaze beyond the wall. "What's the matter, Gwen? What is it? My proposal has come as no shock to you, surely."

"No. It's just that—"

"What?"

She faltered. "I'm . . . I'm no longer certain of my feelings for you, Robyn."

It was not precisely the truth, but she could hardly be honest without causing a terrible row. She wanted to let him down easily, for disappointing him this way made her heartsick and guilty. She wished she could explain, make him understand that the direction of her life had changed. She had stepped out onto a different path and she would not abandon it.

"I don't understand," he persisted. "What do you mean you're no longer certain? What has changed in the space of one week?"

Taking a breath, she stared out to sea and answered steadily. "I'm honored by your proposal, Robyn. It's true I had thought to marry you, but I find myself unable to commit to the marriage now. If I've hurt you too badly, I beg your forgiveness."

"You've near devastated me, for God's sake! I will not accept your refusal." He huffed with frustration and threw up his hands. "Your father was right.

Your nerves have been strained by this trip. You are not yourself, you—"

She turned to him and stayed him with a look. "Robyn, I regard you highly, have always done so. Please don't say something we shall both regret tomorrow. Please accept my refusal with grace."

"I shall not accept it with grace or any way at all! You have been my intended for years and have never objected to it before. This trip has simply made you distraught, irrational, and you'll be yourself again once we are home in Wales. You're bound to realize that your father and I know what is best for you. Now, I suggest you spend more time resting and less time in the sun."

When she did not answer, but stood stubbornly staring out over the palms, he sighed in frustration and turned on his heel, bidding her a quiet good morning.

That afternoon Sir Gerald and Colonel Carstairs announced that they would be traveling to a nearby port town on business and would not return home for several days. After fond goodbyes they departed, and over dinner that evening Libby delivered a piece of news that delighted Gwen. Morgan had sent round a message offering to take them all upon an excursion to the seashore at dawn.

Managing to contain her elation in front of Robyn, Gwen replied casually that an outing sounded quite nice, but she hoped Mr. Riff was not putting himself out. Libby and Sophie gave her sly glances but, heedful of the presence of Lord Breese, said nothing.

At dawn's first light the pearly mist that had rolled in from the sea overnight still drifted through the avenues in gossamer wisps. Its lingering breath cloaked the repugnant odors of Tangier and heightened the fresh perfumes of the garden's exotic blossoms. Gwen breathed deeply and thought of home as she stood with the others on the damp steps of the villa awaiting Morgan.

She saw him emerge out of the haze astride the mettlesome copper horse. Checking an impulse to run forward and greet him, she forced herself to nod demurely when he dismounted and bade her good morning. Eager for the outing, Robyn hovered near, wearing his usual proper English attire and a jaunty straw hat.

Sophie and Libby were excited but somewhat apprehensive, both mumbling anxious words about harems and slavery. Now that Morgan was near, Gwen worried little about such dangers. He carried a revolver at his hip and a rifle hung across his saddle, and she knew how skillfully he could employ them. Moreover, he had brought with him a large band of well-armed Moors riding spirited horses.

"Must all of these men go with us?" Robyn asked, staring at the rough-clad gang who resembled bandits more than escorts.

Morgan turned to adjust his stirrup strap and replied in his laconic way, "Outside the city walls it's wise for Europeans to travel in large parties."

"Are you saying ambush is common?"

"I'm saying Europeans should travel in large parties." Morgan gave the earl a cold glance and nodded at the women, then swung atop his horse.

Sophie and Libby had not heard the exchange, but Gwen stared at the assortment of repeating rifles and cartridges toted by the Moors, and guided her mount close to Morgan's as he unhurriedly led the way down the narrow avenue.

Before they had gone many blocks the mist abruptly cleared, lifting like a veil drawn from the stark white face of Tangier and allowing the sun's rays to glisten excruciatingly off the white ramparts. Directing them through the Kasbah, Morgan pointed out the official buildings, including the law courts, the Pasha's palace, and the prisons. Gwen studied each with interest, noting the crenelated walls and the graceful colonnades whose keyshaped doorways were adorned with pink-and-blue arabesque designs. She thought it a shame that an air of dilapidation hung over the entire government complex, and that the decay was accentuated by the putrid stream of water trickling along the pavement. The scene disgusted her; if Tangier had ever possessed beauty, all traces of it were slowly crumbling beneath indifferent hands.

In front of the Court of Justice the Pasha was publicly engaged in trying a case, sitting at the entrance upon a thronelike chair and garbed in the finest white silk. At Robyn's expression of interest Morgan slowed their progress, and the party watched while a defendant argued for himself in front of the expressionless official. Soldiers swathed in blue burnooses and wearing tall fezzes stood to the side with scimitars in hand.

After a moment of listening to the fast-talking defendant, the Pasha put down the peacock-feather fan he had been using to discourage flies, and raised his arm to signal silence. In a stentorian voice, he then pronounced a sentence.

Immediately the defendant was seized by the sentries and roughly shoved against a wall. The soldiers pinioned his arms high above his head so that the palms of his hands faced outward, prompting a few members of the crowd to wail and call for mercy.

Confused, Gwen frowned when a third soldier came forth wielding a narrow-bladed knife, then watched in horror as the Pasha's justice was cruelly carried out. While the prisoner struggled wildly and cried for the pity of Allah, his palms were cut, sliced from fingertip to wrist until blood streamed down his arms in warm red rivulets.

Sophie and Libby gasped and turned their heads away.

"For God's sake, Morgan," Gwen breathed in a weak voice, "What are they doing to him?"

"It's called the punishment of the salt." He watched the torture with unflinching eyes and explained grimly. "Salt will be packed into the open wounds, then his palms will be placed together, bound, and covered by a wet leather glove. The glove will shrink as it dries."

"My God."

"The torment lasts for days because the wounds can't heal." With a nudge of his boot he started his horse forward, prompting her to follow. "The fellow

113

will likely die of tetanus within a few days—if he doesn't find a way to kill himself first."

As they rode away from the ghastly Kasbah filled with the screams of the suffering prisoner, Robyn condemned the abomination in a perfect echo of Gwen's sentiments. Sophie's face had paled and her eyes were huge with shock. In a nervous chatter Mrs. Carstairs began speaking of the latest gossip surrounding the Royal Family, all while Morgan Riff rode imperturbably onward.

Before long they had passed through the city gates and gone beyond the last white villa. Gwen took a shaky breath and stayed close to Morgan as the countryside unfolded before them in a landscape of ploughed fields, sparse shrubs, and shallow streams. Robyn spurred his mount forward to ride at their escort's side.

"How can you countenance the barbarous punishments that go on here, Riff?" Robyn demanded with the all self-righteousness of a liberally educated Englishman. "Not only that, but what about the slave markets and the selling of white women as concubines? I've read all about them, and fail to comprehend how you and other civilized residents can stand by so unaffected. Why, the treatment of that prisoner was the kind of torture Europe left behind in the Dark Ages, for God's sake."

At the contempt in Robyn's tone Morgan pulled his horse up short, his eyes hard. "That prisoner in the Kasbah would have been an appropriate character for the Dark Ages. How would you punish a man who raped and murdered a young girl and left her body for the carrion to pick?"

114

Robyn set his jaw at the subtle dressing-down, speechless for once, and when Morgan reined his horse about, the earl fell back.

In single file the party followed the path down into a gully, then climbed a promontory strewn with dwarf palms and tufted grass. Daisies grew wild in patches. The air was cool and strong after its skim across the sea, and the women put their hands upon their floppy straw hats to anchor them.

Upon reaching the top of a flat plateau, Morgan halted and, lifting his hand, indicated the splendrous panorama stretching to the north. Before them, the rough Atlantic undulated in variegated stripes of aqua, meeting the pale azure sky in such a subtle blending of hues that the horizon line could scarcely be distinguished. Gwen swiveled in her saddle, finding Tangier nestled behind them like a miniature, its villas myriad squares of alabaster dotted with minarets and fronted by blue straits crowded with wind-buoyed sails.

Morgan looked at her, and she knew that he awaited her reaction to the view. His eyes flickered with expectation, with a hopefulness that she would admit that his land possessed a raw and striking beauty. But the ugliness in the Kasbah was still fresh in her mind; it was one more stain to add to all the other tarnished glories of Morocco, and she made no flattering remark.

Saying nothing, Morgan went on, and the copper horse forged a path over the trail, its hooves picking a way through swatches of aloes, cacti, and marigold. Gwen followed in line, staring at her lover's broad back with a strange sort of ache. She felt as if her silence on the plateau had caused a rift between them, one that might slowly rend the magic of their relationship in two. She longed to stop its splitting, but did not know how.

"I declare, I'm famished after so much arduous riding," Libby announced an hour or so later. "Mr. Riff!" she called out in a querulous voice. "Shall we stop soon and enjoy our picnic?"

He nodded and called out in Arabic for the Moors to halt and make camp. Stopping her horse, Libby clumsily dismounted with the aid of her servants before calling out a cheerful order to Sophie. "Ask Lord Breese to help you find a nice level spot for us to spread the rugs and set up the dining tent, please, dear. I shall ask Selim to unload the baskets of food. After we eat, perhaps Mr. Riff will show us the way down to the beach."

Dismounting, Gwen smiled at Libby's enthusiasm, then caught sight of Morgan, and the tenseness in his watchful pose aroused her concern. Motionless, he sat his horse some distance away and stared out over the barren plain toward the southern horizon. Gwen squinted and looked for an object of interest there, but his eyes seemed to perceive something her own vision failed to detect. For long moments his gaze remained trained upon a fixed spot, and presently a faint haze of dust appeared to hover over the earth.

Gwen straightened. A band of horsemen approached, traveling fast with *haiks* tossed across their dark faces and muskets carried in their upraised arms. Seized with trepidation, she looked to Morgan, but he had already nudged his mount forward and at a leisured pace rode out to greet the leader of the ominous pack. By this time the others of the picnic party had noticed the presence of the newcomers. The Moors remounted and went to form a supportive line behind Morgan, who conducted a brief conversation with the chief of the ragtag group. After a few moments, the latter waved an arm to signal his men to retreat, and without a backward glance, Morgan wheeled the copper horse around and spurred it back to the picnic site.

When he dismounted, Robyn hastened forward with Gwen at his heels. "Who were they?" he asked.

Morgan tethered his stallion to a cork tree, deftly making a slip knot in the reins. "Thieves and assassins for the most part."

"The devil you say," Robyn exclaimed, looking again in the direction of the disappearing company. "What did they want?"

One of Libby's mauve linen napkins escaped the picnic basket and the wind blew it across Morgan's boot. He leaned to retrieve it and replied with his usual brand of coolly delivered humor. "To murder and pillage, I would assume."

"And what did you say to them?"

"I persuaded them to go and find another picnic of Europeans to annoy."

"And who are you to turn aside a group of desperate men with nothing more than a few of your sarcastic words?"

Morgan stuffed the napkin in the pocket of the earl's jacket. "I believe I've already introduced myself."

The tension between the two men was escalating

toward a dangerous clash, and Gwen interrupted in a tone of forced brightness. "Look! The food is all laid out for us. Doesn't it look good? Robyn, why don't you take a seat over there?"

Both men ducked beneath the makeshift dining tent and, after the ladies had all been seated, eased down at opposite ends upon the spread rug. As Sophie distributed glasses of lemonade she inquired about the group of mounted visitors, and Morgan replied glibly that the men had lost their way and were asking for directions, a lie which the nervous young woman readily accepted. Beside her Libby Carstairs looked doubtful, but said nothing, busying herself instead with apportioning silverware.

The meal went pleasantly enough after that, with the sharing of crusty bread, cheeses, fruit, and sugared almonds. The mood lightened, and Gwen suspected she was the only one to notice the underlying strain stretching between the two men who each had an interest in her.

She tried not to look in Morgan's direction too often, afraid her feelings for him would be evident to the watchful earl. But her eyes lifted again and again to observe the man she loved. He sat a little across from her on the pile of richly hued rugs, one knee upraised, the other leg outstretched in a relaxed fashion, his strong jaw working as he chewed. When Sophie expressed an interest in the country, he spoke at length about the history of Morocco, and about its present sultan who claimed to be a direct descendant of Muhammad.

After a leisured hour, Mrs. Carstairs suggested they all walk down to the shore, and with Morgan

118

in the lead they descended a steep path to a stretch of sunny beach aglitter with sand crystals. Exhilarated by the refreshing air, the Europeans wandered in different directions, exploring, picking up shells and bits of mother-of-pearl tossed ashore by the tide. As Gwen bent to retrieve a half-submerged conch from the froth, Morgan came up behind her. She had known he was near, lounging in the shade of the overhanging cliff and watching her with his vigilant eyes. Taking the shell from her grasp, he rinsed it in a curling wave, then set it aside upon a rock before silently taking hold of her hand.

He led her up the path again, away from the others, guiding her over beds of asphodels and thyme, through a cork grove until they came to a jumble of rock, which upon closer inspection proved to be the entrance to a grotto. Crouching down, Morgan entered first, then reached out his hands to help Gwen through the narrow passageway. He guided her between the dark natural corridor smelling of damp earth and seawater until they came to another opening, which put them upon a ledge overlooking a breathtaking vista.

The rock formations created a jagged natural window, a hole cut through the heart of the cliff facing the sea. Its opening framed spirited waves that bucked and reared against the promontory like a hundred white horses, while sunlight created radiant stars upon the fury of foam and spray. The wind blew bracingly. It whipped Gwen's skirts and made her sway so that Morgan put an arm about her waist to steady her balance. For a moment, she could only hold her breath, awed by the view.

"My father's people say that an ancient god carved out this window with his hands," Morgan said.

She smiled. "He must have been quite a strong god."

"The story goes that in the days before man, an enchanted mermaid sunned herself upon those rocks down there. She caught the fancy of a young god, and he flew down from heaven one day to get a closer look. But she was very shy, and when she saw him ogling her from the cliff, she dived back into the sea. Not to be thwarted, he carved this hidden ledge so that he could spy upon her whenever she bathed."

"He wasn't a very noble god, was he?" Gwen teased.

"Perhaps not. But he was clever. Knowing her fondness for music, he played a love song upon his harp, and hearing it, she leapt from the waves and landed here, where she spent a day and a night in the young god's arms."

Gwen glanced at her escort, thinking to find the shine of humor in his eyes, but they were sober. "And did they have a happy ending?"

He turned his gaze back to the view. "I don't know. It would have been difficult, wouldn't it? For he was born of the heavens, and she of the sea."

Gwen stared at his profile in thoughtful silence, then shifted her eyes to watch the galloping waves rush forward and dash against the rock face. "The cliffs of Hiraeth are just as picturesque as these," she commented softly. "Black and fierce, but beautiful."

"I remember."

"Do you?"

"Yes." He turned to regard her with a museful expression, and the breeze ruffled the sleeves of his shirt, outlining the shape of his vigorous arms. "Hiraeth calls to me sometimes, quite unexpectedly. I've wondered over it. It must be something inborn, for I was not there to develop an affection for the place."

Gwenllian searched the blue eyes that reflected the unsettled sea, and she yearned to ask him to heed the call, yearned to ask him to go back with her to Wales. She knew beseechment shone in her face, but Morgan chose not to address it. Instead he bent his head to kiss her lips. And as she pressed herself closer to his body, she thought of the mermaid and the god.

Then while the sun beat down and the sea simmered, she lost herself in the heat of his attentions, forgetting time when his hands roved over her form and invaded the barrier of her blouse, which billowed about her breasts like a white cambric cloud. Closing her eyes, she slipped a hand between the buttons of his shirt and felt the damp flesh beneath it, felt the ridges that his ribs made, and the valley of his spine. Her mouth grew swollen with his kisses.

"By whose leave do you take liberties with Miss Evans?!"

The enraged voice reverberated through the passageway behind, glancing off the walls of the ancient god's retreat and disturbing the rhythms of the lovers' breathless bodies. Morgan raised his head with a snap, and savagery narrowed the eyes that had been tender with love.

Lord Breese stood facing them, shaking with rage as he snarled a furious curse. "Damn you, Riff!"

"Robyn!" Gwen cried.

He ignored her, stalking forth to challenge his adversary. "You are indeed the ruffian they brand you! A product of this despicable land. Daring to paw the woman who is betrothed to another man! I ask you again, by whose leave do you take such liberties?"

"By my own."

The words were low and chilling, and Gwen clenched Morgan's arm in a petition that he provoke no further conflict, for already his fists had tensed in the way of a man on the brink of a brawl.

Robyn had balled his own fists and crouched into a fighting stance, his tailored London suit and necktie making him an unlikely foe. "We may be in an uncivilized land, Riff, but that does not give you an excuse to overstep the bounds of propriety with *my* intended. If I had a pistol I would use it on you—"

"He took no liberties, Robyn!" Gwen exclaimed, blurting out the truth to avert disaster. "Morgan did nothing that I did not allow!"

The earl's face froze as his eyes raked her disordered hair and mussed white blouse. His chest heaved and his fists quivered with the need to lunge forward and attack his rival. When he growled and raised an arm to strike out, Morgan stayed it in one swift move.

"There'll come a day of reckoning between us,

Breese," he warned. "But I'll not have it forced upon me here and now in the way of schoolboys."

His eyes shifted to Gwen's and she stammered, "I—I'll be along in a minute. Go without me."

After regarding her in silence for a few seconds, he turned around, and with a quick step, abandoned the window of the god.

Leaning to retrieve Robyn's expensive hat from the mud, Gwen held it out to him.

"How could you?" he asked furiously, snatching at it. "How could you?"

Six

Sir Gerald had summoned his daughter to the library. Dreading the interview, Gwenllian tarried in the corridor, surreptitiously peering into the room to see if she could judge his mood by the expression on his face. He sat behind the colonel's desk with tiny pots of watercolors, bottles of ink, and an assortment of pens neatly ordered around an unrolled map. She had always known that he loved maps. After his retirement as a cartographer for the navy he had created a special room at Ardderyd to house his collection of globes and charts, and she often found him there, even very late at night. So, she thought nothing of his poring over dotted boundaries and penciled roads with Colonel Carstairs here in Morocco. Even Morgan's involvement failed to rouse her curiosity, for she assumed that, as a resident of the country, he was helping them accurately chart the environs of Tangier for some European publication.

"You wanted to see me, Papa . . . ?"

Sir Gerald glanced up. "Ah! Gwenllian, come

in." Rising from his chair, he slid a piece of clean paper over the map from which he had just lifted his pen, making the gesture smooth and scarcely perceptible. Although Gwen noticed the move, she was too preoccupied with thoughts of the coming interview to wonder long over his furtiveness.

She had little doubt as to the reason for her sire's wishing to see her. He and the colonel had arrived home last evening from their journey out of town, and after breakfast this morning, Robyn had wasted no time arranging a private interview with Sir Gerald. She assumed her scandalous behavior with Morgan had been their topic of conversation.

"What did you want to speak with me about, Papa?" she prompted now, looking up at him from beneath innocently raised brows.

Her sire cleared his throat with a loud harrumph. "Er—Robyn spoke with me this morning, Gwenllian. Quite disturbed he was. He said that he had proposed marriage to ye while I was away. He had spoken to me first, of course, to receive permission, which I quite willingly granted."

Pausing expectantly, Sir Gerald stared at her as if hoping she would volunteer an explanation and spare him further elaboration. When she did not, he clasped his hands behind his back and went on. "Ye've always known that Robyn will be my heir—master of Ardderyd, and I've always thought it fitting that ye should wed him. It would be a comfort to me knowing ye were happily married to a suitable man, a man of my choosing. But Robyn told me ye refused his proposal outright."

"It's true, Papa."

He eyed her from beneath his tangled brows as if she were not quite sane. "Great Elysuim! Why, daughter? Why?"

Gwen knew that she could not admit the truth, for her confession would only ignite a furious outburst of accusations, disappointment, and a probable charge that she had dishonored her sire with her waywardness. Of course, some day she would have to face the music, let the anger fly and have it over. But she wanted to delay that confrontation, for she hoped that she could somehow formulate a way to appease the two men she was bound to hurt by loving Morgan Riff. She had talked her father around to her way of thinking many times before; with good fortune and cleverness she could do it again.

"I've discovered that I don't love Robyn, Papa," she murmured with her head lowered in an artful pose. "He and I are impossibly different, you know. For instance, he likes London society and I don't care for it at all. He enjoys the bustle of the city and I prefer the country. He is gregarious and I'm a stay-at-home. And besides all that, he—he seems to enjoy the bottle a bit too much. It would probably lead to a great deal of squabbling between us if we were husband and wife." Disparaging the earl made her feel guilty, but she needed to strengthen her case in order to win her father's support.

Sir Gerald threw up his hands in exasperation. "Daughter, all gentlemen enjoy their liquor. I don't know anyone who doesn't fall into his cups now and again. Why, when I was a young sailor I used to drink myself under the table more often than I care to remember. There's nothing wrong with that."

Gwen pursed her lips and idly ran a finger over the row of books on the library shelf, stopping when she came to the ponderous volume that Morgan had chosen for her several nights ago in his plot to see her alone. With a moody sigh she murmured, "I thought you would understand."

"Don't think to soften me this time, Gwenllian," Sir Gerald warned behind her. "Yer moping and yer tears will not persuade me to relent, for I know what is best for ye. If I must put my foot down in this matter, I will."

She whirled about. "Why would you make me miserable, Papa? Why would you force me into an arranged marriage? You've always respected my independent spirit before and encouraged me to do my own thinking. Have you forgotten how you raised me? Don't you care for my happiness?"

"I care very much for yer happiness and always have done, as ye well know," he shot back. "Spoiled ye've been from the first, and more so after yer mother died. But a father's wisdom should be respected in the matter of marriage, and mine will be!"

Stepping forward, he examined her flushed face and blazing eyes with growing suspicion. "I want ye to tell me why it is ye've so suddenly changed yer mind, Gwenllian. Not a week ago ye were content to be Robyn's wife and live at Ardderyd. Why not now?"

As Gwen met her father's searching eyes, it occurred to her that Robyn might have said nothing about discovering her in Morgan's embrace. Had the earl's pride kept him from it, or had he remained silent in defense of her honor? She speculated. If her father did not know how far the relationship with Morgan had progressed, perhaps his wrath could be avoided and the situation salvaged.

But before she could speak Sir Gerald came to his own conclusion. "Ye've been taken in by that scoundrel Morgan Riff, haven't ye, girl? I saw the glances passing between the two of ye the other night, in this very room. I saw the bold way he looked at ye, and it did not even bring a blush to yer cheeks. Ye've been smitten by him, haven't ye?"

"Yes!" Gwen cried, pushed into a confession. "Yes! And you have no good cause to disapprove of him, Papa. He's a gentleman, and heir to the finest piece of property in Wales."

"The man is not who ye think he is, and I will not have ye involved with him!"

"I'll see him if I please and you cannot stop me!"

"You dare to rebel against my authority, girl?" Sir Gerald bellowed. "You dare to ignore my good judgment?"

"Father," she said in a pleading voice. "In the past we have always enjoyed a close relationship, and while I may have been a bit difficult at times, I've always been an obedient daughter. But I'm eighteen now, a woman with a mind of my own. And in this matter of the heart I must rely upon my own instincts."

"But ye are not using sound judgment, daughter! Ye are letting a schoolgirl crush over a man ye know nothing about sway your normally good sense! By God, I'll send for Morgan Riff this very hour and tell him in no uncertain terms how I feel. He will not come within a mile of ye again!"

"You can't tell him what to do! No one can. He is his own man and if he decides to see me, he will!"

"The devil he will!"

Too furious to speak further, knowing argument useless now, Gwen wheeled about in a swirl of skirts and ran from the room, hardly noticing Libby Carstairs' shocked expression and Sophie's stricken face as she passed the open parlor. She dashed along to her bedroom, slammed the door, and threw herself across the bed, shaken by the first violent argument she had ever had with her father.

Down the corridor Sir Gerald paced the library floor in an attempt to cool his anger, halting his furious strides only when Robyn rapped quietly upon the door.

"Well," the older man grumbled with a heavy sigh. "I daresay the entire household heard the row between my daughter and me."

"It couldn't have been avoided," Robyn replied diplomatically. "Gwen has become high-strung since coming to Tangier. Hot words between you were inevitable. Perhaps now that she has been chastised she will settle down and be herself again."

Sir Gerald shook his head in bewilderment, absently stoppering the ink bottles on the desk. "I cannot believe her infatuation with Riff has sprung up so fast. She hasn't even been in his company more than three or four times. Admittedly the man has a certain charm for the ladies, but—"

"He is a damned blackguard!" Robyn cursed with an uncharacteristic ardor. "He's a libertine, a product of this barbarous society. No gentleman I've ever known would dare to dally with another's intended."

The older man's hand stilled upon the bottles. "Are ye saying Riff has taken liberties with my daughter?"

Robyn hesitated, unwilling to admit his unvaliant reaction on the sea ledge. Any gentleman defending his own honor and that of his lady would have fought Riff without a second's deliberation. But Robyn had been a coward, knowing himself no match for the ruthless foreigner who had stolen Gwen's affection. He was used to gentility and convention and, most of all, to a respect that his English title did not earn him in Morocco.

"If given the chance, I'm certain Riff would take whatever liberties he pleased with Gwen," Robyn said to fuel the fire of her father's wrath.

"Then she will be forbidden to see him."

"Will you speak with Riff, as well?"

Sir Gerald riffled the pages of an atlas lying open upon the desk. "I hardly know how to handle this situation. My association with Riff is a bit . . . delicate at the moment. And then there are the Carstairs to consider. They seem to like him well enough, and I'm a guest in their home. It wouldn't do for me to create some sort of a nasty scene when we'll be leaving in a few more weeks. Besides," he grumbled, "Riff is unpredictable. I don't trust him. If I were to demand that he leave Gwenllian be, he

130

would likely defy me upon principle, for I sense the fellow takes orders from no one."

Robyn snorted. "As I said, he has no honor."

"On the contrary," the older man countered in a grudging way. "I suspect he possesses a great deal of honor. It's just not of the same code to which we are accustomed."

The earl raised a disdainful brow. "Well, they say there is honor even among thieves."

Sir Gerald walked to the terrace doors and opened them to let in the warm breeze. With effort he mustered a few words of optimism. "Don't fret, Robyn. Gwen will be yers again when we leave Morocco, and all this business involving Morgan Riff will likely fade from her memory even before we reach the shores of England."

Robyn murmured a doubtful response, his attention suddenly arrested by the half-concealed map spread upon the desktop. "What is this work you and the colonel are doing with Morgan Riff—if I may ask, of course?"

"I'm not at liberty to say, truth to tell."

"Forgive me. It was impolite to ask—"

"No, no," the older man relented. "Close the door and sit down. I'll take ye into my confidence and tell ye a bit about Mr. Riff. But ye must keep it under yer hat. I'd rather Gwenllian not be told."

"Gwen . . . ? *Gwen!*" Sophie called through the bolted door, her soft voice anxious. "May I come in? I've brought you some lemonade."

Gwen rose from her hot, disordered bed and unlocked the portal, closing it again after her friend proceeded through with the refreshments.

"I suppose you heard my argument with Papa," she sighed, taking the tray and setting it down upon the vanity stool. "Vulgar of us to shout so at each other, wasn't it? I fear emotion got the better of us."

"Did you really tell Lord Breese you wouldn't marry him?"

Gwen nodded and poured two glasses of lemonade, handing one to the incredulous blonde. "I'm afraid so."

"Will you marry Mr. Riff, then?"

"Sophie!"

"Well, do you think that I'm blind?"

Gwen sipped her drink, made a face at its sourness, and put it aside before restlessly moving to the shutters. Toying with their slats, she caused sunlight to flash upon the tiles in intermittent bands of saffron. "He hasn't asked me."

"Do you expect he will?"

"I don't know."

Sophie threw up her hands. "But what do you *think*?"

Gwen shook her head. "There's a great deal about Morgan that's mysterious to me. Even though his manner is bold, there's a side of his nature that he carefully guards. I feel that I don't really know him, and yet from the moment we met I knew that I belonged at his side. And I believe he shares that feeling."

"Poor Robyn is no match for him at all, is he?" Sophie commented in sympathy for the earl, leaning down to stroke Buff's head when the whining dog demanded attention. "Mr. Riff is so—so . . . formidable and fierce. And yet, his fierceness is charming, isn't it? So different from the men we meet in Britain. You're fortunate to have captured his interest, Gwen," she added with unmasked envy. "I can't blame you for standing up to Sir Gerald. Timid as I am, I would stand up to him rather than lose such a handsome suitor."

"Still," Gwen sighed with a troubled frown. "I've never fought so bitterly with Papa. In the past, our arguments have been over small matters, and regardless of their outcome, they never left scars between us. But now . . ."

"He and Robyn won't make it easy for you to see Mr. Riff again," Sophie predicted, adding a lump of sugar to her lemonade. "What will you do if Sir Gerald forbids him to call again?"

Gwen gave a short laugh. "I don't believe Morgan can be forbidden to do anything. But if I have to, I'll find some way to circumvent Papa. It'll pain me to do that. Oh, why can't he be *reasonable*?"

"Fathers are never reasonable where daughters are concerned," Sophie said with a knowledgeable nod of her head. "But just think! You came all the way from Wales to Tangier, and who should you find here but the mysterious Squire of Hiraeth! It must be an omen, a sign that the relationship between you is meant to be. And if you marry him, why, surely the two of you will return to Wales and live at Hiraeth. That should please your father."

Gwen said nothing. She only stared at the hot bars of sun that striped the floor and evaporated the beads of condensation dripping from Sophie's glass, and remembered the strange tale of a god and a mermaid.

"At any rate," Sophie went on, interrupting her thoughts, "your dashing beau has an appointment to see the colonel tonight at ten o'clock. I heard Mrs. Carstairs mention it after breakfast."

Gwen glanced up sharply at the news, murmuring, "And Papa is having dinner at the embassy. I wonder . . ."

The pointed brass hands of the parlor clock crept toward the hour of ten. Sir Gerald was still out, and Libby and Sophie had gone to bed. With no enthusiasm, Gwen played a game of chess with the sullen earl, eyeing him as he poured a third glass of claret and made a clever move with a carved black pawn. Her ear was cocked to the street sounds and, with her attention so claimed by every clopping hoof and thudding footstep, concentration upon the board grew difficult. After rubbing her brow in distraction, she slid her white queen forward in a countermove.

Suddenly she heard the *tramp, tramp, tramp* of a horse. Briskly, it trotted down the avenue, its iron shoes slithering upon the broken cobbles as its rider drew the reins up short.

"Unwise strategy," Robyn commented, studying her last move so raptly that he failed to note the rider's arrival. "I'm surprised at you, Gwen. You're usually more astute. The knight was the piece to move."

"I—I guess I wasn't concentrating upon the game."

At the breathlessness in her voice, Robyn lifted his gaze. "What *were* you concentrating upon?"

There was no need to answer, for the sound of a distinctive male voice drifted from the vestibule and into the parlor. Robyn's eyes met Gwen's over the chessboard and his fingers tightened upon the black queen he prepared to move. Tension stretched between them as Colonel Carstairs greeted his guest and led him past the closed doors of the parlor toward the library.

Neither Gwen nor Robyn spoke as they continued their solemn contest over the board, but from time to time Morgan's voice drifted through the wall, interrupting the strained hush to insinuate itself between the edgy players. Although Gwen longed to escape the watchful eyes of her spurned suitor, she forced herself to play out the interminable game, her hand trembling each time she positioned a pawn.

An hour passed. Lord Breese poured another glass of claret and, studying the board carefully, moved his king. "Checkmate!"

An abrupt knock rattled the front door. They heard Selim admit a man who introduced himself as a military attaché from the embassy. When he said he bore a message for Colonel Carstairs, the servant hurried off on slippered feet to summon his employer to the vestibule.

Now that the colonel was away from Morgan Riff, Lord Breese downed the last of his claret and rose from his seat on unsteady legs. With a bravado fortified by the spirits, he threw open the parlor doors and stalked in the direction of the library.

"Robyn," Gwen called in an anxious voice, afraid that he intended to provoke a scene with Morgan. "Robyn!"

But her distress did not stay him, and with growing trepidation, she pushed back her chair and followed fast upon his lurching heels. She saw Morgan sitting at the colonel's enormous mahogany desk with a colored map spread out before him. An untouched snifter of brandy held down the curling edge of one corner of the chart. In the long fingers of his left hand, he loosely gripped a pen, which he set aside when Robyn marched into the room full of bluster. At the sight of the earl's contentious stance, malice immediately darkened the blue of his eyes, and Gwen hastened forward to draw his gaze in her direction.

He drew up his sprawled legs and stood, the movement of his body so controlled it resembled the lazy stretch of an animal. "Gwenllian," he addressed her quietly in his familiar way, ignoring the earl. "I hope the evening finds you well?"

While she murmured some inane but appropriate reply, Robyn sauntered forth, thrusting himself with reckless courage between the two of them. Full of daring, the inebriated aristocrat leaned to rest a palm upon the desk, where he tapped the crinkled edges of the chart with his fingernails and drawled, "You seem to spend quite a lot of your time here, Riff. Drawing maps, are you . . . ?"

Morgan folded his arms across his chest and straightened, his height dwarfing that of the other man. "I'm sure you intend to make a point, Breese. Why don't you save us time and get on with it?"

With a haughty tilt of his head, Robyn regarded him. "It's amazing what one can learn in the cafes around here," he said in a slurred voice, "especially when a few coins are spread around. I've discovered that the natives particularly enjoy talking politics. They go on and on about the interfering Christian infidels who are attempting to overrun their country. Of course, it's no secret Britain has an interest in Tangier. If the city were to fall into the wrong hands, Gibraltar may be threatened, and that would not be at all the thing. France already has Algeria . . . do we allow her to have Morocco, as well?"

"I'm sure your political views are fascinating," Morgan cut in. "But I haven't the time nor the inclination to listen to them."

He made to roll up the map on the desk but Robyn pressed both palms to the paper, holding the edges firmly down. "I know what you're doing here, Riff. And I believe that the sultan of this contemptible country that you call home would be interested to know, as well."

Morgan's eyes glittered at the threat, and Gwen held her breath. She watched in alarm while he leaned forward, and in a slow, deliberate fashion rested his knuckles upon the map that Robyn held down. "Do you threaten me, Breese . . . ?"

Uttered with an icy smoothness, the question hung upon the air. The seconds stretched, counted by the *tsk tsk tsk* of the grandfather clock that glowered beside the bookshelf. Gwen stood rooted, afraid to interfere in the dreadful contest of wills.

"Maybe I do," Robyn answered at last, his face pinkening with brashness and wine. "Maybe I do."

"You are undecided?" the other mocked, still with his eyes affixed to Robyn's. "Perhaps the bottle has given you more courage than you can handle." With a quick move he jerked the map from beneath the earl's sweating palms.

The gesture energized the rage of the bested Lord Breese. He charged forward with his slender fists bared and his face contorted in ire, intent upon landing a blow.

Gwen cried out, alerting Colonel Carstairs, who crossed the threshold just in time to size up the situation in a glance. The coolheaded officer seized the posturing earl by his shoulders and pulled him back from the man who stood more than ready to meet the challenge. Infuriated, Robyn struggled to free himself from his host's determined grip, growling a slurred order at him not to interfere.

But the older man ignored him, and hissed, "For God's sake, Breese, provoke him no further! I know him well enough to know that he will kill you for the girl!"

Seven

Nearly a week passed after the dreadful incident in the library, and during that time Morgan did not return to the Carstairs' villa. Gwenllian began to despair, for her father said that if all went according to schedule they would be sailing for Wales at the end of the month. If so, what would become of her relationship with the Squire of Hiraeth?

She had no doubt that if the strong-willed Mr. Riff intended to see her again he would find a way to do it, regardless of her father's mandate against it, and in spite of Robyn's protestations. But much to her vexation, the earl had hovered about her side with untiring persistence until she began to liken him to a sentry posted to guard her virtue. She suspected that it was the earl's intent to personally prevent her from seeing Morgan Riff again during these remaining weeks in Morocco, and then, once they returned home, to continue with their marriage plans as if his proposal had never been refused.

She was relieved when the three men of the

household decided one afternoon to indulge in a game of billiards and took themselves off to an establishment providing such entertainment. Libby Carstairs had gone earlier to spend the day with a friend, and although she had extended the invitation to include the girls, they had politely declined in favor of resting quietly upon the shaded terrace.

"I can't wait to go home," Sophie commented when they were alone and lounging in wicker chairs angled beneath the lacy shade of a cherry laurel. Sighing, she put aside a piece of needlepoint, pronouncing the weather too hot to work with the heavy woolen skeins. "I feel as if my clothes are always clinging to me, even though I change linen twice a day. Just think how cool it must be in Wales now," she went on with a pensive sigh. "As a matter of fact, I received a letter from Aunt Tansy today, and she spoke of how pretty the frost was upon she grass, and how the mist had rolled cold and damp off the sea even while she sat at her writing desk. Funny how home is more appealing when you're far away from it than it ever is when you're there."

The high-pitched tones of *"Allah Akhbar, Allah Akhbar!"* floated across the fringed green palms, prompting Gwen to answer in a cross voice. "I'll be glad when I don't have to listen to the whining of that *muezzin* five times every day. It grates upon my nerves."

"Mine, too." Sophie lifted a languid hand, sipping her iced punch. "It's much more pleasant to be awakened every morning by the crowing of that old rooster my papa keeps in the stable yard. Remember how we used to torment him when we were children, Gwen?"

Watching the play of light as it filtered through the leaves and trembled upon her lace-edged sleeve, Gwen nodded, admitting that thoughts of home were sweet. But privately she agonized, for sailing away from the port of Tangier would mean sailing away from Morgan Riff. Would he come to tell her goodbye? Would he let her go?

She had become so preoccupied with contemplating his intentions that she could scarcely concentrate upon anything else. Pushing the damp hair off her brow, she murmured appropriate answers to her friend's continuing idle chatter, then in a fit of restlessness, flounced out of the chair and paced the sun-dappled flagstones beneath the canopy of nodding trees. The heat intensified, and when a wilting Sophie excused herself to go and bathe her face, Gwen roamed about the terrace, first peering down at the street, then gazing out to sea. Exhausted by the temperature, she at last returned to her wicker chaise lounge and, picking up Libby's tattered copy of *Madame Bovary*, plopped down upon the chintz cushion to lose herself within its pages.

"Her trouble was boredom, wouldn't you say . . . ?"

Starting so violently that the novel tumbled from her grasp, Gwen glanced up, afraid to believe she had heard the deep and mellow voice that had haunted her for days. But her eyes did not deceive her, for only a few yards away, Morgan Riff stood heart-stoppingly real upon the terrace.

"Madame Bovary's trouble, I mean," he explained, slanting a smile at her when she continued to stare.

Flustered over his unexpected appearance and the heady pleasure of seeing him again, Gwenllian scooped the upended novel from the ground, wondering how his eyes had been able to read the faded title at such a distance.

He followed her gaze and seemed to catch her thought, but instead of commenting on it, only quirked his mouth again. She found herself unable to tear her eyes from his well-made length, from the generous shoulders beneath their snowy shirt and the athletic legs encased in breeches and boots.

"I'm so glad you've come," she breathed.

"Did you fear that I would not?"

She lowered her eyes while he strolled to the foot of her chaise lounge. "I didn't know what to think," she murmured. "Papa and Robyn have been watching me like hawks. I feared they had asked Colonel Carstairs to forbid you to come to his house again."

"And you believe that would have kept me from seeing you?"

At the confident glint in his eyes, Gwen's uncertainty abandoned her in a rush. "Would you like refreshment?" she asked brightly, indicating the pitcher of sweet cherry punch circled by a lazy honeybee.

He shook his head. "Actually, I came to invite you to the home of one of my friends. I thought you might enjoy seeing the inside of a Moorish house." His glance swept the terrace, then the adjoining parlor before he ruefully added, "Since they haven't come barreling down the corridor brandish-

142

ing their pistols at me, I assume your father and Lord Breese are out."

Gwen smiled and nodded her head in confirmation. "They're gone for the afternoon, and Libby is visiting a friend. I'm here alone with Sophie, who has gone inside to escape the heat. I'll just let her know you're escorting me on an outing."

She made to excuse herself, but he thwarted her progress, clasping her arm with his long brown fingers. "I don't have a care in the world for my own reputation, Gwen," he said quietly, "but I do have a care for yours. Let's not flaunt impropriety and goad your father's already sore temper any more than necessary. Ask Sophie to join us today."

She raised her lashes to his face, revering him all the more for his consideration of her honor. Then lifting her fingers, she trailed them down the granite line of his jaw in a tender gesture of gratitude that caused him to take her hand and kiss it.

When she turned to go, he detained her again. "This may be our only time alone today. We should make good use of it, don't you think?"

He took her in his arms, and she slid her hands about his neck, her fingers threading through the crispness of his hair while her body pressed against his with a natural compulsion. After a moment, when he would have asserted his self-control and reined the two of them off the dangerous racecourse they followed, Gwen brazenly continued the kiss, testing her feminine powers against his cool good judgment. To her satisfaction he relented beneath the persuasion, turning the kiss into a deeper intimacy, but even as he gave way to her seduction he made his own mastery of the situation clear.

Still, in those next few seconds of gasping pleasure, Gwen told herself with triumph that there would come a time when she could seduce him away from this heathenish land and into the fortress where he belonged.

A while later she breathlessly informed Sophie of the outing planned with Morgan. The girl's eyes widened and she shook her head in remonstrance. "Gwenllian, you daren't go! Your father will be in a most dreadful temper when he finds out. There's no saying what he and Lord Breese will do."

"I don't care. My mind is made up." Seizing two floppy brimmed hats from the pegs on the back of Sophie's door, Gwen sailed one in her friend's direction. "Put it on to shade that disapproving face of yours, and follow me. Morgan is waiting for us."

Before long the threesome joined the slipper-shod pedestrians on the street and forged their way around a line of graceful Negresses carrying bundles of *rhibieh*, which was sold as camel fodder in the markets. They turned a corner, only to find a flock of bleating sheep swelling the avenue. Morgan took hold of the ladies' arms and carved out a passageway through the wooly press, only to be hindered by a ragged boy who tugged at his shirtsleeve like a persistent puppy.

In his filthy hands the engaging child clutched posies of marigolds, and even while the women were jostled by the trotting sheep, he waved the blossoms in tempting arcs before their eyes and smiled an angel's smile. With an admirable effort

144

at salesmanship, the enterprising urchin then convinced their tall escort to exchange coins for the bouquets. Sketching a bow, Morgan handed Sophie her knot of half-mangled flowers, then leaned to tuck the other into the pocket of Gwen's blouse.

They walked on, the girls drawing sidelong looks from every dark male gaze that happened to alight upon their pastel skirts and unveiled faces. But none of the admirers dared give bolder scrutiny, for the gentleman strolling beside them deceived none with his lazy air.

Just as she had before, Gwen surmised that many upon the streets knew Morgan Riff, but no one directly acknowledged that acquaintance. Pedestrians either lowered their eyes and gave him wide berth or elbowed their companions to point out his presence. Gwen knew he was aware of them, aware of every movement on the street. Whenever horsemen trotted by, his eyes moved to their visages in quick examination before flashing to assess the weapons slung over their shoulders or saddlebows. By contrast, he paid little attention to the bell-clad minstrels or to the emaciated sorcerers or to the leather sellers with purple-dyed arms who hawked their wares.

"What's happening over there?" Gwen asked a time later, pointing to a crowd. The group of jeering men were laughing at a huddle of Jews who knelt in the street with their heads bent low in prayer.

"There's a rather cruel legend here," Morgan told her with a sober glance at the spectacle. "When the Arabs want rain, they sometimes command Jews

145

to pray for it, believing that Allah will be so offended by the racket that he'll bring a thunderstorm just to stop the noise."

"What a merciless sport." Gwen pulled Sophie along when the girl would gawk at the offensive display, then gasped as an ancient holy man strolled past without a scrap of clothing concealing the particulars of his withered frame.

Morgan smiled at her maidenly outrage, and with no effort to hide her disdain, she snapped, "Life in Tangier is never tame, is it?"

His brow lifted, and he spoke with his usual sangfroid air, "I thought Welshwomen were adventuresome."

Too proud to reply to the contrary, she tilted her chin, and with dignity, sidestepped a flapping chicken who was being chased by an army of screeching children.

Viewed from the outside, Sid Boazzin's house was an unprepossessing edifice, its lichen-covered plaster peeling in the way of many Moroccan dwellings. Gwen was surprised to discover the interior courtyard cool and neatly tiled, pleasant to the eye if not to the nose, for if her sense of smell could be trusted, its central fountain spewed foul water.

They passed beneath a row of colonnades and entered a pavilion of sorts, where they were met by a turbaned man with mirthful black eyes and an amiable smile. With a vigorous slap to the shoulder he greeted Morgan, then turned his attention to the ladies. In English Morgan introduced them, putting a hand to Gwen's waist and drawing her forward.

With grace Sid Boazzin touched her hands and then his heart, saluting her with the word, *"Marhaba bikum."*

"It means welcome," Morgan said.

"What is the word for many thanks?" Gwen asked, wanting to learn.

"Baraka."

After a moment more of clumsy but genial conversation between the women and their host, Morgan explained the social etiquette of the native household. "It's customary for women and men to dine apart. Though I hate to forgo the pleasure of your company at the table, ladies, I think you'll enjoy visiting with Sid Boazzin's wives and seeing their apartments. One of them speaks English, I believe," he finished, turning inquiringly to his host.

"Fatima does, yes," affirmed the native. "She will be excited by your visit, as will the younger wives—they have never entertained any European ladies before. I will instruct my servant to guide Miss Evans and Miss Kirkland to their wing."

The servant took them through a breezeway draped with honeysuckle and flanked by a towering white wall whose serpentine length vibrated with climbing roses the color of fuchsia. Gwen looked over a shoulder for a last glimpse of Morgan and his host, who were strolling in the opposite direction. The wind caught their voices and carried them back to her ears.

"So, you have chosen a wife for yourself at last, Rhaman," Sid Boazzin said with a jovial taunt. "You are slow, my friend. I have four already."

"And how many children?"

"Fourteen. One born last month."

"You are a busy man," Morgan laughed.

Gwen's steps faltered upon the slick tiles and she glanced at Sophie. But preoccupied with her mysterious surroundings, the girl missed the exchange, sidling along as if afraid she would be enslaved at any second for the pleasure of some slippered pasha. A moment later, when the servant unlocked an iron-studded door resembling the entrance to some medieval dungeon, Sophie looked panicked, but Gwen only beamed at her inanely, still thinking of the conversation she had overheard.

With a wave of his chocolate-colored hand, the servant indicated that the two women should proceed alone through the narrow corridor. Sophie wanted to follow him back to the sunlit courtyard, but Gwen pulled her forward, and before long they came to a vast breeze-filled chamber.

The high frescoed walls were hung with fringed tapestries and hand-painted silks, and thick Casablanca carpets covered the cold blue tiles. Everywhere brass urns and ornaments gleamed, their polished surfaces highlighted by sun that streamed in from a small secluded courtyard, and the strong scent of burning incense and exotic perfume filled the air. Ballooned by the soft crosswinds, gauzy draperies undulated like wraiths in obscured passageways.

Suddenly, the tittering of melodious voices arrested Gwen's attention and she turned her head to find three women sitting close upon a gold-brocaded divan. None of them wore veils, and their unbound obsidian hair hung to slender waists girdled in gold links. A fourth woman glided forward, garbed similarly in embroidered silk, her limbs adorned with bracelets, necklaces, and anklets. Upon her dusky forehead dangled a double row of pearls and silver sequins. Each of the women was pretty and possessed a certain gazellelike grace, but the fourth was the most comely of all.

"I am Fatima," she said with a shy smile. "My husband told me I might have one visitor today. I am pleased to find two."

With that she stepped to the door, which had not been locked, and removed both red slippers from her tiny feet before setting them out in the corridor. At Gwen's perplexed frown she explained. "A wife always puts out her slippers when she is entertaining female visitors. Upon seeing them, her husband knows not to enter, for to look upon the unveiled face of a woman who is not his wife or concubine is forbidden to the men of our faith."

Sophie and Gwen exchanged glances, both thinking the gesture nonsensical since Sid Boazzin had already seen their faces quite clearly. But neither commented, fearing to offend.

Their hostess went on to introduce the three other wives, who had come forward in a chattering flock and reached out with henna-tinted hands to touch the jewelry of the Europeans. With no abashment they admired pearl earbobs, opal and amethyst brooches, and delicate gold bracelets that accessorized the Western fashions. When Gwen drew out the large uncut aquamarine dangling on the chain between her breasts, they clapped their hands and squealed with childish delight.

"It was a gift from my father," Gwen explained to Fatima while the oldest wife translated. "He gave it to me on my twelfth birthday. It's from India. When Papa was in the navy he saved the life of a wealthy man in Calcutta, who gifted him with the jewel to show appreciation. As you can imagine, it's very special to me."

Beside her, Sophie suddenly uttered a cry of pleasure and pointed to a basket suspended from the ceiling on thick cords of braided silk. Peering closer, Gwen was astonished to see a curly-haired infant nestled inside. Dressed in an elaborate gown, the girl child stared up at her with twinkling eyes enhanced with kohl while waving dimpled arms as smooth as brown velvet.

"She is my third daughter," Fatima said fondly, touching the gossamer curls of her child before uttering a wistful sigh. "Alas, I have borne my husband no sons. But Allah has graciously blessed the others with many healthy boys."

Gwen glanced at the three younger wives, then back at the stately woman dressed in her diaphanous blue garments. Astonished, she wondered how Fatima could possible share her husband with all the other beguiling creatures. What would it be like to watch him embrace one of the sultry-eyed girls, and know that he would lie with her all night in order to conceive another child?

While Gwen inwardly disparaged the heathenish practice, she surmised Sophie did the same, for her friend's innocent eyes kept shifting from one seductive countenance to another before alighting again upon the flowerlike baby curled in its airborne cradle.

Fatima clapped her hands, and through a curtained passage two Negresses emerged—slaves, Gwen assumed with further censure—who were bedecked with earrings and bracelets of polished copper.

"Will you and Miss Kirkland dine with us?" Fatima asked politely.

"We'd be charmed," Gwen replied with equal grace. Following example she and Sophie sat on the floor with the other women, forming a circle about a low teakwood table.

One of the slaves poured tea from a Russian samovar, and Gwen found the brew sweet and flavored with mint. A dish of meat and raisins cooked in olive oil was passed around next, along with peeled fruit and a basket of honey-dipped cakes.

"Rhaman has never brought a woman here before," Fatima commented with a soft but suggestive smile. "Perhaps you will be married soon? I am not familiar with the customs of the West."

Feeling Sophie's sharp eyes upon her face, Gwen shook her head and murmured, "He's not proposed marriage just yet. But . . . I am hopeful."

Fatima paused in her eating to translate when the other three wives demanded it. Then, a bit apologetically, she interpreted their excited chatter. "Usually a man does not see his bride unveiled before they are wed. We are curious that your traditions are so different from ours."

Sophie answered with a rare dry wit. "There

aren't any men in Britain who would wed a wife without seeing her first. They're far too cowardly."

When Fatima repeated the quip, the three young wives seemed to find it exceedingly amusing, tittering and chattering for several moments before the oldest wife quieted them. "They want to know if in your country you are taught the art of pleasing a man before you marry him. "They think Rhaman quite—" She tapped her milk-white teeth, searching for the proper word. "Healthy. They say he will likely take much, much pleasing."

Again there came a round of spirited laughter and Gwen blushed, both with embarrassment and indignation. "We are taught no such things," she bristled. "But how do you know Morg—Rhaman? I was under the impression a Muslim wife was forbidden to speak with any man but her husband."

"Oh, that is true," Fatima affirmed, pouring more tea amidst a chiming of silver bracelets. "We have never spoken to him. But sometimes our benevolent husband allows us to sit behind a lattice and view his guests."

Gwen shook her head at such restrictions. "Women have a great deal of freedom in the West. We always sit at the table with male guests. For that matter, we even dance with men who are not our husbands."

Fatima frowned and interpreted the conversation for the other wives, who gave the visitors vague looks of disapproval through slanted ebony eyes.

After that the dishes were removed, replaced by an assortment of sticky sweetmeats rich with dates and almonds. When they had all finished eating,

Sophie withdrew a small mirror from her reticule and, viewing her mouth, dabbed at a spot of honey there.

The youngest wife, a girl of no more than fourteen, immediately spied the glass and exclaimed over it with an excited clap. Sophie relinquished it to her greedy fingers and offered it as a gift, but Fatima confiscated the frippery with a stern maternal frown before chastising the pouting adolescent wife.

"I am sorry to be so impolite," she apologized, returning the glass to Sophie. "But the ownership of mirrors is forbidden to us."

Just then one of the Negresses appeared again and whispered to Fatima, who arose in a swish of silk. "Rhaman awaits you in the courtyard, Miss Evans. The servant outside the door will escort you there."

After courteous goodbyes, Sophie and Gwen departed, feeling almost relieved to quit the exotic apartment with its pampered wives, red slippers and incomprehensible customs.

"Can you imagine . . . ?" Sophie whispered a moment later as they trailed the stiff-backed servant. "Locked up all together and having children by the same man? Scandalous! And I was astounded when Fatima would not even allow that poor young girl to keep a pocket mirror!"

"I'd do without a husband before I'd share him with *one* woman, much less three," Gwen scorned, her soft voice echoing off the faded blue columns of the pavilion.

Morgan awaited them in the courtyard, his well-conditioned frame limned by a shaft of sunlight. "Did you enjoy Sid Boazzin's wives?" he asked while swinging open the scrolled iron gate leading out to the street.

"Oh, yes!" Sophie replied with more enthusiasm than necessary. "It was quite nice of you to bring us here. So—so educational." Sweetly she smiled at him before nearly tripping over the broken pavement strewn with vegetable peels.

He took her arm and steadied her, then turned his gaze to Gwen and tucked her hand in the warm place between his elbow and ribs. "You're unusually quiet. How did you find the wives?"

"Unfathomable," she said bluntly. "I don't understand how they can live like prisoners, forbidden to do almost everything except please their husband."

"You must remember that polygamy has been the custom here for centuries. To them it's normal, a part of their faith, and likely they feel no sense of oppression at all. Even now, they're probably discussing you, wondering how you can be so brazen as to go about the streets hanging on to my arm."

His voice contained a hint of teasing, but Gwen knew Morgan always chose his words with care, so that even levity often had an underlying point.

"I'll never understand them or their culture," she said. "And I'm sure they'll never understand mine."

"Perhaps not."

She glanced at her escort's face from beneath the brim of her hat and spoke earnestly. "Please don't think I condemn the women for their way of life,

154

Morgan. I'm trying not to be judgmental. I just can't imagine such an existence for myself."

Before he could reply, Sophie interrupted, asking if she could stop and peruse the lengths of bright-colored silks displayed in an outdoor stall. Morgan agreed to wait as long as she liked, guiding Gwen beneath the shade of an awning where they watched three men load the back of an ill-tempered camel.

"I could never share my husband with another woman," Gwen said after a moment, the vision of Fatima and the alluring younger women still strong in her memory. She kept her eyes lowered to the ground, avoiding the keen scrutiny of the man at her side. "Could you share a wife with other men?"

He waited until she raised her lashes and met his eyes. "What do you think?"

She blushed and stared harder at the groaning camel.

"There's plenty of jealousy among Muslim wives," Morgan commented. "Occasionally one hears tales of poisonings—a favored wife finds a little something other than honey and mint in her tea. And then, there are problems with the concubines—Sid Boazzin keeps at least a dozen of those."

Gwen stared at him in astonishment.

"It's all legal," Morgan went on with a careless shrug, and Gwen suspected she was about to receive a dose of his tongue-in-cheek humor. "And sanctified. The Talmud says that nine parts of passion are given to the Arabs, and the remaining one part divided amongst the other races of the world."

Color rose in Gwen's cheeks and although she did not meet Morgan's eye she knew that he flashed a grin. Staring straight ahead at the camel's twitching ears, she said, "And you, Mr. Riff? How many concubines do you keep?"

He crossed his arms and leaned back against the sun-warmed wall. "I'm not an Arab. Why should I have any?"

Gwen had no intention of exploring the delicate subject any further, especially since her escort seemed to find so much humor in it. With her lips pursed, she stood watching a dancing minstrel while Morgan bought and peeled an orange, and after handing her a slice, smiled broadly over her petulance.

Her shopping complete, Sophie rushed to display the bolt of gold silk she had purchased, and the trio progressed slowly homeward. The sun faded, growing from acid yellow to a cooler butter tone, and the crowd thinned, retreating indoors for the evening meal. As Morgan led them around a corner and into the Carstairs' quiet neighborhood a muleteer trotted past in a clatter of hooves, his scarlet saddle cloth and green turban a colorful blur amidst an eddy of dust. Just as he passed, a thudding of feet sounded, springing to life in the adjoining alleyway. Morgan wheeled about, and Gwen screamed as two men lunged forward to block their path.

Swathed in white, both wore *haiks* tossed about their faces, and a sword of silver glistened in the dark hand of one. He swung it in a vicious arc, hurling himself in Morgan's direction.

Instantly Riff thrust the women in a doorway, then ducked his head lest it be taken off by the savage swipe of the attacker's sword. The blow glanced off the side of a crumbling column and unsettled its precarious balance, sending a large chunk tumbling to the ground in a splintering crash. The assailant spun about and made ready to attack again, raising his sword and uttering a spine-chilling cry in the manner of a warrior rushing into battle. At the same time, the second man seized Gwen and jerked her forward, struggling to drag her away.

Pistol drawn, Morgan shielded himself behind the broken pillar and fired at Gwen's abductor. The victim groaned as the bullet pierced his rough bur-noose, and releasing his hold on Gwen, he floun-dered backward and toppled to the ground with a strangled cry. Seeing his partner fallen, the other swordsman fled, dashing across the street to vanish over a rusted courtyard gate.

Sophie stared down at the dead man and ex-claimed hysterically, "He intended to capture Gwen and sell her as a slave, didn't he! Libby told us about such outrages! God save us from this horrid coun-try!"

Gwen had flown into Morgan's arms but, witness-ing her friend's terror, moved to calm her. Still with his pistol cocked, Morgan surveyed the alley, the terraces and the hand-printed walls flanking the narrow street and, satisfied with his inspection, nudged the fallen man with the toe of his boot. Then he leaned to pull the *haik* aside and regard the swarthy visage. Making no comment, he recov-ered the face, then turned and spoke gently to So-phie, displaying a composure that no amount of trouble ever seemed to shake. "You've nothing to fear now. We're near the Carstairs' house—only a block away. Can you manage the distance, Miss Kirkland?"

She nodded with tears in her eyes, faltering on trembling legs as Morgan took hold of her arm. Nauseous and shivering herself, Gwen attempted to put up a more intrepid front, but every shadow seemed to hold menace. Twisting her head all about in fear of some new attack, she pressed herself close to their escort's solid frame. She had lost her hat in the scuffle and Morgan bent to retrieve the now crumpled accessory before tucking it under his arm.

Gwen was relieved to find the house empty. Sophie slipped gratefully inside while the two lovers tarried for a moment beneath the courtyard trees. Gwen clung to Morgan, reaction to the dreadful scare making her loath to release his comforting length. He seemed indomitable, and she tightened her hold about his shoulders as if to borrow a measure of his strength.

"This is not the first time I've been a target for evil, Morgan," she confessed. "I don't understand it. Last week, when Libby took us to the fruit market, there was an awful man on horseback there. He singled me out in the square and wouldn't let me pass. He was disfigured, had only one eye—"

"Don't go out again," he interrupted. "Not without me, not for any reason."

At the curt command, Gwen searched Morgan's face. The lines about his mouth were carved deeper

158

than usual with strain, and the assailant's sword had left a scratch below his eye.

"Do not," he repeated, taking hold of her arms. "Not even with your father and Lord Breese as escorts. Swear to me."

His tone contained a kind of harshness she had never heard before, and his fingers squeezed her arms ungently.

"But why must I be a prisoner—"

"Swear to me!"

Swallowing, she nodded obediently. "I swear."

Frightened of his anger, of the strange and dangerous world in which she had been thrust, she was relieved when he encircled her with his arms again. He pulled her head to his chest and she heard his heart thunder at her ear. Its drumming was loud and rapid, and for a fleeting moment she had the oddest notion that he was frightened, too. Drawing back, she lifted her eyes in a questioning way. But he only pulled her close again as if unwilling to have her read his expression, and the pressure of his embrace crushed the flowers tucked at her breast until they released sweet, bruised scents upon the air.

"I must leave Tangier day after tomorrow, Gwen," Morgan whispered. "I'm not certain how long I'll be away, it could stretch into weeks. But I'll call tomorrow to say goodbye. In the meantime, you must promise me that you'll keep yourself safe."

At his announcement Gwen shoved him away, staring up into his face with devastated eyes.

Misunderstanding, he made to cradle her stiffened body again and said in a soothing tone, "I'll be back, Gwen. Surely you understand that."

"But *I* won't be!" she cried, refusing to be held. "We're sailing home in two weeks—three at the most!"

"You're not staying through the winter season?" His tone was full of chagrin.

"No! Even the Carstairs are leaving. The colonel has been assigned to a post in America."

Frowning, Morgan considered her revelation, remaining silent a moment as if pondering some dilemma. He shook his head. "I cannot alter my plans. But I'll come to see you tomorrow and we'll talk awhile. There are things we should discuss." With a gentle hand he set her hat atop her head and tilted it at an impudent angle.

Refusing to be cajoled, afraid that some circumstance would prevent his return and force her to sail home with only memories, Gwen dragged it off again in a contrary gesture.

"Gwen, if I choose to be with you," Morgan said soberly, "do you believe anything can keep me from it?"

"I don't know, Morgan, I don't know! Everything is so complicated. There's my father's disapproval and Robyn's persistence, and most of all, there's a side of you that you won't allow me to know. It frightens me—"

He cut off her anxious words, kissing her until she gave herself up to the pleasure. She closed her eyes, shutting out the mosque's outline behind his head as if she could shut out Tangier and all its grim realities.

"I'll be back tomorrow," he promised in a husky breath. "Keep yourself safe."

"Morgan." She held on to his sleeve when he would move away. "Who were those men who attacked us? You know, don't you?"

"Gwen, now is not the time—"

"Why? Why isn't it the time? After the savagery I've already seen, what can you possibly tell me that will disturb me more?"

He regarded her directly. "I could tell you several things."

"Then start by telling me how you can live in this place! All the killing and the butchery. Oh, Morgan," she cried, leaning against him. "Come back to Wales. Please come back to Wales!"

"This is my home, Gwenllian."

The words were uttered with such a cold finality that she stepped back as if she had received a smarting slap to her cheek.

"Morgan . . ." she said haltingly, reaching out an imploring hand.

But he only brushed her fingers with his lips and said, "Remember what I told you about staying safe. Good night."

Eight

No amount of pleading could convince the distraught Sophie to hold her tongue. She was adamant that Sir Gerald should know exactly what had occurred upon the streets of Tangier and be informed of the dreadful fate that had nearly befallen his daughter. Gwenllian's protests that her sire's temper would explode and bring turmoil upon the household when he learned of Morgan's escort did nothing to persuade the usually malleable Sophie to relent. And so it was when her father, Colonel Carstairs, and Lord Breese entered the house full of good cheer from their day out, they found themselves confronted by an agitated, hollow-eyed girl spewing a tale of harems, kidnappers, and death.

Gwen stood stoically just behind her, head held high, eyes defiant, watching the emotions cross her sire's visage as her friend related in a breathless rush the spine-chilling details of their afternoon. Sir Gerald listened in silence, his expression growing darker by the minute, his snapping eyes exchanging with Colonel Carstairs some privately understood message.

"No one was hurt?" he asked in concern when Sophie had finished her dutiful betrayal.

"No," the blonde reassured him, twisting her hands and avoiding the accusation in Gwen's eyes. "Only frightened near to death."

Robyn had listened to the story with his green gaze fastened hard upon Gwenllian. Now he stepped forward in fury. "You were out with *him?*"

"Robyn!" Sir Gerald snapped. "I will speak to my daughter alone regarding this matter."

For a moment Gwen thought that Lord Breese would ignore her sire's authority and unleash his indignation full measure. She could tell that the earl was well plied with liquor; his naturally sanguine complexion was ruddier than ever and he swayed slightly upon his feet. But Sir Gerald shot him a glare that warned against interference, and the weaker-willed Robyn yielded, spinning about on an unsteady heel.

As the earl's fine leather soles rapped across the tiles in retreat, Colonel Carstairs cleared his throat in embarrassment and, taking Sophie's arm, led her out of the tension-fraught vestibule.

Gwen remained rooted in place, standing her ground but feeling girlish beside the bearlike form of her angry father. When his voice came low and woeful, she was somewhat abashed, for his pain wounded her far more than any fiery outburst.

"I asked ye not to see him again, daughter," he said, holding up his palms in confoundment. For a moment he searched her face as if he no longer recognized it and hunted for the wee lass who had once sat upon his knee. "Do ye care so little for my honor that ye would defy me this way?"

"It has nothing to do with your honor, Papa. It—"

"It has everything to do with my honor!" he cut in, his careful composure short-lived. "Ye have embarrassed me before Colonel Carstairs with yer rebelliousness. Ye have made your intended look the fool. Most of all, ye have endangered yerself by associating with a man ye know nothing at all about. Traipsing about the city with him," Sir Gerald growled, "allowing him to take ye to a *harem,* for God's sake!"

"It wasn't a harem—"

"I don't care what name ye choose to put to it. The fact remains that ye disobeyed me, flagrantly disobeyed me. I would like to delude myself into thinking that ye misunderstood my wishes, or did not take them seriously. If that's the case, then, once and for all, I forbid ye to see Morgan Riff. And if ye think to try my resolution, then think upon it again!"

Gwen did not recall ever seeing her sire's face so overblown with umbrage. His burly chest heaved with it. And yet, she would not capitulate. It seemed that a final breach between them was inescapable now, and although she would like to temporize, it was better to carry through to the end. After all, she was not the first young woman to defy a parent's wishes for the sake of loving the wrong man, and she would persevere in order to champion her own happiness.

Inhaling a deep breath, forcing calm into her voice, she met the simmering glower of the man who had raised her. He was the widower who had dandled her upon his knee, the father who had arranged her suitable marriage, the obstacle who now stood prepared to circumvent her dreams. To cross swords with him was painful, like rending a heartstring with one fell blow.

She took a breath and thrust her dagger. "I love Morgan Riff, Papa. In spite of what you may think, my feeling for him is not a schoolgirl crush or a passing fancy, but something quite deep that I cannot explain to you. I wish I could. But at least I've tried to make you understand. I regret you do not." She drew herself up and finished, "I will continue to see him. I will. One way or another, with or without your blessing."

Sir Gerald had the look of a thwarted parent who wished he could drag his daughter to her room and lock her up to force compliance, but knew that the child was a child no more and must be handled with an adult's reason. With effort he governed his emotions, and at the same time his massive shoulders slumped.

"Very well," he said with resignation. "I won't stand here and argue with ye more, Gwenllian. Ye have forced me to deal with ye on different terms than ever before. I'll have to think about what ye've said, and decide what should be done."

With that pronouncement, he turned away, and as she listened to the ponderous step of his retreat, Gwen was uncertain as to who had claimed victory in the argument.

* * *

The following evening the Carstairs offered a most delicious dinner. The roasted capon, split pea soup, cheese souffle, and brandied peaches were served in candlelight, with the terrace doors flung wide to admit air cooled by a gentle rain. But the company who sat gathered around the lace-draped table seemed to relish little the culinary delights.

While Gwen toyed with the meringue of her dessert, her gaze swept the circumference of the table. She wondered why the faces of all the other diners appeared so strained, wondered why the conversation lagged no matter what topic was introduced. She, of course, had good reason to be tense, for Morgan had promised to call today, and heaven only knew what fireworks his presence would ignite amidst this edgy gathering.

Yet, no one else knew he was to arrive at any moment. What unease plagued the others? Even Sophie refused to meet her eye. The elusive blonde had stayed ensconced in her room all day, and when the two girls had filed into the dining room a while ago, she had kept her lashes lowered to avoid Gwen's reproachful gaze. Now, she glanced up briefly, and Gwen saw a trace of tears sparkling in her soulful eyes.

Across from her, Robyn's face was stony in the arc of candlelight. All evening he had been uncommunicative, far from the witty conversationalist famed at the supper clubs in Britain. Even Libby Carstairs was quiet, although her fluttering hands betrayed anxiety while her husband dutifully carried on a monologue in which no one seemed particularly interested. Sir Gerald appeared the only relaxed diner, offering Gwen a fond smile when he caught her observing him.

At last the interminable meal ended. Unable to endure a moment more of the company, Gwen declined to join the ladies in the parlor, begging off with a headache. The anticipation of Morgan's arrival had stretched her nerves as tight as a bowstring, and awaiting him in solitude was preferable to being surrounded by people who were inexplicably mute.

Just as she entered her room, however, the expected knock sounded upon the door and reverberated through the house like a shot. Well aware that her father would be uncivil to Morgan and try to send him away, Gwen rushed from her room, frantic to head off disaster. But Robyn materialized in the corridor and barred her passage when she made to push past. Before she could utter an indignant word, he seized her arms and clapped a hand over her mouth to stifle her outraged cries.

Voices rang in the vestibule. One was her father's, and the other, low and familiar, belonged to Morgan. She struggled, twisting her head from side to side in an effort to shake loose Robyn's squeezing hands. But he was determined, and kept her arms pinioned tight behind her back despite the kicks she delivered to his shins.

"Your father has booked passage for you on a ship home," he hissed in her ear even while she fought. "You sail tomorrow with me and Sophie."

Provoked beyond words, Gwen renewed her endeavor to break free. But although she clawed at Robyn's arms and bent her head in an effort to bite his hand, her efforts proved vain against his greater strength.

Just a few rooms away, Sir Gerald faced the foreigner who appeared more fearsome than ever with a saber cut beneath his eye and his jaw clamped against a waning patience. Riff's gaze cautioned, and his stance resembled that of a duelist prepared to fence.

"Your business with me is finished, Riff," the older man announced, his brittle veneer of civility nearly cracking.

"Indeed," came the level reply. "But my relationship with your daughter is not."

"I beg to differ with you. The continuance of that relationship is not possible."

The younger man's eyes flickered. "It damned well better be possible."

Colonel Carstairs interrupted in an attempt to head off open warfare. "Morgan, perhaps another time—"

"This doesn't concern you, Frank. I'm here to speak with Miss Evans."

"She's not here," Sir Gerald announced curtly. "She's out of your reach."

Seizing the older man's lapels so swiftly that he had no time to react, Morgan growled, "What have you done with her?"

Sir Gerald glared manfully back at the cutting blue eyes. Morgan Riff was a man whose fighting prowess he well respected, but the older man had learned long ago when to fight a physical battle and when to use words as a more effective weapon.

"Gwenllian is aboard a ship," he flatly lied. "Well away from Tangier. I've sent her home."

The declaration struck its target like a blow. Both Sir Gerald and Colonel Carstairs tensed, fearing that the foiled suitor would react with violence. Indeed, he seemed to hover on the verge of it, yearning to take retribution against the father who had thwarted him.

But Morgan mustered reason over the instinct to retaliate. Although the ferocity of his gaze did not lessen, the energy in his hands did. While raking Sir Gerald with a long and trenchant stare, he released his crumpled jacket. Then pivoting about to open the door, he flung words over his shoulder in a voice that chilled. "You have not seen the last of me."

Down the corridor, Robyn released Gwenllian only after it was too late for her to run after Morgan Riff. When he freed her aching arms, she spun around and struck him hard across the face. "By what right do you keep me from him?!" she cried in a voice so vicious that he flinched. "By what right do you lay your hands upon me and hold me against my will? You are not my betrothed. And I am not a child to be told what to do!"

"I did not relish the need to use force against you," he shouted back. "But it was for your own good, and upon your father's instructions."

"My father!" she exclaimed bitterly. Shoving past Robyn, she stormed into the vestibule where Sir Gerald stood waiting with his legs planted, prepared to receive the brunt of his offspring's rage.

169

"You *lied* to him!" she accused before she had even come to a stop. "You told him I was gone!"

"Ye will be tomorrow."

"And so will *he!* He came to say goodbye to me. But instead of having the decency to allow him a few words, you deceived him, and had Robyn restrain me in the hallway like a child!"

"Gwenllian, when a father is fearful for his daughter he will stop at nothing to protect her. Ye must understand that."

"I understand nothing except that you have hurt me! I understand nothing except that you want to command my life when you have not the least notion of how I feel. You have sent away the man I love, and I will not easily forgive you for it!"

She turned her back upon him.

"Gwenllian!"

But she ignored his angry plea and, fleeing his presence, swept past Robyn with a glance that shattered the aristocrat.

A quarter hour later, Sophie tapped upon the panels of her friend's door, and when no answer came, slipped inside as meekly as a dormouse.

Preoccupied with stuffing clothes in an open valise, Gwen scarcely spared her a glance.

"What on earth are you doing?" Sophie asked in alarm, staring at the strewn gowns, paired stockings, and scattered slippers that were heaped upon the bed.

"I'm leaving to find Morgan. And if you run and tattle to Papa, Sophie Kirkland, I swear our friendship is ended here and now."

"Gwen!" Rushing to her friend's side, Sophie

spoke in horrified disbelief. "You aren't going out into the streets *alone?* It's madness even to contemplate such a thing!"

"But I am. I know the name of the hotel where Morgan is staying and I'm going there, even if I have to run all the way with the hounds of hell themselves snapping at my heels. A pox on Tangier!"

"You don't intend to *run away with him?*"

"I certainly do, if he asks me."

"Do you realize what such a thing would do to your father?"

Without answering, Gwen slid her silver-backed brush into the overflowing bag, and bent to fold a gown.

In dismay Sophie stared at her friend. "Don't you think it's a—a *brazen* thing to do?"

Ceasing her slapdash packing, Gwen sighed and turned to the girl who had been her favorite companion since childhood. "Sophie, Papa plans to send me home tomorrow. Don't you understand what that means to me? If I go, I'll likely never see Morgan again, and I'm not willing to give him up. I'm not willing to abandon what is between us."

"Do you care for him that much?"

Gwen lowered her lashes and did not answer.

The other's soft eyes grew moist and she reached to take the hands of the black-haired girl in her own thin cold ones. "I'm afraid for you. As dearly as I love you and want to see you happy, I'm tempted to run from the room and summon Sir Gerald to keep you safe."

"No, Sophie," Gwen said. Although she was

about to embark on a madcap flight to find her lover, her reasoning was mature. "It's time that I was allowed to exercise my own judgment. I'll endure the consequences, whatever they may be. I appreciate your concern, but neither of us is a schoolgirl with a duty to run to an adult at the first sign of trouble. I am a woman, and you must respect me as such."

"But so many mistakes have been made by young women in love with men who are not what they seem."

"If I make a mistake, then at least it's my own—not one my father has made for me." She touched Sophie's sleeve. "Now, leave my room quietly and say nothing. If Morgan is not at his hotel, I'll return by way of the terrace. Otherwise, I'll send a letter to Papa tomorrow, assuring him I am well."

Sophie clasped her close in an outburst of tearful emotion. "I may not see you again for ages. Take care, Gwenllian, whatever you do!"

"I will." Drawing back, Gwen reached to fasten the valise, then clenched its handle and made for the terrace doors. "Look after Papa and Buff for me."

The sable vestment of night turned the streets into stygian mazes. The horrid odors that drifted up from unnameable refuse, the undefinable shapes dumped upon the cobbles, and the ghostly figures lurking in doorways made Gwenllian feel as if she walked through the perils of an earthly Hades. She thought she would never forget her terrifying journey down the avenues of mysterious traditions and dangerous fanaticism, at whose end waited nothing but uncertainty. For she had no inkling how Morgan would receive her and her bulging valise, especially since he planned to depart from Tangier tomorrow. Was it possible that he would bid her a fond farewell and send her back to Papa?

She did not believe so.

She knew the route to the Hotel La Villa de France, having passed it the day before on the outing to Sid Boazzin's home, but the way was long and menacing in the darkness, and to avoid notice she slipped into courtyards whenever the pale outline of a burnoose loomed in the moonlight.

Climbing the steep hill toward the lodging place, she stumbled into a pool of filth, and had to clap a handkerchief to her nose while she scurried onward in ruined shoes. Everywhere vagrant Moors slept in huddled clumps with their heads resting upon drawn-up knees and their backs propped against oily walls. Somewhere a gimbri strummed an eerie tune, its melody accompanying the sounds that floated from packed cafes where turbaned men chortled and smoked hashish. In skulking knots, stray dogs snuffled about the garbage heaps for scraps of rotten food.

Finally, Gwen came upon a large open square and, skittering through its rusted gate, wended her way past a group of Arabs squatting upon the ground and guarding their loaded camels. Catching her scent, the animals snuffled and lifted their haughty heads. One of the drivers called out to her, likely uttering some lewd proposal or condemning her Christian soul to Gehenna. With a hammering heart she scurried away, the sound of their guttural laughter following behind.

At last she spied the clean, European-style hotel with its clay planters and weeded flower beds, whose swatches of pale-colored blooms sweetly masked the lingering odor of camel dung. At the welcome sight of its lamplit windows, she whimpered in relief.

At the open door a porter offered to take her valise, but she declined his aid, going directly to the desk to speak with a clerk there. "I must see Mr. Morgan Riff," she told him in a breathless rush. "Can you take a message to his room?"

The small black eyes of the clerk flicked over her baggage, filthy shoes, and muddied hem, but remained without expression. "I am sorry, miss, but I happen to know he is not in at the moment."

She had not planned for such a contingency. Desolate, she glanced about the deserted foyer with its white paneled walls. The ticking rococco clock hanging upon the wall above the desk declared the hour a minute shy of midnight. What was she to do?

"I'll wait over there," she said, mustering an imperious mien in case the clerk should think to keep her from loitering.

"As you wish," he nodded with a trace of disapproval.

And so she sat and watched the hands of the clock glide, wondering if she had been a fool, wondering if Morgan would return. Perhaps he had already departed on his journey, and she would witness alone the blistering Tangier dawn as it set the terraces ablaze with day. Perhaps she would have to tramp through the horrid streets again and return to the arms of her self-satisfied sire who would surely say, "I told ye so."

Sighing, she laid her head back and closed her eyes.

She did not know how much time had passed when she was startled awake by the feel of a hand clasping her own. It was a warm hand, the fingers hard, thin, and familiar. Her eyes flew open.

Morgan knelt beside her in creased clothes and with his jaw shadowed by the bristle of a day-old beard. The lines on either side of his mouth were strained with care, and his eyes reflected such a sharp emotion that she likened it to pain. "Do Welshwomen make a habit of sleeping in hotel lobbies?" he asked softly.

"I feared you'd gone away . . ." Her relief was so great that the words came out as whispers. "I feared you'd left the city."

He smoothed the fragile ridge of her cold knuckles with the pad of his thumb. "I've been at the Customs House all night, bribing the officials there. They finally let me look at the names of the Europeans who've sailed from Tangier in the last twenty-four hours. Needless to say, your name wasn't in the book. Your father was about to receive another visit from me at dawn—quite an unpleasant visit."

"I wasn't to sail until tomorrow. Papa lied to make you leave me alone."

"How did you know where to find me?"

"Libby Carstairs mentioned the name of the hotel once."

His black brows slid together into a frown. "And you came alone, through the darkness?"

She nodded and endured the heat of his admonishing gaze for several seconds, until his eyes shifted to the bulging tapestried valise at her side. With no change of expression he then regarded her blushing face.

"I thought . . ." She left the sentence unfinished, for she was not bold enough to state the workings of her mind.

Morgan scrutinized her trusting expression, then looked away, out through the carved doors of the hotel, which were propped open with an imitation Louis XIV chair. He did not seem to be contemplating the night scene outside but deliberating some weighty problem with his quick mind, for his eyes grew dark with concentration. Whatever dilemma he pondered, it did not pose an easy solution. Broodingly, he ran a hand through his disordered black hair and his jaw tautened until its muscles stood out in sharp relief.

"Wait here for me," he said at last, as if coming to a decision. He signaled the jacketed man lounging by the desk. "Porter! Take the lady's valise to my room."

When the man hastened to obey, Morgan excused himself from Gwen's presence and stepped to the desk, where he conversed with the clerk in tones too low for her to hear. He must have made some request that was not well received, for the clerk emphatically shook his head. But not to be denied,

Morgan removed money from his pocket and passed it across the counter with a smooth slide of his hand.

Shrugging, the greedy fellow took up the coins before abandoning his desk and ascending the red-carpeted stairway. A few moments later he returned in the company of a sleepy-eyed old gentleman whose thin white hair stood on end and whose spectacles only half rested upon his bulbous nose. Motioning to Morgan, the clerk led the way into what looked to be a well-furnished private dining room.

Baffled by the activity, Gwen sat down again and watched the hands of the desk clock curve patiently around its circle of gilded numerals. At last Morgan reappeared and, after taking hold of her arm without a word, ushered her into the chamber he had just vacated.

In the center of that room the white-haired elderly gentleman yawned while trying to fasten the small top button of a shirt that was only partially tucked into his baggy trousers. His stodgy, comical figure was flanked by the stiffly erect clerk and porter, who beamed foolish smiles and handed her bunches of gladiolus which appeared to have been hastily snatched from a china vase beside the door.

When Gwenllian stared at them in bewilderment, clutching the drooping flowers, Morgan put a hand to her waist and propelled her forward.

"This is Reverend Montgomery," he announced, indicating the groggy old man with a wave of his hand. "I'm afraid we roused him from his bed rather rudely. He's American—a Methodist. But he assures me that he's quite capable of legally binding

177

together a man and woman who cannot wait to be married. Even in Tangier."

Gwen froze. She stared not at the minister, but into a pair of extraordinary blue eyes. They were quite serious.

Nine

She had become the wife of the Squire of Hiraeth, a lifetime partner to that elusive, mythical being she had discovered to be real. It was a wonder that she was not more bedazzled by this sudden and unplanned union, but some part of her had surely always known an affinity with him was inevitable. And now, it had been sanctioned by law, and awaited only a physical joining to be fully realized.

While Morgan stayed behind to speak with Reverend Montgomery the porter escorted Gwen to her husband's room. How strange she felt when the obsequious employee unlocked the door, then set her valise inside and scurried away. Upon impulse she almost followed after him, disconcerted to be left alone in a gentleman's suite in soiled shoes and with bedraggled hair, a bride without raiment or ring.

She looked about. The room was shadowed with night, the furnishings simple, consisting of a highly carved wardrobe, two chairs, a table, and the bed. She turned her eyes from its white-shrouded shape to find Morgan's jacket draped across a chair. Reaching out a hand to feel its texture, she marveled that she was now at liberty to touch his belongings and be a part of his intimate life.

Made anxious by such a notion, she moved to the open terrace doors, through which dim light shone from a brass lantern hung outside. She supposed the moon hid somewhere in the foreign sky she viewed, perhaps behind the mosque with its pointed minaret, but she could not find its cold half-face. A sense of unreality beset her as she gazed upon shrouded minarets and silvered domes, and like her first day in Morocco, she felt as if she stood in another universe where nothing was secure.

But soon, Morgan would come, the man she valued above everything else in life, even above her father's love. She had risked much to be with him, given away an existence safely planned for her where every day would be a familiar routine and every year predictable. She had traded it all for an exhilarating but uncertain future with a man she had known less than a month.

Shivering, she realized the full significance of the hasty ritual to which she had just assented. She was united now to a man her father seemed to fear in some peculiar way. What would her life be now? What would it be like to lie beside the prepossessing Morgan Riff, who seemed so freeborn and subject to none? Would she come to know his mystery, or become a part of it herself?

She rubbed her arms and stared down at the sleeping city she so despised. Somewhere in the hot maze of cramped humanity, a musician played upon an Arab pipe. The sound was doleful and unpleasant, a fitting partner to the indefinable odor of the streets, which not even the moist sea breeze could completely eradicate with its tang.

How she wanted to leave Morocco, leave without delay! But she must make Morgan want to leave with her as well. She must summon up all the feminine power she possessed and force the Squire to take her home.

With sudden purpose, she reached to fumble with her hair and pull loose the combs that fettered its braided knot. When the heavy masses fell to her waist, she artfully fanned them out about her shoulders in a soft arrangement she thought might tempt a man. The ruined shoes she kicked off with disgust, before removing her silk stockings and modestly stuffing them in the valise. Afterward, she stood uncertainly, not knowing what further steps to take in her seduction. She had had too little experience with men to know what pleased them, and the thought of Morgan's worldliness was daunting. With begrudged envy, she thought of the prenuptial instruction that Sid Boazzin's wives had received in the tradition of their faith.

Growing more apprehensive by the minute, she clenched the warm terrace railing with icy hands and awaited the sound of footsteps in the corridor. But Morgan's tread was noiseless this night. Without warning, the door opened and he crossed the threshold, a tall shadow holding a marriage paper bound by a silver ribbon.

Although Gwen stood fully clothed in a pale yellow skirt and blouse, her bare feet and unbound hair created the provocative pose she had earlier intended. Halting in midstride, Morgan let the paper drop from his hand to the bed.

Gwenllian remained rooted in place, and the hush between the newly wedded pair stretched into minutes. His eyes were fastened upon her silhouette and she fancied she could feel their scrutiny sweep up and down. As his silence continued, it occurred to her that Morgan was disconcerted too by the unplanned circumstances of the night. But where she was fearful, he appeared enthralled, perhaps even beguiled by the sight of his waiting young bride. Gwen yearned for him to speak, offer even some meaningless dialogue to ease the awkwardness of the moment. But he had never been a man to waste words.

Walking slowly forward, he came to stand before her, so that she had to lift up her face to see his shadowed visage. She trembled, overwhelmed by his proximity. The nebulous light softened the harder edges of his face, making it more youthful, almost vulnerable, while the breeze blew short strands of hair across his brow.

Mesmerized by his gaze, she remained motionless as he reached out and touched her arms, ran his fingers over the sleeves in strokes so light her flesh rose. It was the first sensual contact they had made as husband and wife. Disconcerted, Gwen lowered her lashes, then looked up at him again with beseechment in her eyes.

He did not mistake the plea in them, and placed a tender hand to her head, stroking her unloosed hair from nape to ends until the physical awareness between them increased to tension. As he touched her she could see his face change, grow taut with readiness to complete the act he had now begun. She thought of his mastery with reins and rifle, and knew his hands would be no less skillful, no less certain in their holding of her tonight.

And yet, as he took her face in his palms she detected a quiver in them, and as his mouth came to hers, a low sound caught in his throat as if the drive to possess was too strong to be silenced. She smiled against his lips. But it was a private smile. She had made the indomitable Squire of Hiraeth need her, and her sense of triumph tasted sweet.

His hands slipped to the small of her back and pressed while his mouth trailed from her lips to the vee of her blouse. She yielded to his practiced moves and to the heat of his body, feeling his shirt grow damp beneath her hands, noticing that the darkness of his flesh showed through the thin linen fabric. Twining her arms about his neck, she parted her lips, for she wanted the seduction to be hers as well as his. She closed her eyes when his hands caressed her ribs and waist before moving over the flat span of her stomach downward, until they pulled her hips more fittingly into his. But when he began to work the fastenings of her blouse, push the tiny pearl buttons through their silken loops, she clutched his hand to stay it.

"What is it?" he asked, his voice as warm as the night. "You're not afraid?"

She bent her head so that the smooth crest of her cheekbone pressed against his shirtfront, and murmured distressfully, "Yes."

"Of me?"

"No . . . not of you." Lowering her eyes, she stared at his hand where it lay poised above her heart, then reached to trace its knuckles and the valleys in between each one. "I'm afraid of tonight . . . of the things I do not know."

His forefinger outlined the arched and fleshy bow of her upper lip, which was still moist from his own mouth. "But that fear is the thing that charms me," he said in a low voice, a melting voice that made the reserve in her give way.

Trusting now, she dropped her hand from his so that he could draw apart the blouse like one draws back the folded wrapping from a fragile present.

When the faint, hazy light revealed her feminine shape, the fire of hunger overtook Morgan, and before long Gwenllian's instincts were roused in kind. She pushed the shirt from the rise of his shoulders, then closed her eyes when he pulled her close and their flesh met in a warm and dewy seal. In slow, tandem steps he backed her toward the bed, and when she had fallen softly amidst its pillows, he covered her body with his. Urgency increased, and he murmured words against her mouth in a language she did not comprehend. But the soft heat of the syllables told her that she was painfully desired.

They were lost, breathing amidst a fevered cloud of necessity when a sudden resounding crash arrested them. They broke apart as the door to the room slammed into the wall and reverberated. Clad in nothing but his trousers, Morgan leapt off the bed and prepared to fly at the intruder. But his progress was stayed by the threatening glint of a revolver and Sir Gerald's commanding bellow.

"Ask him who he is, Gwenllian!"

Almost witless with the shock of seeing her father standing in their room with a weapon trained upon her husband, Gwen grappled for the sheets to cover her nakedness. Frozen with fear that Morgan would leap at Sir Gerald and prompt her father's pulling of the trigger, she cried out. "Papa—"

"Ask him who he is!" he repeated in a roar, his burly chest heaving with a fury he could barely contain.

Bewildered and afraid, Gwen looked at Morgan.

"He has not told ye yet, has he?" Sir Gerald said with a sneer. "Well, ask him where he will be taking ye tomorrow. Ye did not suppose the two of ye'd be going back to Hiraeth, now did ye, daughter? Humph! Ye shall not, I'll wager, never till hell freezes over. Ye'll be going to the desert, by God. Little better than a damned nomad, your romantic Mr. Riff is. Or didn't ye know? A savage, a war lord who spends his life fighting and killing. By damn, ask yer fine new husband how many wives he has already—how many more he's likely to take for himself upon a fancy. Shall ye relish such a life, girl?"

Gwenllian simply stared at her father, wondering if he had gone mad and blabbed nonsense. Coldness clutched at her heart, and she again glanced up at Morgan.

"Leave us," he ordered, speaking to her father.

"I'll not leave her alone another minute with the likes of ye—"

"By God, you will!" Morgan shouted in a dangerous voice. "She is my wife, wed to me an hour past, and you will give us the privacy to speak alone. Afterward, she may go with you or stay with me as she pleases. I'll not toss her atop my horse and carry her away, if that's what you're afraid of."

Hesitating, Sir Gerald glanced from the half-naked form of Morgan Riff to his daughter. At the sight of her agonized posture upon a bed still warm from her tumble with the man, his eyes lowered with embarrassment and pain, and slowly he sheathed the pistol. "I'll be waiting for ye in the lobby, Gwenllian," he growled. "I'll not leave till ye come down and speak with me."

A moment of excruciating silence followed his retreat down the corridor. Running a hand through his hair, Morgan pivoted on a heel and stalked out to the terrace, where he gripped the curled black railing in the same way he would a weapon. Speechless, Gwen watched while he inhaled deeply to quell the ire that coiled every muscle in his rigid frame. She let several moments pass, struggling to grasp the situation, waiting until his hands relaxed their clench upon the iron rail.

"Is what he says the truth, Morgan?" Her words were jerky, fearful breaths finally squeezed out from her chest.

He sighed gustily, then inclined his head. "Most of it."

"Most of it?"

"I'm the man you met upon your arrival in Tangier, the man some call the English—although I believe you had a less charitable title for me that day."

Gwenllian's mouth opened, but no words came

186

out. Vivid scenes were flashing across her mind in a confusing sequence, including a picture of a ferocious native wearing a bloodstained burnoose. She felt dizzy. Morgan Riff was not the urbane European she had believed him to be, not the Squire of Hiraeth on a sojourn from his Welsh estate but, at heart, a savage who resided among the savage.

"You are one of them," she said in disbelief. "You're—"

"A barbarian. Go ahead and say the word, for God's sake, and get it over with, since you seem so taken with it."

"If I could think of a worse name I'd use it instead," she countered in growing horror. "Papa said you were a—a war lord. Is that true, too?"

"Such a word gets your father's point across well enough."

She stared at him and shook her head, incredulous. "I feel as if I've suddenly been dropped in the midst of a nightmare. I can't believe you could keep such a thing from me—I can't believe you *would!* What did you think to gain from it?"

"I'm surprised you need to ask."

Infuriated by his dispassionate response she shouted at him. *"Why didn't you tell me?* Why didn't you tell me who you were?"

"When?" he demanded with a short laugh, turning about to face her. "When would you have had me tell you? At the Carstairs' over dinner? At the horse fair, or while we stood necking at the colonel's front door? Perhaps tonight would have been a more appropriate time," he suggested with unsparing sarcasm. "When we were in bed together."

"A decent man knows the truth is appropriate at any time!"

"What else does a decent man know, Gwenllian? Tell me. Does he know to turn away a girl standing at his hotel door in the middle of the night with a valise in her hand?"

At his implication that her own behavior was not above reproach, she glared at him. "You're a cad to say such a thing."

"Your list of unflattering nouns grows by the minute. Before the night is over, it should be quite long."

"Yes, it should, shouldn't it!"

He turned from the railing and stepped to the French doors, where he braced a bare shoulder against the frame and lifted a hand to rub his brow in a gesture of frustration. "Tell me something, just for the sake of argument. If I'd come to dine at the Carstairs in my burnoose, carrying my rifle and sword, what would you have said? How would you have received me?"

She only scoffed, folding her arms across her sheet-draped chest in a pointed attitude of rejection.

"I believe my point has been made," he said.

She did not reply, and with bleak eyes he eyed her fragile form, which was huddled in a forlorn way within the ruination of a lovers' bed. She looked like a child who had just awakened from a frightening dream and in bewilderment struggled to separate fantasy from reality. He felt a pain in his belly, and turned his head away.

"I'll give you all the explanations you want,

Gwen," he said quietly a moment later. "But I warn you, you won't care for them."

"How good of you to tell me now." Bitterly, she shoved one of the rumpled bed pillows from her legs so that it slid to the floor with a swish. "I feel as if I've been a part of some conspiracy that no one bothered to tell me about. Why did my father wait until now to come bursting in with his interesting bit of news?"

"Because he wanted to keep my identity a secret."

"Why?"

"I can't discuss the reasons now. But the fact is, I am a Berber chieftain."

She threw up her hands. "How charming!"

"You have a right to feel betrayed."

"Betrayed? That's putting it mildly, don't you think? Of course, now that I know who you are I understand your disregard for my feelings. I am only a woman, after all."

"The values of one's upbringing are not easily discarded in a day, Gwen. Nor is it an easy task for me to jump from one culture to another, to become a European gentleman with the accompanying social attitudes simply by changing my clothes."

"But you played the part of a gentleman well enough to deceive me, didn't you?" she said in a scathing tone.

"Obviously."

"Why?"

"Because I was interested in you," he said with a frankness that galled her. "I knew who you were when I saw you in the marketplace with your father—he and I had previously met here three months ago and planned a series of subsequent meetings. But after your parting compliment in the butcher's stall," he drawled, "I was not about to show up at the Carstairs in my burnoose and sword and suffer another dose of your self-righteous superiority."

His shirt lay at his feet, and picking it up, he tossed it into a chair. "Now that you know the truth, feel free to call me a reprobate, a savage, or any other derogatory word that comes to mind. I married you without first telling you the truth, and I deserve a fit of female histrionics." He shook his head and snorted. "Hell, maybe I thought it wouldn't matter."

His words stung, and Gwen clamped her lips together against a shrill retort. A hush followed, and neither she nor Morgan moved. They simply listened to the sound of a cat yowling on the street, and to the breeze that whispered through the room and rustled the white cotton canopy of the bed like a sail. And they listened to the sound of their own breaths, and felt the wounds of their new sorrow.

"Maybe I am self-righteous," Gwen murmured. "But at least I'm honest."

"Much to your credit, I'm sure."

"When would you have told me about yourself, Morgan?" she asked grimly. "Tonight? Tomorrow?"

"I hadn't had time to decide yet," he said, throwing her a caustic glance. "Up until a few minutes ago I was too preoccupied with thoughts of other things."

Feeling wretched in her half-dressed state amidst

the decimation of their relationship, she said tersely, "Will you hand me my blouse, please?"

He regarded her with a slight smile, delaying the request, and she thought it was the first deliberate act of mercilessness he had ever shown her. When he finally bent to retrieve the blouse, he draped it with a purposefully negligent hand across the foot of her bed.

Snatching it, she turned her back and shoved her arms through the sleeves, hastily fastening the buttons down the front while she slipped out of bed. When she finished she stood staring at the wardrobe across the room. Its door was ajar and she could just discern the shape of Morgan's clothes inside. Hanging beside the elegantly cut jackets and trousers was a chestnut-colored burnoose.

The sight of the garment was all the confirmation she needed of his dual identity; until now, she had scarcely been able to grasp the fact that Morgan Riff and the sabre-wielding man in the marketplace were one and the same.

"Shall I put it on for you?" he asked with a cruel twist of irony.

She raised her eyes and it seemed to her that he had already transformed himself without any donning of costume. He was Rhaman, no less formidable, no less handsome than before, but alien to the world that gave her meaning and safety. Gwen watched him. In a daze of pain, the sort of pain that comes with heartbreak, she let her eyes wander over the angles of his profile, the curve of his naked shoulders, the line of his capable hands which were held half open at his sides. Oddly, in spite of her bitterness, a part of her still longed to feel them hold her again. She still loved him—love could not be slain in the space of an hour—but he was not what she wanted him to be.

"I can scarcely take it in . . ." she breathed, speaking her thoughts aloud.

Though her small voice cracked with the shattering of her adoration, Morgan did not comfort her. Instead he turned his head away to contemplate the inscrutable streets. "Some part of you knew who I was from the beginning, Gwenllian. Like it or not, you *knew*."

"But instead of confirming it," she accused, "you told me you were the Squire."

"I told you what you wanted to hear, which just happened to be the truth."

Unable to dispute his claim, Gwenllian had no retort. For a moment she listened to the haunting music of the Arab pipe that had resumed its mournful melody, then asked in a disrespectful tone, "Why do the natives seem to know you and yet give you wide berth? Do you have such a reputation for killing that they fear you'll strike them down upon a whim?"

Folding his arms across his chest, Morgan leaned back against the folded terrace doors as if unperturbed by the insult. "Berber tribes are scattered all across Morocco. We're not Arabs, but Aryan descendants with our own language, and for years we've rebelled against the sultan and battled among ourselves for land. Consequently, we've earned a reputation for fierce fighting, and are feared by many. To say that 'the Berbers are coming' in Morocco is rather like saying in the Wild West that 'the Indians are coming.' "

"You paint quite a flattering picture of yourself."

"You wanted the truth—brutally delivered or not, I assumed."

"Would that your compunction had not kept you from it earlier," she scorned.

"I gambled and lost, it would seem. Eh, Mrs. Riff . . . ?"

"Don't call me that!"

"My apologies. Perhaps you would prefer the title. As the Squire of Hiraeth I hold a baronetcy, I believe. So you are by all rights Lady Riff."

She turned on him. "And how many other *Lady* Riffs are there, Morgan? I believe your faith permits you a total of four."

"Perhaps you would care to come with me and discover the number for yourself."

"Shall I don a veil? Hide my face with it? Follow you into the desert like the silly meek creatures that tiptoe about Sid Boazzin's house?"

He ignored her derision with his usual placability. "I don't live in the desert. Your father was misinformed on that point. My home is in the mountains of Atlas. As for the veil, you would be expected to wear appropriate native dress, of course, for prudence's sake—not that I prefer it, mind you, being more inclined toward the philosophy that pretty faces should be uncovered and viewed at a man's leisure."

At his deliberate baiting, Gwen snapped, "You must have been crazy to think I would agree to such a life!"

193

"It would seem so, wouldn't it?"

She turned her back upon him, and after the passage of a few moments, said more quietly, "You have no intention of ever returning to Wales, do you? You have no desire to be master of Hiraeth."

"If you were ever under such a delusion, I'm sorry, Gwen. Truly I am."

She turned and looked at him, for his voice held genuine regret, and the deep sound of it wrenched her. As she regarded the hard planes of his face, touched now by the pale light that heralded the coming of a vermillion dawn, she unwillingly remembered the moment she had seen him step into the Carstairs' dining room. She recalled how her heart had convulsed when she had recognized the being who could fill its emptiness. She remembered how splendid he had looked. He looked splendid still.

In that terrible moment she almost flew to him. She longed to be held in his arms and made secure, she yearned to have him soothe her with promises that all would be well. She wanted to turn back the clock and resume what they had begun before her father's intrusion.

But Gwen was logical enough to understand that although rapture might be tasted many times in Morgan Riff's arms by night, by day she would be a Berber chieftain's wife. And that title she knew she could never endure with grace. There would be terror and violence in a life shared with him, and what sort of a toll would that take upon her love? Before long resentment would sour the feeling she shared with Morgan, and then kill it entirely.

194

Wasn't it better to make a quick ending of the relationship here, rather than allow it to suffer months or years of a more agonizing demise?

She saw Morgan contemplating her in his perceptive way, just before he stepped across the room to stand close. His nearness unstrung her and made her resolve weak. She put her hands behind her back, fearing he would touch them. If he did, she would cry.

"I made you my wife because I wanted to, Gwenllian. But it was inadvisable, decided in the madness of a moment. I'm sorry."

Such earnestness shone in his eyes that she had to blink away tears. When he continued in a quiet and compassionate tone, she smothered a sob.

"The life I lead would be a grueling one for any woman not bred for it—a hellish life for you. I won't ask you to endure it for me. It's best for you to return to your father—to Wales. It's where you belong, just as I belong here. The marriage can be annulled. I give you leave to do it."

She lowered her head. She could not bear to continue looking at the eyes she loved and see in them the shimmering of anguish; they were not supposed to be anguished. They were not supposed to be vulnerable.

Her throat closed. "Morgan . . ." The cry broke upon her lips.

He touched her face, and although his voice was sorrowful, it was strengthened with the type of wisdom that only a veteran of hardship owns. "It wasn't meant to be after all, I'm afraid."

Tears spilled over her lashes and ran into the corners of her mouth. He brushed them away with a thumb, and said softly to her in parting, "Look after Hiraeth for me. Will you . . . ? You'll make a far better guardian to it than I could ever be."

Ten

When she arrived at the Carstairs' villa, Gwenllian was so numb that she scarcely felt the humiliation of being escorted home like a wayward child on the arm of her father. Pausing at the threshold, Sir Gerald set her valise down upon the sun-scorched pavement and spoke in a quiet, troubled tone.

"Gwenllian, I understand yer dejection, believe me, I do. I suffered a disappointment myself once long ago. But ye've done the thing that's best for ye, and in the end it will all come out as it should. Ye'll see."

Too dispirited to argue, she nodded. His tender concern had put her on the verge of tears again, which she had valiantly restrained since watching Morgan walk away.

With obvious relief that his dutiful but awkward task of comfort was done, Sir Gerald announced, "The ship home sails at one o'clock. Can ye be ready?"

"Yes, Papa."

"Good." Picking up her bag he ushered her in-

197

side, and as she walked toward her room on wooden legs, she saw Sophie, Robyn and Libby Carstairs watching her through the parlor doors, their countenances relieved. Her father escorted her to her door, patted her on the shoulder wordlessly, and left her to the solitude she craved.

She leaned against the closed door and laid her head back. Buff whimpered at her feet, begging attention, and she scooped him up. But his wriggling presence served only to remind her of the man who had rescued him. And with remembrance of Morgan Riff—in whatever guise he wore—came the tears, which she lay down and shed as if she would drown in them.

The departure from the Carstairs' villa occurred amidst a bustle of trunk-wielding servants and quiet farewells. Little was said to Gwen. Colonel and Mrs. Carstairs bade perfunctory adieus while Sophie and Robyn kept at a sensitive distance, respecting her reddened eyes and grief-worn face by making no comment upon their cause.

The company set out, retracing the route they had traveled upon their arrival a few weeks ago. Just as before, Sir Gerald took the lead with Sophie upon his arm, while Robyn towed Gwen along as if her dazed mien were normal. Although the sun licked at her voile-covered arms and caused perspiration to gather beneath her hatband, Gwen shivered with cold. And although donkeys brayed and caravan drivers bellowed, she heard only a dull roar. The gaudy silks in the stalls shimmered, but they were nothing more than blurs through her tears. With irony she recalled how, only last night, she had yearned to leave behind the filth and din of the city. But she had envisioned fleeing Tangier in Morgan's company, not like this, not alone.

Where was he now? Did he cross the vast plains toward the mountains he called Atlas, ride to meet his clansmen and plot another war? She imagined him in his native garb astride the copper horse, his hand resting upon a sabre or a rifle, his brilliant eyes aware of every swirl of sand and cast of shadow. Even while she held on to Robyn's arm and let him pull her through the jostling crowd, she saw herself running after Rhaman, her shoes filling with sand as she screamed at him to stop. She imagined him wheeling his mount about and scooping her up to carry her to his home.

Regret overwhelmed her in one swift blow, and she faltered in her step. Had she done the wrong thing? Should she have ridden away with Morgan no matter what his lifestyle, no matter what dangers Morocco promised? Surely no existence could be more brutal than the numb, confused one she suffered now.

Tears filled her eyes so she could hardly see the cracked pavement with its crisscross of hurrying sandals. With every wrenching decision made in life did there always follow remorse and self-doubt, a questioning of one's own good judgment in the matter? She did not know. She only knew that she had made an irreversible decision, and felt desperate because there was no turning back.

Three women swept past, their eyes meeting hers

timidly above their veils, and she wondered if they were the wives of Sid Boazzin, those creatures she had so pitied for their lack of freedom. Remembering them, her faith in her own convictions restored itself a little, for she realized anew that she could never join their ranks, not even for Morgan. But the reaffirmation did nothing to lessen the torment of the loss.

During the next hour, the ordeal in the Custom's Office tired her, and she sat fanning herself in the stuffy place. She felt guilty turning away the attentions of the well-meaning Sophie, and even more wretched when Robyn brought her a glass of lemonade and she uncharitably pushed his hand away. But she wanted to suffer her grief alone.

At last, their trunks were tossed into the rowboats that would transfer them to the anchored steamer, and Sir Gerald stepped up to speak with Gwen in private. "Well, daughter," he said gruffly, removing his brown felt hat and worrying it between his freckled hands. "Have a safe voyage home. Take care of yerself. I'm sorry it was not a more pleasant holiday for ye."

She stared at him. "Are you not going with us, Papa . . . ?"

"No. I'm staying on here a week or two. But I'll be back at Ardderyd before yer birthday," he vowed. "And be bringing with me a fine present for my best girl."

Gwenllian was dismayed. She needed his large comforting presence beside her at home. Groping for a way to persuade him to change his mind, she looked out toward the pier where the rowboats bucked like ponies. Their wooden hulls rubbed against the wooden pilings and made a grating sound. Time slipped away and she glanced with beseeching eyes at her father's face, noting that his hatband had left a pink crease across his forehead and put a crimp in his hair. He looked old. Fear pricked her. And she was struck by a sudden, shattering premonition of disaster that flashed behind her eyes like a blinding light.

"Come home, Papa!" she cried on impulse, throwing her arms about his heavy neck. "Come home with me."

"Hey, what is this all about now?" he asked. "Are ye going to miss yer old curmudgeon of a sire? Well, well, it does my heart good to hear it."

She clung to him. "It's just that—"

But her anxious words were interrupted by the whistle blasts of the waiting steamer and on the pier two officials waved at her to step aboard the rowboat.

"Gwen," Sir Gerald said gently, pulling her head against his chest. "I know what's burdening ye, I know yer heart's fair bursting with grief. I wish that I could take it all into my own heart and suffer it for ye. But I can't. How I regret it!"

At his show of tenderness she quieted, soothed by the familiar scent of his cigars and hair pomade while he rocked her in his arms. "He was a beguiling man, yer Mr. Riff," he sympathized, "I'll give ye that. Romantic, aye, and strong, with eyes guaranteed to stir the vitals of any young woman, especially one as sheltered as ye have been. But, my darling, he was not meant for ye. And ye must be-

201

lieve it, strive to forget. Will ye promise to do that before I send ye off?"

She nodded, knowing that a promise to forget Morgan Riff was an empty one.

Home. She drew strength from it in the way she had always done, and yet, she found herself viewing it through much different eyes, eyes disillusioned with the knowledge that life did not yield to dreams.

She had not been at Ardderyd a day when she abandoned all of its pressing duties and forsook even the watchful company of Sophie and Robyn in order to ride to Hiraeth. Too impatient to summon a groom and wait for his dawdling hands to do the task, she saddled a horse herself and mounted unaided from the block in the stable yard. Applying her heels to his flanks, she sent the scrappy pony clattering over the rain-slick cobbles, then in a fit of mischief allowed him to gallop across the soft, perfectly manicured lawn.

The clouds roiled, swollen with seeping rain that drifted down in a mist over the moors fronting the sea. To the east, white daubs of wooly sheep dotted the landscape, whose palette of colors included all hues of emerald and slate, and shaggy cattle roamed the pastures pocked with puddles. Not far away heather and bare rock tumbled toward the wild Atlantic, where the cold spindrift conjured images of the Celtic spirit world.

How cool was the rain! It beaded upon Gwen's cheeks and made her hair heavy. She gloried in it, and realized that it was a gift from Wales, a blessing that quickened her spirit with a shred of happiness. But it was a fleeting thing, a fragile light that the cloak of sadness quickly smothered.

In the distance she could see the squire's domain, the fortress he had forsaken. It rose up from the craggy earth as if it were a part of the firmament itself, reigning over the forbidding frost-riven cliffs where sea birds wheeled and shrieked their lonely cries. Halting her mount, Gwen stared at the ancient structure, feeling its solitude poignantly, like her own. She was unsure why she had rushed pell-mell through the rain to contemplate it. Except that Hiraeth was the only connection she retained with Morgan Riff, the only link left. Perhaps she hoped to find a trace of him somewhere within its empty halls. It was his birthright, after all, bequeathed to him by generations of past squires whose proud Welsh blood ran in his veins. And he had been here once, a long time ago . . .

She nudged the pony into an easy walk and, at the gate, tethered him while the wet sea winds whipped his tail and made the reins slick. Her hands were numb from cold, and using the iron knockers, she rapped clumsily upon the massive portals of the estate, finally eliciting a response from the elderly caretaker. He did not act surprised to see her, welcoming her with particular deference as he ushered her inside. He probably knew that she now belonged to Hiraeth, for the efficient grapevine utilized by all Welsh servants would have informed him without delay. Perversely, she had imparted the news of her marriage to a maid at Ard-deryd this morning, ignoring the fact that Papa would be outraged over her flaunting of the title. Before she had departed Tangier, he had secured annulment papers for her through the embassy and asked her to sign them. But she had put him off with the promise that she would do so upon her arrival home. She would feel up to it then, she had assured him, and would post the signed papers to his solicitors in London within thirty days.

And yet, as she stood in the great hall of Hiraeth and stared up at its dour but magnificent clerestories, she wavered. Perhaps she would never sign away her marriage. Perhaps she would always remain the lady of the place she loved, be mistress to it, walk its deserted grounds in the misty evenings. She would be called eccentric by the villagers, of course, who would whisper that she waited in vain for her half-foreign groom to come home.

"Petwyn," she said, addressing the caretaker who busied himself with her dripping cape and hat. "I'd like to explore the rooms. Can you fetch me some keys?"

"Oh, aye, mum." He removed a ring from his pocket and handed it over. "Would you like me to take you round myself, tell you what I know about the old place?"

"That would be lovely. Please do."

And so Gwen toured every dusty chamber and every echoing hallway in the fortress, experiencing such a deep sense of pride at its history that she decided to review its accounts soon and try to make the estate profitable once more.

The bedchamber of Morgan's mother interested her more than any other. Little had been changed since Marian's residence at Hiraeth some forty years ago. Although draped in dust covers, the furnishings were still intact, arranged just as they had been when the girl had primped before the cheval mirror, or reposed like a princess upon the bed hung with faded velvet. Excited, Gwen swept the shrouds aside, exclaiming over the mirrored vanity, the tapestried chairs and twin clothes presses. She discovered trunks packed with lacy shawls, fur pelisses, and slender elbow-length gloves. One small japanned trunk contained a collection of letters, fragile yellowed things tossed together with no particular care, some only half crammed into envelopes adorned with exotic stamps. Perusing one, then another, Gwen realized they were love letters, ardently penned and signed always with the scrawled and intriguing signature of *Ulysses*.

"Petwyn," she said, frowning, refolding a crackling page. "Tell me what you know about Marian. Were you here during her time?"

The toothless old man had bent to inspect a crack below a casement window where damp seeped in. He straightened and shook his head. "Oh, nay, mum. I came just after she went away. But I gathered a good deal of information about her over the years. She lived here with her grandfather for a spell in between his foreign travels. Quite rebellious she was, they tell me, going about as independent as you please, with no reprimands from the old squire, who only seemed to find her headstrong ways amusing."

"The man she married," Gwen asked, "do you know anything about him?"

"Only a bit. It seems young Marian met him in London. He was a foreigner from some African country, come to see the Great Exhibition at the Crystal Palace. She ran off with him lickety-split, which caused quite a stir hereabouts, considering she was already betrothed to a Welshman."

"I suppose these are the Welshman's letters," Gwen mused thoughtfully. With a vague sense of guilt over prying into the private life of young Marian, she snapped the lid shut.

"I wouldn't know, mum. But 'twould make sense, wouldn't it?"

Gwen took one last look around the chamber, touching a few of the personal belongings that a spirited young girl had abandoned for the love of a man. Marian must have possessed great courage to relinquish her life here, trade all things familiar and cherished for the unknown perils of another land. Gwen wondered if Morgan's mother had ever regretted her decision, ever wept silently for home while lying in the arms of her Berber mate upon some desolate mountain range. Marian had never returned to Hiraeth. She had tried once, after her husband's death. She had tried to bring Morgan home to safety, but failed. How different his life might have been had she accomplished her journey!

"Pardon my asking, mum," the caretaker said sheepishly, "but will the squire be coming home afore long?"

The words took Gwenllian aback, made the answer hard to give. "No, Petwyn," she said. "The squire will not be coming home at all."

206

When she descended the monstrous flight of stairs a moment later she discovered Robyn waiting for her at the last step, holding his rain-soaked hat in his hands and frowning up at her hollowed face.

"I was worried about you, Gwen. Riding out in the rain the way you did with scarcely a word to anyone, staying gone for hours. I didn't know what to think."

"I appreciate your concern, Robyn. But as you can see, I'm perfectly fine."

Truthfully, she was annoyed that he had followed, more annoyed still that he stood atop the same step young Rhaman had occupied when she had glimpsed him for the first time. Taking the earl's arm, she directed him to the blazing hearth in the great hall, and as she did so, her callousness pricked her conscience. Robyn's affection must be genuine to persist with such a courtship. Most suitors with his pride would have been put off by a woman's consorting with another man, especially when that affair had resulted in a marriage—no matter how brief and foolish. She had been Robyn's intended, after all. It would be his right to turn his back upon her, even blacken her name in social circles. And yet, because his pride was so considerable, Gwen guessed he wished to salvage it by excusing her attachment to Morgan Riff as either girlish folly or some temporary lapse in sanity brought on by the heat of Tangier.

She moved to warm her hands before the fire, and rubbing them, eyed the earl askance as he examined the walls of Hiraeth with a critical gaze. He was in his element again, she thought, his hauteur was fully restored. Some might even consider him pleasant looking in an effete way, with his trim mustache, patrician profile, and smart London tweeds. She smiled to herself, for in his ever fastidious manner, the earl had even worn spatterdashes to protect his boots from the muddy ride over.

His eyes met hers with a questioning flicker then, as if he knew she appraised him, and he hoped for a favorable comment. She pitied him all at once, sensing that he felt for her the same wrenching sort of love she felt for Morgan. She said quietly, "I've decided to live here, you know. Live at Hiraeth."

He looked at her in astonishment. "What?"

"As wife to the squire, I have a right to move in. The place desperately needs a mistress to look after it, don't you think?"

"But your marriage to him is to be annulled," he said in incredulous protest. "What can you be thinking?"

She strolled to the enormous painting hanging beside the hearth in its gilt-framed canvas. It depicted the clashing Welsh warriors of centuries past, and their blood flowed freely over the land for which they fought and fell. "I haven't signed the papers yet. I'm not certain that I will."

"Gwenllian!" Robyn exclaimed. "You can't mean this. Why in heaven's name would you stay married to a man you'll never see again?"

"It's ironic, don't you think?" she went on as if he hadn't spoken. "As a girl I always entertained fantasies about Hiraeth. And now, through a set of extraordinary circumstances, it's mine to keep—for all practical purposes, at least. I loved him, Robyn," she confided in an impulsive whisper. "I love him still."

For a moment the earl stood staring at her, the skin about his mouth turning white with pique. Then he retrieved his dripping hat from the mantel, and with a snap of his wrist shook the raindrops off its brim and onto the cold stone floor. "So you do. Well, you'll get over it."

The weeks crept by. Gwen's birthday arrived and departed, and no word from Sir Gerald came to Ardderyd. She began to fret, for it was unlike her father to be so inconsiderate. She knew Morocco had no postal system, but the British post was quite efficient there, and mail packets embarked on regular routes from Tangier.

Apprehensive, she penned a letter to her father and sent it in care of Colonel Carstairs, hoping he and Libby had not yet departed for his new assignment in America. At the same time, for good measure, she dispatched an inquiry to the British Embassy in Tangier, knowing Sir Gerald had connections there.

With each day that passed she grew more anxious, for she could not help but recall the disquieting premonition that had seized her during their farewell on the dock; it had clung to her even after her return to Wales.

A fortnight later, still having no word from him, she prepared to go to the village to collect the estate mail herself, too restless to await a servant's round trip to fetch it. The day was cold, the ground little more than mire, and her pony's hooves sank deep into the earth, sucking and splashing while his labored breaths made silver clouds in the air. The village was wreathed in smoke curls wending from squat stone chimneys, and its streets were crowded with patrons gathering for the Thursday horse fair. Greetings to Gwen were plentiful, made more affectionate by fond remembrances of the pretty lass who had ridden pillion on Sir Gerald's bay hunter in years past.

The postmistress smiled a gap-toothed greeting as Gwen requested the Ardderyd mail, and after a loquacious discourse on the foulness of the weather, she finally handed over the small bundle of letters.

Gwen sorted through them with such eager hands that some fluttered to the floor. But at the bottom of the stack she discovered a flimsy envelope much the worse for wear that was addressed to her in her father's handwriting. The scrawled words were so poorly formed they could scarcely be read.

"What is it? What's the matter?" the postmistress asked as Gwen tore at the seal with trembling hands.

But the squire's wife ignored her, too intent upon reading the hastily penned scribble.

In desperate straits. Need help. Contact Morgan Riff immediately. Message for him enclosed.

She read the lines again and again with a frenzied gaze. What had happened to her father? Fear besieged her. Was he injured, dying?

Her hands shook so badly she could hardly unfold the message enclosed for Morgan, which was nothing more than a tattered scrap stained with brown smudges. She feverishly scanned its spidery letters for a clue of her father's predicament, then groaned.

It had been written in Arabic.

Eleven

Never had Gwenllian ridden so furiously, heedless of her mount's safety as she forced him to fly over drenched turf and tumbled rock. Dismounting before he had even slid to a stop, she dashed into Ardderyd and up the stairs, breathlessly ordering her maid to pack the trunks she had just stored in the attic a few weeks past.

Having witnessed the stormy entrance, Robyn abandoned the perusal of his morning paper and climbed the steps in her wake. In Sir Gerald's absence he had assumed the role of master, taking it upon himself to aid Gwenllian in the managing of the estate despite her unwillingness to accept it.

"What is it, Gwen? Has news of your father come?"

Pulling the letter from her pocket, she held it out with a grave expression. He scanned it, then frowned and unfolded the second missive scrawled in Arabic. "Good lord . . . this doesn't bode well."

"I'm leaving for Tangier," she declared, yanking

clothes out of a wardrobe. "Just as soon as my things are packed."

He rushed forward and stayed her arm. "No. Let me deliver the message to Morgan Riff. Stay here where you're safe."

She shook her head. "I'm going, Robyn. You can't stop me. And that's an end to it."

"Then I shall go with you."

She glanced up at him. Traipsing about Tangier making inquiries into the whereabouts of a Berber chieftain would prove a difficult task for an unescorted European woman. Having a man at her side—ineffectual as Robyn may be in the foreign environment—would make the endeavor less dangerous. She had expected his offer to join her, of course, but a rush of gratitude prompted her to touch his sleeve in a more tender gesture than she had shown in weeks. "Thank you, Robyn. But what can it mean?" she cried. "What could have happened to Papa?"

The earl shook his head in consternation. "He and Carstairs were involved in affairs they should not have been. Riff was connected as well, in an unscrupulous way. I'm afraid Sir Gerald has been caught in the business, though by what party of miscreants I can't begin to imagine."

"What sort of affairs do you mean?" Gwen demanded. "Was it something to do with the embassy, some—some government business?"

"Yes. But your father asked me to keep it to myself, and I shall. At least for now."

"But discretion hardly matters at this point. I should like to know—"

"No, Gwen. Get on with your packing. I'll go and have my valet begin mine."

What mingled emotions the return to Morocco rekindled! When Gwen put her foot down upon the soil of that sun-baked land for the second time, she hardly noticed the dreadful and stirring sights that had so appalled her on the previous journey. She could think of nothing but her father's peril. She could think of nothing but seeing Morgan Riff again.

After sending their trunks to the Hotel la Villa de France, Gwen and Robyn proceeded directly to the British Embassy where Lord Breese made inquiries as to the whereabouts of both Colonel Carstairs and Sir Gerald. He was informed by a terse official that the former had been dispatched to America, and that the latter was unknown to them.

"Liars!" Robyn exclaimed as he joined Gwen beneath the hoisted Union Jack outside. "They know him quite well, I'll wager. Their denial of it only suggests that he was involved in their intrigue more deeply than I guessed."

"Come, then." Gwen tugged upon his arm, wanting to lose no time. She tried not to dwell on the amount of days that had elapsed already since her father's penning of the appeal. "Let's go to Sid Boazzin's address. And pray that he knows how to reach Morgan."

Memories assailed her along the way. She could recall vividly her previous trek through the hot streets on Morgan's arm, recall his mood, his voice, every aspect of his person as he had strolled with his easy step among the vibrant jumble of kaftans and copper sellers. Where her time apart from him in Wales had brought desolate emptiness, her return amplified the yearning to be in his presence again.

"Should we show Sid Boazzin the message written to Morgan and have him interpret it for us, Robyn?" she asked as they awaited the Arab in his courtyard a time later.

"I'd rather not," he said, watching the shadows. "I know nothing about the fellow, but if he's like most of the people in this godforsaken country, he's hardly to be trusted, especially when dealing with Europeans. Besides, the message might contain some reference to the sensitive business in which Sir Gerald has embroiled himself. No, let us be discreet."

And so, when their smiling host greeted them with a cordial *"Marhaba bikum!"* Robyn simply asked Sid Boazzin if he could be called upon to contact Morgan Riff. For good measure Gwen added that she was now Morgan's wife, and some emergency had prompted her need of him.

If Sid Boazzin thought it a rather extraordinary interview—the bride of a most celebrated Berber chieftain in the company of another man—his demeanor never belied it. Moreover, he seemed unsurprised by the news of the wedding, and after offering felicitations, assured them that he would endeavor to send a dispatch to Morgan. But its reaching the chieftain, he added with a sympathetic shrug, could take time.

"You see," he elaborated, "I have no way of knowing how far into the mountains my friend has gone. By the time he is found and returns to Tangier—" he opened his palms—"many weeks could have passed. I hope your . . . emergency is not so terrible that it can't withstand this delay."

Gwen and Robyn exchanged sober looks. "We have little choice but to wait," the latter returned. "And we're most grateful for your help."

"Do you have some written words you would like my messenger to deliver to Rhaman?"

Gwen withdrew an envelope from her pocket. "Yes. If you could see that he receives this . . . ?"

Morgan had not gone into the mountains after all. He and a few of his men were in the lowlands, securing an alliance with another clan so that his forces might be increased in the battles against his enemy.

They were just breaking camp early one morning, unhobbling the horses and setting saddles atop their backs, when a horseman appeared. Morgan set aside his cup of coffee and took up his rifle, then walked out to meet the rider, who he quickly recognized as a servant of Sid Boazzin's. After exchanging hearty greetings, the fellow delivered Gwen's letter, which Morgan did not open until the messenger had gone to share coffee with the men. The tall chieftain strolled off alone then, his eyes surveying the landscape in the instinctive sweep that had been his habit since boyhood, and unconsciously learned from his father as the first rule of survival. Assured that no unwelcome company approached from any direction, he halted upon a rise and broke the seal upon the letter.

Morgan. I have returned to the Hotel la Villa de France. I must see you. Please come with all speed to Tangier. The reason is more urgent than I'm prepared to put down on paper. Gwenllian

For a moment Morgan contemplated the lines, then raised his eyes to stare unseeing at the distant mountains tinted palest purple. The morning air ruffled his garments and tossed strands of hair across his brow, but for once he was unaware of any motion or sound surrounding him. He was engrossed with thoughts of Gwenllian, and speculating upon the significance of her message.

Did she intend to be his wife?

The possibility brought him such unreasoned happiness that he closed his eyes and savored it. These past weeks he had seen her face behind every veil and in the mirages that shimmered above the sands like long-limbed wraiths. He saw it at night in dreams so sensual he had to clamp his teeth in order not to groan her name aloud. He had sought distraction by pushing himself and his men to longer rides with less rest, and by plotting battles and eluding the sultan's army, all to little purpose. Remembrance of Gwenllian clung to him until he felt he would go mad with its haunting. Every day he cursed it, and cursed himself for yielding his imagination to it. Having indulged only in the carnal attachments of early manhood, he had never experienced the deeper wound of Cupid's dart before. But the allure of the Welsh girl had struck

217

him hard. Although not prone to fancy, he had realized that Gwenllian's nature answered some calling in his, and set out to have her. Untutored by tender emotion, bred to fight ruthlessly in the Berber tradition, he had been unprepared for the intensity of feeling that accompanied the hurried courtship. Through the course of it, he felt as if he had fallen from some great height, then soared to heaven, only to plummet downward again.

He fingered the letter in his hand. For a time he had believed Gwenllian loved him enough to abandon her home and live the Berber life, just as his mother had done for his father. Of course, Marian had suffered for her sacrifice. As a child Morgan had seen her take out keepsakes from the past and weep over them in private. The sound of her crying had wrenched him, and it was that memory that had caused him to release Gwen from her vows, when by rights he could have forced her to stay with him and fulfil the duties of a wife.

Still, he had been bitterly disappointed over her decision to go. It was not until he had ridden hellbent across the plains of Morocco and beheld again his beloved mountains that he been able to forgive her for her desertion. For what was he without his country? His soul was here, his purpose. And Gwenllian's were in a place called Wales. The two of them shared a strange and compelling affinity, but as misfortune would have it, they were born of different worlds.

Folding the letter, Morgan turned about. He would hope for a reconciliation, hope that Gwenllian had returned with a vow to be his wife.

But experience had taught him to be a cautious man in human relationships, and he would not hope too hard.

The weeks spent waiting at the hotel were the most tedious Gwen had ever endured. There was little to occupy her time, for she hardly cared to brave the squalid streets to find diversion. Even Robyn proved a poor companion, for he had fallen in with a group of rowdy London blades who spent their days playing cards and frequenting the famous British drink shops which the natives called the scourge of the infidels. There was no female company in the hotel, and with thoughts of her father's fate and Morgan's return harrowing her peace, she could do little each day but fret.

One afternoon, as she idly picked at a tray of dates, Gwen was startled to hear a rap upon the door. Assuming Robyn had taken a sojourn from his carousing, she called for him to enter, only to find the porter peeking round the door with a message in his hand. Breaking open its envelope, she read.

I await you at Sid Boazzin's villa. Morgan.

Her heart thumped. He had come!

Yanking a hat from its peg, Gwen rushed out, only to recross the threshold when her vanity called her back. Consulting the mirror, she found her face drawn and her mouth pale, and ran her teeth over her bottom lip to draw out its deeper color. The heat had made tendrils of hair curl about her cheeks, but too impatient to rearrange the heavy chignon, she set the straw hat atop her head in an artful tilt.

She would have preferred to go alone to see Morgan, but as she hastened through the lobby a moment later Robyn caught sight of her and, after learning her mission, insisted upon escorting her. His excuse, he stated, was to protect her from the unsafe streets, but privately Gwen thought he nursed some jealous notion of chaperoning her in Morgan's presence.

Some time later they were admitted into the courtyard of Sid Boazzin's villa, and with anxious eyes Gwen glanced about its colonnaded square. It was tranquil and empty. The fountain splashed, and sunlight turned its trembling drops into necklaces of molten gold. She twisted her hands, yearning to see the man who was still her husband, but afraid of her own response at the confrontation. If his manner were warm and familiar could she keep from rushing forward with her arms outstretched? She had the insane notion that she might do just that, that she might forget wisdom and agree to be his wife in spite of all the reasons she could not. On the other hand, if Morgan behaved coldly, as if he had never shared with her any intimacy, would she be too shattered to speak?

All at once, beneath the shade of the portico, the glint of light upon polished metal caught her eye. She pivoted. Morgan was standing beside one of the pillars, and she guessed that he had been there all along, watching her in his observant way. Her eyes consumed him, catching impressions of a chiseled chin and jaw, a shadowed throat, and an angular cheekbone sharply defined. He wore his native attire without the *haik*, the hood of his chestnut burnoose lying down about his shoulders so that his head was bare. A sheathed sword hung from his hip and its ornate hilt reflected shards of sun in bright pinpoints of silver.

She felt as if her heart quivered in his hands. Her calm fled, and some instinctive urge told her to run to him, promising that if she were brave enough to seek it, happiness dwelled in the strength of his arms.

But seeing him in his native dress with a sword at his side caused her to remember who he was, remember the lifestyle that he had chosen.

His eyes scrutinized every aspect of her appearance with thoroughness, until she knew he could have described the fashionable hat and the clothes she wore in minutest detail. She tried to read his expression and glean his thoughts, but could not. After a few seconds his gaze flickered over Robyn's dapper, stiffly held figure, then returned to rest upon her face again, which blushed to a delicate tint of rose.

"Gwenllian, Lord Breese," he acknowledged quietly with his usual self-possession. Strolling into the full glare of sunlight, the sword swaying at his side, he looked directly at Gwen. "I've traveled many miles to get here, with as much speed as possible. I hope I've not come too late."

The sound of his voice affected her, touched her even more deeply than she had feared. She wanted to be alone with him. The veins in her temples throbbed and she felt faint with both heat and emotion. "Robyn," she breathed, her eyes affixed to Morgan's. "Please leave us for a while."

The earl glanced from Gwen's strained countenance to the eyes of the Berber, which were narrow blue slashes beneath lowered brows. "I hardly think—"

"Please, Robyn."

At the agitation in Gwen's voice the young aristocrat hesitated, feeling as if he fought a battle in which he had been given no weapons. Loath to provoke a confrontation and appear the loser again, he shrugged his rigid shoulders and, with a hostile parting glance at Morgan, retreated to cool his heels upon the street.

His footsteps faded, leaving a hush behind. The fountain trilled, and a fly hummed, circling the mossy lip of the brimming basin where patches of thyme flourished on spilled moisture. Gwen wetted her lips with her tongue and looked at Morgan. Pain swelled beneath her breastbone. All at once she wanted to admit to him that she had been lonely, admit that unhappiness and regret sat like a stone upon her heart. But as she examined the sober visage of the man before her, she detected no invitation for such a tender unburdening, no yielding of his features.

"Are . . . are you well?" she asked just to break the silence, for no man could look more fit and healthy than Morgan Riff.

His eyes glistened at the break in her voice but he spoke like a stranger. "Quite well, thank you. And you?"

She nodded, swept her lashes down, and clenched

her hands over a fold in her flowered skirt. "I—I know I haven't a right to impose a favor, Morgan, but—" She dipped her head, then reached into her pocket and drew out the envelope from Sir Gerald. "I received this from my father nearly five weeks ago. You'll see there's a message for you enclosed, written in Arabic. I don't know what it says, of course—I felt I could trust no one to interpret it but you." She extended the wrinkled envelope, which trembled with the unsteadiness of her fingers.

Morgan's hand did not touch hers as he reached out to take it. With jangled nerves Gwen searched his face while he read, studying the dark features with trepidation as she sought a clue to her father's predicament. But his expression remained impassive.

She could not know that he struggled with his own emotions. He had ridden hard for two weeks, snatched no more than three or four hours of sleep a night and nearly ruined his horse. Looking like some bearded ruffian, he had galloped directly to Sid Boazzin's house and begged a hasty bath and shave before sending for Gwenllian. As he had awaited her, his heart had thundered, for optimism had gotten the better of him during the long journey to Tangier. But the instant he had seen her slide a quivering hand into the pocket of her summer gown and withdraw the envelope, his hopes had been dashed. She had not come back to be his wife.

For a moment he kept his eyes fixed to the letter so that she could not see them, and when he spoke no trace of heartbreak marked his voice. "Your father's message is unsettling."

"What does it say?" she asked anxiously. "Surely I'm entitled to know."

"Your father likely wrote in Arabic so that you would not be upset—"

"But I am upset. And I should not have to be protected from whatever it is he has written."

"No, you should not." He considered her for a second. "Although the contents of the letter aren't pleasant, I daresay your father doesn't give you enough credit. When circumstances demand it, you can be quite stoical."

At the ruefulness of his tone, her brow arched. "Thank you very much."

Morgan returned the letter. Careful not to touch his fingers, she took it, then slid it slowly back inside her pocket with a long and sinuous hand. The motion stirred the thin fabric of her skirt, rippled it about her shoes and revealed a froth of lace petticoat the color of raw meringue. The sun streamed through it transparently, streamed through the loose weave of her straw hat brim and sprinkled her cheeks and mouth with dots of shifting light. He felt sick with desire, and dragged his eyes away.

"According to the letter," he explained in a tightened voice, "your father has been captured by a tribe of men called the Zemours. I regret to say they are an unsavory band of scoundrels. He gives the location where he was captured, but likely the tribe was on the move, traveling fast. It's my guess he bribed one of them to send this letter."

"Captured?" Gwen cried. "Here in Tangier?

Could these—these Zemours have been so bold as to simply sweep Papa off the street and ride away with him?"

"He was not taken here, but in a place called Mequinez."

"Where is that?" she asked, fear making her voice quaver.

"Some distance away. I warned him not to go without my escort, but after our . . . falling out, I suppose he ignored my cautions."

"I understand none of this!" she exclaimed. "What in heaven's name was he doing wandering about Morocco?"

Morgan crossed his arms and leaned back against the pillar. A sunray slanted across his shoulders and made a pool of lemon at his boots, which were covered with a fine film of dust from his gallop over the plains. "He was spying on the French."

"What?"

"Don't judge him too harshly. All men have their causes, and Sir Gerald fancied himself loyal to his country. It's my understanding he's been making government maps for years, ever since he sailed with the Royal Navy."

"But what was Papa doing in Morocco? The French are not here."

"Ah, but the French are in possession of Algeria, and may have designs upon Morocco as well, especially since our esteemed sultan is so ineffectual at running his country. Britain isn't quite certain she wants Morocco to fall into French hands, because her own interests in Gibraltar may be threatened as a consequence. At any rate, your father and Car-

225

stairs were compiling charts of French telegraph and cable lines along the Algerian border. They were also documenting information on the state of the sultan's military. Unfortunately, instead of relying solely upon the intelligence I provided him, Sir Gerald made a few trips on his own."

Gwen took a moment to assimilate the information before pinning her eyes to Morgan's. "And what was your reason for helping them?"

"I'm afraid my motives were not quite so patriotic as your father's and the colonel's. At the risk you'll think less of me than you already do," he quipped with a wry smile, "I'll explain my reasons. But I'd appreciate it if you didn't spread them about Tangier like your friend Breese once threatened to do. I wouldn't want the sultan to grow any more disenchanted with me than he already is."

"You can be certain of my discretion, of course," she answered tersely, offended that he would feel it necessary to suggest otherwise. "And Robyn will say nothing."

"Very well. Your father has made it his business to keep track of me since my childhood visit to Hiraeth. Colonel Carstairs and the British Embassy are acquainted with me as well, and agreed that I could help them chart French activities. They knew I'd be able to travel freely around Morocco without suspicion. Having no care one way or another for British and French politics, I agreed to aid them, for a price."

Gwen raised a finely sketched brow. "And what price was that?"

"A supply of arms for my men, and money to finance my interests."

"Your *wars*, you mean."

Unmoved by her censure, he raised his eyes to watch a stork gliding on the air above the courtyard. In a flutter of wings, it descended and, after a wary glance, sauntered upon sticklike legs to steal a drink from the fountain. "They're sacred here, you know," Morgan commented. "Storks, I mean. The Moors believe the birds carry the souls of their ancestors."

Gwen looked at the inelegant creature with no interest. "Where do you think my father is, Morgan?"

He shook his head. "I don't know. The Zemour tribe is nomadic. They could be anywhere in Morocco."

"Do you believe he's alive?" She spoke with reluctance, and steeled herself for the answer.

"I'd rather not speculate. Actually, I think there's a very good chance that the Zemours are trying to find a way to ransom him."

"But who would be willing to ransom him other than his relatives or the government? I've not been contacted. And the Embassy has flatly denied acquaintance with him."

Morgan lifted a shoulder. "Governments are only as loyal as prudence permits. As for a ransom, let's not theorize now. The thing to do is to find Sir Gerald as soon as possible."

"And, you're willing to do that . . . ?"

He did not answer immediately. The stork abandoned the courtyard, leaving one white feather behind, which seesawed on the air and landed in the rippling water of the basin. Round and round it swirled like a tiny rudderless craft. Hunkering down, Morgan balanced on the balls of his feet and retrieved the bedraggled token, brushing the wet white tip of it over his palm. Gwen watched the play of the long fingers for a moment, then took a small step toward him, her shoe scraping upon a pebble.

He glanced at her from beneath his brows, stood up, and dropped the feather. Assuming he was on the verge of refusing, Gwen blurted out a plea. "I know it's much to ask of you, Morgan—under the circumstances. You have every right to refuse. But, will you please help me?"

He kept his gaze upon her pale parted lips. "I'm offended that you think there's a chance I would not."

"I'm sorry," she murmured with pain in her eyes. A tiny green lizard skittered between her feet and darted into the moss at the fountain's edge, and she made a pretense of watching it. "It's just that . . . well, that I feel we're such strangers. Despite all that's passed between us."

Morgan leaned his head back as if to study the sky, which was only bare and blue. "I'll set out tomorrow in an effort to locate your father. It might take weeks, even months. I'd advise you to return to Wales and await word there, but I'm sure you'd only refuse. Perhaps you can rent a villa here in Tangier for the duration."

Gwen stared at him. "Surely you don't believe I would consent to stay behind? Why, I've nearly gone mad with the waiting as it is! I'm not about to languish in Tangier, on tenterhooks, while you do the searching for Papa alone. I expect to accompany you—under your conditions, of course. I wouldn't want to be a hindrance."

Morgan made a derisive sound. "You've scarcely been able to withstand the savagery, as you call it, in Tangier. Let me assure you, it's the most civilized place in the country."

"I understand that—"

"No, you do not understand that," he cut in. "You don't understand that in some parts of Morocco Europeans are slain simply for being Europeans, and that there are bands of robbers in the interior who kill human beings with no more compunction than they kill game. The dangers are far greater than you can imagine."

She locked her gaze with his. "And yet, you were prepared to take me there as your wife."

"A proposition which you flatly refused as I recall. I find it a contradiction that you are so willing to brave it now."

"The circumstances are quite different," she argued. "I would have had to abandon every safe and familiar thing I've ever known in order to spend my life with you."

"Precisely." Somehow the inflection of the word undermined her choice.

Feeling as if she were losing ground, able to think of no words with which to persuade him, Gwen despaired. The heat was stifling, and she stepped back a few feet beneath the shade, fearing she would faint. At such a sign of weakness Morgan would never let her accompany him. Reaching to drag the hat from her hair, she used it as a fan, waving it to and fro across her face with a lively sway of her wrist. Spirals of hair danced about her cheeks and she tilted her head back so that the air could cool the flushed length of her neck.

Although he was experienced with women, Gwen's gesture was so natural, so casually feminine, that Morgan could not decide if it had been an unconscious act or a coquettish ploy. Regardless, he found himself stirred to the point of distraction, drunk with her sensuousness. Her elegance in the pale flowered green gown, the lustre of heat upon her brow, and the slant of her half-closed eyes beneath the round, graceful hat brim all combined to test his reason. He told himself that if he took her across Morocco, he would be able to spend weeks in her company, see her every dawn upon waking and every dusk before retiring. Despite her objections and his own good judgment, in the deepest part of his being he still believed that she belonged with him.

"Very well," he said looking into her eyes with no trace of his yearning revealed. "I'll allow you to come. Provided you do as I say."

He thought for a moment that she would press his hand in gratefulness, for she extended her fingers in a spontaneous jerk, then drew them back to clutch at the beribboned hat dangling from her other hand.

"And Robyn . . . ?" she asked. "He'll insist upon going with us. You have no objections, do you?"

For the first time Morgan suffered jealousy toward the other man, a rival he had heretofore dismissed as no serious competitor for Gwenllian's affections. The sting of it pierced his belly and made the muscles tense.

"Very well," he returned with an edge in his tone. "But dress him as a Moor and make him keep his mouth shut. Otherwise, I'll feed him to the natives without a qualm."

Twelve

They were to depart from Tangier at dawn. In semidarkness Gwen fumbled about her hotel room, attempting to properly arrange the strange bundle of clothing that Morgan had had delivered last night. There was a white undergarment with a drawstring at the throat, then another shapeless drape to wear atop it, which was of fine embroidered linen fastened with countless soft buttons that slipped into loops. A silk belt completed the ensemble, except for ten yards of *haik*, which she inexpertly wound about her head and shoulders. She was sorry to abandon her comfortable walking boots for the less substantial red leather slippers Moorish women wore and, in a fit of defiance, refused, stuffing the flimsy footwear back into the bag she had packed.

She walked to the mirror and peered at herself in the dim lamplight. What a transformation the clothing had wrought! Drawing the *haik* over her face so that only her eyes showed, she thought Gwenllian of Wales could have been any one of the shy, mysterious females gliding through the native streets. She glanced down at an object in her hand, a silver container engraved with an elaborate arabesque. It seemed ages ago that she had admired it in the souk, but Morgan had obviously noticed her interest and purchased the jar of kohl as a gift. It had been carefully nestled in silver paper and wrapped in the *haik*.

Almost reluctant to convert herself into the species of woman she pitied, she applied the black paint, using the small pointed brush that had come attached to it. Her rendering was clumsy and slow, but achieved the usual beguiling effect by elongating the shape of her eyes. She stared at herself. The strangeness of her image disturbed her, and she turned away from it.

Even though he wore his costume with all the scrupulous correctness that he would a Bond Street suit, Lord Breese made an unlikely Moor. She suspected he had called in the porter to aid his toilette, for, unlike her *haik*, the folds of his own were meticulously arranged and did not slide off his shoulders. When they hurried out of the lobby together just as morning shimmered over the horizon, Robyn even managed to walk as if he had been accustomed to wearing the voluminous drapes for years.

Morgan had sent horses for them, along with a muleteer who strapped their bags on a packsaddle and bade them follow him through streets where huddles of Moors were rousing from their slumber. Just beyond the massive city gates the Berbers and their chieftain awaited in an ordered assembly.

There were a dozen in all, Gwen counted, each astride a vigorous horse and all well armed with rifles. The band members made a handsome spectacle in their chestnut garments cinched with wide crimson belts, and their mounts sported ornate saddles and bridles festooned with colored tassels.

Gwen recognized one of the group. He was the red-haired Berber who had rescued her from the rider with the scarred eyelid on her outing at the fruit market. She realized that, without her knowledge, Morgan must have sent an escort with her each time she had ventured out of the Carstairses' house. But why? Had he known then that she was not safe? Were his enemies now her enemies, just by her association with him?

"His name is Hassan," Morgan commented, noting the direction of her gaze as he reined his stallion close.

"I've seen him before, in the fruit market."

She hoped for an explanation, but he gave none. Instead, his eyes swept over her kohl-painted lids with an assessing regard, then moved down to peruse the native garb she wore with so little grace. She lowered her lashes, feeling uncomfortable in the strange clothes, feeling out of place amidst the stark landscape which seemed so befitting to Morgan's nature.

Leaning over his saddle, he rearranged her *haik* with an expert touch until it rested naturally across her shoulders and did not slip down to impede the movement of her arms. She wondered if he liked her outfitted in the way of the native women he had been raised to admire, but when she risked a glance at his face, she found it unreadable in the soft apricot light.

A huddle of beggars had gathered amidst the Berber party, and the collection of blind, lame, and leprous wretches was so appalling that Gwen could hardly look at them. Hastily she withdrew coins from the small purse attached to her belt and tossed them into the poor withered hands, which only stretched out for more. Robyn dispersed them with a few threatening swipes of his riding crop.

"I say, Riff," he addressed their leader, shifting upon the hard Moorish saddle. "Just where are we going today?"

Morgan reined his horse about. "Toward Fez. We'll be traveling fast. If you can't spend ten hours a day in a saddle I suggest you say so now."

"I daresay I can ride as well as any one of this group. Yourself included."

Morgan's mouth twisted. "Then see that you do."

The party set out without delay after that, Morgan assuming the lead, drawing up the hood of his burnoose to protect his head from the dust and the increasing fire of the sun. There were no roads out of Tangier, only crude tracks, but the hard ugly furrows were at least relieved by borders of cacti, aloes, and palms. Streamlets abounded, too, their yellow clay banks covered in anemones and gentians, and the sea breeze swept away the lingering odors of habitation. Infrequently they passed mud huts and the desolate ruins of battlements, but little else suggested civilization in the undulating hills except for one or two shepherds playing pipes for their grazing charges.

Gwen took a deep breath, wondering where this trek through the wilds of Morocco would lead them, wondering what circumstances her father endured, and wondering what sort of exotic locales and unimaginable perils would be encountered in the effort to find him. Touching the coarse mane of her mare, she murmured a prayer that all would be well, hoping that the experience would at least provide a key to help her understand Morgan's love for this land.

Staring ahead at his stalwart outline astride the copper steed, she recalled the day the two of them had enjoyed the horse fair, and then remembered with a bitter smile how she had believed their relationship would end happily with a return to Hiraeth. Instead, she rode behind the Berber chieftain over a sun-baked goat track, while her father's life hung upon the whim of a band of native thieves.

Morgan did not ride with her, but kept well ahead and pushed their pace. The heat scorched the earth as they journeyed. Gwen had never felt temperatures so hot, and grew grateful for the lightweight *haik,* which protected her cheeks from a dreadful burn. Robyn's equally fair complexion was already roasting, for he disdained to cover his face. But in spite of his discomfort, he kept up a cavalier front, occasionally drawing out a flask and downing gulps of brandy.

By late afternoon, Gwen was wearier than she would have dreamed possible, and began to fear that Morgan would never allow them to stop for the night. Although she was an accomplished equestrienne, she was not used to riding astride for endless hours. But in spite of her aching muscles and the grueling heat, she did not complain; she would prefer to suffer agonies rather than hinder their progress to find her father.

They met no one upon the road except herders driving their animals to market. Having expected demon riders like those in Tangier, who would swoop down upon them in ambush, Gwen relaxed during the course of the day. She soon grew to trust completely the keen eyes of Morgan Riff, whose vigilance never waned. If he put his water flask to his lips and drank, or conversed with one of his men, his scrutiny of the landscape never ceased. Nor was his rifle out of easy reach.

At dusk, he finally held up an arm to halt their progress, and within minutes the men were unpacking tents, setting poles, and fastening halyards to the pegs. Camel-hair mats were removed from the mules' backs and laid down as pallets inside the canvas dwellings, and a fire was started with dried palm leaves, upon which stones were heated. Gwen saw Hassan tend the fire, prepare the meal and, after kneading barley dough, make cakes of it, which he set upon the stones and baked. She yearned to express her gratitude for his rescue in the fruit market, but he avoided her glances with studious determination, leaving her to conclude that his faith kept him from making social contact with a woman whose face was unveiled. Either that, or he judged it unwise to converse with the chieftain's female.

Besides bread, plenty of dried fruits and cheeses were served at dinner. Gwen and Robyn squatted down upon the sand close to the fire and ate alone after the Berbers formed their own convivial circle. Morgan joined neither party, but remained on watch. Gwen followed him with her eyes as he strolled away from camp, watched his tall form leave the glaze of firelight to be silhouetted against a fading sky. Leaning upon the breech of his rifle in a brooding pose, he considered the vastness of the country that surrounded him.

Gwen considered it, too, looked at the plateaus whose shapes resembled crouching dinosaurs, and at the clouds leaping off the horizon like pouncing lions. The ageless landscape seemed to swallow her up, and she shivered, drawing closer to Robyn, wishing that she could draw closer to Morgan instead. He had not spoken to her all day.

The worship hour came, proclaimed by no one but instinctively realized by all. Not for the first time, she noted that only a handful of the Berbers took out their prayer rugs and prostrated themselves. The others, Morgan included, gave the holy silence due respect, but showed no particular piousness.

Tiredly, Gwen bade Robyn good night and entered the tent that Hassan had designated as her own. A candle and a copper urn of water awaited her there, and removing the dusty *haik,* she set about trying to wash the grime and perspiration from her skin, wincing as she passed fingers over her tender nose. Her hair she unbound and let fall, too tired to fish a brush from her bag and untangle it. She tried to imagine herself living this way as Morgan's wife, traipsing over the Moroccan earth bearing children along the way, but failed to conjure up more than a blurred half-dream.

She heard the strum of a gimbri, the guitarlike instrument she had heard played many times in Tangier. Its melody proved a dolorous one that suited her mood. She lay down and, finding the camel-hair mat a hard bed, raised up again to sit with her chin propped upon her palm. Sighing, she listened to the plaintive music, and smelled the odor of the coarse grass squashed beneath her mat as it mingled with the Spanish *kif* the Berbers smoked. Feeling miserable and alone, she thought how every scent, every sound and vision were alien to those she knew and loved. She wished for home.

Suddenly the flap of her tent was thrust aside and Morgan ducked beneath the opening, his eyes fastening to hers with their usual concentration. She was so grateful to see him that she almost cried out his name. He seemed equally moved, for the hard line of his mouth softened at the sight of her.

The tent was only five feet high, and he bent down. Balancing on his heels, he extended a hand and offered her a green glass jar. "Lotion for your nose," he said.

With a shy smile, she thanked him and applied the soothing balm. He followed the motion of her fingers with his eyes until a self-conscious blush rose to her cheeks. "Just as well I didn't bring a mirror," she murmured with a nervous laugh. "Unsightly, I guess . . ."

"On the contrary."

His words, spoken with such blunt admiration, served to put an intimacy between them, and although Gwen longed for intimacy, she knew to encourage it was a foolish and hopeless urge.

Morgan caught the direction of her thoughts. Gwenllian desired him, but at the same time desired more strongly an avoidance of the entanglement that the physical act would bring. He believed that if he were to take her in his arms and hold her there, she would be subdued with little effort. But he did not want to subdue her; he wanted her to come to him in willingness. He let his eyes wander over her slender form. He looked at her hands as they recorked the lotion. He looked at her legs. They were tucked beneath her, and their graceful curve beneath the white burnoose reminded him of a pair of swans' necks.

"We'll go toward Arzilah tomorrow," he said, forcing his eyes back to her sunburnt face. "It'll be a hard trip, but there are people along the way who might know where to find the Zemour tribe. If we're fortunate, we may even hear rumors of your father."

"Will we be crossing the desert?"

"No. The Sahara is south of Fez, beyond the Atlas range."

The Atlas range . . . his home . . . the land that separated the two of them.

A silence fell and they listened to the sound of rain as it pattered over the hard dirt outside. The gimbri player ceased his song with an abrupt twanging of strings, and the storm began in earnest, making the canvas overhead shiver and bounce.

"Hail," Morgan commented, raising his eyes toward the ceiling.

"Hail?"

"Quite common this time of year."

"Oh." Gwen nodded, then searched for something else to say. She felt awkward sitting so close to the man who was still her husband, but not really her husband. He sat with one knee upraised and a forearm draped across it; the other leg was stretched out, angled across the edge of her mat. Rather than look at it, she contemplated the jar of lotion in her hand.

The minutes stretched by and the tent shook with wind, but Morgan seemed in no hurry to leave. Shifting slightly, he pulled a small bag of pistachio nuts from his pocket, and after shaking a few in his palm, offered them to her.

She shook her head, then changed her mind and scooped them up. "Why is it some of your men do not pray with the others?" she asked, chewing. "I thought it was required of all the faithful."

"We're on the move most of the time and it's inconvenient to perform the religious rituals. But if you ask the men, all of them will tell you that their hearts are pure, and that they despise all enemies to Islam—Europeans, Americans, anyone who is not traditionally of their faith."

"Then, how is it they do not despise you for your mother's blood?"

"They respect me more for my father's. In Morocco, the man who is most deadly with a rifle and sword earns the greatest esteem, grudging or not."

"And you are more deadly than any?"

At the slight edge of censure in her tone he closed his fist over the nutshells. "I have survived."

241

"You could have *survived* at Hiraeth without ever having to fire a rifle."

He raised his eyes, and they were dark with both reproof and honesty. "No, Gwen. I could not have survived."

She studied the frayed tassels sewn to the sash around her waist and twisted them between her fingers. "Are you certain?"

He dropped the nutshells in the sand, and they scattered, wobbling like tiny ships in the sand. Lifting his eyes to Gwen's, he stared straight into them with a grave and unswerving message. "I'm certain.

She watched him stand up and open the tent flap then, and exit into the night, amidst the hailstones.

In spite of her exhaustion, Gwen managed to snatch only an hour or two of sleep, for the lack of simple creature comforts kept her tossing. The rain continued its unrelenting cadence, sending rivulets of water snaking beneath the tent bottom while the wind threatened to make the shelter airborne, so that men came to pound its pegs deeper into the earth with heavy mallets. She shivered with cold as well, drawing the wool blanket over her aching bones until its weave prickled and she had to shove it off again. Finally, she sat up, waiting for the empty blackness and the howling wind to pass while she thought of Morgan.

The morning dawned clear and fresh smelling, and after a hastily snatched breakfast of coffee and hard rolls, the party set out. Many travelers plodded along the trail, and with interest Gwen noted the lines of country folk herding their bony-framed oxen and donkeys. The men were stalwart and tough-skinned while the youthful, unveiled girls strode along with the grace of deer, their foreheads tattooed and their hair plaited in braids joined at the back. Most of them offered something for sale. Holding out eggs or bundles of wood, they ran up to Morgan's horse and, with white smiles set in tawny faces, implored him to buy. Invariably, he obliged.

About midday the group arrived at a wide, swollen river. It swirled palm leaves and rotted logs like spinning tops, and foamed about the jagged rocks that straddled its middle. In resignation, the men began removing the heavy supplies from the backs of the mules and wrapping them in canvas before tying them securely with rope.

"There's a ferry downstream," Morgan told Gwen, "but it's miles out of our way. We'll have to ford here. It's the shallowest point."

She looked at the wildly dashing river, then back at him.

"Just keep a cool head and put your mare to it," he said calmly, as if she had no reason to feel anxious. "When she reaches swimming depth, slide off the saddle so you don't weigh her down. Keep hold of her tail and let her tow you across. Understand?"

Despite her uncertainty, Gwen nodded, determined not to slow their progress. Reaching to grasp her reins to tug the reluctant mare forward, Morgan spurred his stallion to the shoreline. The mare slithered down the muddy descent to follow his lead. Gwen glanced back at Robyn, who appeared put out with the daunting prospect of this new ordeal. But after fortifying himself with courage from the silver flask, he dug his heels into his horse's sides.

When the rushing water reached the level of her thighs, Gwen tensed and prepared for a complete dousing. It happened suddenly as the mare found herself without purchase on the soft river bottom. But after floundering for a moment, the valiant beast began to swim with a strong stride. As Morgan had advised, Gwen slipped off the saddle to relieve the animal of added weight, but the current was so forceful that she was nearly swept away before her hands could grasp a strand of the flowing tail. Battling to keep her chin above water, she looked for Morgan and found his dark head breaking the surface a few yards away. He inhaled a breath and kept his eyes upon hers as their horses struggled to maintain a steady course.

Upstream, one of the men lost his grip upon a bundle of stores wrapped in canvas, and no one could rescue the precious cargo. The torrent whirled the bundle toward Gwen, and extending her free arm, she managed to clutch its trailing rope. But the wet fibers unraveled and snapped loose, so that she had to dive forward in a second attempt.

She caught the rope again, but as she twisted to wind it more securely about her hand, she lost her hold upon the mare's tail. The weight of her garments and the boiling torrent sucked her down immediately. Water filled her mouth, and although she thrashed about to find something stationary to grasp, no anchor came her way. She and the bundle glided pell-mell downstream, tumbled about in the rough white water. She gasped and fought desperately to surface.

Just as she believed herself lost, an arm encircled her neck and dragged her up. Resisting an impulse to drape her body over the stronger one, she relaxed and allowed herself to be towed along, her fingers still frozen about the trailing rope. At last, warm air touched her face and she again had plenty to breathe. Clutching Morgan's shoulders, she staggered, trying to stand up in the clinging burnoose.

"Easy," he said, supporting her weight as she sputtered and choked. "You needn't prove yourself to anyone. Take a rest."

"Riff!" Lord Breese shouted, stumbling forward to join them in his sodden clothes. "You should never have expected her to cross such a dangerous stretch! She nearly drowned, for God's sake. You can't continue to put her through such ordeals. She's a lady, not some Moorish peasant bred in a thatched hovel. Or don't you know the difference?"

Morgan had been about to shoulder the bundle of supplies Gwen had saved, but at the earl's scathing words, he halted. Then, with his eyes glinting, he tossed the cumbersome burden across the mud so that it landed with a thud at Robyn's boots. "I know the difference between an ass and a man. Carry it."

For once, Gwen was grateful for the heat. It dried her soaking garments and took the chill from her body. She even disdained the use of the *haik*, drawing its folds down off her head so that her hair would dry in the arid wind. Since Morgan's men rode behind her now in double columns, she thought nothing of uncovering her face for a while.

Up ahead, Morgan glanced over his shoulder to check the pace of those behind him. Spying her, his eyes narrowed, and within a second the expression on his face altered into a harder look. He reined his stallion around in a churn of hooves and drew it up beside the mare.

"Get your head covered."

Piqued over such a blunt address, Gwen thought to challenge him, but upon meeting his eyes decided to hold her tongue. He was jealous. She had no doubt of it. The chieftain wanted no other male eyes to tarry upon the hair he himself would like leave to touch.

She returned his stare, letting him know with a sweep of her lashes that she had read his envy. Then she lifted her hair and let its shiny masses slither down into the folds of her hood, before slowly sliding up the *haik* to conceal all but her eyes from his gaze.

The sere land through which they passed was hilly, barren except for isolated clusters of cork trees which shaded crumbling ruins and rude farms. The shimmering heat intensified until breathing became a chore. Sweat darkened the hides of the animals and lathered girths and bits. Miserable, Gwen looked without interest at the tufts of wild daisies withering in the torrid breeze and, closing her eyes, tried to picture the rain in Wales.

When she opened her stinging lids again, a group of horsemen formed a line along the top of a distant ridge. A half dozen strong, the band sat motionless, watching the progress of Morgan's party with their rifle butts braced against their stirrups. Although they made no move to advance, the very stillness of their posture was intimidating.

Morgan halted his horse. For several moments he sat in his saddle and returned the regard of the distant leader, and although the space separating the two men was considerable, bridged by the vast field of drooping flowers, the air vibrated with a sudden hostile tension.

With a drumming heart Gwen looked from Morgan's straight back to the other menacing form poised upon the ridge, afraid that the straining stillness would shatter into violence at any second. But after a moment, Morgan gave a curt signal to his men to continue on their way. Each one of them, she noticed, carried his rifle with more alertness. Fretful, she continued to look over her shoulder until the ominous line of watching horsemen retreated in the opposite direction.

"I wonder who the deuce they were?" Robyn mused, nudging his horse close to hers. "Uncivil-looking band."

She agreed, unable to shake uneasiness; in her short experience with Morocco, she had learned to expect little else but incivility.

Awhile later they approached a town, and at first she thought the place appeared quaint with its lime-washed walls and flat roofs. Painted arabesques decorated its huge white gateway, which shone with a pristine brightness in the harsh light. But as she neared, she saw that the walls were crumbling like all their Moroccan sisters, undermined by a deteriorating foundation and the insidious roots of an ancient clematis vine.

Without a word exchanged, two members of Morgan's band veered from the group to post themselves like sentries at either side of the gate, while the rest paraded through in single file. After passing beneath the horseshoe arches, they entered the streets to find dilapidation everywhere. Gwen grimaced. The amount of decay and rubbish was worse than in Tangier, and the reek stronger, perhaps because the heat was more brutal here and sharpened the rotting odors. At the sight of the black open sewers, piles of old rags and shattered furniture eroding in the arid weather, her stomach rebelled.

And the children! Naked and potbellied, they scurried about on spindly legs, begging for money in shrill voices and plucking at Morgan's stirrups. Adults sat upon the pavement smoking or telling the beads of their Islamic rosaries, and watched the newcomers through slitted eyes, making no move to rouse themselves in the heat. Lepers squatted in huddles beneath trellises of barren grapevines, and in the middle of the street a wizened seer told fortunes with a collection of tiny shells.

The souk they entered sold the usual goods of the country, but all pretense of hygiene was abandoned. Opened containers of sugar swarmed with wasps, fruit lay in broken crates unprotected from the dust, and the butcher hacked away at a sheep carcass with his clothes covered in blood.

"Ghastly, isn't it?" Robyn commented, wiping his brow with a monogrammed handkerchief. The party halted and he swung a leg over the saddle, still contemplating the appalling sights. "Unspeakable filth. Far worse than Tangier. Look there—the shops are little more than caves and the houses have no doors. Odd that there are so many broken plows lying about in the streets. I wonder why no one bothers to mend them."

"Probably because it's too hot," Gwen groaned, dabbing at her fiery cheeks.

Robyn helped her dismount with a shaking hand, and she feared that he was in worse condition than she. His skin felt clammy and his face was swollen with the heat.

"Go stand under the shade," she advised worriedly. "And get something to drink."

Obediently, he strolled off for the shade of a portico and, after taking out his silver flask, drank from it with one boot propped upon the mouth of an eroding Spanish cannon.

The Berbers sought refreshment in the souk. They bought tea from huge urns and had no qualms about buying the spitted mutton roasted on open fires. Morgan bought lemons and water from a water seller who wore Medusa-like braids and carried a goatskin vessel. With distaste Gwen noticed that the hairy shape of the container still resembled its previous owner. But clear water trickled from it, caught in shining copper cups. Balancing the brimming containers in his hands, Morgan approached her.

"Step back into the shade," he said gently, escorting her to a tattered awning. "You look as if you're about to faint at my boots."

She pulled the *haik* away from her mouth and drank the water he gave her greedily, for it was cooler and less bitter than the dregs in her canteen. Finally, after wiping her lips with her sleeve, she leaned back against a chalky wall and closed her eyes.

"Gwen . . . ?" Morgan asked in concern, reaching to put an arm about her waist. He took a lemon from his pocket and, biting into it, tore a bit of the peel away. Then he rubbed the fruit over her cheeks and neck, so that the juice cooled her skin.

She opened her eyes and looked at him. Beads of moisture gathered above the curve of his well-molded upper lip, the ends of his hair dripped, and his handsome face was flushed with the virile health of young manhood. The temperature caused his pulse to beat at a slightly quickened rate so that the veins in his neck coursed full with blood. He smiled at her, frowning a little as if wondering at her stare. His teeth were white and perfect.

"What does the lemon do?" she asked, unable to tear her eyes away.

"I don't know," he admitted with a shrug and a wider smile. "But the caravan drivers of the Sahara swear by it." He put the lemon in her hand. "Feel better?"

She smiled. "Like new."

"You are diplomatic." He offered her more water

from his own cup, which she declined. "I must leave you for a while, Gwen. I'm going to speak with the *kaid* here—the local official. If we're lucky he may have word of the Zemours, or even know something of your father. As you can imagine, any European passing through this place would be noticed and well remembered."

She nodded and turned her gaze to the streets, where the idle inhabitants watched the movement of the Berbers with distrustful eyes. "They seem to see everything."

"They do." Reaching out a hand, he covered her face with the *haik* again. Then he made to go, stopping first to retrieve his rifle from the stallion's saddle. "By the way, don't get too close to the children—they're verminous and will infect you before you can bat an eye. Keep your face covered and don't call notice to yourself. Remember, in Morocco women don't challenge butchers."

His words were imparted with humor and a warm look, which Gwen returned. She watched him as he made his way down the street to a stuccoed villa where a huge black man in a lemon-colored robe stood guarding a door.

After awhile, she shifted restively, for the flies were a persistent plague. Hardly interested in perusing the hideous shops, she ambled toward Robyn, noting that he had removed his hat from his saddle horn and angled it jauntily atop his head. The straw boater caused an instant sensation. The curious natives stared at it, watching him narrowly as he moved to sit down upon the cannon muzzle and gulp the contents of his flask.

Stare for stare, the earl returned the observation of his hostile audience. Much to her dismay, Gwen noted that a few of Morgan's men even eyed the Welshman with frank contempt. Wanting to advise him to be more circumspect, she hurried across the street, but a group of children hindered her. They had encircled Robyn as if he were a circus clown, laughing at his headwear while attempting to pluck it off his head.

"Begone, you little guttersnipes!" he ordered. "Begone! I've got no coins to toss." His refined British tones echoed around the square, so that any who had not already been gawking stopped to do so now.

"*Anasera!* Christian dog!" one of the older children cried. "May the true God strike you down!"

"Go away I said!" Robyn barked as the youngsters began to spit and curse him in their native tongue. "Damn you, look there! My shoes are crawling with your filth and fleas!"

The Berbers guffawed at the Welshman's plight. Aggravated and afraid, Gwen attempted to pull the uncooperative earl off the cannon. "Robyn!" she hissed, clutching at his arm. "For God's sake, come with me."

Just as she yanked him to his feet, Morgan stepped out of the *kaid*'s house. His eyes hardened at the scene, and as he stalked the length of the street, he shifted the rifle in his hand as if sorely tempted to use it. The children ran from him, and the Berbers quickly erased their amused expressions.

"Get atop your horse, Breese," he commanded

through his teeth. He gripped the earl's arm with a bruising hand and lifted him from the cannon. "Drunkenness is despised here almost as much as the Christian who practices it. If you'd tried to make a spectacle of yourself, you couldn't have done a better job of it."

"Have a sense of humor, Riff," Robyn cajoled, jerking his arm free. "Nothing else to do in this bloody country but drink."

"There's plenty else to do—protecting your hide, for instance. In another minute those people would have stoned you to death. But what the hell—you wouldn't have felt it anyway." Jerking Robyn's reins free from their tether, he gathered them up for the indignant earl.

"Morgan!" Gwenllian interrupted as the earl was shoved atop his saddle. "Did you hear any news about my father?"

Morgan paused. Above the *haik*, Gwen's blue eyes searched his, desperate for a shred of hope. He clamped his jaw and lied. "No. The *kaid* knew nothing."

He helped her upon her horse then, and went to mount his own with rifle still in hand. But before he had slid a boot into the stirrup, one of the crenellated rooftops moved with sudden life. In the blink of an eye a turbaned man raised a weapon and aimed it at the chieftain's chest.

Gwen screamed. But the Berber leader's keen instinct had not failed him, and shouldering the breech of his own weapon with scarcely believable speed, he sighted the threat and fired.

A double report rent the air, and a second later a limp and bloodied body toppled from the rooftop.

The marketplace babbled in excitement. Everyone cast admiring glances in the chieftain's direction, and before the dust had quite settled, the children went to rob the body of its clothing.

With rifles cocked, the Berbers sprinted in all directions. They skirted the porticos, inspected the shops, and secured the other rooftops. But they found no other attackers lurking in the squalid shadows and, at a brusque word from their chieftain, returned to mount their horses. Gwen stared at Morgan, still stunned by the violence that had lasted no more than a minute.

With his rifle cradled in the hollow of one arm, he swung atop his saddle and took up the reins. "Let us go, Gwen," he ordered quietly.

She obeyed, nudging her mare with knees that quivered. And as she followed the invincible being she loved and feared, she began to realize that all encounters—no matter how dire—were merely a matter of course to Morgan Riff.

Thirteen

That evening, restlessness plagued the camp. While the Berbers put up tents and hobbled horses, their fierce eyes roved over the purple landscape, and their ears seemed more attuned than usual to the wind's whine over sand and scrub. Gwen thought that each of them heard and saw more than she did, and wondered at the sharpness of their senses.

In the far distance curls of smoke wafted against the dying pink sky, and the men gazed speculatively at the gray smudges from time to time, especially Morgan, whose whole body seemed tense with watchfulness. A sense of foreboding hovered in the air, in its heat, and Gwen found herself more fearful than she had ever been, even though no tangible thing threatened now, not as it had earlier in that dreadful place in Arzilah. She had known for a long time that Morgan had enemies, but somehow those enemies seemed more ubiquitous than ever here in the open desolation of the plains.

Last night, with her head upon the camel mat,

she had had a dream in which she lived with Morgan in this land. But as she gazed out now at the scarred landscape cloaked with night, and breathed in the scents of dust and smoke, she knew with certainty that she could never exist here. How could she awake each day fearing for the man she loved, and for the children she might bear him?

No, dreams were not to be found here, at least not those she required. And yet, during her remaining time in Morocco she wanted to be with Morgan Riff every moment possible, so that during the endless winter nights at home she would have more treasures to pull out of her chest of memories and cherish.

She went in search of him, but found that he had mounted his horse and ridden to the top of a hill to survey the distant ridges. What an image he created, Gwen thought. He could have been a warrior from any age. And how she loved him. And how that love, which could not be fulfilled in the way she desired it to be, jabbed her like a wound.

Robyn quietly joined her then, and she turned her eyes from Morgan's roughcast silhouette to the earl's haggard face. Gone, she realized in that moment of contemplation, was the arrogant aristocrat whose step was supremely confident in streets jammed with gliding carriages and top-hatted citizens. Uncertainty lurked now in the once merry eyes, in the chapped hands, and in the words uttered through sunburnt lips. It was the sort of uncertainty, she thought, that stripped a man of his manhood.

Taking hold of his arm, she asked, "What is it, Robyn? Are you unwell?"

He shook his head and for a moment remained thoughtfully silent. "This place, the men here," he finally said. "It's a mad world, isn't it, Gwen? A world I can't fathom. I keep wishing I were back in London, playing faro at the club and discussing Lord Edrington's latest fiasco at the tables. But I have the oddest notion I never will again. I used to think," he rushed on before she could protest, "that I'd like to be an officer in the Grenadiers, carry a sword and wear gold lace on my lapels. I thought you'd be impressed. But, well, I hadn't the nerve to join, I guess." He smiled in self-deprecation. "No wonder you prefer the valiant Mr. Riff."

"Oh, Robyn," she breathed, putting her arms about his waist and holding him as one would a boy in need of comfort.

"You know what I've discovered, Gwen . . . ?" he asked against her hair, giving a surprised laugh. "While I've discovered my own cursed cowardice, I've found that you have an extraordinary nerve— no, don't argue. It's true. You love that Berber knight out there, but you're strong enough to keep yourself away from him, because you know it would never do. Do you realize how rare you are? Any other woman in your place would throw herself at his head with no thought for tomorrow."

Clasping her closer, he whispered, "I do love you. I know my feelings aren't reciprocated, but when we return to Wales can't we make a go of it? Can't we ride and dance and dandle our babies on our knees, go to London in season, to Brighton in August, have grand country fetes at Christmastime? *I* can be content with that . . . can't you, Gwen?"

His plea wrenched her in the deepest place, and she took a shaky breath, wishing it were so simple to plot a life, to make it pleasant and whole. For even though Robyn's scheme sounded satisfying, she could imagine emptiness in it too. Something vital would be missing. There was an alternative, of course, one filled with passion and love, but also with violence and death. The choices seemed cruel ones.

"I can make no promises to you, Robyn," she answered finally, with great tenderness. Her eyes filled as she looked over his shoulder and regarded the figure on the ridge. "Not now, not here. Perhaps . . . perhaps when this is over, and we're home again."

He pressed her hands and straightened himself as if to regain a measure of his dignity. "Yes. When we're home again."

Leaving Gwen to her view of the other man, he walked over the stony ground and, easing down, tarried in solitude beside the sputtering fire.

Pensive, Gwen sat down upon a rock, and after awhile saw Morgan return to camp by the glow of the round-faced moon. She watched him pull the saddle from his horse and lay it down beneath a cork tree, then run his hands over the back of his steed as if to soothe it. For a long while she observed the companionship between man and creature, watched Morgan's hands as he rubbed a cloth over the copper hide. He treated the beast as if it were a friend, murmuring to it in his native tongue, and when he regretfully slipped the leather hobbles over the fleet legs, the stallion craned its neck to nuzzle his master's shoulder.

With a quiet tread Gwen moved forward, knowing her approach in the blackness did not startle him, for nothing ever startled Morgan Riff. "What do you call him?" she asked.

He turned to face her. "Koummite. It means burnt chestnut, which is the most prized color for an Arabian stallion."

"And the other one . . . ?" she breathed, remembering the splendid gray who had died in the service of his master. "What did you call him?"

Morgan glanced skyward. "Maarouf. The Acquaintance."

Gwen could not help but shift her eyes to the heavens, too, as if she would find the gray stallion flying somewhere among the stars. She vividly recalled the time when she had viewed these same constellations with another man. He had been a gentleman attired in European clothes with a starched white collar and a waistcoat lined in satin.

Morgan sensed her sudden reminiscing, and his own was no less poignant. Seeking to dull the sharpness of the memory, he touched the stallion's muzzle and spoke in a voice full of warmth and whimsy. "It's said that when the world began, God commanded the South Wind to condense itself. Well, the South Wind condensed, and God seized a handful of it and fashioned the original chestnut stallion—an Arabian, of course."

Gwen smiled. "Englishmen revere their horses, but their devotion hardly compares to yours."

"Where would I be without Koummite?" Morgan said, indicating the vast landscape with a negligent hand. "An Arabian is swift, and can carry a rider and his weapons all day without water or food. On the back of a brave stallion a chieftain can attack his enemies, defend his home, or flee if necessary. His horse is his comrade in arms."

War, always war, Gwen thought. Turning her back in irritation, making no secret of her pique, she went to stand beneath the cork tree where she plucked moodily at its drooping leaves. Morgan resumed his grooming of the horse, and a hush fell between them. The night sounds sharpened so keenly that the soft swish of the stallion's tail, its breathing through velvet nostrils, and the breeze drifting beneath its flanks seemed loud. Across the way Robyn's feet crunched in the sand. Gwen glanced up, watched him amble to his tent and struggle to remove his boots before emptying them of pebbles. In a neat alignment he set them beside the flap, then regarded his damp sand-caked stockings with something akin to bafflement. She pitied him all at once; Lord Breese had never been without a valet.

"I shouldn't have brought him," Morgan said behind her in the darkness. "I shouldn't have brought you."

At his confession of self-blame she turned her head to stare at him, then cast down her eyes to regard the hem of her burnoose. "That man today in Arzilah—"

"He was one of many, sent by my enemy."

"Sent by your enemy?"

260

"Yes."

She searched his face. "Why is he your enemy? Why does he go to such lengths to kill you?"

Morgan lifted a shoulder. "It's not easy to explain why men fight, Gwen. The reasons are complicated—most of the time, anyway. That's probably why we use words like patriotism and honor and duty."

"I would add hatred and insanity."

"Ah, you are a realist rather than an idealist."

"Perhaps."

Morgan put a hand to the stallion's neck. His long-jointed fingers combed through the mane, pulling loose a burr entangled in it. "My people fight for land, for water and livestock, even for women—all things essential to the survival of a tribe. We winter in the lowlands, but in the summer we go to the high mountain pastures to graze our animals and grow crops. If our land has been taken by a stronger tribe, existence becomes hard, and we go to war hoping to recapture it. In my part of the world that sort of struggle has been an endless cycle for many generations."

He paused, gazing out at the sable-wrapped hills with eyes that seemed to see every stone and blade of grass. "Sometimes I think it's a terrible paradox—fighting for land, I mean. For how can we own the land? It has always seemed to me that the land owns us."

Gwen twisted her head about at his words, sensing that he had expressed a futility often felt but never voiced before. And she sympathized.

"When I was a boy," he continued in his mellow

261

voice, "my father built a sort of fortress for my mother. He was a powerful chieftain with a great deal of land, and many men envied him. Ah, there's another word for our list, Gwen," he said, holding up a finger. "Envy. It makes enemies and wars far faster than any of the other reasons, wouldn't you say?"

"I would have sworn you were an idealist a moment ago."

He smiled briefly. "Perhaps I only wanted you to believe that I was."

"How did your father die, Morgan?"

A burlap bag rested at his feet and he bent to open it, scooping out a measure of barley for the horse. When the sound of its munching filled the night, Morgan dusted his hands and moved to the cork tree, where he crossed his arms and leaned back against the trunk. "When I was fifteen a chieftain called Moussa attacked our fortress. He and his men spitted my father with a spear, then raped my mother. Although I fought him and gave him a near fatal wound, he survived. He and his tribe seized our home. They hold it still."

"You wounded his eye, didn't you?" she asked in sudden enlightenment. "He bears the scars still?"

"Yes."

She crushed a leaf between her fingers. "What a terrible experience for a young boy."

"An early lesson in the harsh realities of life here," he said, contemplating the inky horizon. "At any rate, afterward, my mother insisted that we flee to Wales. Little good it did. Determined that I would never return to avenge my father's death,

262

Moussa sent an assassin after us. My mother took the bullet meant for me."

Gwen stilled, imagining the horror. She glanced at him, at his powerful body braced against the tree. He was so near she could catch the scent of barley and leather on his hands, and the smells reminded her of his affinity with the land, of his sureness amidst its elements. He seemed so stalwart that it was difficult to imagine how deeply he must have suffered during the vulnerable years of his boyhood. "I'm sorry, Morgan," she said. "Truly I am."

He turned his palm over, rubbing at a blister with his thumb. "It seems a very long time ago now."

"Where did you go when you left Hiraeth?"

"I came back here—full of rage and ready for revenge, as you might imagine. But I was only a boy and couldn't begin to rally my father's people and lead them into war. So I went to my mother's uncle in Vienna for a while, then wandered about Europe—waiting upon manhood, you might say. When the time was right, I returned to Morocco."

"And now you fight for your father's land."

Bending down, he retrieved his rifle, which he had earlier propped across the saddle, and his hand automatically caressed the smooth metal barrel with an intimate knowledge. Upending it then, he leaned upon the breech as Gwen had seen him do countless times before. She had come to despise the pose.

"Yes," he answered at last in a low tone. "But even more, I fight to kill Moussa. I think of killing him day and night—have done since I was fifteen. Nothing else has driven me so hard."

263

The words were direct and simply said, but so underpinned with enmity that a chill rose along Gwenllian's arms. "How fiercely you hate," she accused.

He straightened abruptly and took his weight off the rifle, looking at her with eyes that judged in turn. "And how fiercely I love."

She turned away, but he seized her and put his mouth to hers even while she struggled. The bark of the tree scraped her spine, and Morgan's rough chin grazed the tender point of hers, but his hands were warm with life, persuasive with the outburst of his own need. Without breath, without reason, Gwen yielded, wanting to experience what he could teach, clutching at the battle-hard shoulders which curved to fit her frailer ones, grasping the solid arms that could embrace with tenderness or bring death with vengeance.

"Don't fight anymore, Morgan," she pleaded against his lips. "Please! Come and live a different life with me. There's so much more—"

"No. There is nothing more—not for me there isn't."

"You're wrong," she argued, pulling back from his embrace and spreading out her hands. "There's gentility and charity and peace. There are loving neighbors and laughing children who make living to old age a joy. There's an existence without violence, and without the need to wake up every morning afraid of war—or *lusting* for it!"

"In the whole of my life," he declared through his teeth, "I've never found any of those things, not

264

one of them. And maybe—just maybe," he added, turning on his heel, "I damned well don't want to."

When their journey commenced at a bloodless dawn, no words were exchanged between Morgan and Gwenllian. Nor did they speak the dawn after. And that unrelieved pattern continued for days.

As they tramped the endless miles of bleached sand and stone, the air became hotter and more arid, so that in only minutes the lather on the horses' necks evaporated to salt. No running streams crossed the tracks they followed, and the greenest vegetation chose to crowd thirstily around the infrequent wells that dotted the countryside like islands.

One day Morgan halted the party at such a welcome watering place. Parched and wilted by the sun, Gwen dismounted from her saddle in a weary slide while staring at the strange contraption straddling the deep well. A horizontal wheel rested atop a vertical one, and around the creaking apparatus a raw-boned camel lumbered in a circle. As he did, a series of earthen pots tied on ropes descended into the hole before coming up full of water. The motion of the wheel tilted the pots into a wooden drinking trough.

The Moor who oversaw the site grinned at Gwen, and with a bow said, "O Princess of all Women, in the name of Allah, drink!"

Used to such effusive greetings now, she accepted a cup from his leathery hand and, discreetly turning her back to lift the *haik,* drank every drop. Each

265

man followed in turn before the animals were allowed to sink their muzzles deep into the trough and suck cool water through their yellowed teeth.

His pace relentless, Morgan ordered the band to remount before a quarter hour had passed, and they filed back to the gouged trail where the bottoms of their stirrups scraped cacti and thorn shrub. They had not gone far when the smoke of distant fires shimmered like sprites on the melting horizon, and Gwen recalled that she had seen a similar sight once before near Arzilah. While she squinted at the ominous curls and pondered their cause, her mare stumbled, going down on one knee and casting a shoe.

The red-haired Berber named Hassan rode just behind Gwen, and immediately barked out some word to Morgan, who turned his horse about and joined her.

"Are you all right?" he asked.

When Gwen reassured him, he helped her dismount, then bent to pick up the foreleg of her mare. After examining the hoof, he reached to open the flap of her saddlebag, which he had packed at the journey's start, and removed a horseshoe. Gwen knew that all the Berbers carried extra horseshoes, along with any other accessories vital to the welfare of their mounts. They were a people on the move, and acted as their own veterinarians and farriers.

While she watched, Morgan retrieved a hammer and the proper nails from his own saddlebags, along with a camel-hide thong, which he deftly passed over the pommel of her saddle and around the mare's pastern before tying it off, so that the hoof remained lifted. Then, in only a matter of minutes, he set the shoe and began nailing it into place. She watched his hands, fascinated as always by their talents.

When the hood of his burnoose slipped down to leave his hair uncovered, she noted how the sun glossed its blackness, and how the muscles across his shoulders flexed as he labored. The heat was pitiless shimmering off the burning sand, and before long perspiration trickled from his temple into the hollow below his cheekbone. She reached to unhook her water flask from the saddle and offer it to him. He thanked her, and drank sparingly.

"What are those fires to the east there?" she asked, indicating the fingers of smoke still trailing toward the sky.

He returned her flask and wiped his mouth with the back of a hand. "They're Berber villages and homes. The sultan's men have torched them."

"What?"

"His taxes are unjust. Some villages refuse to pay and even do battle with the tax collectors. Those that do are often burned out, or suffer some other form of retaliation. Recently the summer camps of some of my own tribe have gone under the imperial torch, for I have led rebellions against His Majesty over the last few years."

Morgan looked at her, his eyes a startling blue against the darkness of his face. "He's another of my enemies. And he would likely be the least charitable of all—if I were ever careless enough to let him catch up with me."

At her frown he flashed his rare white grin, and Gwen marveled that he could regard all perils with such calm.

"I'd planned to go into Fez," he finished as he retied the flap of her saddlebag. "But I've learned that the sultan and his court are returning to the palace there, so we'll skirt the city and replenish our stores in Mequinez."

"The place where my father was captured?"

At the mention of Sir Gerald, Morgan's eyes moved away from her face to study the braided reins in his hand. "Yes. We're only a few miles away now."

"I pray someone can help us there," she said.

Before long they breached a rocky plateau, whose apex afforded a breathtaking vista of jumbled limestone framed by the snow-peaked Atlas mountains. After pausing to scan the landscape, Morgan led them down a steep decline, and they passed through the imposing gates of the holy city of Mequinez, filing through masses of boisterous pedestrians, camels, and kicking mules, all of whom fought for space in streets sown with thorny weeds and the usual ordure.

Gwen held tight to her reins, jostled on every side by the unruly traffic, sickened by the smells of unclean bodies and mud-caked animals. Holy men prayed amidst the chaos, their flesh emblazoned with self-inflicted wounds, while food sellers ran through the crowd offering roasted mutton. Upon the steps of an enormous mosque tiled in green, beggars praised Allah. Rich Moors dressed in perfumed silks and wooden high heels purchased spices in the adjacent bazaar. The usual ragged children abounded, along with Jews and Negroes, and the calls of the sarsaparilla and tobacco hawkers shrilled above the general clamor.

Gwen pulled the *haik* more securely over her face, suddenly sensing evil dwelling amidst the populated decay. She twisted in the saddle to look for Robyn, relieved to see Hassan riding at his flank. She did not know when Morgan had fallen back to ride beside her, but he had, his hand ready upon the barrel of his rifle. The copper horse snorted beneath his thighs and laid back its ears, nervous in the press of odiferous bodies.

Keeping his eyes on the crowd, Morgan said, "We'll spend the night in the *fondak*—the place set aside for travelers. There are rooms to let there. If you like, you can get a bath."

At that prospect, Gwen could not contain her elation, and although all of the lime-washed buildings in the *fondak* were dilapidated, she waited eagerly while Morgan secured a room. His men watered the horses and smoked *kif* in the shade, laughing and playing some game of chance. With his flask as company, Robyn sat down against a wall whose peeling stucco revealed a foundation of half-crumbled brick.

Before long Morgan escorted Gwen into a tiny chamber framed in cedar beams, whose single unglazed window viewed the street through wrought-iron bars. The grout between the floor tiles was green with mold and the plastered walls were oily, but in the center of the space there stood a wooden tub, a tablet of soap, and bottles of oil and perfume. After spending endless days trudging over dusty paths and sleeping on camel-hair mats, the little room was an oasis.

"Shall I come back for you in, say . . . a half hour?" Morgan asked, amused when she seized the soap and perfume in her hands and lifted them to her nose with a rapturous smile.

"Make it an hour."

He grinned. "An hour then. That'll give me time to stop off at the *hammam*—it's a sort of Turkish bath open to the public."

Recalling the stench outside, she raised a brow. "Which is not as popular as it should be."

He chuckled. "Evidently not."

After he had closed the door, Gwen could not tear off her clothes fast enough. Draping the *haik* over the uncurtained window for privacy, she hopped into the tub and immersed herself in one blissful dive. With a liberal hand she splashed perfume and oil into the clear water, whose bracing chill cooled her skin and made it tingle, so that for an instant she forgot the withering temperatures outside. Grabbing the embroidered shift worn beneath her burnoose, she washed it as she bathed, lathering it with soap, then wringing out the water and spreading it over the tiles beneath the window where the hot breeze blew. Then for another half hour, she simply luxuriated in the tub, her head tilted far back over the rim and her eyes closed as she dreamt of summer days at home beside a river bank edged in violets.

When Morgan returned, he carried a tray in his hands laden with a samovar of sweetened tea and plates of cheeses and almond cakes. Shutting the crude cedar door with his heel, he paused, arrested by the fresh, casual picture of femininity. Gwenllian sat upon a thin pallet beside the tub, her legs tucked in a graceful bent beneath her hips, one arm bracing her weight so that her body created a sinuous line. Her shift was white, heavy with damp, and her black hair tumbled over its folds in wet waves that dripped beads upon her lap. Between the tub and the pallet where she half-reclined, a trail of spilled water glistened upon the tiles, quivering now and then when air whispered through the window.

"Hungry?" he asked in a voice that was not quite normal. The sight of her made his body tense, for he had never seen a woman in such fetching dishabille. He smelled her perfume, noticed how the drying ends of her hair curled slightly about her face, noticed the glimmer of oil upon her lips. She looked very young and very soft. Desire rushed though his blood.

"Starving," she replied.

Her answer made him realize he was still standing with the tray in his hands. He set it down beside her, and she invited him to take a seat upon the pallet, shifting over to give him space. When he eased down and crossed his legs, his shoulder touched hers, and she leaned away a little as if discomfitted by the intimate brush.

"I—I see you got your bath," she ventured awkwardly. "Your hair—it's still wet."

He looked at her, not wanting to talk, not wanting to eat, not wanting to do anything but touch.

Nervous, Gwen lowered her eyes, studying his hand where it rested upon one thigh, noting the way the long fingers curved around one of the little earthen cups from the tray. Strong veins crisscrossed his wrist and his nails were clean and clipped. Lifting her lashes, she followed the line of his arm upward where it met his shoulder and, at last, braved a glance at his eyes.

They were bright with longing and, after skimming over her mouth and hair, alit upon the drawstring tied loosely at her throat. She thought he might reach out and pull it. And if he did, she would not be able to stop him, she would not be able to stop herself.

She gazed at him with direct eyes and extended her fingers to take hold of her burnoose, which was draped limply across the tub. Sliding it across the wet tiles slowly, as if he might stay her hand, she gathered it over her head and then let the white cloud of fabric drop.

Across from her Morgan's eyes darkened, and he set aside the fragile cup he held, which was glazed blue with a lotus painted on the lip. Gwen stared at it to avoid his gaze, and when he had removed his hand, she lifted the samovar and refilled it. Without words, but with eyes that asked forgiveness, she picked up the brimming cup and offered it to him.

Morgan accepted the peace offering, but his expression remained hard, edged with a sullenness he had never displayed to her before. He seemed disinclined to speak, and awkwardly she leaned to slice the pale yellow cheese. As she bent to replace the knife upon its plate, the chain about her neck swung forward and caught the sunlight that

272

streamed through a chink in the wall. The aquamarine pendent sparkled.

Morgan noticed it. "Where did you get that?" he asked, breaking his silence.

His tone was sharp, and Gwen glanced up. "My father gave it to me several years ago, on my birthday. Why?"

"May I see it?"

"Of course." Unhooking the clasp, she transferred it to his palm.

He examined the gem, turned it to capture the light again, then closed his fist over it with a thoughtful expression. "My mother owned a necklace like this," he said with a frown. "In fact, I could swear it was this very jewel. When I was a boy I used to see her take it out of her box of treasures from Wales and look at it. But one day, instead of putting it back, she wrapped it in a package which she addressed and sent off with a servant. I never saw it again."

"Are you certain this is the same necklace?"

He opened his palm. "Yes. It's uncut and distinctively shaped, and the color is exceptional."

She shifted and pushed back the hair falling over her brow, rubbing her temples in a thoughtful gesture. "I think my father loved your mother," she murmured at last.

"What did you say?"

"I believe my father loved your mother. There can be no other explanation, I'm sure of it." Excited, she related the tale Petwyn had told her about Marian's being betrothed to a Welshman before she eloped with Morgan's father. She told him about the carelessly bundled love letters signed with the scrawled name *Ulysses*, and reminded him that Sir Gerald had been a sailor.

Morgan agreed that the relationship might have been possible. Then, for a spell, while the heat evaporated the droplets of water on the floor and dried Gwenllian's hair, the two of them talked quietly about the surprising connection, eating bites of soft cheese and sharing almond-flavored cakes.

"Morgan," Gwen said. "Was . . . was your mother happy?"

The words hung between them, gravely spoken and significant.

"She seemed to be." He raised his eyes, but Gwen looked away, watching water seep through the slats of the tub until he took hold of her hand. Gently, he turned it palm up and dropped the necklace there. The chain slithered between her fingers, and she took hold of it, fumbling to fasten it about her neck again. The clasp tangled in her hair, and Morgan leaned forward to perform the task himself.

Self-conscious, Gwen twisted her head to aid him, feeling his fingers lift her hair and brush across her nape. He inserted one gold end into the other, then slid his hand down the length of the chain to straighten its links. When he was finished, his hand remained resting across her breast.

Gwen looked at it, at the dark thin fingers against the whiteness of her garment, at the straight bone of his wrist and the long sinews. She swallowed and closed her eyes.

He could have pressed her back upon the pallet then and, in the warm room made molten by golden light, finished what he had begun on a night in Tangier. She would have let him.

But he did not. He only took her face between his hands and, after gazing at her through eyes made brilliant with unsaid feeling, whispered, "If anything should happen to me, depend upon Hassan."

She searched his face with sudden alarm. "Why do you say this, Morgan?"

He brushed her cheek with a forefinger, and one corner of his mouth lifted in a smile meant to reassure. "To put my mind at ease, that's all. I must spend the afternoon away. The local pasha and his son have invited me to their home, and it would be unwise to refuse them. Besides, the pasha has a great deal of influence and power in this region, and may be able to help us in the search for your father."

"I pray he can. So much time has passed already."

Morgan rose and went to the door, and when he opened it the sunlight flashed in and made a pool of fire upon the tiles. For a second he looked back at her as if to squeeze one more glance into time.

"Finish your cake," he said, smiling softly. Then he shut the door.

Fourteen

After removing the sword from his saddle, Morgan gestured for Hassan to leave his game under the shade and join him. The young Berber immediately complied, walking noiselessly in his goatskin boots with his double-pouched ammunition bag swinging at his waist.

"See that Miss Evans gets anything she might require," the chieftain instructed in a low voice. Shifting his gaze to the caravan drivers who had led their dusty camels into the *fondak* to drink, he added, "Don't let her out of your sight. I could be gone hours—these damned feasts the pasha hosts are interminable, and the foolish old peacock may not be inclined to give me an audience until he's spent half the day stuffing himself with French bonbons."

"You can depend upon me," Hassan said.

Nodding, Morgan turned about to depart, and caught sight of Robyn Breese, who lay snoring with his back against a column, oblivious to the flies that crawled over his face. "And keep an eye on him," he added dryly, "since he can't seem to be trusted to do it himself."

The two men exchanged looks, and Morgan left the run-down square to shoulder his way past the fortune-tellers, carpet sellers, and bands of roving children. Close by, Gwen watched him, standing on tiptoe at the barred window, pressing her face against it until his dark head, which rose above all the others on the street, finally disappeared from view. Feeling insecure now that he was no longer near, she sought the comfort of the pallet, where she stretched out on her stomach and drew up her burnoose to let the air cool her legs. The room was hot, and she soon perspired so that her garments clung uncomfortably to her skin. Rolling onto her back, she tried to ignore the din outside in the bazaar, and flung a hand over her eyes as if to shut out the disturbing visions that the sounds aroused. But when she closed her lids she saw terrifying images of her father in the hands of savage men. And she saw the disfigured face of Morgan's enemy, who the proud Berber chieftain would fight until his sense of honor was finally appeased. Or, until he was killed.

Too agitated to sleep, Gwen veiled her face with the *haik* and ventured with a tentative step out into the *fondak* to seek a breath of air. The late afternoon temperature had soared high enough to sap the energy from even the most stalwart natives, and most had sought the shelter of the indoor cafes, leaving the square tranquil. Only the wind moved with any vigor, whirling dust and rubbish into stinging eddies that cavorted through the streets. The Berbers lounged in the shade, and Robyn still dozed against a column with his legs sprawled.

Before she had gone many steps Hassan materialized beside her like a huge red-haired guardian angel. She smiled at him and he called to a water seller who loitered near with his swollen goatskin bag. After buying her a cup of water, the Berber handed it over, careful not to meet her eyes or let his fingers brush against hers when it was passed.

Putting a hand upon his sleeve, Gwen said, *"Baraka,"* which she knew to mean "many thanks."

For an instant his light-colored gaze met hers and a grin touched his sunburnt lips. "God bless you, miss," he returned in clumsy English. Then he backed away to stand at a respectful distance.

Nearby, his comrades laughed together in a relaxed group, and she thought of the village boys at home idling in front of the tobacconist on Saturday mornings. They were not so different, really, she supposed. While she smiled at the comparison and watched one of the Berbers toss a playing piece high in the air, a resounding crack shattered the agreeable atmosphere.

Whirling about, Gwen witnessed a scene that was more spine-chilling than any she had yet encountered. Screaming men descended upon the square en masse, running forward with their rifles aimed, the muzzles flashing fire. The Berbers reached for their own weapons, but the savages bearing down like a vicious tide gave them little time to act. Such chaos reigned that Gwen could only stand paralyzed for several nightmarish seconds, seeing men fall all about her while swords slashed and poniards stabbed in the turmoil of hand-to-hand combat. The sounds of clashing steel echoed off the eroding walls, and animals bolted wildly through the melee, jumping over writhing bodies while their churning hooves added to the cloud of dust already thick enough to clog the throat. Men grunted in anguish and effort, shrieked eerie battle cries as they stormed their foes.

Insensible with panic, Gwen backed beneath the portico, and stumbling over the ends of her garment, fell hard against a column. Only a few yards away Hassan ravaged an attacker with his sword, and the victim's blood spattered crimson on a lime-washed wall. She screamed. Robyn staggered toward her and flung his body across her length. Clasping each other, they watched the continuing carnage in utter horror.

Outnumbered and with their small force quickly dwindling, the Berbers intensified their efforts. They fought valiantly, more skillfully than the others, with their powerful arms slicing and hacking, and when weapons were gone they smashed faces with their fists. With a sort of terrible beauty they battled, toiled, charged to save their honor. Hassan warred more fiercely than any, cutting down man after man, his huge body the only shield, save Robyn, between Gwenllian and the menace that threatened her life.

And then, two devils besieged Hassan at once. With one arm wounded, the young Berber began to flag, and Gwenllian feared that he would soon be bested. Although Robyn clutched at her clothes in an effort to keep her down, she leapt up and seized a fallen sword from the ground. Rage gave her the strength to lift the heavy weapon, and with a ferocious effort, she ran forward and swung its blade at the monster who attacked the redhead.

She clearly saw the face of the man she murdered; it was not ugly or inhuman. But even as his blood stained her hem, she felt no remorse, only an odd, empty sense of elation as he crumpled at her shoes.

Hassan dealt his own deathblow to the second adversary, thrusting steel through his chest. Still holding the sword, Gwen glanced frantically about. Morgan's men littered the square like toppled giants, their bodies fallen across those of their enemy. Except for the injured Hassan, who stood bent double at her side, only two antagonists remained alive, and they fought each other to the death. And then, within minutes, the Berber fell.

The devil who had killed him charged forward to challenge the beleaguered Hassan, who recovered himself with incredible determination and stood with his sword raised high. He parried and thrust, feinted and lunged, but his wound was critical. His strength seeped speedily away. Hysteria squeezed Gwen's chest when Hassan sank to the ground and groaned.

His murderer's mouth twisted into a gruesome smile, and when she made to escape, he grasped her clothes with his bloodied fingers. Sword still in hand, she turned on him in a desperate struggle to defend herself.

A shot rang out. Her captor's body jerked, and she felt her garments freed as he collapsed to the ground. Robyn stood behind her holding a pointed revolver, and his hand shook so violently that Gwen was astounded his aim had been true.

For a moment the two Europeans only stared at each other, dazed. The smoky silence about them was profound, a silence of sacrilege and massacred flesh. Slowly they turned their eyes to view each angle of the scene, wondering that they stood alive upon such a battlefield. For a long while they stood motionless, too shocked to move. And then, when the dust began to clear, an army of flies invaded and, showing no more respect than the insects, nimble-fingered beggars crept forward to rob the bodies.

Gwen dropped the sword, and its strident clangor made her jump. With a whimper, she sank down at the fallen Hassan's side and closed her eyes against the sight of his mangled body. Robyn knelt, too, and quivering, dropped the revolver. He scrabbled about on his knees to find his flask, seized it, and gulped its contents, failing to hear the sound of hooves as a horse picked its way through the field of vanquished warriors.

But the sound penetrated Gwen's dim consciousness, and she jerked reflexively, her nerves stretched to the snapping point. She glanced up. Her eyes widened with utter dread.

The rider smiled at her in a grimace of triumph, and his smile embodied more evil she had ever seen in the face of any man. He had only one eye, for Morgan had left one sightless. She remembered well the seamed visage and the necklace of claws that adorned his chest.

Astride the monstrous Barb, whose sides showed flecks of blood from the jab of vicious spurs,

Moussa waved his revolver at her peremptorily, barking a command in some language she did not understand. She stood frozen, afraid to turn about and look at Robyn lest Moussa be alerted. But she prayed the earl would pick up his pistol and fire it.

He did, but not before Moussa detected the movement and emptied his own revolver with a much greater skill.

Pivoting about, Gwen saw the earl sprawled face-down, dead, the last drops of his fine English brandy spilling in the dust. She cried his name, and her scream shrilled off the peeling stucco walls in an echo that seemed to resound a thousand times.

Morgan had already spent endless hours at the pasha's table, sitting cross-legged on the jewel-colored carpet with two dozen other guests. The bowl and ewer for hand washing were passed round yet again, then robed slaves brought in more platters of food covered with gold beehive-shaped lids. He tasted the roasted fowls, the vegetables, the mutton and stews, all with little appetite, for he did not like to be away from his camp so long. But the pasha had proven as stubbornly unavailable as Morgan had predicted, sitting at his place of honor on a satin pillow, and licking his fat fingers while food dribbled on his clothes. With an imperious wave of his hand, he ordered still more delicacies to be brought forth.

Sweetmeats were passed round, and then a loaf of sugar on a jeweled platter, which some of the guests cut and ate raw. Slaves refilled the silver samovars many times. Morgan shifted in his place, his eyes roaming restlessly about the chamber graced with polished marble pillars and cedar doors inlaid with copper. If the meal did not end soon, he would risk a breach of protocol and leave.

At last, the pasha heaved himself up, clapped his small soft hands and waddled off to sit beneath the embroidered canopy erected above his throne.

"Remind your master that I'd like a word with him," Morgan said to one of the slaves, for to approach the pasha directly was forbidden.

"My master says that he will give audience to no one until after the Dance of the Bee," came the lazy reply.

Grinding his teeth with the continued delay, Morgan went to stand alone in the courtyard, detaching himself from the other guests as the musicians began their play. He had seen the Dance of the Bee performed many times; it was provocative entertainment, but he hardly cared to watch it today.

A dozen of the pasha's concubines filed in, veiled and garbed in kaftans and transparent surplices, their heads covered with turbanlike *nantouze*, whose spangled ribbons fluttered like strung butterflies to their breasts. Sensually they undulated to the rhythm of the music, which slowly crescendoed until it reached a frenzied pitch. As the dance required, each woman pretended she had been stung by a bee, and began to cast off her clothing as if to find the place of the sting.

Unmoved, Morgan watched their oiled bodies, glistening and red-brown, but he saw only

Gwenllian, just as she had looked when he had earlier left her.

The music stopped and the performers trotted out with sly, inviting smiles for each gentleman. Evening approached and the brass lamps were lit, and while Morgan strolled impatiently about the courtyard, he was at last summoned by the unhelpful servant who announced dispassionately that his master had granted an interview.

Although the pasha's flesh was dissipated and his teeth rotten, the official possessed shrewd eyes. And whenever his ripe lips lifted into a false smile, the gesture reflected the cunning mind of its owner. Morgan did not trust the petty official in most matters, but knew that every snippet of gossip in Mequinez filtered up to him, and, with luck, he might relate it.

So after accomplishing the usual insincere greetings, Morgan wasted no time with his inquiry. "Have you any knowledge of an Englishman by the name of Sir Gerald Evans?" he asked bluntly. "I've been told that the Zemours captured him here in Mequinez."

The pasha stared at him from beneath the folds of dusky eyelids. "The fate of an Englishman is as Allah wills," he pronounced in a bored tone. "The infidels defile our cities, overrun our country, bring the sin of drunkenness to our streets. They should be condemned to the fires of Gehenna if they are so careless to fall into the hands of true believers."

"Nevertheless," Morgan persisted. "I have an interest in this particular Englishman and would like to know his whereabouts."

The pasha regarded him with a malignant gaze, taking a few moments to chew a sugared almond. "It is true that the Zemour tribe captured the Christian here in our holy streets," he drawled at last. "I believe they wanted to receive gold in exchange for his heathenish hide—which at least makes it useful for some earthly purpose. They thought perhaps the soldiers of the French would lighten their purses for such an exchange."

Morgan waited while his host dipped a tiny hand into the sweets bowl again and popped another almond into his rosebud mouth. Then he asked, "Which French soldiers?"

"There is an outpost on the Algerian border, near Figuig. Perhaps you can find this dog of the Gentile there." The pasha shrugged and picked his teeth with a long, pointed nail. "And then again, perhaps not."

He made a signal for Morgan to depart, and the dismissed guest inclined his head in a curt nod; it was the closest the chieftain would ever come to bowing to any man, despite the demands of protocol.

As he turned about, the pasha's son, a youth of no more than eighteen, attempted to detain him with an effusive invitation to stay and listen to the Moorish bagpipes. But a sudden odd feeling of unease had settled over Morgan in the last few minutes, an indefinable oppressiveness in which reason had no part, only intuition. Pausing in midstride, he listened to the sounds of the city outside the palace, tense and alert.

Beside him, the sullen boy fell back, frightened

by the sudden look of fierce concentration on the chieftain's face. Morgan turned a hard, speculative eye upon the toadlike form of the pasha, who had waddled to a striped divan and plopped down upon it. Their eyes met across the chamber, and the sly ones in the fleshy countenance danced with wickedness.

I have been betrayed, Morgan thought.

Sprinting toward the gate, he pushed past two sentries in tall black fezzes before rushing out onto the dusk-shaded street. The *fondak* lay situated at the opposite end of the city, blocks away, and Morgan cursed the distance. Running with the swiftness and endurance of a man conditioned by war, he wended in and out of milling pedestrians, shoving them aside with a hand if they cleared the way too slowly. With every step his dread increased, for as he neared his destination he sensed a change in the pattern of the crowd, and the atmosphere of the streets grew more quiet, the shouts of hawkers absent. Even the beggars had vanished. As he ran, he unsheathed his sword, his breaths coming fast and strong, his brow furrowed with concern for what he would discover.

Up ahead, through the fall of eventide, the buildings of the *fondak* came into view, and surrounding them a mob of people shoved and elbowed for space, obviously attempting to view some spectacle of interest. Morgan's dread was now verified, and it quickly congealed into fear as he burst through their ranks like a vengeful angel.

He came upon a scene devastating enough to rob him of his breath.

Standing stock-still with sweat running down his face and his chest heaving from the run, Morgan's eyes reflected the slaughter of his men. Their blood colored the earth. He had seen the toll of war many times, and death in its most horrendous forms, but never before had he been absent during its heat, or allowed one of his tribe to fight without his presence. Nor had his emotions been so tied to those he had abandoned in the *fondak* today.

And there was one even more important to him than all his men combined . . .

"*Gwenllian!*

His cry was wild. He glanced about the square, his violent eyes alighting upon every burnoose, every crumpled frame. Failing to find the one he sought, he bounded forward, propelled by the rage of fear. All around him beggars scurried through the carnage like stray dogs and robbed bodies before the inept but ruthless officials could arrive and stop them. Seeing their filthy hands pawing Berber sashes, pouches, even boots, Morgan charged, swinging his sword while he snarled, "Leave them alone! Leave them alone or I'll cut you down where you stand!"

Staring at him as if he were a warrior from hell sent to sentence them all to damnation, they scattered like mice, furtively watching him make a swift circuit through the waste of bodies with his boots ringing against strewn swords.

Discovering Hassan, Morgan went down upon a knee to touch the still warm shoulders of his most trusted friend, but his eyes did not dwell long upon the noble face. Frantically they searched for

Gwenllian in the dim light, finding Robyn Breese instead, who lay facedown beneath the portico with a bullet in his chest.

Morgan had learned to master his emotions long ago, but the sight of the dead aristocrat wrenched a low and agonized groan from his throat. Once again, with explosive and desperate energy, he circled the terrible scene of butchery hunting for Gwenllian. Although he knew it to be a useless effort, he sprinted to the room he had let for her, and kicking open its door, searched the shadows. All remained just as he had seen it last, the jars of perfume and oil, the tablet of soap balanced on the tub rim. The pallet linen was disturbed, still impressed with the form which had reposed earlier upon it, and her bag of belongings sat beside the door.

He returned to the square, to his comrades who lay spread upon the dirt. Moussa's work. And Moussa had taken the woman Rhaman loved.

Gwenllian!

It was a silent cry, which only the ears of the dead could hear.

Fifteen

Darkness was his foe. It was ally to his enemy, and likely an alliance deliberately wooed. The pasha had betrayed Morgan, inviting him to the feast of his table, detaining him, so that Moussa could better ambush his unwary men . . . and seize in his hands the woman Rhaman loved.

No trail could be discerned in blackness, no hoof prints or other signs of passage. And although his heart was raw with anxiety and his rage demanding retribution, Morgan's cool power of reason, that judgment for which he was legendary, steadied the course of his passionate emotions. He would wait for dawn and then go in search of Moussa's path. He prayed that Gwenllian could hold on to her courage until he could find her. And when he did find her and had her safe within his arms again, he would send her away from this unsettled land, away from his side. He would send her home to Wales.

And Moussa would live only to beg for his life, and then, beg to have it ended.

He learned from witnesses that his enemy had

flown Mequinez and that no men had accompanied him. It was grim comfort to Morgan that it had taken every warrior with whom Moussa had been traveling to defeat the small valiant band of Berbers.

When the first violet smudge touched the ramparts of the city, Morgan exited through the time-worn gates. He leaned well over his saddle, studying the hard baked earth with its confused prints of camel, horse, and human passage, and searched diligently for two particular sets of hooves emerging out of all the others. Around and around he went, skirting the ramparts while he kept the stallion's pace checked.

After a half hour, when the sun rose to her relentless splendor, bringing sweat to the steed's sleek flanks and to its master's rugged lineaments, a crowd had gathered to observe, shading their eyes against the glint of sunlight on stirrups and sword. With great concentration the chieftain continued to scrutinize the marks scattered across the earth. Suddenly he pulled the horse up short, dismounted, knelt, touched the dirt and traced with his forefinger the shape of a print.

He did not need to examine his discovery long to recognize the imprint of the shoe he had nailed upon the near front hoof of Gwenllian's mare on their journey to Mequinez. Less worn than the other three, the point was distinctive. He had forged the shoe himself last winter when the farrier in his village had fallen ill. And beside it were the prints of a larger set, those of Moussa's Barb.

In a flash he was astride again. The mighty haunches of the stallion bunched and flexed, and the beast sprang forward to fairly fly over the rocky plain and leave behind no more than a rising gauze of dust.

For hours Morgan rode without stopping, and he created a solitary, commanding figure who caused all he thundered past to pause and stare. At midday, when the sun reached her zenith, he rested the flagging steed beneath the shade of a palm. He waited until the blowing breaths of the animal decreased, walking him a bit to keep him from stiffening, then took reins in hand again and mounted up. And so his journey went, taking him even into darkness, when nothing but starlight and the moon's porcelain face lit his way. Through villages and terraced farmland he followed the trail, all the way to the edge of the great mountain ranges, where his enemy likely gathered a few more men before riding the plains again.

And then, after several more days of hard travel, Morgan no longer needed to see the pair of tracks; he knew where Moussa went. He went into the city of Fez.

The sultan and his court were due to arrive there at any time, and to enter the city would be a dangerous prospect for Morgan, for if he were recognized, the army would try to arrest him. But that consideration gave him no pause, for he was accustomed to disregarding personal danger in the pursuit of honor in any form. He could think no thoughts of self-peril, only thoughts of Gwenllian and vengeance. And so, he put spurs to the stallion when he would slow, and then praised the valiant beast in the hush of night, just before he removed the still warm saddle and lay his head upon it to rest no more than a pair of hours.

After days of grueling travel he reached the last ridge above the old capital of Fez, an ancient city infinitely holy, and flanked by two high Atlas peaks, the whole protected by crenellated ramparts and square watch towers. Within, innumerable terraces and minarets crowded for space, and without, orchards of orange and lime striped the fields. As he paused upon the ridge Morgan scanned the trails leading into the city, noting a hovering of dust in the distance. Two caravans approached, both long ribbons of camels that bore captives to be sold as slaves. Shepherds herded flocks to market, country folk trudged with baskets of ripe fruit upon their heads. And one other menagerie journeyed on the trail.

Morgan swore. Below, the royal procession moved ponderously toward the great Gate of the Lion's Hill, entrance to the city. The sultan's entire court traveled in a straggling line: the elite corps of soldiers uniformed in red, members of the royal harem attended by ladies-in-waiting, and dozens of servants toting sumptuous striped tents, baggage, and ammunition. Towed by mules, a complement of cannon brought up the rear, and on foot at the end of the long line danced the painted strumpets who followed the army everywhere.

Morgan's gaze shifted to the figure leading the ostentatious parade, the *Kaid el Meshwar,* or Grand Master of Ceremonies. And just behind, straddling a milk-colored horse and accompanied by a slave holding a monstrous parasol, rode the white-robed sultan himself.

Wanting to waste not a moment of time, Morgan reined his stallion around and rode to a secluded meadow he knew. He left the animal hobbled there, for his entry into the city must be as unremarkable as possible. On foot he approached the gate, timing his arrival to coincide with that of the royal procession. With *haik* in place, he stood aside like any other spectator.

The country's ruler passed through the ogee gate and nodded approvingly at the three human skulls displayed on tall pikes above it—victims of his bloodthirsty decrees—before barking at his slave to position the parasol more favorably to his complexion. Once the crowd's attention was fixed upon the sultan, Morgan stepped in line with the bevy of servants who marched along bearing the royal furniture. Making himself inconspicuous, he managed to pass through the gate without catching notice of the guards.

Once inside, he found himself in a city throbbing with activity. Overcrowded with caravans and the sultan's train, the streets roared. Outdoor kitchens, barbers, and tea sellers found more patrons than they could serve. Cafes turned thirsty travelers away. Pushing his way through the complaining masses, Morgan paused long enough to buy a drink of water. As he downed it, his vitals tensed with the knowledge that his enemy and Gwenllian were near. His own journey's pace had been so swift that Moussa could not possibly have arrived in Fez more than a few hours earlier. It would be Morgan's task now to make discreet inquiries in an attempt to discover where the monster lodged.

The knowledge proved easy to glean, for the scoundrel with the sightless eye was well known here, and his arrival with a woman in tow was news for gossip. In the bazaar Morgan bought a white burnoose in exchange for the chestnut one that was more distinctive to his tribe, then set off for a particular address, wending through streets so mazelike and narrow that the stirrups of riders scraped the walls of facing buildings. An hour remained until twilight and he knew he must tarry until then, observe the comings and goings from Moussa's address while plotting a way to breach the walls and access the rooftop.

He fastened his gaze to the lodging place and eyed the crude cedar door. Then he calculated the height of the mud facade and that of the building at the end of the street, judging the latter elevation to be lower. The minutes ticked by, and pedestrians slowly vanished in order to go inside to partake of the evening meal. Then came the *muezzin*'s call to prayer, and an hour or so later, the sound of feminine chatter floating on the air. Moroccan women traditionally spent their evenings upon the roof terraces, which were built so close together that neighbors could gossip without leaving their own embroidered cushions. With their veils cast aside, the females of Fez nightly shared with friends and family the boxes of sticky candies to which they were famously partial.

Listening to the soft murmur above his head, Morgan continued to watch Moussa's door for another half hour until the streets stood almost empty. Then, rechecking his pistol and fingering the hilt of his sword, he judged the night dark enough to suit his purpose.

A mule stood tethered nearby, and as the street was too narrow for the animal to turn about, Morgan backed it up several paces to the end of the row of dwellings. Climbing upon its rump, he straightened and grasped the bars of an upper story window before hoisting himself onto the building's roof. Crouching low, he paused to study the sea of terraces surrounding him, and saw that the vague shapes of lounging, pale-garbed women decorated almost every one. A few of their dusky, unveiled faces were dimly illuminated by the flicker of brass oil lamps fending off the close of early night. Morgan knew he would have to be careful, and very fortunate in his trek across this lofty territory forbidden to his gender. Moorish law decreed that if any man were discovered violating this most sacred feminine domain, he would be promptly arrested, fined, and imprisoned.

Unfortunately, Moussa's building was hemmed on three sides by terraces. After a moment of deliberation, Morgan decided to cross the westerly one, for its kohl-eyed occupant reclined alone upon her pile of cushions.

She spotted him immediately, for she was just lighting a lamp when he boldly stepped around the bordering wall. The yellow arc fell full upon his face, and with a gasp the youthful girl stared at him with indignation, her mouth opening to scream. But he made no threatening move in her direction, only smiled and begged her pardon in a most gallant voice.

For a second or two he thought she would screech an alert anyway, but slowly her lips closed, then curved shyly in response to his affecting grin. Perhaps she decided he went to meet a lover, for after a wistful sigh the girl blew out her lamp and allowed him to pass in conspiratorial darkness.

The terraces were all accessed by sets of winding stairs leading down into open courtyards flanked by rooms, and Moussa's lodging was no different. Drawing his revolver, Morgan noiselessly descended a few steps while hugging the plaster wall and listening for sounds below. A burst of low male laughter arrested his progress. He stilled, and smelled the strong odor of *kif*.

With a stealth that came as second nature, he crept onward, hugging the curved wall until a faint glow of lamplight spilled over his boots. One more step and the courtyard came into view below. Gwenllian sat huddled upon its tiles, her hands bound in her lap, a thong looped about her neck and tethered to a ring in the pink-tinted wall. Her hair was tangled and unbound, falling half over her lowered sunburnt face. Her garments were filthy and stained with long-dried blood. A lamp flickered close to her feet, and next to it sat a tray of untouched food.

She was alive. In spite of her disheveled appearance, a relieved sigh hissed through Morgan's teeth. Regardless of what treatment she had suffered at Moussa's hands, Gwenllian was alive.

He could see no sign of her captors, and their voices no longer penetrated the night, leaving Morgan to suspect they occupied one of the rooms off the courtyard. His boots soundless, he warily closed the distance between Gwen and himself, his crossing not immediately catching the notice of her downcast eyes. Then, startled by his shadow, she glanced up.

When she would have cried out and struggled to her feet, he signaled for her silence, then removed the poniard from his boot and in a deft slice freed her from her bonds. All the while she clung wildly to him, and although caution and time forbade it, he folded her in his arms for several frantic seconds. The sight of her face sent wrath spiralling through his chest and he cursed beneath his breath. She had been ill-treated, her lips and jaw bruised and bloodied.

"Where's Moussa?" he hissed, gently touching her tangled hair. His eyes swept the dark recesses of the pillared courtyard and its corridors.

"Not here. But there are three other men—in the room to the left."

"Keep behind me. Move with no noise."

They started forward to cross the length of the courtyard. But fortune would not allow them an easy escape. Goatskin soles pounded upon the tiles all at once, and before Gwen could blink, two of her ruthless wardens emerged from the gloomy corridor.

Faster than thought, and with exceeding skill, Morgan fired his pistol and shot them both. He hesitated a few seconds then, waiting with the weapon poised for the third man to appear. When he did not, Morgan gripped Gwen's arm to pull her toward the narrow stairway that led down to the street. Before they had taken two steps, a figure leapt from the blackness, and his body hurtled into

297

the chieftain's to slam him against the unyielding tiles. The weight of the huge attacker pinned the leaner man, but Morgan managed to seize the poniard from his boot and roll, and raised an arm to stab the burly chest. In a countermove, his foe lunged and pinioned the Berber's arm. A mortal struggle followed.

Gwen frenziedly scrabbled about the floor to find the fallen revolver. At last she seized it, but before she could put a finger to the trigger and properly aim, Morgan wrestled free and again made good use of his poniard. Not hesitating a second after his brutal but necessary deed, he captured Gwenllian's hand and pulled her down the stair. For a moment he stood on the threshold surveying the tranquil street, then bade her run with him as fast as she could.

They sprinted over endless blocks. When Gwenllian's pace flagged, Morgan dragged her along with an arm about her waist, and when anyone passed, he drew her into the shadows and buried her face against his chest to smother the sound of her labored breathing. They dashed past a palatial mosque where amber light splashed from the holy interior and revealed rows of worshippers prostrate upon gold-fringed rugs. Passing a sluggish canal, they heard the sound of a rolling millwheel churning water afloat with cattle carcasses. Flutes and bagpipes played mournful tunes in accompaniment to their flight, and the lingering scent of incense and tobacco drifted upon the air to sting their nostrils.

At last they neared the city gates, and Morgan

halted their headlong pace with an abrupt tug upon her sleeve. "Damn!" he cursed, his breath coming fast from the long run. "The gates are closed already! We've arrived too late."

Doubled over with the ache in her lungs, Gwen regarded him fearfully through the fall of her hair.

At once remorseful, Morgan put a hand to her head and drew her close, his voice quiet with reassurance. "It's all right, it's all right. We'll stay until morning, get food and an extra horse. Come on." He clasped her about the shoulders and helped her over the uneven ground that was strewn with broken crates. "We'll find some place to rest and wait out the night."

All the shops in the bazaar were closed, and knowing that Gwen's bloodstained apparel would arouse curiosity in the morning light, Morgan asked her to keep an eye out for a new wardrobe. Before she scarcely understood his meaning, he guided her beneath a clothesline strung between two tumbledown dwellings, and told her to wait. Then, eyeing each flapping garment in turn, he climbed upon a wooden trough and, with one agile leap, yanked a burnoose loose from its moorings.

"Morgan!" she whispered in outrage, glancing up at the windows of the house.

Tucking the stolen garment beneath his arm, he grinned with all the charm of a mischievous boy. "Sometimes necessity makes a thief, eh?"

He led her through more black, labyrinthine streets until they came to a square where the huddled forms of sleeping Moors resembled heaps of forgotten rags.

"It's not quite the Hotel la Villa de France, is it?" Morgan quipped with a rueful look around. "I'm sorry I can't do better than this, Gwen. But it would be risky to seek lodging anywhere. My face is too well known here."

"The sultan . . . ?"

"He arrived today. Unfortunately I must postpone the pleasure of hunting Moussa for the time being, and get you away from Fez as quickly as possible. He and the sultan aren't the only threats here. We must make certain you draw no attention to yourself. Whatever you do, speak no words of English. Few Christians have ever penetrated the walls of this city. It's holy—full of shrines and such—and the natives would consider your presence a sacrilege."

"I—I understand."

He thought her manner seemed odd all at once, reticent and strained.

"What is it, Gwen?"

"Nothing." Twisting her hands, she made to sit down upon an upturned crate, only to realize that it was full of rotten fruit.

Morgan regarded her through the darkness. She looked forlorn and lost, and he wanted to comfort her, wanted no restraint between them. There were too many things they needed to speak about, not the least of which was the death of Robyn Breese. And although the thought twisted his belly, he wanted to know all that had happened to her while she had been in the hands of his enemy.

Reaching out his arms, he took her cold, stiffened body into his embrace, but Gwen would not respond to his attempts at comfort. She stood rigidly with her legs trembling and her face averted, and after a moment he drew her down upon the warm dusty pavement. She sat ramrod straight, hugged herself with her arms, and did not touch him. He did not know what to say, did not know what was wrong with her. For a moment they both stared out at the eerily tranquil square and its slumbering mounds, and heard nothing but the distant bray of a donkey and the yowl of a hound. The world seemed very lonely.

Heartsick, unable to resist Gwen's warmth, Morgan placed his hands upon either side of her face. Earlier, she had drawn the *haik* over its lower half, and now he made to pull the linen free. But she stayed his hand, looking straight ahead at the harsh shadow-line of the city ramparts and avoiding his eyes with studious care. "Don't," she said curtly.

Angered and confused, Morgan desisted in his efforts to touch her for the time being, hoping to hearten her with news he had gleaned from the pasha in Mequinez. "I think I know where your father is, Gwen."

She twisted her head to look at him.

"He may be in the hands of French authorities—there's a military outpost on the Algerian border where the Zemours could have left him. But you mustn't get your hopes up too high, because the information came from the pasha, who I can't trust. He bribed Moussa to detain me at the feast. But it would be his way to speak the truth even as he betrayed me."

"You found Robyn, I suppose," Gwen murmured after a moment, looking skyward.

"Yes. I'm sorry." Morgan made to take her hand, but she slid it away.

"I've been concerned about . . ." She faltered and the sentence trailed away.

Morgan read her thoughts. "I had Robyn buried with my men."

She made a bitter sound. "He would have hated being buried here, in this country."

Morgan wanted to apologize, but found the depth of his feelings, and his guilt, inexpressible. He rubbed a palm against his thigh and let the moments pass.

"Hassan fought bravely," Gwen murmured, drawing up her knees and laying her cheek against them. "They all did. You have a right to be proud." She turned her face in the opposite direction, away from him, and let it rest upon her knees again. "I killed one of Moussa's men. Hacked him with a sword. It's odd—how I feel no remorse over it. Maybe I'll be judged for that." She hesitated. "Do you think so?"

"I think the Almighty will be too busy dealing with me to bother."

She did not smile at his attempt at dark humor, but stared into the blackness of the African night, still removed.

Wanting to be gentle, but losing patience, Morgan reached to take her face within his palms again, brooking no evasion. He dragged the *haik* away, and although there was only moonlight to limn the delicate features, he saw again the bruises that smudged the corners of her mouth. Steeling himself for her answer, his stomach knotting peculiarly, he asked in a low voice, "What did Moussa do, Gwen? Tell me . . . it's time to tell me."

She bent her head so that her brow just touched his chest, but did not answer.

"Gwen . . . ?"

She began to shiver and, abandoning her aloofness all at once, slid her arms about his shoulders and clenched his back until he felt the bite of her nails through his burnoose. "Did he touch you?" he asked in a voice that was almost strangled.

Seconds passed. "Yes."

The world spun. "What else?"

She said nothing and he closed his eyes and laid back his head, swallowing against the tightness that squeezed his throat. Then he buried his fingers deep in her tangled hair and forced her chin up. He wanted to know everything, every detail. And, he did not want to know. *"What else?"* he demanded.

She stared at him through lids that were half closed. "Nothing. Nothing."

A series of pictures flashed across Morgan's mind. He could not shut them out. "Tell me the truth, Gwen. Damn it, tell me the truth. Did he—"

"I told you!" She wrenched out of his hold and shifted away from him on the hard ground, jerking her sleeve from his fingers. "I told you."

Morgan rose to his feet, and pulling her up, thrust the wad of stolen burnoose into her arms. "Put it on," he said, directing her back into the deepest shadows. "Take the others off."

She stared at the bundle with her teeth a-chatter. *"Do* it!" he ordered.

Frightened by his vehemence, she turned her

back in modesty and sidled between two rows of the stacked fruit crates. After giving him another apprehensive glance, she slowly unsashed the stained garments. Pushing the burnoose off her shoulders she dropped it to the ground, then untied the drawstring of the shift, which she let slither past her waist and down beyond her freezing thighs.

As the last garment fell Morgan turned his head and looked back over a shoulder.

Gwenllian glanced up, caught him regarding the pale form of her nude young body. In his handsome face she saw not only love, but something else akin to both anguished pain and helpless rage that made her instantly raise a hand and strike his face.

"Don't look at me like that!" she said through clenched teeth. "Don't *ever* look at me like you're seeing me with *him!*"

Morgan did not flinch when she delivered the stinging blow. Nor did he say a word or take his eyes from her. He only waited until she had donned the clean, stolen clothing, and then he reached out his arms and drew her close, sinking to the ground with her clasped against his chest. He stroked her head, murmured low words, rocked her in the way male comforts female and lover comforts lover.

Rocked and rocked, until all the tears that could ever be spent over the loss of innocence were spent.

Sixteen

She thought it strange how the brutal circumstances that had both calloused and strengthened her had likewise made the man who loved her vulnerable. But in the space of that heart-wounding night, the two of them, the Welshwoman and the Berber chieftain, had altered.

When the darkness glided away on velvet slippers to allow dawn's creep across the almond skies, Morgan shifted in his sitting position, waking her, and as she opened her eyes and looked full into his face, she read the changes there.

She knew he had not slept at all. He had kept his eyes open and watched all night . . . thought all night. His gaze was bright, hard, the dark rims of the irises blacker than ever about the paler blue. And she thought, he is mad with vengeance, with guilt. He blames himself. And his love for me . . . he wears it full in his eyes.

The mingled expressions and what they would motivate him to do frightened her, and she threw both arms about his neck. He breathed a sigh against her hair and held her in response, but only for a moment. Then he gently disengaged himself, and said in a voice husky with the remnants of deep emotion, "Let us go to the marketplace and get something to eat. The horse sellers will be there soon. We'll buy a mount for you, then leave Fez before the hour is up. I am taking you back to Tangier."

He grasped her hand and pulled her to her feet, his manner tender just as it had been all night, but also grimly sober. And she did not dare to question his plans, although her heart was heavy with thoughts of what the future would hold.

He led her through back passageways whose squalid courts were not yet rousing, past holy shrines where the dead lay beneath inlaid stones bordered with wild poppies, past a raving holy woman with a stork perched upon her shoulder. On the outskirts of the souk he stopped to buy her a roll richly flavored with cinnamon and dates, and a cup of fragrant coffee from a copper urn. He stood in the shade with the hood of his burnoose pulled up over his head, making himself as inconspicuous as a man of his stature could possibly be, always keeping her protected in the shadow of his body. She stood eating in silence, and glanced askance at him as he took his own meal. His eyes never ceased to study the faces of all who passed, and she knew he watched for Moussa, and for the sultan's sentries.

The hush between them grew long, and nodding toward the tumbledown buildings with their canopies of ancient grapevines, she said, "Why does it seem that all of Morocco is crumbling, Morgan? Why does no one repair the ruins to what they once were?"

"There is a saying here—when Fortune has brought great happiness, it is followed by great sorrow, and when a thing comes to be perfect, it soon begins to fade."

"How cynical."

He shook his head. "It's not considered cynical, merely an acceptance of fate."

While she stood considering such a philosophy, he lightened the conversation. "Those children there—do you know why the barber is shaving their heads and leaving one long lock dangling behind the ears?"

She shook her head and observed the outdoor hairdresser with curiosity.

"It's so that Sidna Azrain—the Angel of Death—can reach down, and with one quick snatch haul them up to Paradise. He's a blind angel, you know."

When she smiled he glanced down at her, his face relaxing just long enough so that the lines at both corners of his mouth deepened nicely.

"Put the veil back up," he said then. "And let's go look at horses."

As they hastened past the lines of shops, avoiding a noisy troop of musicians beating their tom-toms and tambourines, three soldiers in the red coats of the sultan's corps suddenly appeared around a corner. Before Gwen had scarcely glimpsed them, Morgan pulled her inside a leather shop where the two of them waited until the danger had passed.

When the way was clear again, he led her to a

busy section of the market, where many wealthy Moors in fine dress congregated. Trotting alongside Morgan, keeping up with his urgent stride, Gwen found herself searching faces as thoroughly as he. She hunted for Moussa's horrible visage, terrified that she would suddenly see it emerge from some shop or leer down at her from the back of his snorting Barb. But there was no sight of him, and at last they arrived at the souk where a pipe-smoking Arab had tethered a line of horses for sale. Slowing his step, Morgan inspected the animals while Gwen hung back and listened to the trader haggle with exaggerated respect. While she waited, she observed the activity a few yards away. Upon a huge wooden platform in the center of the square, a group of bedraggled women and female children crouched, huddling closer when they were given some barked command by a turbaned Arab who flourished a long whip. Well-dressed Moorish gentlemen circled about the collection of frightened women, scrutinizing each in turn, and sometimes they stepped up on the platform to touch them.

"I have purchased the black mare for you," Morgan said, coming up behind Gwen with the horse in tow. "She's not as fine as I would like, but the best of the lot."

"They're being sold as slaves, aren't they?" she said in outrage, indicating the group of wretched women with a nod of her head.

"It's called the *Sok-el-rhazel*—the Market of the Gazelles. Three or four thousand of them are sold each year. Most are Sudanese, captured in their villages and transported here. The rest are of various nationalities, travelers perhaps, who were unlucky enough to fall into the wrong hands."

Appalled, Gwen stared, scarcely believing that slave trafficking was so blatantly conducted at the close of the century. "What will happen to them?"

"Most will become house slaves, or concubines of the gentlemen who are looking at them now. But let us go," he said in a hushed voice, indicating that she should mount. "And keep your eyes lowered when we pass beneath the arches. We don't want to catch the notice of the guards at the gate."

Moments later, as they approached the huge ogee gate with its decoration of bleached skulls, Gwen was beset with apprehension, likening the exit to an open prison door guarded by uncharitable wardens. She felt they could not walk through quickly enough, and grew impatient with Morgan's unhurried pace. He strolled beside the shoulder of her horse, and casually reached to adjust the *haik* about his face as any traveler would do who was preparing to journey upon the dusty trails outside. And yet, despite his air of calm, she saw the muscles along his shoulders tense at sight of the two guards posted at the great portal.

With their rifles resting at their sides and their legs crossed at the ankles in a relaxed pose against the wall, they seemed to pay no particular attention to the tall man and the woman he escorted, and Gwen released her indrawn breath, thinking that they were to be allowed to pass with no detainment. But before she could whisper her relief to Morgan, a dozen soldiers suddenly appeared atop the ramparts and formed a solid, ominous line that stretched the length of it. They carried rifles and raised them to their shoulders while a half dozen more red-coated men rushed forward from the guard house.

Gwen froze in terror with the realization that she and Morgan were not to escape the city. He had been recognized.

His composure in the face of the ensuing uproar astounded her. While the approaching soldiers growled commands at him and cocked their pistols, he leaned close and in a quiet voice ordered, "Go to the *fondak*, Gwen—to the caravan drivers heading north. Tell them you are the wife of Rhaman. Here's some money—"

He surreptitiously passed a flat wallet beneath her knee which was trembling against the saddle leather. "Pay them well and they'll take you safely to Tangier. When you arrive there, book passage home immediately."

"No!" she cried, glancing from the bellowing soldier to Morgan's face. "I'll not go! I'll stay here, close to you."

He gripped her hand hard where it lay atop his shoulder and hissed, "I forbid it. You can do nothing here, you're in danger. Do as I told you. *Swear to me.*"

With their revolvers aimed at his chest, two soldiers barked at him to step away from the horse and relinquish his weapons.

"Swear it, Gwen!" he commanded again through his teeth. "For God's sake, do it for me!"

He was glaring at her furiously even as the soldiers seized his arms and pinioned them. Throwing off their hands, he struggled to turn about again, shouting at Gwen to obey. But his concern for her earned him nothing but a swift and unsparing blow to the back of the shoulder with a revolver butt.

He staggered beneath the force of it, and with brutal hands three of the soldiers shoved him to the ground and stripped him of his weapons, while a cavalry mount caparisoned in scarlet was led forward by a guard. The resisting prisoner was yanked to his feet and handcuffed then, but all the while he kept his eyes fixed upon Gwen. He shouted over his bloodied shoulder for her to follow his orders, but his efforts gained him nothing but another silencing blow, and after he was slung groaning atop the saddle, the soldiers fell in around him and whipped up his steed.

"Morgan!" Gwen screamed, instinctively reaching out her hands. *"Morgan!"*

In the company of soldiers the Berber chieftain was led into the great courtyard of the sultan's palace, the whole of which was enclosed in gray battlements and guarded by a lofty bastion decorated with pink and blue archways. Though some areas were under repair and the bastion itself newly whitewashed, the same general air of decay pervaded here as it did everywhere in Morocco. Incongruously, in the center of the vast courtyard sat an ornate carriage—the only one in the country—that Queen Victoria had given the sultan as a gift of goodwill. Morgan gave it little notice, too preoccupied with evaluating the security of the entrances

311

and exits, and noting the number of sentries and their weapons. After several seconds of calculation, he knew escape was impossible.

It seemed the Commander of the Faithful had been out riding, for suddenly he appeared trotting across the courtyard upon his white charger, surrounded by guards and by two bearded Negroes who waved the flies from his face with enormous reed fans. His stirrups glittered gold, and his garments of white silk enshrouded his stout figure in a mummylike fashion. Morgan had never received the dubious honor of a personal interview before, and he assessed now the visage of his country's ruler, who, according to the belief of the faithful, was the true successor to the Prophet.

His Royalty's skin was as crinkled as dark parchment, and his eyes stared out from beneath lids that were only half open, giving the impression that nothing roused him to any great display of energy. Indeed, an air of ennui surrounded him as he motionlessly sat his horse and stared with an obsidian gaze at the prized prisoner circled by three dozen ruthless sentries.

In a show of obeisance, the soldiers dismounted and bowed before their potentate, and Morgan was flung to the ground as well, his treatment no more gentle than it had been at the gate.

"So," the sultan finally pronounced in a lazy drawl, letting his gaze flick over the swelling eye and bleeding nose of his captive. "I have caught up with you at last, Rhaman."

"It would seem so."

The sultan's steed pawed and nipped a fly from

its shoulder, which went to circle about the sultan's face. One of the fan-wielding slaves vigorously brushed it away. "I am surprised," the tyrant said. "Surprised that you made it so easy for me."

"Sorry to give you so little challenge."

The sarcasm was ignored by the ruler. "I am curious. I know you to be a dauntless man, Rhaman, but also quite prudent, especially when it comes to eluding me. What cause was so important that it brought you into Fez?"

Morgan's hands were still bound and he lifted a shoulder to wipe the blood from his eye. "A cause I prefer to keep private."

The arrogant response angered the sultan, and although the boredom-dulled eyes did not snap, the thin mouth turned down at the corners in the manner of a thwarted child. Speculatively, he gazed at the man who showed neither intimidation nor respect, and his tone hardened. "You are a most exasperating fellow, Rhaman, and the reckoning between us has come due at last. You should be less insolent, for your life is hanging in the balance. However, to your good fortune, I am renowned for my benignity, and I will grant you the benefit of a hearing like any other prisoner. You are charged with inciting the mountain people, with persuading them that my taxation practices are unjust and should therefore be ignored. You have led them into war against me, and slain many of my soldiers. Do you deny these charges?"

"I deny none of them," Morgan answered. His mouth curved. "But then, you didn't expect me to, did you?"

"One never knows how Allah may visit the heart of a sinner and move him to repent. And I have been known to be lenient on occasion, when proper repentance is displayed." He observed the prisoner from beneath his brown papery lids, his expression one of vague regret, for he rued the destruction of anything that could be of possible value to him.

"Well," Morgan said, "Allah has not visited my heart. Either it is too hard or not sufficiently humble to invite a divine call."

"Spoken as I suspected it would be," the sultan pronounced with a sigh. "Alas, 'tis a pity to destroy you. You are famed for your horsemanship, for your skill with weapons, and for the coolness of your reason. You could have commanded the elite corps of my soldiers had you chosen to follow the divine path of Allah and serve the descendant of his Prophet. But you have chosen a life of rebellion and war instead, and shall earn a fitting punishment for it." He waved a hand to terminate the interview. "It is as Allah wills."

Gwen sat alone amidst a sea of hostile natives, who, should they discover her nationality, would at the very least refuse to give her food and lodging. At the very worst, they would kill her. She did not dwell long upon the thought; already she hovered on the verge of panic at the direness of her predicament. Not only was she without an ally, but she spoke no more than a few useless phrases of Arabic; if she should open her mouth and utter one word of English, she was doomed.

314

For long moments she simply sat atop the saddle, staring at the notched prints in the dust where the cavalry mounts had lurched forward carrying their riders. A film of dust still hovered from the galloping hooves, and it was circumnavigated by an army of vicious flies that made Gwen's patient mare stamp and swish her tail. When the horse swung her head around and nudged the stirrup, Gwen whispered, *"What am I to do? What am I to do?"*

She decided that leaving was out of the question. To ride away from Fez without a backward glance and abandon Morgan to an uncertain fate was more than she could bear. But how could she survive here alone, even for a brief spell? And even if she found Morgan in the hands of the sultan, what could she possibly do to assist him? She assumed he would be taken to the ruler's palace where charges would be brought against him and a sentence passed.

She shuddered as she contemplated the punishment that would be meted out by the dictator of such a barbarous place. Imprisonment in some foul jail would probably be a kind fate compared to the other forms of torture she had seen practiced in Morocco.

Forlorn, she searched the dark foreign faces of the crowd and found them all unfriendly. Some gave her sidelong glances as they passed, for women did not usually go out unescorted. She slumped a bit to make herself less conspicuous, for somewhere in the city, Moussa might still be hunting for his lost captive.

The usual traffic clogged most of the avenues, so when Gwen prodded the mare into the chaotic midst of it and trotted along with the jostling flow, few took time to notice her. In an aimless, desperate path she wandered up and down the streets, frantic to think of some plausible plan of action. She ignored the beggars who snatched at her stirrups, clutching more tightly to the money purse hidden in the folds of her burnoose. She was parched with thirst but too fearful to approach a water seller lest her pale blue eyes and unescorted status pique his interest.

At last, quite by accident, she discovered the gray and desolate walls of the prison, whose only entrance was secured by iron-bound oaken doors inset with a single barred window. For a while she observed the activity about the jail, noting that visitors seemed to be allowed to speak to inmates through the window bars. Only one guard was visible. He wore a fez tipped back over his sweating brow, and lazed in the shade with his outdated rifle propped against a wall. His relaxed posture suggested negligence, as if it had never occurred to him that the security of his fortress could be threatened in any way.

Looking about, Gwen searched for a place to wait, a place where she could watch the comings and goings of the prison without attracting notice. Across the street, a few wooden vats used for dying leather sat abandoned in rows, and after tethering her horse behind them, Gwen eased down amidst the slatted vessels. With her *haik* pulled high over her nose, she watched the street for a while, noticing how the shimmering waves of heat made the pedestrians look like undulating wraiths. The sun beat down upon her head, and she rested it upon her knees, swallowing against both the dryness of her throat and a lump of anguish. She tried to think of Wales, remember its cool mists and gentle rains and the safety of Ardderyd, but she could not hold on to the elusive images long, seeing instead a vision of the Squire of Hiraeth as he stood before a merciless sultan. What would his sentence be? Would the young chieftain spend his days locked in that crumbling fortress with its lazy guard, or suffer some swifter end?

"God help him," she breathed, feeling sick. "And tell me what to do . . ."

After a moment she lifted her head again and focused on the crowd, watching a boy on the corner as he tried to sell week-old French newspapers. She had seen other boys do the same in Tangier, but this lad was particularly enterprising and energetic, hawking his papers while offering to do any number of other odd services for prospective patrons. He worked tirelessly in the heat on bare, dusty legs, smiling and bowing with an engaging manner whenever he accepted the coins tossed out to him. Gwen's interest sharpened when the urchin carried a cup of water to the prison sentry, who flicked a coin at his feet in payment.

But much to her disappointment, the waif vanished after that, and with her energies sapped by heat and fear, Gwen folded her arms across her knees and laid her head down, dozing for nearly an hour before the clatter of hooves startled her awake.

She quickly pressed herself closer to the vat, peering around it to see a detachment of red-coated soldiers thundering down the avenue, riding two abreast and carrying fixed bayonets that flashed in the sun like bolts of lightning. In the midst of their terror-inspiring lines, Morgan rode, his hands bound together atop the saddle pommel.

Gwen rose to her feet with her heart throbbing. She watched while two soldiers seized the prisoner by his arms and hauled him from the saddle. They barked a command to the indolent guard, who briskly snapped to attention at the prison gate. Gwen despaired as she realized that Morgan was to be confined in the terrible place and, forgetting her own danger, stepped out from her hiding place.

Morgan's keen eyes spied the sudden movement, and narrowed in distress as they alit upon her poised figure across the street.

She put a hand to her throat, hovering on the verge of calling out, but he shook his head to stop the dangerous impulse. He had been dragging his feet, and one of the soldiers struck him across the shoulder in a cruel blow that made him sway. He grunted, lifted his head, and fastened his eyes to Gwen's again, and their fierce expression clearly commanded her to leave without delay.

After the guard unlocked the forbidding prison gate, the soldiers shoved their captive inside, then swung the massive portal shut again amidst a rasping of unyielding iron. The sepulchre boom of its closing chilled Gwenllian, and after watching the soldiers remount and spur their horses out of the square, she hastened across the street.

All day she had seen visitors speak with inmates

through the bars, and even pass them clothing, and so she moved toward the iron grill with confidence that she would be allowed to do the same. The guard eyed her with interest, but she kept walking in a straight course and struggled to hide her fear of him. He raked her with his gaze, then grabbed his rifle and with a swift motion stabbed at a basket of oranges beside the wall, spearing one with his fixed bayonet.

The action made her start. He laughed, then removed the gruesomely spitted fruit and tore into its peel with his teeth, ignoring her as she sidled to the gate. Standing on tiptoe, she peered through the bars and focused her eyes in the gloom, surveying the vast interior courtyard where Morgan had been abandoned. She recoiled. Conditions inside were so appalling, and the stench so overpowering, that she had to step back and cover her mouth in reaction.

The guard smirked while juice from the orange dribbled down his mouth. She turned away from him and, steeling herself, raised up for another look.

The prison was a sort of unpaved square open to the air and devoid of cells, designed as nothing more than a holding space for countless inmates who shambled about its befouled and putrid-smelling space like lost souls draped in rags. All manner of pathetic humanity huddled dumbly in its corners and beside its noxious fountain, while bearded madmen resembling animals babbled dementedly with their legs fettered in chains. Other wretches sat lifelessly against the walls or slept curled in the shade. Sanitation was nonexistent and all around the perimeter of the awful place, wide sewers ran in blackened streams that invited pestilence.

Gwen despaired. *Morgan was to exist here*.

He moved out of the shadows, his tall healthy frame a contrast to all the others. With a cry, she thrust her hands through the bars and he seized them between his own.

"Why did you disobey me, Gwen?" he demanded without preamble. Anguish darkened the blue of his gaze and made his voice harsh. "You can do nothing for me now. You only risk your own life by staying here."

Her eyes filled with tears and she gripped his hands in a frantic way. "What will happen to you, Morgan? What will they do?"

"Go," he said urgently, refusing to answer. "Go to the *fondak* and pay the caravan drivers to take you to Tangier before it's too late. Go home. I want to be able to think of you there. I want to think of you safe, at Ardderyd."

"You can't ask it of me, Morgan," she argued, tormented. "I won't leave you! If the circumstances were reversed and I were in trouble, you would never walk away."

"No, I'd move heaven and earth for you, Gwen. But there are times when circumstances cannot be changed, no matter what anyone wills. I've led a dangerous life, one of my own choosing. I've warred against the sultan knowing the consequences if I fell into his hands. Now I must accept my fate, and I could do that with dignity, even here—" He waved his hand at the abominable space behind him. "Except for you. Oh, Gwen, to what pass have I brought us? My God, I want to rip these bars away so that I can make you safe. Don't you understand the danger, don't you realize what could happen to you in this city?"

"I realize nothing except that I want to help you!"

He put his hands through the bars and took her flushed face between them, speaking with such tenderness that fresh tears spilled from her lashes. "You can only help me by going to the *fondak* now. By letting me kiss your hands one more time before watching you walk away. You must have the courage to do that, Gwen. You must have the courage to say goodbye."

"I can't, I can't," she whimpered, leaning her brow against the bars and closing her eyes.

"Yes, you can. I know you have courage."

"It has deserted me now! Oh, Morgan, must you spend your life locked in this wretched place? Tell me! What will happen to you? Are you to endure some terrible punishment? I won't go unless you tell me—I must *know.*"

But he only shook his head and took hold of her fingers again. And at the touch of his warm flesh, a sudden spiraling tremor shook her body, for she vividly remembered a man whose palms had been sliced with a dagger in Tangier, then bound together by a leather glove that shrank with the sun.

"The punishment of the salt," she gasped, breath deserting her. "Is that to be your fate, Morgan. Is it? *Is it?*"

When he made no reply she scrabbled to draw his fine and skillful hands to her lips as if she could protect them, whimpering, her anguish too great to utter.

"Gwen," she heard him say in a voice thick with emotion. "Go now. Please go."

Unable to look into his eyes again, she clenched his hands in one last spasm of grief. Then she turned away. Running blindly across the street, ignoring his anguished call, she thought of the torture he was to endure, of the death that would be slow and excruciating. *It must not happen! She must prevent it!*

Stumbling back to her hiding place, she squatted behind a vat and put her head in her hands. Silently she keened. What was she to do? What *could* she do? With feverish hands she pulled out the wallet of money Morgan had given her and counted it with clumsy fingers. It was a substantial amount, much more than she had expected, and she realized it was probably the money paid to Morgan by the British government for his assistance with their espionage.

A plan began to form in her brain as she counted the notes a second time, but she could think of no way to carry it out. She looked about, frowning, and her gaze happened upon the boy on the corner that she had seen earlier selling French newspapers. He was taking a rest from his endeavors, and sat in the shade nearby with one of his papers spread out on his knees, which he appeared to be reading. He pointed to the printed words with a skinny forefinger and murmured aloud, stumbling over some of the pronunciations. She wondered how well he understood the language. She knew travelers regularly journeyed to Fez from French-held Algeria, and francs had been accepted currency in Morocco for years.

"*Parlez-vous français?*" she asked him a moment later, breathless with hope.

In surprise the youngster jerked his head up. Then he smiled, and the band of white teeth lit his dark pointed face. "Some. I am learning. I have a friend from Algiers who sometimes teaches me the sounds."

He had replied in a garbled tongue that was a massacre of the French language. But Gwen understood. "I'll help you, if you like," she offered, hardly able to keep her voice steady.

For a moment he studied her eyes with his own bright black ones, obviously curious over the identity of this strange unescorted female who offered to tutor a paper seller in a foreign language. But he was young enough not to question kindness or be suspicious of it and, shrugging, pointed out a few words on the page he did not know how to pronounce.

After an hour the pair grew comfortable with one another, and once they had perused the entire news sheet, the boy named Kelab laid it aside with a great show of contented pride. "The next time my friend comes to Fez," he declared, beating his chest with a dirty fist, "I will show him how well I can speak."

"Kelab," Gwen said. "That guard over there—the prison guard. I'm wondering . . . do you know him?"

"Oh, yes," he returned with an important nod. "I fetch water for him every day he is on duty."

"Would you say that he is an agreeable sort, or one to be avoided? Pleasant, or cruel?"

The boy cocked his head thoughtfully and put his arm about a skinny stray dog that had been nosing about for scraps. "When he wants me to fetch him *kif* or water he can be quite agreeable, yes."

She nodded, choosing her words with care. "There's a man, a prisoner that the soldiers brought in today. His name is Rhaman."

Letting go of the dog, the boy turned his head and observed her with speculation in his large clever eyes. "I know of Rhaman. Everyone does. I saw him locked away in the prison today."

Gwen lowered her lashes and waited while a group of ragged musicians passed. "I would like to help Rhaman get out of that dreadful place, but . . . I need assistance."

"What kind of assistance?"

"I—if the guard were offered money," she said, "a great deal of money, do you think he would release Rhaman?"

"You are wanting to know if he can be bribed?"

"Yes."

Kelab stared straight ahead at two turbaned men who trotted by on shiny liver-colored mules, and his manner suddenly evolved from mischievous to wise. "There is not an official in all of Fez, mademoiselle, who will not take a bribe, if it is big enough."

Gwen's heart fairly leapt at his bald statement, and she eased out her wallet so that it remained half hidden in the folds of her robe. "Is—is five hundred francs a big bribe, Kelab?"

His stared at her. "It is very big."

"Then, if I were to go to the guard, would you escort me and speak on my behalf? I'll pay you handsomely for your help."

At first she thought he might refuse the payment on the basis of their brief but cordial friendship, but, if so, his entrepreneurial spirit quickly rose to the fore and smothered any trace of charity, so that he held out a flat brown palm to be crossed.

"Better to wait until dark when few are about," he advised, dropping his payment in the scarred leather pouch he carried strapped to his waist. "Another hour. Then we go and talk to the guard, just before he goes off duty."

She nodded and, committing a breach of Islamic etiquette, squeezed his hand.

Before long the shops began to close up for the day, and the traffic thinned to a laggard flow as twilight descended over the square like a hazy blue vapor puffed from the sky. Gwen watched every movement of the guard, watched him stroll restively, then smoke, then pace up and down the weed-lined prison wall. As she searched his face beneath his tasseled fez, she prayed a feverish prayer that he was a greedy soul.

At last, Kelab pronounced it dark enough, and set off to the prison in a jaunty march, where he greeted the guard with a flourish of his hand before sidling close to speak. After pointing to Gwen, who hung back in the shadows with her veil drawn close, he spoke Arabic in low and earnest tones.

Immediately the guard smiled, then laughed, his teeth flashing ivory in the gathering darkness. He gave some answer to Kelab, who, after arguing a bit, turned back to Gwenllian with a scowl upon his face and his arms crossed in an attitude of annoyance.

"He says five hundred francs is not enough to risk his life, mademoiselle. He says Rhaman was sentenced by the sultan himself, and to release him would be a fool's mission. I am sorry."

"Wait, Kelab," she said, realizing that the cooperation of this guard was Morgan's only hope. She took hold of her *haik,* and feeling along its hem, ripped out a small section of stitching and forced out the treasure she had hidden there. "Look at this."

Kelab stared at the gemstone cradled in her hand. Then a huge smile split his dark cherubic face.

"You tell him it will be his," Gwen instructed, "together with the money, if he will find a way to free Rhaman."

"I go to tell him now," Kelab declared. "You wait for me here."

He almost swaggered back to the guard then, and Gwen thought surely the resourceful urchin delivered the grandest sales pitch of his career before he signaled her to come forward with the gem.

The guard let his eyes roam over Gwen's veiled face and slender form. He was young, she realized, not much older than herself, but he possessed a shrewd and opportunistic countenance that warned her not to trust him far. In silence she glided closer to the lantern affixed to the outer prison wall and opened her hand to let him view the gem, certain that its unusual beauty and shape would be evident even to one who knew nothing at all of stones.

For long moments the young man studied it. Then he reached to stroke his unshaven chin in a contemplative way, which prompted Kelab to resume his persuasive dialogue in low but rapid tones. Glancing furtively about as if wary of watching eyes, the guard deliberated for long, vacillating moments, and at last gave an answer to the boy, which was curt and coolly delivered. After speaking, he waved Kelab away with both hands as if the sight of him had become a nuisance.

Motioning for Gwen to follow, Kelab stalked off, and when they were a little distance away from the prison, he turned to whisper, "I regret to tell you that the guard will make no promises, mademoiselle. But he says you may go outside the gates now and wait for him beside the south tower of the ramparts. Perhaps he will meet you there, he says, and bring with him what you want. Perhaps he will not. It is as Allah wills now."

Kelab raised his hands in an eloquent gesture. "The guard is afraid, and who would not be, eh? The money, the beautiful stone will be no use to him if he is caught and loses his head."

Her spirits not to be dampened, Gwen squeezed Kelab's shoulder in gratefulness, thanking him for his assistance and friendship.

"You should hurry," he prompted, sheepish with her effusiveness. "The gates will be closed soon."

When Gwen remounted the mare and approached the crouching Gate of Lion's Hill, its piked skulls shadowed now in the amethyst cloak of evening, she gripped the mare's reins hard. With dread, she eyed the keepers of the exit, terrified that they would detain her for some reason. They looked up, gave her curious glances, but made no move to stay her progress. When they cupped their hands and lit cigarettes of *kif,* the yellow glow of the flaring matches seemed to twist their faces into devil's masks.

The subsequent hours seemed endless. Alone and afraid, Gwen waited beside the ramparts, whose construction was so ancient and bleached that the structure resembled the hump-backed form of some fossilized beast. The moon rose high in the heavens, and spilled from her round silver countenance light so cold and dispassionate that the sphere seemed detached from her African domain. Gwen shivered, sitting her horse like a statue, listening, wondering, knowing if the guard did not soon appear all hope was lost for Morgan. And then, what would become of her? She had seen the caravan drivers depart for Tangier hours earlier.

Just as she began to despair, she heard the scrape of heavy boots. She stiffened and, leaning forward in the saddle, stared through the blackness to see who approached. Two figures walked alongside the wall. One of them was tall and had his hands bound together.

She slid off her horse and ran forward, but before she could get close, the guard made a harsh sound in Arabic to stop her. Then he turned to Morgan and, hauling back a fist, savagely sank it deep into the prisoner's middle. With a grunt, Morgan doubled over and fell to his knees, only to be sent sprawling by a kick to the small of his back.

The callous guard then barked some command at Gwen and barred her way when she would have flown to Morgan's side. Fearfully she stood staring up at him, not understanding a word of his gibberish.

"He's says . . . to give him what is his," Morgan interpreted in a thick voice, slowly raising up on all fours. "I suggest you do it . . . quickly."

Gwen drew out first the wallet, then the aquamarine on its golden chain. With a soft laugh the guard snatched them and riffled through the money to make certain that he had not been tricked. Satisfied, he removed a key from his pocket and cast it down upon the sand at Morgan's boots, then pivoted on a heel and left them.

Gwen flew to Morgan's side to help him to his feet, trembling with both relief and indignation. "Why did he hit you and knock you to the ground? It was a brutal thing to do!"

Morgan grunted. "I'm sure he felt I deserved a little battering since I was relieved of the sultan's punishment—and its unpleasant aftereffects."

Gwen fumbled in the dark to unlock his fettered wrists, and made a sound of disgust. "Daggers, rubbing salt in wounds, administering cruel and lingering deaths. In Wales they simply hang criminals and have done with it."

"In Wales," he returned, lifting a now freed hand to touch her face, "they breed remarkable women."

Seventeen

In their flight from Fez they retrieved the copper stallion from the meadow where it was hidden, and then rode as swiftly as their horses could carry them through the dangerous darkness. After several hours, when Gwen began to droop with fatigue, Morgan halted their progress and, throwing her saddle to the ground, bade her lie down.

"I'm taking you to Tangier," he said quietly as he covered her with the blanket still warm from the mare's back. "But I must go first to the mountains and gather some men together for an escort. Traveling with you alone on the open plains is too conspicuous. It invites attack, and there would be little I could do to protect you if we were confronted with a band of cutthroats. Or with Moussa and his men."

"My father," she murmured, her voice slurred with exhaustion. "What is to be done about my father?"

Morgan laid a soothing hand upon her hair. "I'll send some of my men to inquire at the French outpost in Figuig. No matter how long it takes I'll find

330

Sir Gerald, Gwen. But within the month I want you to be safely aboard a ship bound for Wales."

She lay in silence for a time. A field of tall fennel surrounded them, and the wind undulated through its curly tops, so that the stalks resembled green maidens dancing in the night. The plants smelled pungent and clean, she thought, almost like the garden at Ardderyd in summer. But the air here was hot, and when it blew across her face, its particles of sand pelted her flesh. She rested her cheek against the smooth leather of the saddle and put an arm over her eyes to protect them from the sting. Morgan sat close. She felt his presence keenly and grew desperate. The thought of their impending separation wrenched her, and with a determination that she knew was ill-advised, she searched for a way to delay it.

"What if I were to remain with you, Morgan?" she breathed with her face still against the saddle. "With your people in the mountains—just until you have located my father? I—I'm not ready to go home yet, not until I have some word of him."

Morgan had been easing a boot from his foot to empty it of sand. At her words he glanced up sharply, only to find that her face was turned away. He frowned. After the harrowing events of the last days, he had assumed that Gwen would want to flee Morocco as quickly as possible, but obviously he had misjudged her endurance. He knew she had changed, that she was not the same blithe and unworldly girl he had met in Tangier; indeed, when he had rescued her in Fez he had seen the differences all too clearly, and with an aching conscience.

She had suffered and survived, and now looked out at the world with eyes more darkly grave than ever before.

He closed a fist over the top of his boot and blamed himself for the tragedies that had shattered her once-secure life, and he feared that in some deep private part of her being Gwen blamed him, too. If she did not now, she would as time wore on. The thought tormented him. And now, she wanted to stay among his people in the mountains he called home . . .

A corner of his mouth lifted in rue. What did he have to offer her there, besides a mud-walled dwelling and the coarse society of a Berber village who would not understand her language or her ways. The people would accept her, of course, but only because she was the woman of their chieftain. Gwenllian would never be one of them. Marian had never been; the rebellious Welsh lass who had used neither henna nor kohl had spent her life in near social isolation, with only the love of Morgan's father to compensate for all she had sacrificed for him.

Leaning back upon his saddle with his hands behind his head, Morgan stared up at the stars. His eyes were filled with their bright and unreachable glitter, and for the first time in his life he bitterly resented his lack of the permanent things that make existence in the world comfortable.

But his life had been an unindulgent one, a harsh existence full of war and hardship that continued a tradition begun and held sacred by valiant ancestors. He experienced no bitterness over that burden of inheritance, no ire over the dangers his way of life demanded, but he did regret that he had nothing fine, nothing soft to offer the woman he loved. He regretted it sorely.

His eyes returned to Gwen's slender body where it lay curled upon the wind-rippled sand. She had fallen asleep long ago waiting for his answer, and now lay relaxed, one hand coiled close to her slightly parted lips and the other pillowing her tousled head.

Quietly raising up, Morgan shifted so that he could protect her body with the curve of his own, touching the cold rise of her frail shoulder with a hand more used to swordplay than tenderness. She did not awake, and in sudden weariness he bent his head to rest it against the voluptuous warmth of her hair, whose tresses he clenched within his fingers as if to bind himself to their delicate but enduring owner.

At last the two travelers entered the mountains, which were wild jagged things of red sandstone slashed with bottomless gullies. Paths undulated over the ridges like twisted ribbons, and terraced fields of barley graced the valleys. High above, on the limestone escarpments, olive trees clung as if for dear life. The resinous odor of evergreens filled the air, together with wild honeysuckle and rose, whose vines climbed like entwined lovers over rocks and honeycombed fissures.

Gwen stared about her in awe. Some of the trails wending through the ranges were so slippery and steep that she feared the mare would stumble and roll down, or plunge over a beetled cliff even while

Gwen clutched shrieking to the saddle. Morgan seemed unbothered by these precipitate passes, by the dizzying heights and breathtaking vistas. He casually pointed out the villages poised along the way where Berber lads herded goats, and men tended orchards of figs. As she looked out over the panorama, at the limitless spaces and soaring heights flooded with sun and canopied by the blue of heaven, she thought it a fitting land for Morgan Riff. He was truly born of it. The realization stung her.

All at once, he halted and raised a hand to point. Following the line of his finger she saw a fortress perched atop a cragged gray ridge. Built of clay, defended by crenellated walls and two square towers, the solemn bastion reminded her of some feudal keep ruled by a medieval lord. Though it was neither graceful nor elegant, its air of timelessness made it spectacular.

"It is the fortress that your father built for your mother, isn't it?" Gwen asked in wonder.

"Yes." Morgan regarded the structure for long moments with hard and ruthless eyes. "And it will be mine before the year is out."

He uttered the words with such icy calm that Gwen felt chilled. Before long, she knew that Rhaman would go and fight Moussa, and she knew that nothing she could say or do would keep him from it.

As if his threatening words had been heard by other ears, a gunshot exploded suddenly, followed by the ping of a bullet that buried itself in the sandstone cliff not a foot above Morgan's head.

In a flash he was off his horse and dragging

Gwenllian from hers, pulling her against the sheltering cliff face. She pressed herself to the sheer rock in terror, and realized that the enemy was poised above them on the pinnacle. By blocking the path of the slender passageway winding around the mountain, the attackers could pin them here, for she and Morgan were so tightly trapped on the path that the tiniest misstep would send them tumbling into a stony abyss. A few feet away the panicked horses stood perilously close to the edge, and they snorted and rolled their eyes in fear as their hooves sent sprays of sand slithering hundreds of feet down.

The air grew quiet, so that the sound of the cool wind whining around the facets of the vertical rock seemed loud. Listening tensely, Morgan stood with his body protecting Gwen's, while his eyes scrutinized every angle of the view. And then, he slowly raised the breech of the rifle to his shoulder and bent his head, sighting some point on the path that wrapped around the cliff and disappeared.

The flashing glimmer of a white burnoose suddenly appeared in the precise spot he targeted. Morgan fired and sent the sly attacker catapulting over the precipice amidst a small avalanche of bouncing stones. Gwen gasped, but the young chieftain did not lower his weapon or relax his stance. He fired again as two more gun-wielding figures dashed headlong around the rock face.

Crouching lower at his feet, she watched in fearful wonder while he shot, deftly reloaded and emptied the rifle again and again at the single file of men that attempted to besiege them on the treacherous path. Just when she had begun to fear she and Morgan would never escape the apparently endless number of attackers, a volley of gunshots resounded above, then echoed through the narrow canyon before receiving answering fire.

"Reinforcements," Morgan commented without taking his eyes from his rifle sights.

"For whose side?" she quavered.

"Ours."

He climbed a few steps up the rock face, finding toeholds with no less agility than a mountain goat, and poised the rifle at some target she could not see, his shots ringing with the others on the bluff above. For a half hour or so the battle continued to rage while Gwen huddled in her place listening to the erratic reports, watching the nervous horses start each time bullets rained about their lowered heads. Finally, Morgan jumped down from his place and, gripping her arm, instructed her to mount up again.

She faltered, her foot slipping away from the stirrup.

"You're not injured?" Morgan asked with concern.

"No, j-just shaken, I guess."

He enfolded her in his arms for a fleeting spell, and lent her a measure of his calm before he directed her to the horse again. "You must mount, Gwen, and follow me out of here. You've nothing to fear now—it's safe."

She set her foot to the stirrup and took up the reins. And she thought, but did not say, that no place in this wild and heathenish land would ever be safe. Not ever.

She could not have imagined any habitats so fantastical as those aeries Morgan called the villages of his people. A chain of them straggled through the mountains, huddles of clay-modeled structures topped with flat thatched roofs that resembled nothing so much as man-built bird nests. Rudely picturesque, the villages were filled with curiosities, not the least of which were the weatherbeaten denizens draped in garments of goat's hair, whose half-naked children played around the dome-shaped ovens that smoked outside of every hut.

Respectfully, and with something akin to awe, the residents lined up as Morgan rode past at the head of his cavalcade. Some of the men fired guns into the air while the women began a series of shrill, celebratory *you-yous!* to welcome the chieftain home.

Although the poverty in the last village was extreme, it was devoid of the filth of the cities. Here the air was pure and the streets carpeted with sweet tufted grass, and food appeared to be plentiful as well; olive and apricot groves, barley fields, and fat sheep marked the distant ridges.

At the end of one lane, a solitary house stood behind a terraced rise, a structure somewhat larger than the other dwellings they had passed. Just as simply built, its mud face reflected the lemon light of afternoon, and its cedar planks framed windows wreathed with undisciplined honeysuckle.

With rifles in hand, the three dozen men who had escorted them dismounted and formed a line to the cedar door. Morgan swung down from his horse and, after aiding Gwenllian from her saddle, proceeded through the soldierlike ranks of Berbers whose eyes regarded him respectfully, and whose sun-ravaged faces held the ruthlessness of seasoned warriors. His progress was slow, for each man stepped forward to kiss his shoulder in a dramatic show of fealty. Gwen stared at the demonstration in wonder, thinking Morgan could have been a feudal baron of another age surrounded by lieges eager to show their loyalty.

The low door stood ajar, and putting a hand to Gwenllian's waist, he ushered her inside to a tiled court that was neatly swept and flanked by rooms opened to the air. She looked about. Little furniture filled the shadowy apartments, and nothing decorated any part of the simple square dwelling except a series of arabesque designs painted over the archways in patterns of rose, lime, and azure. A few gentians circled a central fountain, and next to its sun-warmed, cracked basin an old woman abandoned her kneading of bread to stand in silent deference.

When an elderly man emerged from one of the apartments and ambled forward to greet his young master with a crooked bow, Morgan said, "This is Haqqi. Kbira is his wife, and the two of them keep house for me. Both were the servants of my parents long before I was born."

He glanced down at Gwen, waiting for her response. But she found she did not know what to say; words completely failed her. This humble, Spartan place was his home, and although situated among the glorious mountains he loved, it was very crude. She could not help but think of Hiraeth, waiting solitary and forsaken, its chambers august with age and grand with the richness of inherited treasures.

She stared into the handsome eyes fastened to her own, and saw that they were naked, vulnerable, perhaps even close to beseechment as he waited for her reaction. And yet, she said nothing, made no remark upon his home.

In silence he led her down a passageway to his quarters. When she stepped inside the room flooded with a light so brilliant and so pure that it dazzled the eyes, she almost gasped.

Here was the splendor, she thought. Beyond the thick walls with their wildly beautiful rugs, shelves of books, and fur-draped pallet, through the open terrace doors, rose the magnificent mountains. They were situated perfectly in the rectangle created by the huge lintel and frame, and the sun streamed between their peaks to form a glistening pond upon the tiles. Atlaslike, their snowy spires seemed to hold up the arching sky, then rise through the wreathing clouds straight into Paradise.

Morgan walked to the center of the room, then turned to face her so that the peaks soared just behind his shoulders. Reluctantly, with a realization that was forced from her heart, Gwen thought, *this is where he belongs.*

"This will be your room for as long as you stay," he said, and something in his voice asked for her approval of it, for her admittance that this place he loved was beautiful. But she did not admit it, for she was sorry it was beautiful, bitterly sorry. In spite of all that had occurred, she had held on to the belief that she could coax the man she loved away from here and make him return to Hiraeth. But as she regarded the face whose planes were as rugged as the country that had shaped it, she realized Morgan's character was as independent as the land itself, and doubted he could ever be lured away.

And yet, how she longed to *try!* Perhaps if she took hold of his shoulders, gripped them tight and made him put his mouth to hers, she could find the power to break Morocco's mighty hold. She had heard of men who had abandoned families, causes, even kingdoms for the love of a woman. Would Rhaman?

A commotion sounded outside. Hearty laughter, whose tenor tones mingled with the lively notes of a gimbri, floated through the open doors, and Gwen walked out upon the terrace. Below her, the villagers danced and sang in a joyful throng that slowly moved up a hill to one of the swallow nest homes tucked within the mountainside. Dressed gaudily, the women wore handkerchiefs over their heads, and their arms were tattooed with intricate blue designs above fingernails that were stained with henna. While some were fair complected, others were dark, with black almond eyes shining above wide white smiles. All were crying the shrill, elated *you-yous!* she had heard before.

"What are they doing?" she asked Morgan in bewilderment.

"Celebrating a wedding," he explained, strolling up behind her. "The villagers accompany the bridegroom to his fiancée's house on the day of his mar-

340

riage, making merry along the way. They love celebrations."

"But the women are unveiled, and they are joining the men."

"Many of the strict laws of Islam are ignored here. The people are less inhibited."

As he spoke a gunshot sounded and the crowd raised an exultant shout. "That's the groom's signal to the bride that he has arrived."

Gwen watched the exuberant guests twirl about in a circle and perform complicated jigs with their arms raised high above their heads. In the rapidly fading day, they carried rushlights to illuminate the groaning tables of food that old women dragged out from tiny homes. Bread and cake and spitted meat were passed hand to hand to be freely shared. And then, toil-worn palms clapped in unison to the beat of tambourines, and the combination created a primeval sort of music appropriate to the wild landscape.

"The bride and bridegroom will go now to his house, where the wedding rites will be performed," Morgan continued. "Then they'll be left alone together for a time while the others dance and feast in the streets. Shall we join them?" he asked, grasping her hand.

Before she could reply he led her out into the midst of the festivities, and with no pause to give her breath, swung her about in his arms. His movements were smooth upon the unlevel ground, compared to Gwen's, which were stiff and unconfident until the dizzying rounds in Morgan's embrace and the thrumming of the tom-toms liberated her spirit. She began to laugh, caught up in the merriment of the moment, and the villagers applauded the pair and circled in prancing steps. Smiling, the brightly dressed women made trilling sounds with their tongues while the young men played rousing songs on the gimbris. Above, the stars new hung low, their fiery points touching the flames of the popping rushlights, and now that twilight had fallen the moon smiled down with a carnal glow upon her brow.

Morgan smiled as well, his face transformed from a chieftain's harsh mien to that of young troubadour lilting with his lady. His shoulders felt warm and vital beneath Gwen's hands, and when his body touched hers she did not want it to draw away. He whirled her until she was dizzy, exhilarated, and stirred. And then he stopped, shouted some jovial parting words to his people, and led Gwen back to the shadowy path.

They entered his quarters breathless, and while Gwen rushed to the terrace to watch more of the spirited scene, the old manservant Haqqi ambled in bearing a tray of food and drink, which he sat upon a low table encircled by a nest of woven pillows.

"Hungry . . . ?" Morgan asked, indicating the little feast with a flourish of his hand.

"Am I ever!"

When she went to sit upon a fringed pillow, he took a place beside her, easing down and folding his legs tailor-fashion. The food smelled delicious, and after pouring rose water over her hands and those of his master, Haqqi conversed with Morgan briefly before backing out of the door.

"I feel as if I'll never learn your language," Gwen

lamented, sipping sweetened tea. "It's so difficult to learn."

Morgan grinned. "Don't worry. In order to get by in the mountains you need only know how to bless with humility and curse with courage—if you have a smile on your face while you're doing it, all the better. I'll teach you the finer points."

She laughed, then lowered her lashes.

The room darkened suddenly as the flamboyant moon hid behind a cloud and left the feeble lantern light alone. Outside, the sounds of the women's cries and the drumming music grew passionate, conjuring lurid pictures, and Gwen felt shy in Morgan's presence, in this strange and stirring place that was his home. So much was unspoken between them, so much was undone. Through instinct, she sensed there was only one way to heal it. And that was a way that Morgan knew.

She looked at him, letting her eyes roam over his chest, his neck, and his finely shaped mouth. Steam wended up in a moist curl from the dishes, and she viewed him through its veil, so that the sharper edges of his face were slightly blurred with vapor. When they had danced, she had tucked a wildflower through one of the loops on his burnoose, and she noted that its exotic hue matched exactly the blue of his eyes.

She watched him tilt the samovar so that its tea trickled chimingly into a handleless cup. She longed to speak to him but did not know what to say, realizing fully that the thing she craved would likely bring greater torment to both of them were it allowed to happen.

He uncovered a dish of vegetables, drew aside the linen from a loaf of bread soaked in honey butter, and then stirred the inevitable Moroccan *couscous* of steamed white millet. He dipped a hand into the latter dish and, as was tradition, made a ball of it with his fingers. "We have a custom here," he said, poising the bite of food. "When we entertain favored guests, we feed them from our own hands."

Raising her gaze, Gwen expected to find the gleam of humor in his eyes, but she did not. She found only gravity, and sensuality, both so affecting that her pulse quickened. "Morgan . . ." she breathed, and there was desire in the word.

He leaned nearer, raised his hands, one to hold the food to her lips, one to catch the falling crumbs. She regarded his fingers, and then parted her lips to accept what they would offer. Chewing slowly, she dipped her own fingers into the bowl of warm nourishment and, after clumsily molding a ball, tremblingly raised it to his mouth. His eyes stayed upon her face while she put it between his lips, and she watched the muscles along his jaw flex when he consumed it.

The sounds of merriment outside increased so that the rumble of male laughter blended with the peals from feminine throats in a natural harmony. And all the while the tom-tom beat, primitive like the throbbing of lovers' blood.

Gwen took a breath and examined the face of the man she loved, wanting to tell him the secret she harbored. But first, a question needed to be asked, one that caused her voice to quaver.

"Morgan," she began, trailing a fingernail through the bead of honey that had spilled upon her burnoose. "I know it's your right—the right of all men here—to have wives and concubines. I could not blame you if you did, for it's a part of your culture, but . . . after the things my father said when he—"

"There is no one else, Gwen."

At his quiet forthrightness, she lifted her lashes. "There never has been."

She was ready to confess. "I—I never dissolved our marriage, Morgan. I never signed the papers."

He stared at her, his eyes changing, narrowing with brief speculation before softening as they discerned the significance of her disclosure. When another shot rang out in the street, followed by much excited shouting, he paid no attention to it. But Gwen asked in sudden fear, "What is it?"

He met her gaze. "It's the bridegroom—he has just consummated his marriage."

As he spoke the words, she knew why she had come to this lost and uncharted place: she wanted to belong to the man called Rhaman. Just for a while, she wanted him to take her to a place she had never been before—not a place of mountains or plains or savage cities, not even to a place named for homesickness. But to a place removed from the world, and even more splendrous than its most famous landscapes. A place where Wales did not exist, a place where Morocco would be forgotten, a place where Morgan and Gwenllian would be no product of cultures or beliefs, but simply a man and a woman who had fallen in love. And with a quiet, a wrenching despair, she wanted him to erase the

345

ugliness that another had left her with during a mockery of touching meant to be sacredly shared.

Morgan took his eyes from hers and fixed them upon the dark stain of tea that had dribbled from the samovar's lip. "I've not been able to ask it of you before, Gwen," he said. "I wanted to—wanted to that night in Fez, but my anger was too great. And then, there seemed no proper time to speak."

He put a hand over the top of his cup to catch the warmth of the steam, and then cast his eyes down as if with guilt. Gwen thought the guilt must be awful to prompt the lowering of such a gaze.

"I should not have left you that day in the *fondak*," he admitted. "I should never have deserted my men. I failed them with my lapse in vigilance, and failed you. I should have been there. If it had meant my death, I would have kept you from what you endured. And now I can't forget it. Sometimes when I look at you now, anger fills me until I can hardly breathe, and I can think of nothing but killing Moussa."

"Oh, Morgan—"

"I must ask something of you—"

"Anything."

His eyes fell upon hers again, and Gwen thought that they were the eyes of the boy Rhaman, vulnerable, just as they had been when he had sat alone upon the stairs of Hiraeth so many years ago.

"Can *you* forget?" he asked.

Gwen swallowed. She could not speak, for to tell him the truth would be to fuel his anger more, add to the fire of his vengeance. Her throat closed. "You mustn't ask, Morgan. I don't want you to ask. I only want—" Her voice broke and she reached to take his hand and kiss the palm, bury her face against its roughness.

Lifting a forefinger to brush her bottom lip, he gently shaped its curve. Then, sliding both hands deep into the warmth of her hair, he drew her head close and murmured his love against her ear. She kissed him.

Seized by an urgency made more impatient by Gwen's response, he gathered close the feminine form that his maleness craved. Settling his mouth upon hers, he pressed hard, his breaths made heavy by a yearning that had been withheld too long. Raising the hair off her neck, he moved his lips along the edge of her jaw to her ear, then to her nape. In turn, she pulled the burnoose from his shoulder, felt the ridges and hollows there, and the firm brown skin. Putting her fingers in his hair, in the thick blackness of it, she drew his head down as she lay back upon the pillows. She traced the line of his jaw, its taut angular plane, its strong point, her eyes fixed to his. His lips found hers again, and she shifted her body into the curve of his, frantic now to experience the wonder of what was about to be.

He exercised little restraint; he had gone beyond it. Yanking the drawstring at her neck, he slipped the layers of linen from her shoulders, and when her breasts were revealed, he slid his hand between them, over them, before laying his cheek against their swell, and closing his eyes.

"I'll take the memory away," he breathed. "The memory of *him*. Just help me, Gwen, just help me . . ."

She answered by dragging the fabric of his garment down, so that the bareness of his flesh could come against the bareness of her own.

"Do you love me?" he asked with a need to hear, his hand moving swiftly over her belly. "You have never said it."

She closed her eyes, feeling him move atop her, his body knowing perfectly what to do. "Yes," she breathed. "Even in Wales, in the days of my childhood, I loved you."

She raised her head to behold him, and although the light was feeble, she could see the strength of his frame, its perfection, the vigorous limbs entwining now with hers. And she touched his length, explored with impatient fingers all the places where his hand guided, and all of the places where it did not.

The glee outside turned to tumult, and the beating of tom-toms crescendoed until Gwenllian laid back her head and relinquished herself, surrendered to the storm of necessity gasping for fulfillment.

And as the moon peered in like a jealous voyeur, Rhaman took the daughter of Wales to that place where she begged to go.

Eighteen

Once during the night she awoke to find him gone. With her head still resting upon the pillow, she moved her gaze about the charcoal room, searching, finding his silhouette where the moonlight limned it on the terrace. He stood staring out at the shifting shadows, whose deep purple shapes were bereft now of flickering rushlights. The sounds of revelry filled the house no more; the merrymakers had returned to their curious homes, taking their music and laughter away. Now only the bark of a jackal moved on the air.

The mountain breezes blew cool through the open door, and Morgan had donned a burnoose. When the wind touched it, the garment rippled, and the movement was the only indication that his statuesque image was that of a breathing man. His posture suggested a brooding spirit, and after a moment he turned his head to contemplate the unsheathed sword hanging upon the wall above his head, whose curved shape resembled a sharply horned moon in the eerie light.

Gwen had noticed it before. Old, dull of finish, it had surely belonged to one of his fierce ancestors, perhaps his father. He took the weapon down from its pegs and, holding it in both hands, contemplated it for several moments, running a finger over its once keen edge. After a time, with a visible sigh, he put it back in place.

Next he withdrew some object from the pocket of the burnoose, turned it over and over between his palms, pondered it at some length. Then he let it dangle from his fingertips, its beaded cord twirling in a half circle before swaying and trembling and growing still. His oddly reverent treatment of it intrigued Gwen, and frowning, she stared hard at the token until moonlight struck its distinctive gold shape. She blinked, then stared at it more intently, astonished by what she saw.

As her husband closed his fist upon the symbol and raised his eyes to the sky, Gwen turned her head and swallowed, feeling as if she had intruded upon a most sacred and personal moment. She allowed him a long spell of privacy, barely breathing while she pondered his astounding secret.

At last, she shifted upon the pallet to face him and said, "Your god is not the god of your people."

The sudden sound of her voice, her pronouncement, did not startle Morgan. He did not even pivot to look at her. He said simply, "No."

"Your mother . . . she brought you up in her faith then."

He lifted his head to regard the black spires of the mountains, rubbing his shoulders as if a chill chased over them. "It caused a bitter argument between her and Father . . . the most bitter one they ever had."

Gwenllian spoke as quietly as he. "If they knew, your people would never accept your leadership."

"No."

"Your men would kill you."

"Possibly."

She looked at him in awe with her brow furrowed, as if just by scrutinizing his wind-ruffled form she could fathom the depths of his character. "You're a complicated man, Morgan Riff," she said. "I don't think I shall ever know you, not really, not as I want to."

He turned his head at that, the slight but marked gesture suggesting the words had somehow wounded him. And then he crossed the room, came back to her, and drawing the burnoose over his body, cast it down like a ghost upon the tiles.

They stayed abed long after dawn, speaking little, only indulging in the pastime whose potency allowed them to forget all things but themselves. For long spells they simply held on to the body of the other, until the husband would become the clever teacher again, and the wife a willing intimate. Clasped close, they watched the sun creep over the tiles before it splashed their faces and made them remember that the cares of the world outside still owned them.

When Morgan arose, Gwen followed him with her gaze, feeling sick with need to draw him back, regarding him with melancholy eyes while he bathed himself from the earthen ewer of cool water set within a niche.

Sensing her observation, he turned his head to glance over a shoulder with beads of water dripping from his hair, and gifted her with his rare smile, so that she blushed. She observed him while he dressed in his unselfconscious way, pulled on breeches first, then the nightshirtlike garment he called a *chamir*, and lastly, a heavy linen *farajia* embroidered down the chest and cinched with a wide leather belt. The burnoose and *haik* he left off . . . but not the revolver and sword; they reminded her who he was, and what he would shortly leave her to do.

She put her face against the pillow to shut out the sight of them, curling her knees upward so that the sheet lay twisted between her thighs, but when a sharp ray of sunshine snaked across the tiles to burn her skin, she drew the linen over one shoulder like a cloud.

An oaken desk graced one corner of the room, and removing paper and pen from it, Morgan scrawled a message. "I'm dispatching some of my men to Figuig with a letter of inquiry for the French officials there," he explained, still writing in his deliberate way. "They should return within the month. If we're fortunate they'll bring word of Sir Gerald."

"And if they do not . . . ?" she murmured, staring at the faint film of sand beneath his desk.

Morgan looked up from the paper. "I will find your father for you, Gwen. Have no doubt of it."

The words were uttered with such a simple, calculable finality that she shivered in her coil of sunshine and, getting up from bed, ran to put her arms around his waist from the back. Laying her head against the curve of his spine, she said, "I'm scared, Morgan. I keep seeing terrifying pictures in my mind, like nightmares, and in them you're always fighting a bloody battle where horses are screaming and swords are cutting men down. I can't stop thinking of the picture, it comes to me unbidden."

Tightening her arms about him, she confessed, "You'll think me silly, but during our time together in Tangier I thought of you as a sort of god—one of those mythical types who are vulnerable to misfortune but immortal—do you know the kind I mean? No matter what danger you encountered you always survived it. It comforted me to think of you that way, as a god. Funny, there are times when I still half believe you are. And others," she breathed, "when I fear that you are not . . ."

He put down his pen and gathered her in his arms. "Ah, Gwen, don't be afraid for me, it's no use being afraid. It spoils the moment. Do you understand?"

"Yes."

He bent his head to kiss her, spending several moments at it before drawing back and touching the tip of her nose with a playful finger. "I wouldn't want to be a god anyway."

"Why not?"

"Because, it would mean missing my appointment with Sidna Azrain."

"The Angel of Death?" she asked, appalled.

"You remembered."

She stared up at him and, folding her arms across her breasts, asked in a scornful way, "Has the fatalism of this place infected even you?"

"Fatalism? No. I simply think an encounter with an angel would be rather exciting, don't you?"

She turned away, disliking his jests about such things.

Morgan drew her back. "On second thought," he said. "I *have* felt somewhat like a god during these last few hours—Eros."

And for another hour, his duties elsewhere continued to know neglect.

Later that morning he strolled with Gwen through the village. The light sparkled off grass made slick with an earlier mist, and the sluggishly evaporating moisture drifted skyward carrying scents of marguerite and marigold. A pair of broom-tailed mules lazed beneath a cork tree, swishing flies so indolently that the effort appeared to tax them, while a hound dozed in the shifting shade cast by an old woman carding wool by the roadside. The sun hung suspended over the homes clinging to the terraced mountain, and in the street donkeys rolled in such langorous delight that their wriggling backs sent up puffs of dust.

Gwen shaded her eyes with a hand, feeling as if she walked across a pocket of lost earth ringed by magic mountains whose circle severed it from the rest of the world. Time did not move in this Atlas village, it was of no importance. The women she saw in the streets were in no hurry to finish their labors; they idled, some admiring the profusion of oleanders spilling over the road, others simply sitting on the grass with sleeping infants in their laps and faces upraised to catch the sun. The children gamboled about the spiny argan trees, plucking the olivelike nuts and tossing them into rippling puddles as if no thought of school or learning intruded upon their carefree thoughts.

Beside her, Morgan remained quiet. She thought perhaps he waited for her questions, and pointing to the hillside, she asked, "What are those, Morgan—some sort of tombs?"

"They're the shrines of the local saints, quite sacred. At certain times the villagers go and sit beside them, often for days, until they're ready to share with the saint their prayers and sorrows. Then they knock three times on the tomb to wake him up."

Gwen smiled. "That reminds me of the holy wells at home. Do you know that people go to some of them and cast curses? They write the curse on a piece of paper, then throw it into the well and hope the resident spirit will rouse himself enough to conjure it up."

"And so cows cease to give milk and pretty maids get warts upon their noses."

She laughed. "Something like that."

They walked along and her expression sobered as she noticed a group of females prostrated before the crumbling wall of a burial yard. "What are those women doing?"

"Mourning their dead. Earlier I gave them the news of the men who were slain in Mequinez. The mother of Hassan is the one there—apart from the others and wearing a black scarf."

Gwen stopped, sorrowfully regarding each bowed

head and prayerful posture. And for a moment she thought reverently of Hassan, of all the men who had died that day in the *fondak*. But most of all, she paid silent homage to Robyn Breese. Remembrance of him and his last act of courage would never leave her.

While she stood in reverie, the tattoo of hooves sounded. In a field at the bottom of the road the men of the village rode their finely accoutered steeds. Before Gwen's dazzled eyes they made their mounts rear and leap to perform agile acts of equine skill. Each horse displayed superb training, each equestrian showed his mastery using signals no more obvious than a sleight of hand upon a braided rein. At a sign, all the riders swung into four straight lines, and waited while Morgan went to stand before them and examine their proud and motionless ranks with critical eyes.

When at last he inclined his head in silent approval, they whooped, saluting him with rifles raised high above their heads.

"They've arranged a *fantasia* in honor of my return," he explained when Gwen came to stand at his shoulder. "It's quite a display, as you'll shortly see."

While he spoke the Berbers put their horses through more daring exercises, wheeling them about upon their great haunches, pivoting them in reckless figure eights as they shouted eerie cries and fired their rifles. When they began to charge each other in frightening maneuvers, she recognized their activity as an exercise in mock warfare; they showed their chieftain a readiness for battle.

As the performance ended and the warriors lined up upon lathered, heaving mounts to receive Morgan's accolades, Gwen experienced a stabbing ache of foreknowledge; before the day was out, Rhaman would ride away with them.

When the two lovers walked back to his villa a time later, a silence stretched between them. In the courtyard a crowd of men awaited beside the trickling fountain, and Gwen watched discreetly from the shadows as they removed their shoes and approached their chieftain across the tiles. Although she could scarcely comprehend a word exchanged, she understood that the villagers asked for his counsel, which made him not only a military leader, but an adviser and judge of his people. One man seemed to be accused of a crime by his angry-eyed escorts, who shoved him forward and condemned him with pointing fingers. Hastily, the defendant removed his slippers, knelt at Morgan's feet, and kissed the back of his hand. Then in a plaintive tone, the supplicant begged for mercy while a group of curious onlookers peeked through the open door.

In a barrage of vehement words, his accusers continued their list of charges until Morgan finally held up a hand and demanded silence. Before Gwen's wondering gaze, the entire crowd lifted up their palms, and turning toward Mecca, began praying ardently to their Most Merciful.

When they had completed their ritual, Morgan drew the accused up from his knees and spoke to him in low earnest tones, his eyes stern as he pronounced a sentence. Immediately the prisoner was hauled to the floor by his indicters and, as he let out a piercing whine, received from one of them three lashing strokes from a bastinado.

When Morgan was free to converse again, Gwen assailed him with questions. "Who were those people? What crime did that poor fellow commit?"

"He loaned a bit of money to his friends and charged them interest. Usury is forbidden by Moslem law."

Her eyes flashed, but she said nothing as he moved to dip a cup of water from the fountain and raise it to his lips.

Over its rim Morgan regarded her face, his eyes keen with the knowledge of her silent censure. "Had he been judged in Fez or Tangier, Gwen, he would have been hung up by his ankles and flogged until he was dead."

Feeling chastised, she trailed disconsolately behind him as he strolled to his quarters. Once there, she saw him raise the lid of a teakwood trunk, remove a box of cartridges and two revolvers, then pack them inside a *chouari*, the leather bag which fastened to his saddle. His manner had grown suddenly purposeful, detached, as if he were mentally distancing himself from her, preparing for the physical separation soon to come.

He is leaving, she thought. *Leaving to find Moussa.*

Unable to stand and watch his preparations, she whirled about and stalked out onto the terrace, staring straight ahead, avoiding the cedar rail where a scorpion clung and sunned its wicked length. Through eyes that shone with welling tears she regarded the mountains, until their solid, unsympa-

358

thetic forms shivered like reflections viewed upon wind-rippled water. Resentment and the ache of love swelled so strong in her chest that she feared she would sob aloud with them, and she clapped a hand to her mouth to smother the sound. And then, she felt a hand clasp the ridge of her shoulder. She quivered at the hardness of it, at the warmth and power flowing through the fingers like a current.

"Don't you want him dead, Gwen?"

She stiffened at his quiet, almost bewildered words, at the heaviness of his hand. The blood of anger rose to her cheeks and suffused them even while her limbs turned icy with fear. How afraid she was of losing the man who was now bound to her by a physical seal! Whirling to face him, she felt her pain give way; it erupted into passionate words.

"Not at the possible cost of your own life, Morgan! Nothing is worth that. *Nothing!* I don't *care* if the monster lives or dies, I have no desire for revenge—you took that away from me last night. Thank God you did! Moussa's death cannot erase what he did to me, and it's sheer madness to believe otherwise!" She knocked his hand away when he tried to touch her and shouted, "And I won't have you riding off to defend my honor in some stupid notion of misplaced chivalry!"

Across from her Morgan clamped his jaw. Her contempt roused his anger, and he stared down at her through narrowed, dangerous eyes. "Gwenllian," he said. "My honor—twisted or not as it may be judged—is the thing that has driven me all my life. I wouldn't know how to exist without it.

It was the code of my father and his father before him. They taught me that the protection of family and the avenging of honor is the test of a man's integrity, and I believe that. Last night—whether you rue it now or not—you became a part of me, the other portion of what I am. And I became a part of you. Your honor is *mine*."

At the fierce philosophy her husband so eloquently communicated, the sting of tears made Gwen's eyes bright, and she blinked them away and averted her head rather than let him see.

"Go then," she whispered through a tightened throat. *"Go."*

For a moment Morgan did not move. He simply stared at her rigid back. From nape to waist it was graced by a fall of tangled hair the color of a mink's breast. The light played over each curl in turn, glossing the fine strands when the breeze whorled them on the air. He wanted to reach out his hand and touch the brightness.

But he did not. Quietly, he leaned to pick up the *chouari* bag and sling it over his shoulder, the weight of its contents reminding him of where he was about to go. He drew in a ponderous breath at the thought and, glancing one more time at the curl-wreathed back, let the bag slide off his shoulder to the tiles again. With noiseless steps he returned to the terrace to stand beside Gwenllian, and the wind that blew down from the mountains dried the moisture in his eyes. Extending a hand, he cupped her quivering chin and pulled it upward until her gaze lifted to meet his own.

"You want to change who I am, Gwen," he said

quietly. "You want to mold me into a gentleman suited to the world you understand, suited to the world that makes you feel safe."

"No!" she argued, turning about. "No. I don't want to change you. I want you to change yourself, admit that you could belong at Hiraeth just as completely as you belong here. I want you to give it a chance!"

"I have given it a chance!" he shouted. "Years ago as a young boy. Even then I knew where I belonged. And you must know it, too, Gwen. Why can't you accept it?"

"Because only a fool would throw away Hiraeth!"

He made to go, shouldering the bag again with his mouth set grimly, but Gwenllian ran to clutch at his sleeve in a frantic effort to pull him back.

"Don't let us part like this!" she cried.

His frustration giving way, Morgan seized her in his arms, the tightness of his embrace expressing his own desolation over the impasse of their lives. "Haqqi and Kbira will care for you while I'm gone," he breathed against her ear. "And I *will* return to you—nothing will keep me away if I know you're here."

Taking hold of her arms then, he kissed her. And then he pulled her clutching hands free from his body, and went down to meet his men.

During the course of the next weeks Gwen remained almost entirely to herself, confined to the room she had shared with Morgan. The ordeal of the last months had exhausted her, and often she rested in the shade when the sun shone hottest. But in the darkness of night when she lay alone and waited for Morgan, staring up at the rough cedar rafters and envisioning dreadful pictures, she found no rest at all.

Occasionally she ventured out to explore the steep village streets which were little more than goat paths, her appearance an instant attraction to the inhabitants, who seemed to find her no less enthralling than the Pied Piper. The children came dashing down from their homes, shadowing her footsteps in the manner of faithful puppies, and the women she met along the way inclined their heads at her respectfully as they slid bread out of their beehive ovens or weeded their gardens. None attempted to address her or to make overtures to friendship. She knew they admired her clothes, for Morgan had given her the blue silk tunic with its embroidery of silver thread from his mother's trunk. Whenever she wore it, Gwen remembered Marian, and sometimes she even had the odd fancy that the long dead lady glided by her side like a guardian lending the encouragement of sagacity. More and more often, Gwen wondered what sort of life her countrywoman had lived in these wild, forbidden mountains so alien from the rain-dashed cliffs and heathered moors of Wales. However had she coped?

At least, the old woman Kbira treated Gwen with an amenable, if gruff, affection. The Welshwoman had been surprised by her knowledge of English, and even though it was of the pidgin variety, it sufficed as a way to communicate.

One day as Gwen wandered aimlessly through the courtyard, the servant arrested her with a preemptorial snap of the fingers. "Come, come!" she commanded in a querulous voice. "Rhaman's lady do no thing every day. Need busy hands."

After giving her a thorough tour of the little den-like kitchen which was hung with a mishmash of bright copper pots, she showed Gwen how to make a flat bread baked with almond slivers. Then she demonstrated the use of an old wooden handmill set upon a mat in the center of the kitchen. A bundle of barley ready for milling sat beside it, bound by twine, and Kbira untied it and began to crank the rustic device. Next, in her typically brusque manner, she insisted that Gwen employ it.

While Gwen clumsily cranked the handle of the instrument, Haqqi stumped in. Taking one look at the Welshwoman, he scowled and stumped out again.

"He not like you," Kbira remarked with bald honesty, irritably wrenching the mill handle out of Gwen's inept hands. "He not like the woman of Rhaman's father either. Christian women are less than dogs, he say."

Smiling toothlessly, the old woman added, "But mostly, he angry that Rhaman not take our granddaughter to wife. Haqqi has offered her many times. Maybe Rhaman will take her to be his second wife next year." She shrugged with the fatalism common to her countrymen. "Maybe he will not."

While Gwen stood faintly taken aback by the conversation, the old woman grabbed her hand and said, "Come. We go to granddaughter's house. You see how pretty she is."

A moment later she towed Gwen down the path. Her rusty black garments brushed wild poppies, snared on blackberry bramble, and scattered lizards while her arthritic feet negotiated the steep decline with amazing agility. The two women climbed up to one of the queer little aeries, and without knocking upon the planked door, Kbira unlatched its bar and thrust Gwen inside.

At her abrupt entrance an assortment of chickens flew in all directions, perching on narrow rafters in a flurry of dirty feathers and shrill squawks. Adjusting her eyes to the interior gloom, Gwen scrutinized the dwelling, deciding that it could be termed nothing more than a hovel. It contained no furniture at all, only reed mats spread haphazardly upon the earthen floor. A set of earthenware was propped on a crude shelf, and a hand-tied ladder led to the roof. Beneath its rungs a black goat stared at her through amber eyes, its presence explaining the pervasive odor.

Gwen shifted her eyes to the other end of the room, where a girl with tawny skin sat cross-legged upon the floor weaving a rug of coarse wool yarn.

"She called Aziza!" Kbira announced to Gwen, pointing with a gnarled, henna-tinted finger. "You talk!"

With that improbable assignment the tyrannical matron then departed. Waddling out, she shooed away a striped cat before slamming the door, and the motion of her exit sent the chicken feathers dancing again.

Clearing her throat, Gwen smiled tentatively at her hostess and murmured, "Hullo."

The girl with slanted hazel eyes and dark frizzed hair nodded in an enthusiastic way and, jumping up, retrieved from the slanted shelf a clay bowl full of eggs, which she held out to her guest in offering.

Gwen stared at the hard-boiled eggs, already peeled, with no inclination to eat them. But fearing to offend, she reached a hand into the bowl and selected one, nibbling at its glossy end while Aziza stared at her expectantly.

The girl was pretty, with smooth skin and white teeth, which she displayed through lips that were full and dusky pink. Although the henna from her palms had run down and made long reddish stains over the inside of her wrists, her hands moved with graceful flourishes, and Gwen thought of the slender-boned wings of the sacred storks. Aziza's coarse-made clothes were not particularly clean, but Gwen had seen the Berber women washing their garments in the stream beside the road, and surmised that the primitive laundering method left much to be desired. Unwittingly thinking of the great steaming washtubs, milled French soap, and sturdy wringers commandeered by a half dozen maids at Ardderyd, she felt ashamed.

Aziza touched her on the shoulder and invited her to inspect the weaving she had earlier abandoned on the floor. Intrigued, Gwen focused her eyes upon the partially completed tapestry rug, its brilliant colors illumined by a shot of sun slanting through the roof hatch. She gasped, for the piece was beautiful, utterly beautiful, a perfected pattern of the twining vines and lotus blossoms she had seen on countless crumbling arches. Its primary colors were so vivid against a background of black that the fabric resembled a net of precious gems.

Gwen glanced at the mud dwelling again in wonder, and realized that the arabesque rug was the only thing of beauty in the dismal habitat, out of place and yet not out of place.

"It's lovely," she proclaimed in awe, kneeling down to touch a finished edge. "It's very, very lovely. You have a gift."

Aziza seemed pleased, sensing the praise in her guest's tone of voice. Eagerly she eased herself behind the loom again and began to demonstrate the art of its use, encouraging Gwen with smiles and exaggerated gestures to try the technique herself.

Gwen complied with both timidity and eagerness, and after an hour of shared feminine laughter and awkward attempts to match the native's talented weaving, the Welshwoman rose from the loom, leaving a noticeable rift in the smoothness of Aziza's flawless work.

She thanked her hostess with a sincere press to the hand, and when the door was closed behind her, stood staring bemused at its rough planks for a moment, comparing them to the polished entrance of Ardderyd. It was odd, she thought, how friendship tiptoed across the most unlikely thresholds to welcome a stranger.

As she negotiated the steep path down, thunder rumbled across the heavens, and Gwen glanced up to find clouds boiling over the mountaintops and obscuring the clear skies of the valley. Large splats of rain descended, striking the hard ground and wetting the fronds of the dwarf palms, which drooped from the weight of the water beads. While sprinting homeward as fast as she could over the melting earth, Gwen drew up the *haik* to keep her hair dry, but by the time she dashed into the house her skin was chilled and damp. Spying one of Morgan's burnooses hanging from a peg in his room, she snatched it and flung it over her shoulders before kicking off her soaking shoes and setting them aside.

Hugging the warm folds of the fabric, she experienced a poignant sense of her absent lover, and went to look out at the mountains through the open door. The rain dashed against the flagstones. She closed her eyes, and the *pat-pat-pats* became hoofbeats, hundreds of them, orchestrated with the clang of swords. She could see men clashing in battle upon muddy hillsides, see horses with bared teeth, their tasseled bridles bright streaks against crimson skies, while their riders cried war with spewing rifles.

Shuddering, Gwen clamped her teeth and folded her arms about her waist. She felt a bulge in the innermost pocket of the burnoose and, sliding her hands into its depths, drew out a small leather-bound journal.

The engraved initials *S G E* glittered upon the corner of the book, but even without the flourished letters, she would have known her father's journal. She had seen the slim volume countless times before, for it had been his habit since early manhood to record the events of his life as they occurred, and this was only one in a set of many diaries packed away at Ardderyd.

With unsteady hands she riffled through the pages, locating the last entries which, according to her calculations, were set down just days after the receipt of her sire's desperate letter in Wales. As her heart throbbed in trepidation she read the lines, scrutinized them over and over for meaning until the words were only shifting characters blurred by welling tears.

How long had Morgan possessed this record of her father's capture? How long had he known the details Sir Gerald's ill-treatment at the hands of his barbarous captors? And above all, why had he kept such knowledge from her?

She closed the diary with a soft press of both hands and, hugging it to her heart, wondered if the concealment meant that her father was dead.

Nineteen

Gwen had discovered a calendar in Morgan's desk, and each afternoon, when the chieftain had not been sighted riding down the rocky stairway leading to his cloistered village, she slashed through the date with a pencil. One day, as she sat with her chin propped upon a palm and formed her twenty-third such slash, she despaired. *Was he ever coming back?*

And what of her father . . . ?

She clenched the pencil harder and ground its tip into the margin of the calendar, unconsciously creating the shape of a curved sword from whose hilt hung a braided cord adorned with thick black tassels. Had she lost her beloved sire to the savagery of Morocco, just as she had lost Robyn Breese? Had she lost Morgan?

Just then, Kbira toddled into the room to collect clothing for the week's wash, and when Gwenllian put down her pencil and stood up from the desk, the servant made a *tsk*ing sound between her teeth. In a purposeful stride, she came forward and thrust a wad of clothing at the younger woman's chest, demanding, "Come! Rhaman's woman come with Kbira."

Accustomed to her abruptness, the Welshwoman followed her out into the sunshine that quivered off the rain-rinsed trees and made a yellow swatch across a hillside scored with shepherds' paths. After a few moments of negotiating the slippery route the two women came upon a stream fed by the melting snows of the high ranges, its water tumbling over rocks that were furred with moss and populated by sunning dragonflies. All along the shore women crouched, washing their clothes, slapping them into the clear water, then rocking to and fro as they rubbed the scraps of laundry over washing stones. When Gwen and Kbira approached, the launderers looked over their sloped shoulders and smiled shyly before turning back to their task and taking up the rhythm once more.

Gwen accepted a pale-colored ball of homemade soap from Kbira's hand and, following example, knelt down upon the muddy bank with her bundle of wash, which she christened with an inexpert plunge into the rushing current. The servant regarded her askance with a protruding brown eye, but said nothing, and Gwen continued in her clumsy fashion. A while later, as she struggled to pull out a sodden burnoose and dash it against the soapy stone, she gazed at the mountain peaks and asked, "When do you think the men will come home, Kbira?"

The old one shrugged her ancient shoulders and settled her bulk more comfortably over her knees until she resembled a nesting hen. Her answer was filled with resigned acceptance. "Who can say? Men fight. Come home. Leave to fight more. That is what they do. Always they do it."

With her eyes reflecting the glitter of sun on water, Gwenllian looked beyond her to the careworn profiles of the toiling women and said, "And some do not come home."

Kbira shrugged again. "As Allah wills."

"Of course. As Allah wills."

In spite of her irreverent mutter, Gwen had tried hard over the last weeks to set aside her intolerance. She had attempted to adapt to the strange existence into which she had been placed, to understand its melancholy religion and abide its absence of luxury. Each day she spent hours pondering the future, hours imagining herself as the wife of a Berber chieftain, a woman exiled from her own people and forever lost in the timelessness of a remote African village. If she agreed to remain his wife, she knew Morgan would make the transition as easy as possible for her, arrange trips to Tangier so that she might socialize with the European community there. Likely, he would even encourage her to journey home to Wales occasionally to dull the edge of her homesickness. But her *life* would be here—here upon the hot banks of a drifting stream guarded by frowning mountains and lined with kohl-eyed women awaiting the return of their warriors. If she stayed, she would learn to perform the labors they performed, enjoy the simple pleasures they enjoyed, and fear as they did that, some day, the warriors would not return from war.

Morgan's father had been such a casualty, leaving behind a grieving widow and son. And after years of sacrificing for him, Marian had found herself alone in the midst of terrifying danger, which caught up with her even as she sought the safety of Hiraeth.

After awhile Gwen learned the rhythm of the laundresses so that her body rocked in tandem with theirs. While the trilling water cooled her reddened, straining hands, the sun beat atop her head, its intensity absorbed by the blackness of her unbound hair. The scents of soap and wet grass filled her nostrils and the buzz of insects droned behind her back, until time fell away and she slipped into a spell of absent dreaming. When the thud of footsteps fell upon the spongy earth close beside her, she scarcely heard them, assuming another village woman had come to do her wash.

Although she did not bother to glance around and acknowledge the newcomer, her companions did, including Kbira, and one by one, each silently gathered her sopping clothes and hastened away. Curious over their behavior, Gwen turned her head and squinted against the glare of the sky.

The linen she wrung dropped from her hands with a splashy thud, and she rose slowly to her feet, her gaze fastened to the eyes of the man standing a few paces away. Although his stance was as straight as ever, his burnoose was stained and dusty, and his face grim, the weariness of its features alleviated only by the slight tilt of the provocative mouth.

He reached out his arms and she fell into them as if they were a safe harbor, pressing her face against his chest and crying out his name. The sun felt hot upon her neck where his hand had carelessly parted her hair, and his heart hammered against her ear in a rhythm louder than the rush of the river. She put her hands upon the warmth of his head and closed her eyes for a second. The reunion was almost sweet enough to vindicate the awful waiting.

"You're wounded," she murmured a moment later, touching the brown rent in his sleeve.

"It's nothing." His eyes were a mirror of the water. "Leave the laundry and let us go home."

"Tell me what happened first, Morgan. I must know. Did you lose many men?"

"Only a handful. But Moussa escaped me. He fled like a jackal to hide in the desert."

"The desert?"

"The Sahara, far from here."

Far from here . . . A reprieve, Gwen thought. She studied him with concern, wondering how many nights had passed since he had managed a restful sleep, how many days since he had tasted a decent meal. Several days' growth of beard shadowed his jaw and lines of fatigue marked the corners of his eyes; seeing him so spent made Gwen yearn to care for him in the way a chieftain's wife would do.

"You are battle weary," she said softly, touching his shoulder. "Come, let me tend you. I've dreamed of your homecoming these many weeks, longed to have you back."

He reached out, took a sun-warmed lock of her hair between his fingers, and answered in a whisper that promised much. "And I have longed to be back."

Hand in hand they walked through the green, spearlike grasses, talking with their heads bent close, and leaving behind a dozen half-rinsed garments that clung to the washing stones like a row of languorous bathers. Occasionally they paused to kiss, but as they climbed the footpath to Morgan's villa, they drew abruptly apart as the sound of hooves pierced the tranquil air.

A rider barreled through the village on a lathered steed, waving his hands and rousing the denizens with a furious hue and cry. Women ran out of their homes and gathered children into their arms while old men dropped garden tools and jabbered excitedly. Beside Morgan's front door, Kbira screeched, *"Allah tif! Allah tif!"*

Bewildered by the disturbance, Gwen plucked anxiously at his sleeve. "What is it? What's happening? What is the rider saying?"

"Go to Kbira, Gwen," he commanded.

"But what is it!" she cried, her distress increasing with the rise of hysteria on the street.

Already he was sprinting down the path. "The sultan's army is on its way. Go with Kbira!"

Several dozen mounted men were already gathering on the road, their battle-worn horses shying and rearing as frightened toddlers screamed in the arms of wailing mothers. Morgan barked orders at them even while Gwen searched fearfully for a glimpse of the descending menace, putting a hand to her brow to shade her eyes against the sun's glare. Finally, upon the steep decline winding down from the mountain face, she saw flashing blurs of crimson through the stunted branches of the argan trees . . . the tunics of the sultan's troops.

The royal steeds galloped down the grade at such a reckless pace that their legs appeared to leave the surface of the ground, and the sound of their rampant hooves and jingling military harness combined to make a fearsome herald. Those soldiers riding at the fore carried torches, and their licking flames reminded Gwen of the pillars of smoke she had seen on the journey to Mequinez, a sign of the sultan's retaliation against a rebellious tribe.

Frozen momentarily by thoughts of the impending battle, she observed the chaos on the road below. In spite of their chieftain's commands, the women and children scurried back to their homes to bundle up armloads of pitiful possessions and to collar squealing animals. Morgan had mounted the copper stallion in one energetic leap and, withdrawing his rifle, organized his men into a cohesive force prepared to confront the enemy. With a wave of his arm he directed another contingent of Berbers high above the village to vantage points that would be strategic to firing down upon the invaders.

Even as the chieftain bellowed a battle cry, the soldiers in their tall black fezzes charged fiercely in a disciplined force. Creating a deafening series of reports, the rank and file emptied their weapons as they spurred their destriers forward. A few royal sentries detached from the line and steered their mounts up the steep rises to the nestled homes, where they tossed smoking torches atop the bristly thatched roofs and watched them explode into brilliant flame. Mud spattered in showers as the troops invaded the narrow rain-fresh streets to clash with savage defenders. Villagers caught within the ferocious attack were ruthlessly shot or trampled.

Before Gwen's eyes Morgan and his men engaged the sultan's army in the mighty crash of warfare, that terrible contest of brutally employed weapons, shrieking horseflesh, and cursing men that echoed the clangor of all the past unsettled centuries here. Horrifically passionate, it was the ultimate test of skill and survival, noble valor and absence of mercy. In a sort of unified awe and horror Gwen watched Morgan swing his rearing stallion about, slap the rifle breech to his shoulder, and slay an antagonist before severing the arm of another foe with one fell swipe of his sword.

Nothing that she had earlier witnessed prepared her for the barbaric spectacle. For here, the innocent were targeted just as deliberately as the warriors. Beneath the torch of the tyrant's agents the wretched homes burned in spirals of evil smoke, and the flourishing orchards and barley fields smoldered likewise. Nothing of the meager Berber existence was spared, not even the crude shrines, which the mounted officers of the army trampled with irreverence.

Watching it all, Gwen experienced a sudden, unexpected vengeance so violent that she might have been witnessing the destruction of her own faraway village. Dashing up to the house, she retrieved a pistol from Morgan's desk and ran outside again. As she descended the path in a mad scramble, her feet lost purchase on the stones, and she almost tumbled onto the road where a hundred horses leapt and plunged.

Crouching in the scrub, Gwen watched while men engaged in hand to hand combat and knocked their foes to the ground with flashing swords and pistols. With shaking fingers she cocked her weapon and aimed it at a torch-bearing soldier who thundered toward Morgan's villa on a flagging steed. Closer and closer he came, zigzagging through the melee while the tassel upon his hat madly bobbed.

She squeezed the trigger.

Her target jerked backward with the blast and tumbled from his mount into a ditch, whose rain-water extinguished the dangerous torch. Closing her eyes against the sight of her victim's body, Gwen breathed deep, then raised her head just enough above the scrub to search for Morgan in the confusion. There was no sign of the copper horse. Terrified, she remained in place and fired at another red tunic with haphazard accuracy, then another and another. She had shot three of the sultan's soldiers before one shrewd veteran discovered her presence and stumbled across two of his fellows' bodies to pursue her on foot. She ran, gasping, grappling for a foothold upon the rocky path as she climbed through the bramble. His heavy boots clapped close upon her heels.

A hundred yards away Morgan rescued one of his youngest men, yanked him off his feet and out of the way of an attacker's vicious scimitar. He fought by instinct only, for his concentration centered entirely upon Gwenllian.

Where was she? A few moments ago he had seen

Kbira disappear safely over the top of the hill, but Gwenllian had not been running at her side. Afraid for his wife, he twisted in his saddle, simultaneously fending off another attacker with a slice of his mighty sword, grunting with the effort of the parry. His stallion flinched and snorted, its haunches nicked by the heels of another steed gone wild amidst the fray. Morgan reined him around, searching through glinting weapons and grimacing faces for a glimpse of a slender girl.

Smoke wreathed the road, burning his eyes and throat, and he cursed, prodding the stallion forward until its great shoulders mowed down an unhorsed soldier. Sick with fear, Morgan peered through the battle haze, searching for sight of the path leading up to his villa. And then he saw her.

On hands and knees, Gwenllian climbed over the terraced slope, her feet slipping upon the rocks while the hem of her burnoose trailed almost within the reach of a pursuing royal soldier. The ruthless officer scrabbled after her, reaching up to snatch his victim's garment and yank her backward. She lost her footing and screamed out as she rolled helplessly at his boots. In one hand he carried a slender sabre, which he raised above Gwenllian's lowered head.

As he witnessed the imminent destruction of his beloved, a cry rose from Morgan's throat and his face twisted in both heartbreak and rage. Viciously he spurred his stallion and sent it plunging through rearing animals and over the fallen bodies of many men. The stallion responded. As his shoulders cut a passageway, his iron shoes slithered through the

378

mire and sparked off the stones of the path. Leaning low over the lathered neck flecked with lather, Morgan freed his boots from the stirrups, leapt from the saddle with a yell, and propelled himself onto the back of Gwenllian's attacker.

Both men jolted to earth in a tangle of limbs, the soldier's sabre flying out of his hand. He slammed a fist into Morgan's belly and rolled away, grappling for his fallen weapon, but the chieftain allowed him no quarter, withdrawing his wicked poniard and slicing through his chest.

Gwenllian looked away. A second later she felt a pair of hands upon her waist, and she clutched them, turning her eyes to the battle again.

The violent struggle diminished. The Berber force was greater in number than the sultan's troops and their familiarity with the terrain, together with the fierce instinct to defend their families, gave them an added edge. The warriors in red tunics wheeled about and retreated in an undisciplined flurry, abandoning to the whooping victors their dead, their weapons, and their riderless steeds.

Gwen stood staring at the churned and bloody earth, at the strewn, lifeless forms, at the exultant Berbers who sat upon steeds so exhausted their heads hung low. Everywhere, smoke undulated from the remains of humble homes while women and children crept cautiously out of the narrow caves that pocked the mountainside.

Beside her, Morgan surveyed the destruction as well, his eyes hard, his burnoose crimson with his enemies' blood, and his face splattered with mud. Gwen looked at him, then moved her gaze slowly

379

to view again the tragic wreck of his village. Sickened, she turned about and relieved her weakened stomach.

"Go inside," Morgan said, touching her shoulder.

But she shook her head and told him no, so that he searched her face with questioning eyes. She held his gaze, and when he walked down the path through a haze of smoke, she followed, prepared to tend the dead and dying of the man she loved.

Morgan did not return to the villa until the moon had thrown her thin cold light over the battered valley. Having bathed and discarded her filthy clothes, Gwen sank down upon the pallet to await him, groaning with weariness and the soreness in her body. She left a lantern burning, and a tray of cheese and bread sat upon the low teakwood table.

At last he entered. The flickering light illumined his grim face and his bruised, scratched hands where they clenched the barrel of his rifle. He propped the weapon against the desk. Seeing Gwen's strained face, he solemnly met her gaze.

She said nothing, but went to pour coffee for him while he tossed his ruined burnoose and *farajia* across a chair. He wore breeches and the white *chamir*, and Gwen suspected that he had bathed himself in the stream, for his hair was wet, and the dirt and blood washed from his face.

Exhaustion showed in the deep lines about his mouth, and in the slight slump of his wide shoulders. Gwen yearned to offer some words of comfort, but she found none. She could think of nothing to say to a man who had suffered devastation.

"Would you like some bread and cheese . . . ?" she asked him after a while. "I—I left a tray."

He declined, and sitting down in the desk chair, unstrapped the mud-caked spurs from his boots. Silence stretched long, and Gwen busied herself with pouring him another cup of coffee. When she handed it to him, he said, "Thank you for settling the women and children in the courtyard. It'll be several weeks before their homes can be rebuilt. Some of the families will have to leave tomorrow and stay with relatives in other villages."

"Has this village been attacked before, burned like this?"

"Yes. Some years ago."

An endless, senseless cycle, she thought.

She watched him remove a cloth from the desk drawer. Picking up the rifle, he began to clean off the grime with a practiced, almost loving hand. The gesture annoyed her, and although she knew the present was hardly a propitious time to ask him about her father's journal, she found it impossible to put it off.

From beneath her pillow she withdrew the volume, and lifting the hem of the nightgown borrowed from Marian's trunk, padded to Morgan's side. Wordlessly, she slid the diary across the surface of his desk.

His eyes flicked over it before locking with her own.

"Is my father dead?" Gwenllian demanded.

He gave her a level stare. "I don't know."

381

"Where did you get this?"

"From the *kaid* in Arzilah. The Zemours had sold him Sir Gerald's surveying kit, and the diary was tucked inside. Having no use for it, he gave it to me when I asked." Pausing, Morgan rubbed a speck of soil from the rifle stock. Then he raised his eyes to hers and added, "I thought it best not to tell you the details of your father's ordeal, Gwen. I thought to spare you."

"Thought to *spare me?*" She exclaimed in a sudden burst of scorn. Crossing her arms, she turned her back upon him. "One is never spared in this country."

"So you have said," he replied in a weary tone, polishing the rifle again.

Not yet finished with her tirade, Gwen paced the length of the room and threw up her hands. "Life in Morocco is outside the bounds of anything even remotely civilized. The people here are of two kinds—those who go about butchering enemies as well as innocents, and those who *are* the innocents. And the innocents sit placidly by in poverty and ignorance, so resigned to their fate that they even style their children's hair in a way convenient for the angel of death! As Allah wills, they say with a shrug of their shoulders, as if there is no such thing as human will. I am sick of hearing it! The country literally crumbles while the ablest men go off to fight each other, and fight again and again. Where is the sense in it all?"

Morgan regarded her without expression, and she shook her head at him in utter frustration. "How can you live this way? How can you keep from being sickened at the sight of your people's children run down by soldiers who have no more compassion than demons? How can you not yearn for civilization—for culture, for order, for a society who has some notion of what it means to be *humane*? No matter what you do, no matter how many wars you fight, Morocco will never change. You can't make me believe that it will. It hasn't relinquished its backward, ruthless ways in centuries. All these petty tribal wars are a way of life, not efforts at reform. And how can you defeat a sultan who—according to the fanatics—rules the country by divine right? What you do is pointless, Morgan, nothing more than vain male pride cloaked in the name of honor!"

Morgan had been sitting calmly in the chair while she raved at him, the rifle lying across his lap. Now he set it aside with care and came slowly to his feet, his form towering above her own. "I will not suffer your scorn, Gwenllian. Do you understand?"

She lifted eyes that were red-rimmed and brimming full, abashed that she had so berated him. "I'm sorry," she whispered, reaching out. "I'm sorry . . ."

He drew her head against his chest and held her in his arms as if there had been no harsh opinions spoken. And yet, when he spoke, the heaviness of his tone evidenced the disharmony that lingered between them like a knife. "Me, too."

They drew apart and Gwen went along to lie down upon the pallet, listening to the soft rubbing noise of the linen cloth as Morgan continued to clean the rifle in silence. After awhile, he set it aside and reached to extinguish the lantern, so that the room was thrown into blackness. He walked toward the pallet and she heard the sound of his undressing, the swish of the clothes as he slid them from his body and laid them aside. He eased down beside her, and like strangers, they lay stiffly together in silence with their backs turned, never touching. If she had not been so weary, Gwenllian would have wept.

But when the sky lightened to the palest mimosa and the first birds stirred, the chieftain and his wife roused, and still half-dreaming, moved together upon the pallet barely rumpled from exhausted sleep. Morgan slid an arm about her waist and she turned to receive his kiss, parting her lips and twining her legs about his stronger ones. He breathed her name. Then he slid a hand down over her hips to grasp the bottom of her gown, and she shifted so that he could draw it up. Still languorous with the remnants of sleep and the heat of his moving body, Gwen kept her eyes closed, but when his lips returned to hers and pressed them hard, she opened her lids to behold Rhaman's flushed and handsome face. Arching, she loved him desperately, as he loved her. Both knew time was their greatest enemy.

Twenty

The village became a hive of activity at dawn's breaking. People from neighboring villages arrived on foot, leading donkeys laden with food and supplies for rebuilding. Families sorted through the burnt rubble of their homes, tearing down charred walls in order to construct new ones, gathering straw and tying it in bundles to form the thatch for roofing.

Morgan worked in the midst of his people, mixing a huge trough of *tabia,* which was the clay compound dug from the mountains and used to construct almost all Berber homes in the Atlas range. The sun shone bright, drying up puddles and making hard ruts in the road, putting the sheen of perspiration on the browned faces of those who toiled with shovel and trowel.

Gwen was not idle, but spent the morning assisting Kbira, doling out sacks of flour to the bedraggled women queued up outside with fretful children clinging to their skirts. Gwen learned to be efficient with the long-handled shovel and the

385

domed oven, baking countless loaves of bread, which she smeared with freshly churned butter and fed to whimpering toddlers sitting spread-legged on the prickly grass. When noon approached, she paused, arched her back against its ache and wiped her sweating brow. Then she put a warm loaf in a basket together with dates and cheese and, making lemonade in an earthen jug, went in search of Morgan.

The acrid odor of ashes lingered, yet the air was clear and perfumed with the spice of juniper and rose. She marveled at the indifference of the earth to human affairs; regardless of the play of turmoil across it, it always kept its enduring order, day and night, summer and winter.

Negotiating the paths notched by the hooves of soldiers' horses, she inhaled and raised her head to study the ranges whose snowy peaks resembled icing applied by a giantess' hand. A little turbaned shepherd with his flock of sheep passed, and the lambs gadded all about, nuzzling at their mothers' hindquarters while they trotted to keep pace. Below, children splashed barelegged in the stream, waving sticks in games of imitation war.

Gwen found Morgan working with a trowel in his hand, which he used to apply thick layers of mud to the wall he had begun. Already she could see patches of it drying in the heat, turning to a lighter ochre color than the fresher applications. Shifting her feet on the pebbly incline, she stood watching, and her basket brushed the tops of the tall wild mint.

Morgan's back was to her, and she admired his

physique, watched the stretch of the *chamir* as it pulled over his flexing shoulders and stuck damply to the warm flesh she had kissed only hours past.

"Haven't you seen enough of me this morning?" he asked without turning around.

She strolled forward and, setting down the basket, murmured huffily, "Eyes in the back of your head, have you now? One of these days I'm going to manage to surprise you, Morgan Riff. Just wait and see."

He grinned. "The suspense will kill me."

She picked up a pebble and flung it at his backside, but he dodged it and threw down the trowel to retaliate.

After scrambling up the slope, Gwen rained gravel down upon his head. He pursued, and she laughed in carefree peals, squeezing through a break in a half-ruined wall. Morgan vaulted over it. Her stumbling flight was no challenge to him, and he reached her in only a few quick strides, capturing the waist of her tunic and pulling her off balance so that she had to fall against his chest or tumble down the rocky descent.

Sinking into a patch of mint, Morgan held her atop him and laughed. Gwen realized that it was the first time she had ever heard him laugh, really laugh, so that his flat belly vibrated with the pleasant effort, and deep lines etched either side of his mouth. She was glad she had been the one to bring him the laughter, glad to see his eyes lighten with it. And in that moment, as she looked down into his smiling face, she yearned to capture time and hold it still. If he remains with me, she thought, if he vows never to go and fight again, I will stay here. In a simple exchange for his presence, I will forsake Wales, my own people, and all the security I've ever known. But if he leaves . . .

They engaged in a spell of kissing then, and Gwenllian's abandon was so complete that Morgan wondered at it, and would have turned the fevered caresses into something more had not a troop of small children discovered them. With shrieks of gaiety the urchins joined hands to make a dancing wreath about the lovers, finding it inordinately funny that their chieftain lay beneath a woman. When he leapt up and growled at them like a charging bear, they screamed in glee and scattered.

After that, Morgan sat with Gwen and lunched, and they spoke of pleasant things, of the books he had read and of the sights he had seen in Vienna long ago. Occasionally he reached to brush a strand of hair from her eyes or put a sticky date between her lips while she told him about her childhood at Ardderyd. Frequently, they touched.

A time later, when a small band of Morgan's men trotted through the busy village, Gwen was so drowsy with sun and completeness that she paid them little heed. But Morgan frowned and, quietly excusing himself, walked down to the road to greet them. Without preamble, he strolled up to the leader of the group and asked, "What did you discover in Figuig, Kifan?"

The travel-stained rider dismounted, his face as impassive as a carved mask of warm wood. He was an older man, proficient in French, cunningly diplomatic and unemotional, and all those attributes had won Morgan's favor years ago.

"The Englishman is in the fort," he reported. "The French received him as a captive, paying many francs to the Zemours."

"Why is he so valuable to the French?"

"It seems he infiltrated Algerian borders for the purpose of charting their telegraph cables, and only narrowly escaped capture by a French officer, who gave up the chase when the Englishman crossed back into Morocco. It was then that the Zemours seized him."

"It is just as I suspected. Has he been tried?"

"Yes. He is to serve ten years—that is, if he lives so long. I was permitted to see him for a few moments only, and he is not well."

Morgan clamped his jaw at the dire pronouncement. "Go and get food for yourself and the men."

"We can wait. There is much rebuilding to do."

"No. You'll leave with me in two hours. Do you think a hundred men will be enough to take the French fort?"

"Yes. It is only an outpost on the border, and there are only three dozen cavalrymen presently stationed there. It is my belief they will not be prepared for an attack."

"Then go and outfit your pick of men." Morgan perused the ruin of his village with grim eyes. "Take less than a hundred if possible. So many are needed here."

Kifan turned to go and Morgan glanced up at Gwen. She still sat among the picnic things in the patch of mint beside the trough of *tabia*, but her pose was no longer a restful one. She stared at him intently. His stomach knotted, and he found he could not bear to give her the news of his departure on the tranquil hillside where the two of them had laughed with such abandon. He would do it later, in privacy, for he sensed their farewell would be a stormy and wrenching one.

A time later he was taking cartridges from the trunk in his room when the sound of Gwenllian's footsteps rang upon the tiles. She entered clutching a bouquet, smiling, still flushed by happiness and sunshine, her hair loose and dancing down to her waist, her eyes alight. But in a second, upon seeing his activity, the dawning of his mission registered in her brain. Her color deepened with sudden dismay while the blossoms fell from her fingers in a descending shower of mauve.

"You are leaving."

Her statement was uttered in such a low tone that it was almost inaudible, but Morgan clearly heard its bitter edge of accusation. "Yes," he said. "I am leaving."

Gwen's face blanched, the radiance draining away so quickly that it became a countenance of shattered disappointment in seconds. He had expected resentment and umbrage, but in her eyes he read something deeper, much deeper, as if his answer had prompted the crossing of some invisible threshold she had privately erected.

She fixed her eyes on his and breathed, "Where are you going?"

He had already decided not to reveal his plan of liberating her father from the French fort, for her

390

anxiety would only be increased twofold. He said simply, "To fight."

"And if I asked you to stay . . . ?" She tilted her head in a gesture of confrontation.

"Gwen."

She ignored his sternness. "If I asked you to stay, Morgan, would you?"

"Do not do this, Gwen."

"Do not do *what*?"

"Force me to make a choice that cannot be a choice!"

"So I am not to ask my lover, my husband, to do his duty by his wife? I am not to ask him to stay by my side and live with me?" She put her hands upon her hips and accused, "It is all very well for me to sacrifice, isn't it, Morgan? *Isn't it?* I'm expected to abandon my home and my country in order to hack out a living in this godforsaken wilderness because *you* chose to love it. I'm expected to live among people I cannot even begin to understand, and who likely despise me even while they smile into my face. But you will not sacrifice for me, will you? Your precious fighting is too important, more important than anything I can give you. Admit it! Say that your love of war is greater than your love for me can ever be! I want to hear it from your lips before you leave!"

Morgan's eyes blazed with anger and he took a threatening step toward her, speaking through his teeth. "I'll be damned in hell before I'll say it."

She backed away beneath his forbidding regard, then watched as he yanked his sword from the chest and, as a symbol of his will, slung the braided cord over his shoulder.

Spurred by his action, Gwen opened her mouth to censure him, but suddenly an arrowlike ray of sun glanced off the edge of the sword, and its reflection hurt her eyes. She blinked, but the weapon still glowed with violet light. The eerie phenomenon caused the hair upon her neck to rise, and in that second she was overwhelmed with the foreknowledge of doom—the same sort of doom she had experienced in Tangier when her father had said goodbye upon the dock. The sensation made her nauseous.

"Morgan . . ." she breathed, reaching out her arms. Stumbling toward him, she sank down at his boots and clutched his burnoose with icy hands. "Don't go. Do not. Something is going to happen to you—happen to us. I know it! Stay here with me. Please, I beg you, I *beg* you!"

Impatiently Morgan reached down to take hold of her arms. "You are overwrought with fancies, Gwenllian. Calm yourself. And do not go down on your knees before me as if you were less than I. Not ever. It is beneath you to beg me for anything."

"Don't go, Morgan, don't go!" she cried again, ignoring his admonishment, desperate to break through the wall of his composure.

Not unaffected by her desperate concern, he enveloped her in his arms and, stroking her hair, allowed a trace of his own wretchedness to escape. "Gwenllian, if I could stay, I would. But I cannot."

"Why, Morgan, why? Why can't you stay here and lead a simple life, sit with me upon the hillside, farm the hills like the others, watch our family grow?"

He grabbed her arms. "Because of duty elsewhere, Gwen. And because I can't live the whole of my life on a damned hillside. Adventure is in my blood. Don't you understand? Without it I would cease to be who I am. Since you insist upon my honesty, I admit that I am stirred by war, that I have a passion for it. But I do not love it. I love you. You have made me vulnerable in ways I never thought to be, ways that give me both pain and pleasure. But don't you see? I can't transform myself into the kind of man you want. I cannot be your Squire of Hiraeth."

He pulled back and searched her eyes then, willed her to understand. But she only lowered her head and did not answer, and although her arms circled his waist, they did not cling as if to bind him. After the passage of a few moments she drew away and turned her back.

Morgan stared at her, his pulse quickening with a sudden dread that he failed to rationalize. He watched her, waiting, knowing she was assembling words which she would soon communicate. The hush increased until the air was devoid of all sound except the thrumming of blood in his ears.

At last he saw her inhale deeply; her shoulders rose and fell with the heaviness of the breath; the hem of her burnoose quivered with the trembling of her legs. She did not turn around to face him, but he heard her voice clearly.

"If you leave me now, Morgan, you will find me gone when you return."

The words sliced the air.

Gwen turned to look at the man who was her husband. His eyes were narrowed in examination of her own. They seemed to read her soul in order to confirm the threat. Slowly, his skillful fists, the hands she loved, curled into hard spheres. He held himself rigidly.

She had carried her trump in hand and played it now. Had it been a mistake? All at once she feared that it had, and panic seized her. She would lose him, for Morgan Riff would not bow to the testing of love, it was not in his nature to do so.

As Allah wills. She imagined she heard the echo of the catechism winging on the tight-strung air. In anguish, she searched the eyes staring back at her. They were full, tender, and shattered in a way she had never imagined they could be. But they were the eyes of Rhaman.

I have lost, she thought. We both have lost. The spirit between us has just torn itself in two.

"A few hours ago on the hillside," he said bleakly, "you swore that you would surprise me one day. Remember?"

She nodded, and he leaned to pick up his rifle, embrace its polished barrel with a hand intimately accustomed to its feel. He contemplated it for a moment, seemed to weigh it, and then raised his eyes to pin Gwenllian's. "Well, now you have."

Twenty-one

She yearned to go home to Wales, to resume the life that had once been properly on course. But nature made her a temporary prisoner. Rain flooded the valleys, cascaded down mountain faces to make muddy rivers of the roads, and to make impassable the passages leading to the world outside. The Berbers could not get to market or work the swollen fields, and even the little sure-footed shepherds kept their flocks near the village rather than risk their getting bogged. Work on the rebuilding of homes stood suspended. Some inhabitants lived in the camel-hair tents they were accustomed to using in nomadic seasons; others trudged the slippery paths to seek shelter in distant villages.

Restless and heartsick, chafing beneath the forced confinement, Gwen often threw a *haik* about her head and went out, caring not that the warm rain pelted her face and soaked her clothes. Sometimes she roamed for hours, climbing about the ruined homes, strolling through dripping groves of pomegranates, finding high vantage points. Images of Morgan lingered everywhere, and she longed to run from them, seek the solace that only Wales could bring.

Ardderyd would hold grievous memories, too, of course, for its halls would be empty of her father's presence, but she knew Morgan would continue to search for him. He had vowed to do so, and above all, he was a man of his word. How well she knew it! He had said repeatedly that he would never leave Morocco, and he had not, not even when she had tested his love with an ultimatum. He had made his choice and she had made hers; they were a man and woman who could not exist in the world of the other.

Nevertheless, in the days following his departure, she clung tenaciously to the hope that he would swiftly return, penitent and loving. But he did not, and she carried in her mind the image of him astride the back of a copper beast, a beast created from a breath of wind divinely condensed. And the image sped ever further away from her side to a place she could not go, could not even conjure in her imagination, though she tried hard during long nights spent within a comfortless bed.

Nearly three rainy weeks passed. One afternoon Gwen sat kneading a mound of dough while Kbira and Aziza chopped vegetables for the *couscous* they would serve for supper. She liked to work in the kitchen, for there was homely comfort not only in the presence of the other women, but in learning the traditional tasks their hands performed. Savory smells filled the air in lazy curls, and Aziza sang a love song in her honeyed voice. "O tribe of Beni-Abess, how I long for thy tents."

Kbira had been painstakingly instructing Gwen in the Shellah language, and recalling the smattering Morgan had already taught her, the Welshwoman found herself able to communicate articulately enough to suffice. She had informed the women of her pending departure, and both had stared at her with incomprehension, as if the notion of a wife leaving her husband was an idea too foreign to grasp.

Haqqi proved a willing aid in her plan to go, however. Even though the rain did not cease, and he surely knew his mission a vain one, the old man hobbled each day down the path to ask about the road conditions. And each day he dutifully reported that the tribesmen could not yet escort the wife of Rhaman to Tangier. Curiously, although Gwen suspected Haqqi knew enough English to do so, he never spoke to her directly, but made Kbira the relator of his messages.

Now, as Gwen sat on the coarse mat of the kitchen turning a ball of dough, the old man stumped in, his horn-nailed toes sticking out of his soiled slippers, which he had failed to remove at the door in the customary way Kbira strictly enforced. Gwen paid little heed to him or to his mate's shrill admonishment over his dirty habits, plunging her hands into the dough and turning it again, listening only absently as the old man jabbered on, too fast for her to comprehend.

Suddenly Aziza and Kbira cried out. The bowls in their laps clattered to the floor in a shower of vegetables. Startled by their behavior, Gwen glanced at their stricken faces, and then at Haqqi.

In his withered hands the old man held a pair of spurs, their polish dulled, the leather straps stiff with dried mud. They were not of the elaborate, sharply roweled variety usually worn by Berber horsemen, but simple and straight. English made.

Gwen's hands slowly left the fragrant warmth of the dough. She stood up.

Laying the spurs on the mat beside her, the old man said in clearest English, "Rhaman has fallen. He is dead."

The sun emerged. Water shivered in the Atlas breeze, evaporating, forming vapors shot with rainbows over shrinking brooklets. Puddles blinked and disappeared while new blossoms crept from clean-washed crevices, and lambs lay soaking in the radiance with twitching tails. Somewhere a shepherd trilled upon his pipe and the melody was timelessly old. The smell of wet clay hung once more upon the air as weathered hands rebuilt their mountain aeries.

Gwen stood on the path of Morgan's villa, her eyes surveying the scene of rebirth. The sight of the activity distracted her thoughts for a moment and she tried to focus upon it, keep her gaze away from the snowy summits that reigned over the realm of a chieftain who would never return.

She swallowed, breathed deep in the way one does to muster courage in the face of an ordeal. At the bottom of the little path her horse waited, surrounded by a mounted group of expressionless men wearing the chestnut burnooses she would forever see in dreams. They were ready to escort her on her journey home, guide her out of the labyrinth through which Morgan had led her. She bit her lip, knowing the Berbers wondered at her hesitation.

Her eyes shifted to the people who lined the pathway down. In silent reverence, every woman and child of the village stood waiting to bid the wife of Rhaman farewell. As she moved forward, each held out a humble parting gift: strung beads, figures of clay, dried fruits, pressed flowers, and from a little boy, a small wooden cross. Every gift was a rich offering given by someone who owned little.

Gwen thought her tears had dried up with the sun, but at the end of the line, when Kbira's granddaughter stepped forward with her gift, the salty drops again spilled over.

Across Aziza's arms lay the tapestry of the arabesques—the only thing of value the girl owned, the only thing of beauty in her life.

At first Gwen shook her head, but Aziza insisted. The Welshwoman clasped the treasure to her breast, and too overwhelmed to speak, embraced the hennaed palms in her own soft white ones. She pressed them hard in the seal of friendship.

A moment later one of the Berber men packed her gifts away and helped her mount. She took up the reins and bit her lip to keep from sobbing. And then, with one last look at the place that her lover had loved, Gwen put her heels to the hide of the horse, leaving behind a country that her heart was no longer certain it despised.

* * *

Finally home, she found comfort in the rich wet soil of the Welsh firmament. It spoke to her in gentle Celtic murmurs her spirit understood, lent her the familiarity of childhood, the safety she had quietly craved. And yet, it could not give back to her the wholeness she had once enjoyed before her adventure of love and death in the land of Morocco.

With the cliffs watching over her like black sentinels, Gwen walked several miles each morning. Her steps were languid and meandering, and as she walked, she thought about many things. She pondered the mystery of love, of sorrow, of calamity, and attempted to reconcile them all in her mind, fathom why destiny had given her such a generous measure of each. The answer was unknowable, of course, but she sensed that the pain of all three led to an understanding she was yet to discover.

For the first three days she stayed away from Hiraeth, but then, drawn irresistibly to its lonely halls, she rode over and ordered an astonished Petwyn to throw open the windows and air the musty chambers. He did what he could to freshen the mansion and make it comfortable, and Gwen established residence again. She spent hours staring up at the warriors painted on the canvas in the great hall, and decided they were not unlike the Berber faces she had left behind.

The estate begged for repair. Wind whistled through its crumbling mortar, windows rattled in loose frames, and slate shingles fell onto its barren lawn. Often Gwen stood upon the drive staring up the mansion's stark profile, thinking that its windows looked colder and grayer than she remembered them, as if the soul of Hiraeth were gradually fading beneath the squire's neglect. Trying to breathe life into it again, she dined in its chilly rooms, brushed her hair before Marian's mirror and slept upon a mattress once graced by a king. And then one morning, after climbing out of bed, she almost fainted, and realized she was to bear the future squire.

The miracle of Morgan's gift provided a great solace. It also gave her an added reason to examine the accounts and plan for the complete restoration of her child's birthright. And yet, even as she hired stone masons and roofers and gardeners, she found herself distressed. One day, would she see her son standing upon the cliffs, black haired and with brilliant blue eyes, staring out to sea in search of another land? Would Morocco call to him with the same siren's song his father had always heard? She wondered. She prayed.

One blustery afternoon a servant from Ardderyd asked that she help solve some pressing matter at her father's estate. After ushering her into the drawing room where a fire kept the chill away, the servant bade her wait. Idly, she strolled about the room, examining the well-remembered bric-a-brac, the volumes of poetry, the miniature ship sailing the marble mantelpiece. The pleasant memories that each object sparked made her decide to add more personal pieces to Hiraeth's cheerless rooms, and she grew so preoccupied with her mental redecorating that she failed to hear footsteps. At the sound of an unexpected voice, she jumped.

"Gwenllian."

She gasped. "Papa!" Running forward, she thrust out her arms and fell into the exuberant embrace of Sir Gerald.

"My girl!" he exclaimed. " 'Tis heaven to hold ye again! I hope my surprise has not shaken ye too badly. Ye're not going to faint, now are ye?"

"Of course not. But I can't believe you're home!"

"Ah, and many were the days when I feared I should not be!"

"I feared the worst, as well," she admitted, drawing back and searching his haggard features. "But you have been ill, haven't you, Papa? I can see it in your face. How thin you are!"

"Cook's meat pies will soon remedy that!"

"But you look pale as if from some illness—"

"Do not fret over me, daughter. I am recovered, and only needed to hold ye in my arms again to feel as right as rain. But let me take a good look at ye—how have ye fared in my absence?"

In spite of herself, Gwen glanced over her father's shoulder, intuitively hunting for a shadow.

"What is it, girl?"

She forced a smile. "Nothing. Did you just arrive?"

"Not more than an hour ago. You're not living over there at Hiraeth, are ye, Gwen? Tell me that what the servants say isn't true."

"Oh, Papa, let's not talk about that now." She wanted to ask him about Morgan. She wanted to know if her husband had lost his life rescuing her father after she had sent him off in anger. Bracing herself for the answer, she breathed, "How did you escape your captors? How did you come to be here?"

"Why, Morgan Riff rescued me." He spoke as if

402

he were surprised to hear her ask. "He led a band of men against the French fort where I was being held. That heathen tribe of Zemours sold me to them like a slave, and the damned Frogs were only too glad to sentence me to jail on trumped-up charges. But, did ye not send Riff to me yerself, Gwen, according to my message?"

Realizing her sire knew nothing at all of the events following her receipt of his cryptic letter, she delayed her explanation, intent only upon gaining more news of Morgan. "Did you speak with him, Papa? When did you see him last?"

Hearing the distress in her voice, Sir Gerald took hold of his daughter's arm and guided her to the sofa. "No, Gwen. I never spoke to Riff, and I only saw him from a distance. He simply raised a hand to me in a sort of salute, then sent me on my way to Tangier with an escort of his men."

"But he was alive when you saw him last?" she cried. "He survived the attack made on the fort?"

"He was very much alive. And on his way to some place in the Sahara—or so one of his men informed me."

Hope fled. Gwen felt the color drain from her face, and instinctively she put a hand to her abdomen. It was as she had suspected. Morgan had gone to the Sahara to fight Moussa, and died there.

"What is it, girl?" Sir Gerald asked with a frown of consternation. "I swear you've turned white as a sheet all in the space of a minute. Ye must tell me all that has passed since ye left me in Tangier."

All that had passed. How could she?

She regarded her father's careworn face, more

aged than it had been before, and knew she would never tell him all that had passed. She only related the barest facts, omitting much of the horror she still strove to forget as she spoke of Robyn Breese and his courageous end. And then, when she spoke of the village in the mountains, her voice lowered. It quavered when she related the news of Morgan's death.

With tender concern Sir Gerald said, "Ye had gone back to him? Ye had decided to be his wife?"

Gwen opened her mouth to answer, then paused in confusion, before saying simply, "Yes. Yes, I loved him very much."

"I'm sorry, so sorry." Her father walked around the sofa and put a hand upon her shoulder. "It's a shame he didn't want to come here to live after the two of ye were married. Things might have been different then . . ." He glanced at her askance. "It would have been the best thing for *you* anyway."

Gwen looked out the window, at the oyster-hued clouds and cold gray sea. "But it would not have been the best thing for him."

Her sire's eyes were full of wisdom. "No. It would not, would it, my girl?"

A moment of silence passed, and Sir Gerald strolled to the mantel, where he retied a loose rigging upon the mast of the miniature ship. "I want to apologize for the arguments we had in Tangier, Gwen. The matter has weighed heavy on my mind. I fretted over it while I was fearing for my life in Morocco. I know I was harsh with ye. But I didn't want ye to be hurt."

"I know about Marian, Papa," she said quietly. "At least, I think I do."

Sir Gerald lifted his shoulders as if unsurprised by her knowledge. "It was a bitter disappointment at the time. How I hated the foreigner who had stolen her away from me! I was so enraged I actually thought about hunting down the scoundrel in Morocco and challenging him to a duel. But then, I met yer mother . . ."

Pouring two glasses of sherry from a decanter, he handed Gwen one, then sipped his own. "When I met Morgan Riff in Tangier, it was as if I were seeing his father. All the old anger of my younger days came flooding back to haunt me. I couldn't bear to have him take my daughter away from me as his father had taken Marian. I was unfair to him, perhaps. For in the end, he proved to be the greatest sort of friend a man can have. He saved my life."

Gwenllian turned the glass of sherry round and round between her palms. She said softly, "Before long, there will be a child."

Her sire wheeled about, scrutinized her face, then leaned back his head in delight. "Ha! A grandson! Well, I never expected this. Just think of it! He will go riding with me and fishing. Ah, and I'll wager ye've got plans for him, too, haven't ye, Gwen. He shall be a proper squire to Hiraeth, eh?"

Gwen lowered her eyes, stared at the braid edging the hem of her new bombazine. "Of course . . ." she murmured. "He will be a proper squire, Papa— a proper squire to Hiraeth."

Twenty-two

Late one day after enjoying tea with her father, Gwen slid on coat and gloves and, declining the use of the carriage, declared she would walk back to Hiraeth. Sir Gerald admonished her, for the afternoon was cold and wet, the winds shrieking over the moors like dervishes bent upon mischief. But his daughter only kissed his leathery cheek and ignored him, and once outside ran like a schoolgirl just released from lessons.

She made for the sea path, climbing high, holding on to her hood when the gusts would snatch it off her head, and at last breached a pinnacle. With the wind buffeting her skirts and stinging her face, she gazed at the ocean as it pounded the cliff face, staring down at the water weeds that danced below the currents, searching for the lost fairy city of the *Tylwth Teg* she had once likened to the skyline of Tangier.

In girlhood, she had always been able to find its golden domes and aery towers in the glimmering deep, but now the enchanting place seemed to have vanished, or at least it no longer deigned to reveal its magic to her eyes.

Sniffling, stamping her feet against the cold, she finally turned away, putting a hand to her middle. In spite of the fragile curled being she carried within her body, her emptiness remained such a determined companion she feared it would never leave. Even her father's return had done little to alleviate her loneliness.

She looked up at the clouds with a sigh. Wind-driven, they cantered across the skies, forming an image of a great gray beast like the one who had once carried a chieftain across a faraway land. "Oh, Morgan . . ." she breathed, the words wrenched from an empty place deep inside. She listened, tried hard to hear an answering call through the surf and rain. But none came.

Forlornly turning from her vantage point, she bowed her head against the gale and began the journey home. Soon the deluge increased so that the boggy turf became an arduous route, and raising her lashes against the sting of drops, Gwen tried to judge the remaining distance to Hiraeth. But instead of seeing its stone chimneys through the storm, she glimpsed a figure standing on the long foam-sprayed headland which jutted out to sea. She blinked and looked again, but had there really been a presence there, it idled in the rain no longer.

Drawing her coat more snugly about her shoulders, Gwen hurried on, keeping her gaze fastened ahead to the place upon the headland. After a moment her vigilance was rewarded, for again, the distant figure of a man materialized.

His features were indistinct, blurred in the downpour, but she could see that he was bareheaded, garbed in a greatcoat with his hands shoved in the pockets. He stared in her direction.

She stopped, wonderstruck and afraid. For several seconds she stood staring with the rain drumming all around. An eerie tingle chased down her spine, one that began as a shiver at the back of her neck and coursed to her heels. And then, she found herself running, stumbling over the earth and crying out words she did not hear.

Wildly she ran, closing the watery distance between herself and the waiting man. As she neared, his figure became a more tangible shape, one tall and solid, breathing and alive . . . the part of herself she had lost.

His arms stretched out, receiving, crushing with such fierceness that her feet left the streaming earth. Gwen clung to him with all her strength, squeezed herself against the wet wool of his coat, whimpered his name, endeavored to get closer by burying her face in the warm rough place beneath his jaw.

"Morgan!" she cried, gasping, fearing to let him go. "Tell me you are real!"

His arms were hard, and still held her off the ground. "I am real. And so glad of it!"

"Don't let me go," she pleaded when he started to move. "Not yet, not yet. I'm still afraid."

He found her mouth with his, and she felt the warm substance of him again, heard again the resonance of his voice when he groaned. He put hands on either side of her face, slid them back beneath her hood to touch the warmth of her curling hair.

"Have you come back from the dead?" She was still breathless from his energy and from her wonder. "Haqqi told us—"

"An old man's mischief," Morgan cut in. "Nothing more than that." And then he smiled with the rain running into the corners of his mouth. "I believe he thought to save me from my infidel wife."

She laughed a bit hysterically, her teeth a-chatter, and Morgan pulled her close. "Come on. You're freezing and I'm impatient. Let us go home."

They ran back to Hiraeth, Gwenllian sheltered by his greatcoat which he unbuttoned and opened out so that she might nestle protected at his side. But when they neared the mansion his brisk steps slowed and he faltered slightly, so that she glanced up with concern to search his face.

He stared at the bleak edifice with its black iron gates and posturing gargoyles, his gaze sweeping over stone and drab facade. They scanned the flooded green lawn and the gray slate roof and the frowning eaves where pigeons huddled. They surveyed the barren, windswept landscape. And his eyes, Gwen thought, were grim with the reflection of what he saw.

Water ran off the edge of his jaw and he clamped his teeth, stepping forward and drawing her with him toward the massive doors studded with iron. He threw them wide and together they crossed the threshold into the body of Hiraeth, their garments dripping rain on the cold slate floor. Slowly, Morgan turned to shut the portals, and the clang of their closure rang loud, echoing with a strangely sepulchre finality through the corridors. The squire surveyed the dim clerestories, the severe stone stairway, the skirmishing Welsh warriors imprisoned in a death struggle upon their canvas plain.

Gwen observed him anxiously, saying nothing, but interpreting the expressions that crossed his face. His eyes were bright, fathomable, and all at once she saw again the boy residing within their glistening depths, remembered young Rhaman standing here, lost and vulnerable. And now, as she assessed his manly face, she thought, *he is out of place and feels it strongly. But, he will not say it.*

The distance between them seemed to widen, stretch into more than just a few short paces, and although Gwen longed to close the alarming gap, she resisted the urge with a wisdom gained by maturity. He must be the first to speak.

He turned to face her. "Gwen—"

She waited, allowed him to take her fingers between hands made brown by the sun of another land. And when he spoke again she knew that a bit of his heart left him, rode fast upon the words that came huskily through his lips. "I'll stay," he said. "I'll stay here at Hiraeth with you."

She closed her eyes, and for a moment savored sweetly the sound of his sacrifice. Reaching up, she cradled his head within her hands, smoothed the sleek dark hair so that its moisture ran between her fingers. She knew what it had cost him to make the promise, knew well the value of the gift. And knew she could not accept it.

Drawing back, she gazed into his face, and in a gentle gesture touched its rugged planes. "No, Morgan," she said through a throat tight with tears. "I love you, but I don't want you to stay, it's too great a price. You don't belong to Hiraeth. You've always known that, and now I know it, too. You must go back to your mountains and your people, to the place where you are meant to live." She smiled bravely. "What would Morocco be without Rhaman? What would Rhaman be without his country? You are who you are, it was wrong of me to try and make you someone else. I want you to go back."

She saw that her words had staggered him. For a few seconds he only stared at her face, and her rejection of his loving offer eclipsed the light in his eyes. He shook his head and held out a hand. "You can't mean that."

"I do."

He opened his mouth, closed it, and then swallowed. And the self-mastery, the composure that nothing could shatter, slowly shattered before Gwen's gaze.

After a few seconds he said, "I did not make this decision lightly—it is not a promise that I'll go back on."

"Oh, Morgan," she cried, "I realize that. I know you're here because you love me, but I also know that you could never be happy at Hiraeth, and I can't accept that sacrifice."

He ran his fingers through his hair. Then, as if struggling with emotion, he turned and paced the length of the great hall before halting at the stairway that curved up into deepest shadow. Putting a hand atop the bannister, he rubbed the wood that was dark with age and oil. "These last months have told me much about myself," he said. "Much about what is important. Until recently I hadn't ever taken much time for reflection, but maybe I should have. Shortly after I left you, I journeyed to the desert to find Moussa—"

"You journeyed to a French fort first," Gwen interrupted in a soft voice. "You should have told me, Morgan."

He touched the elaborate newel-post, the lion's head carved of oak, and shrugged. "Perhaps I should have."

"Thank you for my father's life."

"Is he well?"

"Yes. But older somehow. Much older."

He rested a foot upon the first stair step and rolled his shoulders in the sodden greatcoat. "When my men and I discovered Moussa in the Sahara," he said, "our tribes fought a long and bloody battle. I lost many men, but Moussa lost a great deal more. His horse had been wounded, and he was on foot when I came abreast of him. I stared at his face, and all I could think about was my father and mother. And you. I burned with the desire to kill him. But when I raised my sword and took his life, I found no honor, no satisfaction in the act. I only felt as if I'd done murder."

Gwen frowned at him, and knew that his words had been a difficult admission. She said quietly,

412

"But now you have your father's fortress back. You are master of it, as you should be."

"Yes. I rode there directly, and entered it for the first time since his death. It looked much the same, only in sad disrepair. I sent everyone away for a few hours so that I could walk through its courtyards alone and enjoy my victory. But I felt no triumph there, none of the happiness I had longed to feel for so many years. I couldn't understand it, it made no sense to me. But now it does." He looked at her with eyes that were clear and bright. "Now it does."

"You can't give up your life for me, Morgan," Gwen said in a level voice. "And Morocco is your life."

His expression was sober. "There are things to which a man knows he must surrender, Gwen, even a man like me—especially a man like me. And if he's wise, he knows the time to do it."

"No." She walked forward and, reaching out her arms, embraced him, laid her cheek against the wet, soaked lapel of his coat. He gathered her close and she raggedly breathed in the smell of Welsh wool, shutting her eyes against the sight of the walls that glowed faintly with crested shields and protected the two of them from the storm outside. Clinging to him, she felt his cool cheek pressed against her brow.

"Rhaman surrenders to nothing," she avowed fiercely. "Go back to your people . . . and I will go with you."

Perhaps Hiraeth sensed that its halls were to be abandoned a final time by its most recent squire,

413

perhaps it conspired with nature to verbalize its displeasure, for a frost-driven wind besieged it like a howling king's militia. And yet, inside its ancient walls the chieftain invaded its inner chambers imperturbed, excited by nothing but his lover, whose flesh he sought with his.

The two stood together, and for a discerning moment Gwenllian studied the squire dressed in his fine waistcoat, buff-colored trousers, and polished leather shoes. Then with loving hands she reached to unfasten the buttons of the unbefitting garments, sliding them off the shoulders made hard by the toil of swordplay. She touched the smooth dark flesh of his chest, put her lips against it and found it very warm, as if he had brought with him the heat of his country.

Only a meager light kept the darkness at bay within the tapestry-hung chamber; the fire framed by the marble mantelpiece cast its gold glow in an arc across the floor, touching the bare feet of the lovers and the pooled wet coats surrounding them.

The husband's disrobing of his wife was not done in leisure, and before many moments had passed she lay beneath him upon old embroidered sheets that smelled of camphor and lilac. She lifted her hands, traced the curve of his arms as they flexed to brace his body's weight, and lifted her head to take his thorough kiss. Just behind his head the vibrant hues of the arabesque rug shimmered in the trembling light. She had hung the treasure there upon her return to Hiraeth as a reminder of the beauty of Morgan's land, and had contemplated it often in the nights of her loneliness, sometimes reaching out a hand to follow its intertwined design so that recollection would revive.

Her husband seemed to know at what she stared, for he bent his head to her ear, and in the language of his native tongue, whispered that he loved her. He whispered many things. And Gwenllian understood them all.

He moved then, and familiar with his body's rhythms Gwen moved in tandem, pleasing him as he pleased her until each forgot all but the other. Finally, as frenzied groans calmed to more gentle sounds, Gwen nestled snugly against her counterpart's side, hearing the wind rattle the weathered window frames, watching the sumptuous velvet drapes billow as briny air wended its way over the canopied bed. All at once, against her will, she found herself yearning to get up and run to the rain-splashed panes, look out and see the cliffs and moors of her childhood, reassure herself that they were there, unchanged, as they had always been.

But she resisted the call and, seeking Morgan's warm hand, slid it down over the soft swell of her middle. "Soon I shall bear you a child," she whispered.

He shifted, turned upon his side to peer down with joy into her smiling face. "Gwenllian! When will he come?"

"In summer."

Morgan pushed the sheet aside, his eyes tarrying upon the body of the woman he loved, at that place where their two hands joined. "Then he shall be born here, at Hiraeth."

She searched his expression, opened her mouth

to speak, only to find her protest silenced by the touch of his mouth. "It is right that he should carry some memory of it, Gwen. It's the place that his mother loves."

Laying her head back upon the pillow, Gwen let her eyes travel the length of Hiraeth's lofty ceilings which were still grand with their lavish plaster garlands. With the wisdom of a woman she asked, "But what if it calls him back one day, Morgan, pulls him away from us? What if it pulls him away from the mountains that you will teach him to rule and to love?"

Morgan lifted his eyes and moved them over the same path that her gaze had earlier followed, contemplating the lines of the ancient structure named for homesickness that sheltered them from the night. "Then we will let him go, Gwen. We will let Hiraeth have its squire."

Lifting her head, Gwenllian rested it atop the crest of his shoulder. She entwined her fingers within the dark lean ones calloused from leather reins, and whispered, "Thank you, my love."